# CITY OF WOLVES

*Nightmarked #2*

KAT ROSS

City of Wolves

First Edition



ISBN: 978-1-957358-03-1

Maps by the author.

*For Bean*

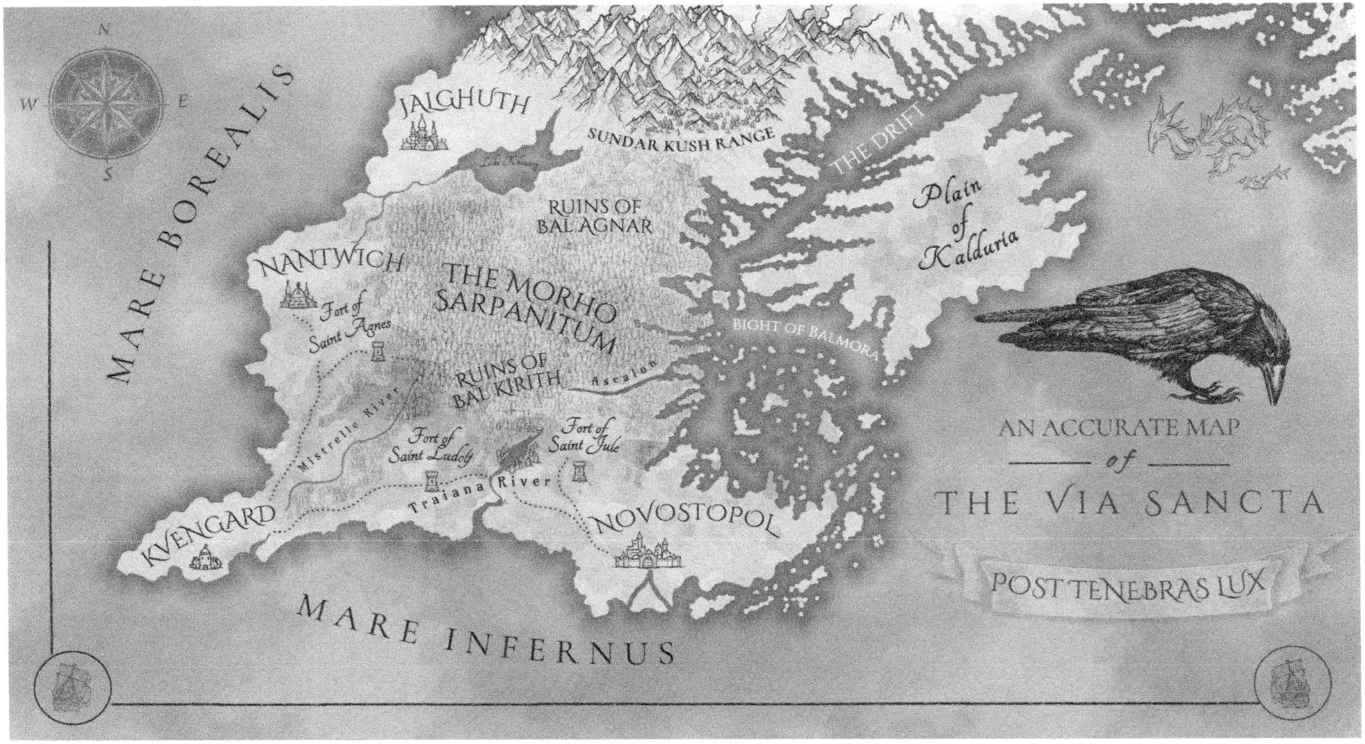

AN ACCURATE MAP
of
THE VIA SANCTA

POST TENEBRAS LUX

MARE BOREALIS
MARE INFERNUS
N
W
E
S
JALGHUTH
SUNDAR KUSH RANGE
THE DRIFT
Plain of Kalduria
RUINS OF BAL AGNAR
NANTWICH
THE MORHO SARPANITUM
BIGHT OF BALMORA
Fort of Saint Agnes
RUINS OF BAL KIRITH
Ascalon
Mistrelle River
Fort of Saint Ludolf
Fort of Saint Jule
Traiana River
KVENGARD
NOVOSTOPOL

PARNASSIAN SEA
YRELLE
Dur Athaara
Caverns
The Creche
TENETHE
The Pit
Temple of Valmitra
Isles of the Eastern Witchdom

Her Skin in divers colors did appeare,
Now Black, then Greene, annon 'twas Red and Cleare.
Oft-times she would sit upright in her Bed,
And then again repose her Troubled Head.

*— ANGELUS SILESIUS, DER CHERUBINISCHER WANDERSMANN*

# Prologue

First came darkness.

A night so long and deep there could be no end to it.

A black sun rose in the fire-streaked heavens, but it gave no warmth or light. A terrible melancholy seized him. He was worth nothing. A crude lump of matter scorched in the black flames. How it stank, that fire! Like the earthy, putrid mould of the grave.

He confessed his sins, throat choked with bile. Was that a hooded figure in the shadows? Watching, listening? If so, it offered no absolution.

Listless misery turned to terror as he felt his very essence dissolving, pulverized to a bitter dust swept away by the wind.

Then, visions. A headless raven, dull feathers the color of tar. It took flight from his pale, bloated corpse.

A boy lying with one arm flung wide on a rocky shore, hair washed by the outgoing tide.

A white peacock in a garden. A two-headed lion spewing darkness.

The Black Sun again, devouring the world.

He tried to scream but had no voice.

*Light.*

The faintest glimmer at first, yet growing brighter with every arduous step. A journey of a thousand years through the blasted landscape of his own private hell.

Slowly, slowly, the foul vapors faded.

Sight returned.

His first thought was, *I am dead.*

The Light was all around him, flowing in whorls and eddies. He remembered the long night, but it was distant now. The Light warmed him. Made him safe and whole.

He turned his head, shocked to find he could.

Thick iron bars framed a window set high in a brick wall. Beyond it, the rolling thunder of the ocean.

*Am I dead?*

*Was it all a dream?*

He felt no hunger or thirst. No pain. If he had a name, he could not recall it.

But when footsteps sounded outside the door, he discovered that he could still feel fear.

# Chapter One

"This is it. Number 26."

Alexei reined up before a white house with mullioned windows and decorative timbers in a crosshatched pattern. Low shrubs, pruned at precise angles, flanked a flagstone walk leading to the front door. The curtains were all drawn, giving the place a grim, shuttered air.

Bishop Morvana Ziegler shot him a hard look. "They speak only Kven. I'll do the talking, Bryce."

He nodded. She delivered the same lecture each time.

"You will not mention anything about Marks, is that clear?"

"I thought you just said they wouldn't understand."

Her pale blonde brows flattened in displeasure.

"*Ja, ja*, I won't bring it up," Alexei said, turning his attention back to the house.

The boy lived in a respectable, well-to-do neighborhood east of the Arx. He was the fifth child to vanish without a trace in the last year. Willem wasn't the most recent. They'd just come from that house, a thatched cottage on the other side of the city. A girl of seven who'd been taken a little over a month before. But Alexei had asked to reinterview each and every family himself. It was his habit when he took on a new case to reassemble the pieces of the puzzle from scratch and see how they fit together. The Polizei might have missed something. Since they had no leads, Morvana had agreed, although she insisted on accompanying him.

He swung down from the saddle. Most of the horses in Kvengard were regular stock, but the Arx used Marksteeds. Creatures bred with ley. Their eyes shone like burnished gold and they faded to shadow when you didn't look at them directly. Riding them took getting used to, not because their gait was any different, but because he had the strange sensation that the tall, blond woman at his side was floating on thin air.

Alexei looked around, the ever-present salt breeze tugging at his cassock. Willem had vanished on this very street at some point between the corner where his school chums said goodbye and the front door of his home. In broad daylight, yet not a single witness had come forward.

Had it been Novostopol, Alexei would have guessed the boy got into a car, most likely driven by someone he knew. But there were no cars in Kvengard. No electricity or telephone service. It could have been a carriage, though his friends hadn't seen one, nor did the neighbors.

A servant admitted them to a dark, stuffy parlor. Solidly middle-class. A portrait of the Pontifex Luk, robed in white, hung over the fireplace. In person, he was thin bordering on cadaverous, but the artist had softened his harsh features and added color to his ashen cheeks. Luk looked almost grandfatherly, if not as hale and benevolent as Dmitry Falke. Luk thought Alexei was Falke's spy, but he seemed to believe the old axiom about keeping friends close and enemies closer. Instead of sending Alexei back to Novostopol in disgrace, he'd been assigned as an aide to Bishop Morvana Ziegler.

She'd made it clear that she disapproved of his service during the war. He still wasn't sure why she'd given him this case. Perhaps just to see him fail—though that wasn't entirely fair. Morvana had agreed to his every request and seemed determined to catch the culprit.

"It's an old family in Kvengard," she said, watching the door. "We must tread carefully."

"Their only son is gone. Surely they understand the need to follow every line of inquiry."

She gave a reluctant nod. "*Ja*, I know."

"What did you tell them about me?"

"The same as the rest. That you're a special investigator from Novo." A small smile. "Most Kvens think your city is a den of iniquity. It makes sense you would have expertise on crimes like these."

Willem's parents appeared, the mother red-eyed, the father stoic and gruff. They showed him a smaller portrait of a handsome boy, dark-haired and blue-eyed. He stood stiffly next to a small white dog, gazing off to the side. It had been painted less than a year ago for his thirteenth birthday.

Alexei ran through his questions. He ordered them deliberately, posing the easiest first and the most uncomfortable last.

Had he made any new friends lately? What about girlfriends? How did he get on at school?

Did he seem unhappy before he disappeared? Nervous or different in any way?

Had any workers come to the house in the last few months? Tradesmen or peddlers?

Did they notice any strangers hanging about the street?

Did they have any enemies? Anyone at all who might want to harm their child?

What about relatives? Were there any falling-outs in the family recently? Old grudges?

Had he ever run away before? Did they have an argument?

It was useful to watch their faces while Morvana translated. The father stiffened most at the part about running away, angrily responding that Willem was a good boy who did well at school and was happy at home. Such a denial was to be expected, but Alexei sensed no anxiety from the mother—not towards her husband, at least. Only grief.

The interview unearthed nothing new. The Polizei had already been through the house, but Alexei wanted to look for himself. He signaled to Morvana.

"May we see his room?" she asked.

They were ushered upstairs to a bedroom overlooking the street. Single bed, neatly made. No posters of starlets or sports heroes like he'd expect to find in Novo. Just a desk with school books and half-finished homework assignments. A chest of old wooden toys that he'd probably outgrown but wasn't ready to part with. Three pairs of polished leather shoes sat lined up under the wardrobe. And a muddy pair of sneakers.

Willem was a runner. He had three first-place trophies from races at school. A fit, athletic boy. It wouldn't have been easy to take him against his will.

"It is just as he left it," the mother said from the doorway. Her face held both bleakness and a terrible hope. "Will took good care of his things."

The room reminded Alexei uncomfortably of his brother, Misha. A dusty shrine to a boy—now a man—who would never return. He prayed it would not be the same with Willem.

Alexei ran a hand beneath the feather mattress, hoping he might find a diary or some other hidden clue indicating that the boy knew his abductor. He lifted the carpet and tested for loose floorboards. Nothing. The forensic team had been thorough. If Willem had something to hide, it wasn't here.

Afterwards, they interviewed the two servants. They were sisters and both had worked for the family for many years. On the day Willem went missing, one was in the kitchen chopping vegetables for supper. The younger was polishing the silver. They swore Willem never arrived home.

"Where's the dog?" Alexei asked. "The one in the painting?"

Morvana conveyed the question. The older sister, a woman of about forty with thick blond braids, answered. "She says it ran away."

He felt a small jolt. This was new. "When?"

Morvana spoke with the woman in Kven for a minute. "Two days after Willem went missing."

That's why it wasn't in the Polizei report.

"She'd taken the carpets outside to beat them. The back door must not have closed properly. The dog got out."

"Did they look for it?"

Alexei waited impatiently through a longish exchange in Kven. Finally, Morvana shook her head. "Not really. She called a few times, hoping it hadn't gone far. She expected it would just show up."

"But it didn't."

"No."

"She feared her masters would be angry, but with their son missing . . . well, they were too frantic about Willem to worry about the dog."

It made sense. "Was it the boy's pet?"

The servant must have understood for she nodded before Morvana translated. "He love very much," she said in thickly accented Osterlish, wiping away a tear with the edge of her apron.

Alexei could think of nothing more to ask. The parents met them at the front door.

"Will you find him?" the mother asked. Pleading. "Do you think he's alive?"

Alexei was far from fluent in Kven, but he understood those questions. He'd heard them at each house they'd visited.

They didn't want the truth. What parent would?

"I'm sure he is," Morvana said firmly. "We're doing everything we can."

She'd repeated the same empty words again and again in the last week.

On his way out, Alexei paused. There was a peculiar smell in the hall. Almost putrid, but with an overlay of sweetness. A row of cloaks hung on pegs. It seemed to be emanating from the wool.

"Did you smell that?" he asked softly, as they stepped outside.

Morvana wrinkled her nose, diamond stud glinting. "It's the tannery. The father owns several in the city. They make gloves."

Kvengard followed a strict interpretation of the *Meliora* that forbade the slaughter of animals for food, but leather remained the most effective medium to block accidental use of the ley. Dairy cows that were old or diseased were humanely killed after an injection of tranquilizer and used at the tanneries. They'd passed near one yesterday. The stench was brutal.

"What did you make of the dog?" she asked.

"I'm not sure. It could be a coincidence."

Morvana had questioned the parents about their whereabouts on the afternoon of the disappearance, and both repeated the stories in the file. The mother had been out shopping with a friend all afternoon. They returned to the house together and discovered Willem hadn't come home from school. The father was at work all day. Both accounts had been confirmed.

"We should see if any other pets are missing," Alexei said.

She nodded. "I'll send some officers, but we have an audience with the Reverend Father at six bells. He wants an update on the investigation."

Outside, the pair of glossy black steeds waited patiently for their masters to return. Just as the hounds were bred to sniff out particular Marks, the horses were bred for docility and speed. Alexei had heard they could outrun an automobile at full gallop, though he'd never had the chance to test it.

Dusk had fallen and the lamp-lighters were out with their ladders. The clatter of iron-rimmed wheels on cobblestones and cries of hawkers seeking a last sale echoed through the narrow, canyon-like streets. Kvengard was a port city, sitting on a rocky promontory above the Southern Ocean. A steady breeze kept the air relatively fresh, though the smell of manure was pervasive. Alexei didn't find it unpleasant. Yet as he rode toward the Arx, his blue eyes swept each carriage that passed, lingering on the expensive lacquered ones with enclosed benches.

If it was just one child, he would suspect the parents or someone else in the household, regardless of their alibis.

But there had been nine.

And whoever was taking them, he didn't think they intended to stop.

---

Alexei left his mount at the stables and climbed the stairs to his apartment in the Wohnturm, a tower house on the grounds of the Arx. He slept in a chair near the window and used the large sleigh bed for his timeline. After hanging up his exorason, the loose outer garment worn over the cassock, he studied the files laid out in two rows on the quilt.

The children all lived in different parts of the city. They attended different schools. Some were wealthy, some not. Some had siblings, others didn't. They ranged in age from eight to fifteen. The older ones had all received their first Marks after the testing.

The first was Noach Beitz, the last little Sofie Arneth.

He could find no pattern, nothing they had in common, except for two things.

First, there was never any sign of violence. Some were taken from their beds in the night without raising an alarm. Others, like Willem, vanished into thin air within sight of their homes. As if they knew and trusted their abductor.

The second was the dates. Nine children over the last year. One every forty days, precisely.

He'd spent hours staring at a calendar, ruling out any connection to lunar cycles or holidays. Yet there must be a reason for it.

How was he choosing them?

Of course, it could be a woman, but Alexei felt that possibility to be remote.

There had been a case in Novo when he was still in law school. An Unmarked man who raped and murdered four women, all strangers, before he was finally arrested. Debate raged over whether this was proof that denying the deviants Marks was correct, or whether it was better to do something to restrain their impulses.

But those were crimes of opportunity. Impulsive and messy. The man was caught when a neighbor saw him entering his flat covered in blood.

This perpetrator was different. Methodical and intelligent.

He would not make a careless mistake.

If not for the children, Alexei would have been gone. It was his tenth day in Kvengard. In the long nights when sleep refused to come, Alexei dwelt on Mikhail and Lezarius, imagining various scenarios, each worse than the last. They must be in the Void somewhere. Lezarius had told Kasia that he planned to raise an army. But who would follow a madman—other than Alexei's mad brother?

Each night, he would vow to slip away on the morrow and search for them. Then he would wake and look at the timeline spread across the bed and think, *one more day*.

He'd grown obsessed with the case.

Kvengard had no newspapers. People knew because of the

missing flyers on every street corner and they were keeping a close watch over their offspring. He wasn't sure it would do any good. It hadn't for Sofie Arneth.

He picked up Willem's file and jotted: *Dog?*

Then he reviewed the other dossiers again, even though he felt certain they hadn't mentioned pets. He'd glimpsed a cat in the Keller house, a fat orange tabby that fled when he'd entered the home. And the dog had disappeared *after* Willem did, making it unlikely that the creature had been disposed of to prevent it from protecting its master or making noise.

The surge of excitement at finding something new faded to a dull ache in his temples, but Alexei kept reading. There had to be *something.*

Shortly after five bells, he made his way to the kennels to see Alice.

She trotted over and licked his hand. As he did every day, Alexei let her sniff Misha's copy of the *Meliora*, the foundational doctrine of the Via Sancta. His brother had read the book so many times the binding was coming loose from the seams. Alexei kept it wrapped in oilcloth so it would hold his brother's scent.

"Venari," he commanded. *Hunt.*

She gave it a snuffle and looked at him—a touch regretfully, he thought.

He didn't really expect Misha to turn up in Kvengard, but it made him feel like he was doing something useful.

"Are you happy here?" he asked, scratching the base of her nubby tail where a scar intersected her muscular haunch.

Alice wriggled and barked.

"You can come sleep with me tonight," he said in a low voice.

*Sleep* being a euphemism for curling up at his feet while he stared at the ceiling—or, as he'd done the last two nights, reread the case files, hoping he'd overlooked some critical clue.

The other Markhounds watched with slitted eyes from

their little straw-filled houses. Alexei hadn't heard them howl once and the Wohnturm was close enough that he couldn't have missed it. He felt sure no one's Marks had inverted since he'd arrived in Kvengard.

He set off through the wooded grounds for the Pontifex's Palace, a colossal limestone rectangle with blue Wolf Wards glowing above the windows and doors. The captain of the knights guarding the brass doors demanded to see his new corax identifying him as a member of the Nuncio's office. The man's chilly light blue eyes, so like Alexei's father's, kept flicking to the Raven on his neck. At last, the knights brusquely waved him through the doors. He strode through the corridors to the audience chamber, reaching it just as the bells tolled six. More knights in green surcoats stood guard outside.

Bishop Morvana waited for him beneath a faded tapestry, having changed into her robe of dark blue silk with gold embroidery along the sleeves.

"You've been to the kennels," she said, eying the short brown hairs clinging to his woolen cassock.

"Just visiting the hound I brought with me."

An appraising look. "I've never met a priest of the Interfectorem who treated them as anything other than working dogs."

"We share a history," he admitted.

Morvana's emerald eyes cooled. "In the war, you mean."

She didn't wait for a response, striding past the knights and pushing through the tall doors to the audience chamber.

Luk sat on a raised dais. His white robes were sleeveless, which Alexei still found faintly shocking. Running Wolves wound down both spindly arms. For all that the Kvens were arch-conservatives, they seemed to find nothing wrong with displaying their Marks for public view.

Alexei lowered his head in deference. "Reverend Father."

"Reverend Father," Morvana echoed, stepping forward to kneel and kiss his offered ring.

The Pontifex of the Southern Curia had a soft, mellow voice, nearly unaccented when he spoke Osterlish.

"So," he said. "How are you getting on?"

"We're finishing up the interviews," Morvana said. "The Polizei were thorough, but Fra Bryce thought it would be worthwhile to reexamine all the evidence."

Alexei suppressed a sardonic smile. He knew what she thought of the Polizei.

"Any theories?" Luk asked, propping his sharp chin on one hand. The heavy gold signet ring gleamed in the standing lamps to either side of the dais.

"It has to be an Unmarked." Morvana glanced at Alexei. He nodded, though he felt a twinge of guilt. Kasia Novak had failed the tests and she was a good person regardless. But it *had* to be. Anything else was impossible. Marks would not allow an individual to commit such evil. They'd already ruled out an Invertido by the simple fact that none of the hounds had barked on any of the days in question.

"What do you recommend?" Luk asked.

"A door-to-door search of the Burwald."

The Burwald was Kvengard's equivalent of Ash Court, a community designated for deviants. Alexei had ridden through it several times in his trips around the city. It was cleaner than the one in Novo, though solidly working class.

"That's a violation of civil rights," Luk pointed out.

"I see no other course." Morvana's jaw set. "We have six days before the next one."

"You're certain of the timing?"

"It's the *only* thing I'm certain of," she admitted grimly.

"Perhaps we can ask for written permission to enter the premises," Alexei ventured. "That's perfectly legal."

Morvana cast him an appraising look. "And if they refuse, at least we have a shorter list of suspects. Clever."

"You have my permission to do so," Luk said, his gaze piercing. "This *must* be stopped."

The pontifex was bald as an egg, which only enhanced the impression of a skeleton draped in skin. Alexei didn't know what was wrong with him and hadn't dared to ask. But he wondered how much longer Luk would wear the white robe.

"I would also suggest an official announcement, Reverend Father," he said. "People should be warned."

Morvana stared at him, though her expression gave little away.

"And what would you have me say? That an Unmarked maniac is loose in our city?" Luk leaned forward. "Tell me, Fra Bryce, what will happen if the Arx issues such a message?"

Alexei remained silent.

"The days of lynch mobs are thankfully over," Luk continued. "But I imagine life would become very unpleasant for the poor souls who failed the tests, most of whom are blameless. I understand the gravity of the situation, but I will not condemn an entire class of human beings to poverty because they lose their livelihoods."

"You needn't say it's an Unmarked—"

"Everyone knows there is no other possibility. I imagine the whispers have already spread and I refuse to give them weight." The mild tone vanished. "Find this person and arrest them. That is the only solution."

"Yes, Reverend Father."

"Now, on to other matters. I've received word from the garrison that the Knights of Saint Jule are marching on the Morho Sarpanitum." He watched Alexei's reaction closely. "They're heading towards Bal Kirith."

"Falke . . . the Reverend Father implied as much when he spoke to me," Alexei said carefully.

"I assume the action is intended to inflict retribution for the Reverend Mother Feizah's murder at the hands of the Nightmage Malach." Luk's thin mouth tightened in a grimace. "He should be brought to justice, but I wonder how many will die in this operation. Morvana, what say you?"

"It is to be expected," she replied crisply. "Dmitry Falke would seize any pretense to invade. We will continue to monitor the situation."

Pretense? A Pontifex was dead. True, Malach hadn't done it, but only Alexei knew that.

"Very good." Luk flicked a finger. "Keep me informed. You're both dismissed."

Two cardinals passed on the way out of the audience chamber. Both eyed Alexei with open hostility. Morvana earned a cold nod.

"Does everyone think I'm a spy?" he wondered.

"I do not know what they think, Fra Bryce."

Morvana's long legs carried her ahead down the stone gallery, hands tucked into her sleeves and a preoccupied expression on her face. He hurried to catch up.

"They don't seem to like you much, either," he observed.

She glanced at him. "I've spent the last five years in Novo. The Arx here is much the same as yours. Some thought I was too young to be nuncio and their opinion has not changed."

"When will we start the search?"

"I must coordinate it with the Polizei and community leaders."

"We have no time for red tape. Why not start tonight?"

"Because we need to do this properly or else any evidence we find might be deemed inadmissible. Surely you know that."

He gave a reluctant nod.

They parted ways outside the palace. The phalanx of heavily armed knights guarding the doors didn't even glance at him as he passed, but his back itched as he walked towards his rooms in the Wohnturm. Kvengard was a peculiar place. Calling it insular would be a laughable understatement. They walled themselves away, renouncing all technology or contact with the outside, but he wondered how long it could endure.

Falke had moved at last. The Curia was headed for war again, whether Luk liked it or not.

The man was a puzzle. Brilliant and difficult, with a tendency to go his own way regardless of what the Pontifical Council decided. From the talk Alexei had overheard in the mess hall, Luk commanded absolute loyalty among the clergy. More than that—an almost divine authority, which was a heretical notion. There was no God but the ley. No heaven or hell but those we create ourselves.

What would the Kvens do when he was gone? Oh, there were always cardinals waiting in the wings. Someone would take the ring. Yet Luk had been Pontifex when Alexei's *father* was still an infant. It was his hand that guided Kvengard in all things. Would he still cling to neutrality if he knew what had happened in Jalghuth?

Luk wouldn't believe me even I told him, Alexei thought. He'd think it was some scheme by Falke to force his hand.

Saints! Intrigues within intrigues. He almost longed for the days when all he had to do was chase down Invertidos. When Lezarius was not a threat to the known world, but just an old man in pajamas bumming cigarettes from the orderlies.

Alexei rubbed his temples. One problem at a time. Something had to break in the case. It *had* to.

He climbed the stairs, lit a candle, and sat down in a chair with the files. By the time he finally nodded off hours later, Alexei had a softly snoring dog at his feet.

# Chapter Two

The curving, sheltered harbor bristled with tall-masted merchant ships laden with goods for the lands of the Golden Imperator across the southern sea.

Kasia Novak had passed her time aboard the *Moonbeam* listening to the sailors talk and thus had learned a good deal about Kvengard. It was the only Curia city to be granted a trade license by the Imperator. Great fortunes had been made from the import market in *bokang*, a dense wood that burned for days and gave off a sweet cedar-like scent. Bokang had the advantage of emitting very little smoke, which was fortunate since the city relied on it for everything from cooking to heating and trades like blacksmithing.

The Kven peninsula was rocky and covered in heath-moors, its own forests having been felled centuries before. Now it was dotted with grazing sheep and cows, and little stone structures where the shepherds dwelt. From the rail, she studied the city itself, mounded above the harbor like—

"Gingerbread," Natalya said at her shoulder. "Delicious gingerbread."

Kasia raised Tessaria's binoculars. "It does, doesn't it?"

The timbered houses were capped with tall spires and

patterned in fanciful designs, with red tile roofs. Horses trotted along the waterfront hauling all manner of conveyances, from rough wagons to elegant coaches with lacquered insignias on the doors.

"I'm glad we get to stay the night," Nashka said. "I want some Kven cheese."

The captain had insisted that his passengers make themselves scarce before customs officers boarded. Tess tried to bully him, but he wouldn't back down. He'd been edgy ever since their dashing escape from Novostopol, despite Tessaria's letter from Dmitry Falke granting them safe passage. The captain promised to take them to Nantwich, but only once his business here was concluded.

"Do you think about anything but food?" Kasia asked.

"Not when I'm starving."

"They did feed us."

"Ship grub," Natalya replied dourly. "It was only edible because I washed it down with ship grog."

Tessaria Foy emerged from belowdecks, a tall, regal woman in her late seventies with a steely gaze and long braids. She aimed a boot at Fra Patryk Spassov, who sat up with a snort. He'd done some damage to the grog the prior evening as well, and looked far worse for it than Natalya, though Kasia had heard them both singing pop songs until the wee hours.

"Can we stay in a decent hotel?" Natalya asked hopefully.

Tess laughed. "And advertise our presence here? Not likely." She cast a baleful look at the captain, who pretended not to notice. "If that man weren't such a coward, I'd keep you both locked in your cabin for the next twenty-four hours."

Behind her, Nashka mimed plunging a dagger into her own chest and stabbing repeatedly.

"But since we're being evicted until dawn, I've made other arrangements."

Tess turned and Natalya gave her a bland stare. "How? Smoke signals?"

"I have my ways," Tessaria replied with an enigmatic smile. "You can buy new clothes, darling."

They both brightened at that.

Tessaria was a vestal, the female equivalent of a priest, supposedly retired. Tess still wore a black cassock from Falke's inauguration, just as the two young women were decked out in tight dresses and torn stockings. Kasia had her heels, though Natalya had lost her shoes in the alley when they were assaulted by masked thugs.

The Order of the Black Sun.

That was the reason Tess was so steamed about them leaving the ship. Kasia thought Kvengard looked harmless enough, but her patron seemed to believe they wouldn't be safe until they reached the Reverend Mother Clavis in Nantwich.

"Ah, here's our dinghy," Tess said, peering over the rail at a waiting oarsman.

Spassov shuffled over, rubbing his bald spot. "Where are we off to?"

"*We*," Tess replied, "are going to stay with friends. *You* will remain at the docks and keep an eye on the *Moonbeam*." She dropped a purse into his meaty paw. "That should cover room and board for a night at one of the waterfront hostels."

He frowned. "What if something happens?"

"Then I shall send for you."

"But I promised Alyosha I'd keep an eye—"

"Yes, yes," she said impatiently. "We'll manage somehow without your masculine protection."

"He's just trying to help," Kasia said. "I'd be in a sack if it wasn't for him."

"Why can't he come?" Natalya put in.

"No, Sor Foy is right," Spassov said quickly. "One of us ought to stay and make sure the captain keeps his word. I don't mind."

Tessaria looked a touch chastened. She leaned over and

whispered in his ear. "You may find us there, Fra Spassov. I assure you, we'll be fine. And it's only a single night. If you hear nothing, we will meet back here in the morning."

He nodded solemnly. "Thank you, Sor Foy."

"Give him your shoes," Natalya advised. "Unless you want to end up in the drink."

Kasia kicked them off. Spassov tucked the pumps into a pocket of his cassock.

"You see?" he said with a grin. "What would you do without me?"

"Perish of boredom," Natalya declared. "Not to mention sobriety."

Kasia detected no sexual tension between them, though Natalya was a terrible rake. Just camaraderie. She'd grown fond of Spassov herself. He resembled a shaved bear, but she got the sense he was more cunning than Tess gave him credit for.

They all climbed a ladder down to the dinghy and rowed across to a series of long stone piers. Sea birds with red-tipped wings clung to the rigging of the schooners at anchor, while smaller fishing skiffs headed out to sea, bobbing as they reached the choppier water of the harbor mouth. Once they'd bid goodbye to Spassov, the three women engaged a horse-drawn cab. Tess spoke to the driver in Kven and and settled back in the seat.

"Draw the curtains," she commanded.

Natalya obeyed, but peered through a crack as they clattered off, the seat jouncing and creaking. "I feel like I'm in a stage play. Something quaint and old-timey."

"Will we have running water?" Kasia wondered. "At this mysterious refuge?"

"They're not barbarians. Once you get used to it, the life here is pleasant. Simple. Plenty of people have emigrated from Novo."

"I prefer my washing machine, thank you, Auntie."

"As do I," Tess said with a laugh. "Now, I will tell you where we're going. A place called Danziger Haus. It belongs to very old, very dear friends." Black eyes twinkled. "We were intelligence agents together during the war."

Natalya let the curtain fall. "I thought the Kvens were neutral."

"Officially, yes. But everyone had spies everywhere, darling."

"Did you blow stuff up?"

"I may have engaged in acts of sabotage," Tess replied cagily. "I spent three years in Bal Agnar." Her face darkened. "It was a terrible time. Public executions every day. Chaos in the streets. Starvation and pestilence. When they sealed the gates, I expected to die there."

"How did you get out?" Kasia asked.

"Lezarius banished the ley. When his army broke through and liberated the city, people fell to their knees and wept. I watched them tear down the gates to Gethsemane Prison. The conditions inside . . . ." She shook her head to dispel the memory. "Well. Our hosts are Jann and Hanne Danziger. We've stayed in touch, though I haven't seen them in a decade or so."

Tessaria turned away, her expression discouraging further questions. They rode in silence for long minutes. Then the sound of the wheels changed from cobbles to dirt. Kasia drew the curtain wider. They were somewhere on the outskirts of the city. Stands of trees appeared, interspersed with rocky meadows and purple-tinged heath.

"The Danzigers made a heap," Tessaria said. "Luk rewarded their loyalty with a trade commission. They've tried to reforest their property."

"A heap is right," Natalya murmured, as a large house came into view.

It conformed to the timbered Kven style, but on a far grander scale. Turrets of various size capped the east and west wings. A stretch of emerald lawn fronted the house, with formal gardens and dark pine woods beyond.

There appeared to be a party going on. Carriages lined the drive and the windows glowed with light. The strains of a string quartet drifted across the lawn.

"I thought they were expecting us," Kasia said in surprise.

"Not exactly." Her guardian looked displeased. She rapped on the roof and the cab drew to a stop. "Wait here."

Tessaria handed the driver some coins with an admonishment that he'd get the rest when she returned. Kasia watched her stride up the drive.

Natalya grinned. "A party? Well, we're dressed for it. I dance better without shoes anyway."

Nashka didn't know about the Order of the Black Sun. She believed their only enemy was Bishop Maria Karolo, last seen dripping on the wharf at Novoport. Why? Because Tess refused to tell her. The woman hoarded secrets like a wyvern with gold. Tess claimed to be retired, but she'd admitted before they left that she'd used both Kasia and Natalya as unwitting informants for years. The betrayal still stung. Kasia knew it stemmed from Tess's devotion to the ideals of her faith, but she'd had enough of the Curia's manipulations.

She decided that Natalya had the right to the truth. Her friend was in as much danger as the rest of them.

Kasia leaned forward. "Those men from the alley? It wasn't random, Nashka. They're some sort of evil alchemists."

Natalya laughed. "If by alchemy, you mean mixing lager with vodka, I heartily agree—"

"No, really. I should have told you before."

"Evil?" Nashka repeated thoughtfully. "As in, diabolical dark forces bent on world destruction?"

"Yes."

"And you know this how?"

"Remember all that talk about *Caput corvi* and *The dragon consumes itself, dying to rise again*?"

"Not really, but I'm sure you do."

Kasia had an extraordinary memory. She could recall entire conversations verbatim, even years afterwards, and mundane, stupid details like what she wore that day, or the precise order and title of every book on a shelf. She had thought everyone remembered things the same way and couldn't understand Tessaria's shock when her guardian realized Kasia's talent—if it could even be called that. She'd never found it particularly useful until now.

"Caput corvi means decapitation of the raven," Kasia explained. "The man said, *The Black Sun rises again.* It's the Mark of the Pontifex Balaur."

"He's dead," Nashka said flatly.

"Maybe they think they can bring him back."

"That's horseshit."

"Probably. But they're very much alive and Tess claims they have secret societies in all the cities."

"Saints. Why didn't you tell me before?" She sighed. "Never mind. I suppose Inquisitor Foy put the screws on you. Well, that explains a few things. Not what they want, but Tess's paranoia." She tilted her head. "Though it isn't paranoia if they really *are* trying to kill you. Go on."

"They call themselves the Order of the Black Sun. I don't know much more, but they seem to be chasing me. I suppose they know about the cards."

Natalya withdrew her feet from the opposite seat. "Do a reading, Kiska."

Kasia realized she was clenching the deck in her pocket and forced her stiff fingers to relax. She hadn't attempted a spread since she'd drawn the Martyr and the Knight of Storms on the ship. Mikhail and Lezarius.

"You think I should?"

"Yes," Natalya said firmly. "The ley never lies."

Kasia leaned her head out of the window. Tess was nowhere in sight.

She snugged her gloves tighter and spread the deck across the seat. Kasia always drew with her left hand. Her fingertips danced over the cards, then slid one from the spread.

The Jack of Wolves.

"Oh, dear," Natalya muttered. "I know that's not good, but remind me of the particulars."

She'd painted the cards herself, but over the years of their partnership, Kasia had naturally taken over the role of cartomancer, allowing Natalya to develop her skill as an artist. Nashka adapted the designs of the ancient pre-Dark Age decks, giving them her own flair—and often incorporating people she knew into the images. But she was less concerned with their complex layers of meaning, leaving Kasia to interpret the significance.

"Jacks are tricky," Kasia said, studying the card. "Wolves means Kvengard, of course. The Jack has a high rank, but not the highest. Those would be the Saints, Cardinals and Bishops. So it's someone of importance, but also the servant of another. The golden crown caught in the tree above means he seeks greater power and authority, yet it lies just out of reach."

"Sounds like most people," Natalya said dryly. "Go on."

"Here's the tricky part. Do you see how the card reveals only one eye? That means a double nature. Showing one face to the world and another in private."

"Again, half the population. What about the peacock?"

The Jack was captured in mid-stride, facing to the left, a stave in his fist. A ruined building that resembled a fort lay in the background, and a white peacock.

"Purity. Innocence. A peculiar combination with the Jack, who represents worldly ambition, especially in the forward motion. Let's try another and see if it sheds light."

Next came the Mage. The first numbered card of the Major Arcana. The figure wore a crimson robe with a deep cowl. It faced the viewer, though the features were cast in shadow. One hand was raised aloft, holding a vial that gave off stylized beams of light.

"Malach?" Natalya asked in alarm.

Kasia firmly shook her head. "No, he's the Fool."

Zero. A Nullity. He preceded the Mage in the pecking order. A vagabond who journeyed beyond civilized realms, he was both naive and cynical, a wily figure with infinite potential for light and darkness both.

Natalya still didn't know all of it. She had no idea that Mikhail Bryce had killed the Pontifex Feizeh. Like everyone else, she thought Malach was to blame and Kasia couldn't tell her the truth without breaking her promise to Alexei.

"Are you certain?" Natalya pressed. "He came after you in the Arx. If he's here, we have to leave even if it means swimming to Nantwich."

Kasia considered it. "Yes, I'm sure. The Major Arcana are powerful archetypes. They wouldn't change."

She'd drawn the Mage before in Novostopol when she did the spread for Ferran Massot—but with a crucial difference. The card had been inverted. Invertido for Mikhail, whose Mark had been flipped by Malach. Upright, it meant someone else.

"But it means a nihilim?"

"Yes. Or someone who wields abyssal ley."

She closed her eyes and drew a third card.

The Lovers.

Kasia stared at it. The man was pictured from the back, which had a Mark of two flaming towers. The woman was dark-haired and full-figured, with an uncanny resemblance to Kasia herself.

"Fra Bryce is here," she said softly.

"Oh-ho!" Nashka fell back in her seat with a satisfied smirk. "I knew it. Do tell."

"He came to the flat while you were at Tess's," she admitted. "I let him sleep there, the poor thing."

"Sleep?" Natalya arched a dark brow. "I hope you're being modest. When you say he's here, do you mean this house?"

"The city, at least. Spassov said he was headed for Kvengard." She gave Natalya a warning look. "Not a word to Tess. She doesn't know."

"That you fell into bed with a priest who's wanted for murder? I'd never. " She sighed. "Too bad we're leaving tomorrow."

Kasia drew another card.

A skeleton with moths resting inside the empty eye sockets. Bony fingers gripped a small golden scythe.

Natalya's breath hissed.

"Don't faint," she said dryly. "Death has many meanings that aren't literal. The end of an old way of life and the birth of a new one is the most common. Letting go of old attachments. Liberation."

Kasia turned over the last card.

The Sun.

She smiled. "You see? It portends good fortune, happiness, and harmony. So all is not lost—"

"She's coming!" Natalya exclaimed.

Kasia swept up the cards and returned the deck to her pocket. Tessaria Foy wasn't alone. A man was with her. A very handsome man in evening wear, with thick blonde hair and light eyes, crinkled at the corners with faint lines that spoke of laughter. He opened the door to the carriage with a grin.

"I've been appointed to spirit you up the back stairs," he said in stage whisper, offering a white gloved hand to Natalya.

She climbed out, wiggling her toes in the grass.

"I can manage, thank you," Kasia said, when he extended his arm to her.

"A lady of independence." The Kven accent was thick.

"Oh Jule, do stop trying to flirt," Tessaria chastised. "You haven't changed since you were a little boy."

He chuckled. "I hope not, Domine Foy. Remember how

you used to let me sit in your lap?"

Tessaria rolled her eyes, but Kasia could see she was fond of him. Jule insisted on paying the driver the remainder of the fare and they cut across the lawn, circling around to the rear of the house. A low murmur of voices drifted through the open windows, and the clink of silver against plates.

"It's the annual fete of the Imperator's ambassador," Jule confided as they approached a smaller set of doors. "These parties are tedious anyway. I'm glad for an excuse to slip away."

He led them through a steamy, bustling kitchen and up a flight of servant's stairs to the third floor of the house. The door opened to a corridor paneled in rich wood and carved moldings. They followed it past a dozen closed doors to a library that occupied a round turret room at the corner of the house. A sweet-smelling bokang fire burned in the hearth.

"Make yourselves comfortable," Jule said, gesturing to an array of heavy upholstered chairs. "I'll fetch my aunt and uncle, though it might be a while. They're in the midst of dinner."

"Don't rush," Tess said, shrugging off her cloak. "It was a long sea journey. We'll just rest for a while."

"I'll send up some refreshments." Jule eyed the younger women with curiosity. "You must be hungry."

"Ravenous," Natalya said with a smile.

A spark lit in Jule's eye. "Then I'll tell the servants to hurry." He gave them each a brief bow from the waist and strode off, closing the door behind him.

Kasia moved to stand by the fire, examining it with interest. The wood was bone-white and looked dense. It didn't seem to burn so much as to hold the dancing flames.

"I'll admit, our timing was poor," Tess conceded. "Luckily, I caught Jule sneaking out for a cigarette. He's discreet."

"What do you plan to tell them?" Kasia asked.

"Nothing of consequence."

"Good."

She thought of the cards she'd drawn in the carriage and longed to do another reading, but Tess would never approve. She didn't trust Kasia to handle the cards without accidentally using the ley. It was all a puzzle, Kasia thought as she stared into the fire. Sometimes she ignited them, but sometimes she didn't. Intention seemed to matter. If she wanted simply to do a foretelling, they behaved as always. Both times she'd used them to wield the ley, her life had been in danger. First with the vestal knights at the Pontifex's Palace, and later with the assailants in the alley.

The newfound power had come shortly after Malach touched her on the rooftop. What had the mage done to her? Did she always have the ability, or had he changed her in some way? She could see the ley now when she concentrated, flowing in currents along the earth. It was sparser on the third floor of the house, thick as a river below. Kasia slipped a gloved hand in her pocket, checking to make sure her deck was still there. When she looked up, Tess was staring at her sharply. Kasia withdrew her hand.

"I can't wait to sleep in a proper bed tonight," Natalya said, curling her feet beneath her in one of the armchairs. "One that doesn't tilt to and fro like a carnival ride."

"Enjoy it while it lasts," Tess said dryly. "The journey to Nantwich will be nearly a week and the crossing can be rough."

Natalya tipped her head back. "Do we have to stay in the Arx when we get there?"

"Yes. Until we get our bearings, at least."

Natalya caught her eye with a slight grimace. Kasia wasn't thrilled at the prospect, either. She knew there was no returning to her old life, but she just wanted to be left alone. Far from the machinations of the church.

"Are you certain the Reverend Mother will even take us in?" she asked.

"I am certain."

A guarded, considering look crossed Tess's face. Kasia didn't like it. Her patron kept too many secrets. She was about to press Tessaria for answers when the door opened and an elderly couple entered. The man wore a somber evening suit that emphasized the extreme pallor of his skin. His hair was silver and leonine, swept back from a high brow. Strong, square features revealed a once-hardy man who suffered from some long illness. He walked stiffly with the aid of a cane.

The woman at his side was small and birdlike, with bright blue eyes and ruddy cheeks. At first, Kasia thought the Marks on her arms were part of her gown. Flowers and vines twined from shoulder to wrist in such thick abundance hardly a centimeter of bare skin showed. Then they flickered with ley. Kasia blinked in startlement.

Tess hurried to embrace them both. The woman laughed, kissing both of her cheeks.

"I'm so sorry to barge in on you like this," Tessaria said. "It's unforgivable."

"Nonsense. You're always welcome here. Now, who have you brought us?"

Tessaria turned. "This is Kasia Novak, my ward."

"Of course!" Her smile was warm and inviting. "I have always wanted to meet you, Kasia. Tessaria spoke of you often in her letters. I am Hanne, and this is my husband, Jann."

He dipped his head. Natalya rose to her feet, joining Kasia at the hearth.

"And this is Natalya Anderle. A dear friend. The Reverend Father Dmitry entrusted me with a bit of Curia business to conduct in Nantwich. Kasia always wanted to see the city, so I offered to take her and Natalya along." She scowled. "There was a mix-up with our luggage. Apparently, it was loaded onto the wrong ship." She cast a wry look at the women. "Natalya was so incensed, she threw her shoes into the sea. It was a childish tantrum, but the girl has an artist's temperament."

Natalya gave Tess a level look but remained silent.

"Hot-headed." Jann chuckled. "It comes from the creative fires, *ja*?"

"She's very talented," Kasia said loyally.

"Well, she had every right to be furious," Hanne Danziger said. "I can't tell you how often we've suffered damage to goods from rough handling by those oafs at the docks. Not to worry, I'll have my seamstress make you some new garments."

"We're only here for one night," Tess said quickly. "I don't wish to trouble you."

"It is no trouble. She is very quick. We just need your measurements. The shoes will take longer. I'll send to the city, but we can have them by morning. In the meantime, I am sure I can find something suitable for Domina Anderle."

"You're too kind," Tess said.

Hanne studied her. "Is it good to see you," she said. "Saints, but it's been too long. You look the same as ever." Her face grew sorrowful. "I am pleased Falke took the ring, but we grieve for the Reverend Mother Feizah. Is it true that a Night-mage entered the Arx?"

"Where did you hear that?" Tessaria asked sharply.

A shrug. "Everyone says it."

Tess sighed. "I suppose it's inevitable the truth would come out. We still don't know how he managed it."

Jann shook his head, lips tight. "We did not give our lives for the nihilim to come and go on holy ground as they please! It is an abomination. I wish—" His knuckles tightened white around the cane. Kasia sensed Marks flaring beneath his clothing, tamping down his anger. "Forgive me," he murmured.

"There is nothing to forgive," Tess said gently. "I share your sentiments. And I'm sure the Reverend Father Dmitry will not allow such a trespass to stand." She paused. "What of your pontifex? Has Luk made any public statement?"

The Danzigers exchanged a glance. "His condolences, of

course. You understand the position of the Southern Curia. We abjure all violence, even in revenge for such a brutal act. Especially then. The nihilim would make beasts of us all."

Tess made a noncommittal sound. It was a long-standing sore point that Luk always stood apart when there was fighting, only to reap the benefits of peace once it was over. An awkward silence ensued.

"We should get back," Hanne said regretfully. "I would much rather stay and catch up, but the Imperator's delegation is touchy about matters of etiquette. They will not take kindly to being abandoned by their hosts in the middle of dessert."

"Of course." Tessaria smiled. "We're tired anyway."

"Your rooms are just down the hall. They are being prepared. We might be quite late so you don't need to wait up. We will see you at breakfast?"

Tess nodded gratefully. Hanne turned to Kasia. "I hope we shall have the opportunity to speak more before the ship departs. I am curious about this cartomancy you practice." Her smile was motherly, yet Kasia had trouble returning it.

The Danzigers left with a promise to send the seamstress. Footmen arrived on their heels, bearing a table covered with a white linen cloth. More servants laid it with a dizzying array of silver, crystal and delicate blue-glazed porcelain. Natalya brightened as they whisked the covers from platters of broiled trout in almond paste, dark seeded bread, and sweet, creamy Kven cheese. Dusty bottles of wine were uncorked and decanted. The moment the servants departed, Kasia turned to Tess.

"She knows?"

"That you play at reading the future for parties? Yes! I told her that ages ago. How could I know it would become a liability?"

Liability? "Well, as long as that's all you told her." Kasia took a sip of wine. "They seem like nice people."

"The very best," Tess said firmly. "Poor Jann. He was

captured, you know. Balaur's agents tortured him at the Arx in Bal Agnar. His legs were broken and never healed right."

"That's horrible." Nashka set her fork down.

"Yes." Tess's gaze grew distant. "I am glad to see them doing well."

"And Jule is their nephew?" Kasia asked.

"On Hanne's side. Her sister's son. Jule's parents were both deployed as neutral observers. They never made it back from the Void. I imagine he'll take over the business when they finally decide to retire. Hanne keeps hoping he'll settle down with a nice girl, but Jule is the restless type."

It was quiet for a while as the women ate, though Kasia noticed that Tess picked at her food. She seemed lost in painful memories. Natalya tried to cheer her with silly jests, but finally gave up and paced over to the tall shelves, idly leafing through the books. They were all in Kven. She finally earned a rueful laugh with her awful reading of a volume of poetry.

The food was excellent. Kasia ate double helpings of everything and had just pushed her plate back with a happy sigh when the seamstress appeared with a tape measure.

"Should I come back later, Domina?" she asked in a thick Kven accent.

Kasia studied her bulging stomach. "No," she said with a sigh. "Just shave a few centimeters off, eh?"

The woman grinned cheerfully. "Of course, Domina. It will all fit perfectly, I promise."

She took out a pencil, pad, and ribbon, and they took turns standing by the fire while she jotted down their measurements. The seamstress was deft and chatty, informing them that she had a sister in Novostopol and was glad for a chance to practice her Osterlish.

"Perhaps I will visit her someday," she said. "I would like to ride in an automobile. Do you enjoy living there?"

"Novo's the best," Natalya said wistfully.

The seamstress lifted her arm and wound the ribbon around her slender bust. "It must be very loud."

Kasia thought of their flat above the curry restaurant. It was popular with students and served until three a.m., so the after-hours crowd often ended up there, congregating in the street.

"You get used to it," she said.

"It sounds exciting. Me, I like the country life." She laughed, tucking a wayward strand of flame-red hair behind her ear. "And out here, it is very peaceful."

"I'd go mad," Natalya muttered.

Tessaria cleared her throat. "Are we nearly finished?"

The seamstress scribbled a number down and rolled up the ribbon. "That will do. Now, what did you have in mind?"

"Something simple," Tessaria said. "But modest. High necks and long sleeves, please."

The seamstress seemed to find this amusing. Her own dress, with its expanse of pale, freckled bosom, would have been utterly scandalous in Novo. "Of course, Sor Foy."

"Trousers and a blouse for me. Dresses for the young ladies."

"I want trousers, too," Natalya objected.

"Fine. Kasia?"

"I'd prefer a dress. Something with pockets, but stylish." She looked at Natalya. "Like my blue one."

"May I borrow your pad?" Natalya asked.

She quickly sketched the dress and handed it over. The seamstress studied the drawing.

"*Ja*, I can make that. What kind of material?"

"Velvet. Dark blue or black. Lace trim, if you can."

"Pretty." She nodded her approval. "You have the figure for it."

"She has the figure for a burlap sack," Natalya said, biting into a carrot with a loud snap.

"Well, you both look fabulous in pantsuits." Kasia eyed

her companions, tall and slim as birch switches. "I, on the other hand, look like a mid-level bureaucrat angling for promotion."

Natalya laughed.

"I'll have the new garments to you by morning," the seamstress promised.

"So quickly?" Kasia said with surprise.

"I use the ley. It is my talent."

Tessaria tried to press some silver coins into her palm, but the woman refused. "You are guests of Domina Danziger. It is my pleasure to serve." She winked. "You can tell your friends that Amelie of Kvengard made these clothes. Perhaps someday I will own my own shop."

She bade them goodnight. Natalya covered a yawn. "Why can't we show a bit of skin like everyone else?"

"Because . . ." Tess scowled. "Just because."

Kasia didn't mind covering herself. It concealed her lack of Marks. "Come, Nashka," she said. "Let's find our rooms."

Tessaria tugged on a tasseled bell pull and two servants magically appeared. Both were dour and unsmiling, with none of Amelie's easy warmth. Maybe they didn't speak Osterlish, Kasia thought, as she followed them down the dim hall. Or maybe they just didn't like foreigners. Either way, she decided she would be glad to leave in the morning.

Tessaria kissed each woman on the cheek, then vanished into her room. Kasia was wordlessly ushered through a door across the way. The servant pointed to another bell pull and mimed yanking on it.

"Yes, I understand. I'll call if I need anything. Thank you."

A brusque nod. Kasia closed the door.

A candelabra next to the four-poster bed gave the only light. All the furnishings were dark and pointy. She kicked off her pumps and tested the feather mattress. Scuffling noises came through the wall. Kasia noticed that a small child-sized door connected to the room next door. She knocked.

"Who is it?" Nashka asked in a fluting voice.

"Me."

Kasia opened the door. The hinges squealed, as if it hadn't been used in years.

Natalya clutched her breast, eyes wide. "Have you come to ravish me?"

"I ate too much cheese to ravish anyone."

"Me, too." Natalya wiggled out of her dress and pulled a white linen nightgown over her head, then admired herself in an oval standing mirror. "Saints, I almost look virginal in this thing."

"*Almost* being the operative word." Kasia drifted over to the windows. They faced the vast lawn at the front of the house. "The guests are starting to leave. Oh, that must be the delegation from the Imperator!"

Natalya stumbled over the long hem in her haste to get to the window.

A group in flowing robes emerged from the house. Torches burned along the drive, illuminating their embroidered turbans and richly colored sashes. The men and women wore identical clothing, though the men were all bearded. Kasia watched in fascination as they climbed into three lacquered carriages. One of the stallions tossed its head, eyes shining like gold coins in the torchlight. An instant later it seemed to vanish into shadow, leaving only a vague afterimage of a regal black horse.

"Marksteeds," Natalya said in awe, staring intently. "They must be. Oh, it makes me dizzy to look at them!"

"Do you know which emirati holds the throne?" Kasia asked.

The Masdar League was comprised of seven kingdoms, each of which occupied the seat of the Golden Imperator for a seven-year term. Their lands lay far across the Southern Ocean.

"Not a clue," Natalya said. "You know I don't follow politics."

"I wonder why they only trade with Kvengard."

"Who can say? It's always been that way."

"Do they have Marks?"

"I don't think so."

"But they must use the ley. The witches do."

"The witches are heathens," Natalya declared piously. "The Masdar League is civilized, at least."

"I wonder what it's like there."

"Burning desert and humped beasts with jewels for eyes," Natalya whispered. "They have eunuch assassins, too, clad in white silk wrappings from head to toe, who can kill with a single breath."

Kasia arched a brow.

"It's all true," Natalya insisted. "They guard the Imperator. He or she is like a god for the seven years they reign in court."

"I thought you didn't follow politics."

"Saints, everyone knows that. You just didn't pay attention in school."

The last of the carriages vanished down the torchlit drive. Others pulled up, bearing away the lesser dignitaries—all Kvens, judging by their dark, long-tailed coats and skimpy evening gowns.

"The Danzigers must be very well-connected," Kasia said.

"Well, they earned it, serving in Bal Agnar. I can't begin to imagine what that was like. Did you see Tessaria at supper?"

"She knows things she's not telling us."

Natalya looked thoughtful. "About the Order of the Black Sun, you mean?"

"I don't know. But she's hiding something."

"More than one thing, I'd wager. Sor Foy keeps the Curia's

secrets. But I trust her. Don't you?"

"Of course," Kasia murmured.

Did she though? The letter of safe passage from Falke seemed too good to be true. So did the Danzigers. Could Tessaria be using them in some intrigue again? It couldn't be ruled out, but they were marooned in the midst of nowhere, among strangers. Kasia had no choice but to go along for now. And she didn't truly believe Tess would let them come to harm. She was loyal and good-hearted, even if she could be overly zealous in her faith.

"We ought to get some sleep. Tomorrow will be a long day."

Natalya made a face. "A week shipboard? Ah, I suppose I can stand it. We're in this together, aren't we?"

"Always." Kasia hugged her close, breathing in Natalya's herb-scented hair.

She returned to her own room and undressed for bed. Some rooting through an impressive ebony cabinet with drawers lined with red morocco unearthed a simple linen nightdress similar to Natalya's. Kasia sat on the bed and took out her cards, spreading them across the coverlet. All lay face down, save one.

The Lovers.

She bit her lip. She would like to see Alexei Bryce—very much. She had a sudden strong urge to steal a horse from the stables and ride out to the Arx. Maybe she had some ravishing in her tonight, after all.

Tess would have a fit.

But that isn't what stopped her. Kasia didn't even know where the Arx was. Nor did she have any clue how to manage a horse.

*Leave it to the ley,* she decided regretfully.

Threads of fate bound them together, that much she knew for certain. She would see him again, though when or how remained a mystery.

A howl from the next room made her turn. The connecting door banged open.

"Tess lied," Nashka announced breathlessly. She'd braided her springy curls for sleep and looked diminished somehow, even though she stood a head above Kasia.

"Tess does that rather frequently. What did she lie about this time?"

Natalya dragged her through the connecting door and pointed at a large ceramic vessel with a lid. "Is that what I think it is?"

Kasia laughed. "You shouldn't have drunk so much wine."

"She said there was *plumbing*."

Kasia recalled the conversation in the carriage perfectly. "No, she said they weren't barbarians."

"A chamber pot is the very definition of barbaric."

"You can always pee out the window."

"I just might," Natalya replied grimly. "If I had a penis, I would."

"Thank the Saints you don't. There'd be a hundred bastard children running around Novostopol."

"What do I use for paper?"

Kasia shrugged. Natalya blew out a breath. "Just wait until it's your turn."

"I'll hold it."

"Until tomorrow?" An incredulous stare.

"Saints, just go pee in the chamber pot. It won't kill you."

Natalya wrinkled her nose. "It's nasty to have it sitting right next to the bed."

"Then put it in the corner."

"I take back all the nice things I said about Kvengard," Natalya declared. "These people are fundamentalist crackpots."

She slammed the door. Then she opened it again. "Good night, darling."

Kasia blew her a kiss.

# Chapter Three

It had rained hard that morning, but the hot midday sun was already drying the tall meadow grasses, dotted with yellow and white wildflowers. Two mating dragonflies flitted over Malach's head, then circled back and landed on his bent knee. Each was the breadth of his thumb, double-wings shimmering metallic green with darker spots of blue.

A breeze ruffled his black hair as he watched Nikola Thorn trot her horse in a wide oval around the Pontifex's park. She wore a green cloak that blended with the trees. Nikola flashed him a smile, silver canine tooth winking in the sun. She looked happy. And why shouldn't she be? He had done everything he could think of to make her stay at Bal Kirith not simply bearable but pleasant. She'd asked for riding lessons so Malach had given her the best mount in the stables, a black stallion named Fortalex. Within a few days, Nikola was galloping around as if she'd been born to the saddle.

When she was hungry, he chivvied the hungover maids from their beds or foraged in the kitchens himself. When she grew bored, he tried to amuse her with stories and bawdy songs. The morning sickness had passed. Nikola seemed well. Yet despite Malach's efforts to lull her into complacency, he knew she chafed at her confinement to the Arx. The previous evening, after a heated argument, she'd hurled a full bowl of soup at his head.

Life had otherwise been peaceful in the fortnight since Dantarion left to hunt Lezarius. About two dozen mages remained, all high-ranking clergy. Beleth waited impatiently for word of his capture, but like the others, she slept all day and debauched herself all night, so Malach had managed to mostly avoid her.

Tashtemir had given him a thick paste for the stab wound in his side with orders to apply it twice a day. The unguent stank, but Malach followed his instructions. His flesh was knitting together even faster than he hoped. He felt stronger every day—though he took care to hide it.

Nikola's belly was starting to swell. She covered it with the cloak, but he knew she was worried. Beleth had no idea she carried Malach's child. Watching her now, he wondered how much longer they could maintain the pretense. Unlike the other women, who'd grown frail and weak as the fetus sucked the life from them, Nikola radiated vitality. Her dark skin glowed, her face fuller and more rounded. She still covered her hair beneath a scarf, but he loved the silky feel of it between his fingers, the tight curls threaded with a few prematurely silver strands that caught the moonlight when she slept.

She will carry the child to term, he thought, still awestruck at the prospect. And then—

The dragonflies took flight as Tristhus and his older sister Sydonie ran out of the woods. Each carried a brace of yellow lizards strung together by the tails. The children wore cloaks identical to Nikola's, their straight black hair raggedly cut above the shoulder. Tristhus hadn't hit his growth spurt yet and his sister was a head taller. If not for the height difference, they could have been twins.

"Hello, Nikola!" Sydonie said with a toothy grin.

Nikola waved and galloped over. "What do you have there?"

"Lunch!"

She dismounted and admired the catch.

"You look pretty today," Tristhus said, shyly offering her a bloody lizard. "Do you want one?"

"Maybe later," she laughed.

Nikola slung an arm around his shoulders, catching Malach's eye with amusement.

After a rocky start in which the children had driven her to shelter at the park's stelae for two days while Malach lay feverish in bed, they got on well. Malach hadn't realized how starved for affection the pair had been before Nikola came along. They lied and manipulated at every turn, but it was their nature. Most of the time they were pleasant company.

"Take the lizards to Cook," Malach said, climbing to his feet with an exaggerated wince. "Tell her we want a stew."

"Nikola promised to play with us," Sydonie said. "Didn't you?"

Nikola opened her mouth to reply.

"After lunch," Malach interrupted. "We have something to do first."

Syd pouted. "But she said—"

"Enough. Do what I tell you."

She cast him a venomous glare, but grabbed her brother's hand. The children darted away. "And tell Cook not so much salt this time!" he shouted.

Syd made a rude gesture. Malach returned it.

"We need to talk," Nikola said once they were out of earshot.

"Of course," he murmured, taking the horse's bridle. "Whatever you say."

Grasshoppers leapt from their path as they walked to the stable, which was in a converted chapel. The groom, a sour-faced man who reeked of wine, took Nikola's mount.

"Where are we going?" she sighed as Malach steered her into one of the overgrown pathways. "You've been putting me off for days. Don't think I don't know what you're up to. But it won't work. I'm not staying here."

"We can talk when we get there."

"How far is it?"

"Not far at all."

They crossed the meadow, thick with ripening blackberries. Malach paused to pluck a handful and give them to Nikola.

"You're buttering me up," she said suspiciously. Then, "Saints, these are sweet. They must thrive on evil."

He smiled and gathered more. The thorns raked his flesh, but he pushed deeper into the thicket where the children had missed the largest, plumpest fruit. Berry juice stained Nikola's lips as they passed through the ruined gates of the Arx and entered the jungle beyond. The scent of stagnant water filled the air, and green growing things.

The land rose and the undergrowth thinned as they entered a cathedral of towering golden-leaved regnans. Malach led her to one whose trunk stood as wide as twenty men. He pulled aside a veil of creepers to reveal a tattered rope ladder. Nikola's gaze followed it up into the gloom.

"Are you sure you can climb this?" she asked dubiously.

"I can't ride yet," he said. "The motion would tear me open again. But my arms are strong."

"Where does it lead?"

"You'll see."

She shrugged and started to climb, Malach just behind. The rope ladder was decades old, rotted through in places, but she stepped without hesitation past the broken strands to the next rung. Halfway up, she turned and looked down at him. They were a good eighty meters from the forest floor.

"How fare you, mage?" she asked easily.

"Well." He smiled, thighs trembling. "Keep going."

They climbed higher into the canopy. A fresh breeze cooled the sweat on his face. Then Nikola disappeared into the huge oval leaves. A few seconds later, Malach joined her, clambering out to a flat branch nearly as broad as the Via Fortuna.

She stood for a moment, catching her breath. "All right," she said at last. "I agree that was worth the effort."

The regnan soared above its sisters, giving a hawk's eye view of the Morho in every direction. Malach handed her a water skin and Nikola drank.

"These trees are older than the Arx," he said. "Much older."

"I bet you bring all the girls up here," she said.

He'd discovered it when he was a child. Malach spent weeks weaving a rope ladder long enough to stretch the length of the trunk. He could haul it up when he wanted to. It was the one place Beleth could never find him.

"No, you're the first," Malach said. "That's the Parnassian Sea." He pointed to a sheet of beaten silver in the distance.

"Are there really a hundred thousand islands?"

Malach smiled. "I've never counted, but it's possible. Some are very small, just a rock with a few pines."

"A smugglers' haven." She sat down cross-legged, palms braced on the smooth wood. "Where do the ships dock?"

He tensed. "Just a few more days and I'll be fit to ride—"

A level stare. "That's what you keep saying, Malach."

"I mean it this time."

"All well and good. But what if something happens to you? I'll have no idea where to go." Her voice hardened. "You can't keep me in the dark any longer. If you do, I'll leave within the hour."

He knew she meant it. "All right. The smugglers drop anchor in hidden spots among the islands. There's usually a few around. Most are legitimate vessels flying flags of convenience from the Masdar League, which are sanctioned to trade with the Curia. It gives them cover. They fill their holds in Kvengard and then stop here to pick up the illegal human cargo bound for Dur-Athaara."

"And you're sure they'll take a passenger? I don't fancy ending up in the slave hold."

"They're mercenaries. If it doesn't get them in trouble with the witches, they'll do anything for gold. Or kaldurite."

The stones were exceedingly rare. They blocked the ley and the witches of Dur-Athaara prized them highly. The drawstring bag in Nikola's pocket represented a decade of savings from her job as a char at the Arx in Novostopol. Since Syd and Trist tried to steal it, Nikola kept the kaldurite on her person at all times.

"How would I make contact?" she pressed.

"There's a cove," he said reluctantly. "Where the mages bring slaves to trade. It's at the mouth of the Escalon River."

Nikola frowned. "And the Curia doesn't know about this?"

"If they do, they turn a blind eye."

"When can we leave?"

"As soon as I can ride."

She eyed him skeptically. "Maybe you can ride now and you're not admitting it."

He stared at her in reproach. "Are you trying to kill me?"

"If I'd wanted to do that, I wouldn't have come here at all." Her lips thinned. "But I won't give birth in this viper's den!"

"I don't want that, either. I told you, you'll be safe in Dur-Athaara by the time you have the baby."

Nikola peered past the spreading treetops to the Arx. The gilded roof of the Pontifex's Palace was just visible. "Dantarion could return any day. You claim she wouldn't consider me a rival, but I find that hard to believe."

Malach had told her about his cousin's pregnancy a week before. He'd never fathered a child before and now two were on the way—one a half-blood, the other a full lucifer. Nikola had taken the news calmly. Too calmly. He'd wanted her to fly into a jealous rage.

"She doesn't love me," he explained. "It was just an occasional tumble."

"Incest." Nikola shook her head. "Why am I even faintly surprised?"

"She's not a mother or sister," Malach protested.

"Still wrong."

"Says who?" he wondered.

"Everyone."

He grinned. "Clearly not *everyone*."

"Well, it's one thing the Curia's probably right about." She frowned. "Do you have a sister?"

The question stirred a sliver of memory. Very old, but still sharp enough to draw blood. He pushed it away. "No, but if I did—"

She raised a palm. "I'll stop you right there, Malach."

He smiled lazily. "I was going to say, I'd leave the choice to her."

After some judicious consideration, Malach had decided not to mention Dantarion's particular tastes. Nikola Thorn wore her toughness like armor, but beneath it he sensed an unworldy innocence. Once he would have delighted in unravelling it, thread by thread. Yet that no longer appealed to him. What he wanted, odd as it seemed, was to preserve it for as long as possible.

"I'm sorry I brought it up," she said. "My point being, even if your cousin doesn't care, I imagine retribution will be coming your way for breaking into the Arx. And I'm not going back there! I'll die first."

"They'll come eventually, yes," Malach conceded. "Given the choice, Falke would invade today, but Feizah has to approve all military actions. She may not know about any of this. Falke's playing his own game. Either way, it'll take weeks for a decision to be made. Except for the outer forts, the knights are demobilized. Restarting the war machinery will take time. In the meantime, the sentries can give us warning if anyone shows up."

She touched the puckered scar across his wrist. "What happened to you in the Arx?"

He'd put her off when she asked before. The terror was too fresh. But time had dulled it—a little bit.

"Falke tried to sever me," he said roughly. Nikola looked blank. "To cut my hands off so I could never touch the ley again."

Nikola looked shocked. "Saints!"

He still felt the pressure of the blade sometimes, so sharp it hardly hurt. Severing had been practiced by both sides during the war. The Curia viewed it as some brand of perverse compromise. A way of sparing the heretics but rendering them harmless.

There was no remedy for severing. Malach couldn't think of a worse fate.

"Our child will be powerful," he said, pulse racing as he thought of Falke. "Maybe strong enough to destroy them."

Her eyes turned inward. A hand stole to her belly. "Why are half-bloods so powerful, Malach?"

"I don't know, but they are. Part lucifer, part human."

"I could still lose it like the others."

"You won't."

Her eyes met his, demanding an answer. "How do you know?"

Malach had thought long and hard about it. "You're Unmarked. I think that's the secret."

She frowned. "What difference would it make?"

"I don't know, but you *are* different. Something about you makes it possible for the child to grow without hurting you." His hand stroked her knee. "You're special."

Nikola shook her head, suddenly angry. Her moods

changed like quicksilver now. "Why do you think we're given menial jobs, Malach?"

He shrugged. "Punishment?"

"No, because we're unreliable. We have short tempers and poor impulse control. In no way are we better than other people."

"That's propaganda. Why did they keep you on at the Arx?"

"I made an effort. Not because I cared about what they thought of me. I wanted the money."

"So you could run away?"

"Yes."

He gazed at her, full of strange, unfamiliar longing. "What will you do in Dur-Athaara?"

"Find a job. I don't care what it is, so long as I don't have to scrub floors."

"That's all you want?"

"I want to walk down the street and not be stared at."

"That's a lie," he said stonily.

She arched a brow.

"When I first saw you, you flaunted your lack of Marks. You could have passed if you wanted to."

"I didn't care enough to bother."

"I think you enjoyed provoking them."

Her gaze flicked away. "Maybe I was bored."

"Are you still bored?"

"With crocodilians on one side and Beleth on the other?" She eyed him in exasperation. "No, Malach, I'm not bored. I'm scared."

"I thought psychopaths didn't feel fear."

She laughed. "Like you, you mean? Well, I'm not a psychopath. I'm a sociopath."

"What's the difference?" He'd heard the terms before, but the Curia's labels held little interest for Malach.

"I'm not totally cold-blooded. I brought you here, didn't

I?" She hugged her knees. "We're not violent criminals. We're the friend who never remembers your birthday. The one who lets your plant die when we flat-sit and can't keep a lover for longer than two months."

*We'll see about that*, he thought.

Nikola gave a hollow laugh. "The true psychopaths are clever enough to pass the tests. They're experts at mimicking normal. I suspect there are more of them out there than the Church will ever admit, all of them Marked and leading respectable lives. Some might even be in positions of authority. Master manipulators."

He thought of Cardinal Falke. The emotional detachment as he parted Malach's skin with his scalpel.

"That's an interesting theory," he said. "You called me a psychopath."

"Because you are."

He frowned. "I have feelings."

Nikola seemed to find this amusing. "It's not about *your* feelings. It's about empathy for other people's feelings."

"Oh." That made more sense. "What kind of questions do they ask on the tests?"

She thought for a minute. "You have two children. A boy and a girl. The girl is your favorite. The boy loves you the most. You take them to the beach and when you turn your back, they run into the water for a swim. The current is powerful and pulls them quickly out to sea. You're a strong swimmer. You know you can save one, but if you try to save both, you could all die. What do you do?"

He smiled. "Let them save themselves, if they can."

She patted his hand. "You'll make a wonderful father, Malach."

"Just kidding. I'd save our child. Dante's can drown."

Her lips twitched.

"But the answer the Curia is looking for would be to try to save them both and risk killing everyone."

She tilted her head. "Why? I chose to save the child I liked least because it seemed the more selfless choice."

Malach held his hands up like a balance scale. "The choice is between actively causing one person's death and passively allowing others to die. The church believes in the sanctity of each individual life, period. They think it would be wrong to deliberately allow a child to drown, even if that choice saves more lives. It's not what I would really do, but the correct answer is obvious."

"See?" She slapped the trunk with a snort. "You're proving my point. A mage! And they would have held you up as a paragon of moral virtue."

A grumble of thunder. Fat drops of lukewarm rain pattered down.

"I could give you power," he said, leaning closer. "Deep down, you want more. I know you do—"

"This is clearly hard for you to grasp, Malach, but I don't want your Mark." Nikola's voice was almost pitying, which irritated him beyond measure. "I don't want to owe you anything. And I don't want to touch the ley. *Ever*. I just want to be left alone."

"That's what you keep saying, but I'm not sure I believe you."

"Believe what you like," she hissed. "I'm telling the truth."

They glared at each other. Then she was suddenly astride him, strong thighs clamping around his hips. Malach fell back on the broad trunk as she fumbled with his trousers. He pulled her down and tasted her tongue, still tart-sweet from the berries. Desire consumed him instantly, hot and urgent, but he sensed a trap.

"I know you want me." Nikola's warm breath tickled his ear. "Please, I've been aching. You have no idea."

He groaned in frustration. "I can't," he muttered weakly.

She cupped him through his pants. "No?"

"No!" He fended her off and rolled away, aroused to the

point of agony but determined not to take the bait, luscious as it was. "I'm sorry. The wound . . . ." Malach studied her from beneath his eyelashes.

The attempt might have begun as a test of his mettle, but he could tell she was burning for him now. It gave him no satisfaction whatsoever. Nikola rearranged her clothing and looked away, jaw tight. "I'm sorry," she said.

"No, no." He sat up and put his arms around her. "You've no idea how badly I want to. I just can't. Yet."

He kissed her neck and she pushed him away. "Don't start anything you can't finish, Malach," she warned, rising and walking to the rope ladder. "I'm tired. I think I'll go . . . take a nap."

He watched her start to descend, then stood and followed.

In truth, he had no plan. He knew she couldn't stay here, but the thought of losing her forever left him in a cold sweat. He would go to Dur-Athaara in a heartbeat, except for the inconvenient fact that the witches killed his kind on sight.

You have to give her what *she* wants, he thought unhappily. Not what *you* want.

Empathy.

Malach's mouth twisted as if at a bitter taste. He slung a leg over the trunk and started down, still punished with unspent lust.

---

Nikola was still in a foul temper as they readied for bed that night. She'd spoken barely a word to him all afternoon. In desperation, he'd torn himself to ribbons picking more blackberries, which sat untouched in a bowl on the table.

Raucous laughter drifted up from the meadow. A few cardinals frolicked below, playing some obscene version of hide and seek with the footmen. Malach sat on the broad marble windowsill as a full moon rose over the Arx. He felt a peculiar weight in his chest, like a sharp stone lodged there. Surely not . . . *guilt*?

He swallowed a mouthful of wine, hoping to dull the unpleasant sensation.

"Can I get you anything?" he asked as Nikola unbound the scarf from her hair.

"How about a ticket out of here?" she muttered.

Malach set the goblet down. "Two days," he said heavily. "I'll take you to the coast in two days."

She looked up sharply. The nights were warm and humid in the Morho and Nikola wore only her own skin—likely to make him suffer. If so, it was working. His eyes skimmed over the sinuous lines of hips and belly. The small toes, still bearing a hint of blue polish.

"You've said that before."

"I mean it this time."

"Do you swear?"

"I swear." He touched the Broken Chain Mark at his collarbone.

She closed her eyes and released a soft breath. "Thank you, Malach."

"You can have the child in Dur-Athaara. I'll send someone to get it." His voice sounded cold and empty. Malach tried to soften it. This wasn't her fault. "There's an inn called the Mother's Rest. It's down at the docks. I'll leave a message for you there."

She nodded. "The Mother's Rest. I'll remember it."

The drunken laughter outside had faded. A symphony of night insects whirred and chirped in the darkness.

"In the meantime," he said, "I have a present for you."

She sat on the edge of the bed and started finger-combing her hair. "How exciting."

Malach went to the tall, ornately carved cabinet where he kept his scarlet robes and opened a hidden compartment at the back. He slid out a lacquered box and unlocked it with a tiny key he kept stashed atop the window molding.

"Don't let the children see it," he warned, opening the box.

A black metal object nestled within. "What is that?" Nikola asked, frowning.

"A handgun."

She recoiled as if the box held a live snake. "Where did it come from?"

"I stole it from the Museum of Antiquities in Novostopol. I know one of the curators."

"Well, I've never been. I polished enough fogging antiquities in the Arx. Seeing more on my day off didn't hold much appeal." Nikola studied the weapon in morbid fascination. "Does it work?"

Malach nodded. "The bullets were harder to come by. I only have a few."

He took the gun from its velvet case and showed her how to load it.

"You just point that end at whatever you want to kill and press this part with your finger. I tested it once."

"On what?"

"A Perditae."

She eyed him in disgust.

"It wanted to eat me," he said reasonably.

"Still." Nikola scowled. "A gun!"

Malach found it amusing that the Curia approved the manufacture of much larger guns for the purpose of shelling his city, yet enforced a strict ban on small firearms, insisting that knights carry swords as they did in the olden days. The reasoning was that once you started making them, the weapons would inevitably find their way into the wrong hands —*his* hands. This gun was at least a thousand years old. He'd kept it as a curiosity, nothing more. Malach hoped she'd never have to fire it.

"You might need it for protection. I don't want anything to happen to you after . . ." He looked away, studying the fresco of three blue-winged herons fleeing a storm. "After you're gone."

"Well, thanks." She laughed. "You're an incurable romantic, Malach."

He liked that. "Only with you."

She closed the lid and set it aside. "Now I know why you don't want the children to get their bloody little hands on my gift."

He gave a shudder, only partly in jest. "They're terrifying enough with knives."

"True. They're clever though, and loyal—up to a point. You should be kinder to them."

Malach snorted. "They'd see it as weakness."

"How would you know? I doubt you've ever tried." Nikola crawled under the blankets and patted his pillow. "Don't be afraid, we'll just spoon." A chuckle. "I promise your virtue is safe."

He wanted her—oh, so desperately—but that would mean admitting he'd lied earlier. Malach shucked his clothes off and climbed into bed next to her. The sheets were cold, but her body felt warm, fiercely so, as though a furnace burned inside her.

"I'm glad I met you, Nikola Thorn," he said gravely as she snuggled into his shoulder.

"And I you, Malach."

She sounded like she meant it. The truce held as the rains came in a torrential downpour. Wind fluttered the heavy drapes and water pooled on the floor, but Malach didn't get up to close the windows.

So little time, he thought drowsily, content just to hold her in his arms. This is all I want. *Just this.*

# Chapter Four

Leaf rot and stagnant water. Rich black loam squishing underfoot in the green dimness. Ferns the size of trees, each frond beaded with fat raindrops that showered down at the slightest brush. Fluttering wings and the hoots of the ring-tailed creatures that swung through moss-draped branches.

The Morho Sarpanitum was a world unto itself. A living, breathing animal that never fell silent, never slept. Every square meter was home to *something*. Lezarius stepped over a rotten log and grimaced as a millipede the length of his arm undulated from a dark hole. He barely remembered the last time he'd seen the sun. Its existence could only be inferred from the weak shafts that occasionally broke through the canopy far overhead. The most ancient of the trees dwarfed even the gilded dome of the basilica in Jalghuth, which measured a hundred meters at its apex.

In the Old Tongue, the name Morho Sarpanitum meant Forest of Clouds. It had been a beautiful place once, and still was in many ways, but the corrupted ley that flowed from Bal Agnar and Bal Kirith for so many years still lingered. Lezarius couldn't shake the sensation that jungle was watching. Toying with them until the trap snapped shut.

A dew-spangled spiderweb tickled his face. He brushed it aside, clambering over the enormous roots that burst from the earth like the bones of a prehistoric monster.

After the sterile, hushed atmosphere of the Batavia Institute, where each day was identical to the last, the jungle assaulted his fragile senses. He liked the birds best, darting flashes of red and blue singing pretty trills. He didn't mind the gentle patter of rain sifting through the leaves or the cathedral-like glory of the massive trunks. But there was one sound he had come to despise with all his soul. The high, thin whine of the bloodsuckers.

Lezarius slapped at a mosquito, leaving a bright smear across his palm. A cloud of them followed the two men, blackening the rivulets of sweat running down Mikhail's broad back as the knight hacked a path through the dense undergrowth. Torrential rains pounded the Morho every morning. They only lasted an hour or so, leaving pools of muddy water. Then the heat would come and battalions of mosquitoes would rise up from the ground.

Suddenly, Mikhail stopped, his head cocked.

"What is it?" Lezarius whispered.

The forest worked in shifts. Daytime was for lizards and snakes and the ring-tails. The denizens that woke at dusk were the most dangerous. They'd been stalked by something in the darkness that snarled but never attacked—leery of Mikhail's sword, perhaps.

He lowered the blade and took out his belt knife. Lezarius watched with puzzlement as he carved a line through the bark of a small, bulbous tree. Sticky white sap oozed out. He coated his hands with it, rubbing it across his face and neck. Mikhail gestured for Lezarius to do the same. The sap had no odor that Lezarius could detect, but within a minute, the droning cloud began to disperse.

The mad Pontifex broke into a gap-toothed grin. "That is

a fine trick! I think I've lost a liter of blood since we entered this cursed place."

He stomped over to Mikhail and kissed his gaunt cheek. Mikhail looked startled. Then his mouth twitched. The first hint of a smile Lezarius had ever seen.

"Here, give me your back."

Lezarius smeared it over the knight's skin. Mikhail flinched a little as it touched his scrapes and bites, but remained still for the procedure. Lezarius didn't blame him for going shirtless. The air was thick as honey and hot as a forge fire. But some part of him still recoiled every time he looked at the Nightmark. A blindfolded man with a dagger to his throat. The smile was the most disturbing part. As if he embraced death with open arms.

Lezarius never mentioned it. Mikhail lacked the ability to explain why he had accepted the mage's Mark so there was little point in asking.

They sat down on one of the colossal roots. Lezarius rummaged through his pack and found a tin of sardines. It was the last of their food. He'd hoped the stores would last longer, but Mikhail ate enough for three men. The knight was stronger now, though he still looked thin. Food didn't stick to his bones. Perhaps it was the feverish energy.

The smell of the sardines prompted a plaintive mewing. Lezarius opened another flap and took out a small black cat. He had named her Greylight, a sardonic nod to the eternal gloaming of the forest. Lezarius divided the tin, giving half to Mikhail and half to his cat. Greylight wolfed it down, slapping a paw over the largest chunk in case he changed his mind and tried to take it back.

The knight frowned, pushing half of his share toward Lezarius.

"I'm not hungry," he lied. "You have it."

He took out his crumpled package of Keefs and lit one, inhaling deeply. His jangling nerves calmed as the sweet smoke permeated his lungs. The constant ache in his belly dulled.

"Did you know," Lezarius said, gesturing with the cigarette, "that many aeons ago, all realms were one?"

Mikhail chewed and swallowed, blue eyes roaming the forest.

"There was a great land mass that broke into pieces. The largest is the one we journey across now. The isles of the witches and the golden dunes of the Masdar League used to be joined to it. The world is comprised of plates, you see. The force of the ley makes them move. Only a few inches a year, but it adds up to great distances in geological time, Mikhail."

The knight gave no sign he heard, but Lezarius knew he was listening.

"Two plates met along the boundary of the Northern Curia. The pressure of this collision forged the mountains of my home. As the range took shape, wind and rain dug deep valleys that carried snowmelt from the peaks. It left a lowland basin behind, rich in sediment. And that became the Morho Sarpanitum."

Lezarius had trained as a geologist when he was young, before taking the robes of the Pontifex. The Morho had always fascinated him. The last old-growth forest on the continent. Much of it was comprised of swampy lakes. They'd slogged through those wetlands for the last week, camping wherever they could find a Wardstone. But as they went deeper, he'd made a disturbing discovery. Tiny holes pitted the stelae as though they rotted from within. Many were covered in choking creepers, the tendrils prying at the stonework like tiny chisels.

"The Void is an offense to Nature," he said softly. "I think the Morho will break the stelae someday. It seeks to restore a state of balance. To bring the ley back. But I had no choice! I created the Void to avoid the bloodshed of a civil war."

Lezarius gave a bitter laugh. "You know better than

anyone what a vain hope that was. Luk was the only one who held to the *Meliora*. The only one who believed the rebels had been punished enough and should be left alone." His brows lowered. "I do not blame you for fighting, Mikhail. You were only following Feizah's orders."

Mikhail's shoulders stiffened at the name. He turned to Lezarius, sweat slicking his dark hair. A muscle twitched in his jaw. A tiny movement, but Lezarius read his ambivalence.

"Should we have shown her mercy? No! She was in league with our enemies. She sent priests to murder us at the Institute! She would have killed you herself at the Arx if I had not stopped her. No, no, we did as we had to." Lezarius sucked his teeth, anger simmering. "I showed mercy once before and look what it bought me."

They'd eluded the last pack of Markhounds, yet the forest itself had turned against them. It was clever, oh yes. At first it had offered them easy game trails—all headed in the wrong direction. When its quarry persisted in taking a different route, woody vines snagged their feet at every step. Dense thickets and treacherous mires closed the way ahead, trying to force them northward.

Towards Bal Kirith.

Lezarius had not seen the city since it fell to Curia knights three decades before. Once it had been a place of otherworldly beauty. The Arx there was the first to be built by the Praefators, founders of his faith, and remained unsurpassed by any of the five that came after. In a sudden vivid flash, he remembered the heady perfume of the scarlet poppies that grew in thick abundance through the park that sat like a verdant gem at its heart. He had strolled its pathways with the Pontifex Beleth, sunlight dappling the manicured grass. It was the first time he had seen the great regnan trees, their white boles stretching towards the dome of the sky like pillars. Both of them were young then. It would be years more before the city openly rejected the Via Sancta. Yet he had sensed dangerous currents in Beleth even then. A slow twisting of her mind.

*To feel deeply, without restraint, demands the freedom to explore primitive impulses*, she had said to him. *How may we evolve otherwise?*

*You speak of the shadow side?* he asked with a frown.

Beleth had smiled. *I speak of human nature.*

*The basest aspects of it!* he replied indignantly.

*We would make self-interest a crime. Yet are not the rights of the individual of equal weight to the rights of the whole?* She laughed at his obvious discomfort. *Never fear to debate these questions, Lezarius. Let us merely be grateful there is no Hell, for if there were, I imagine it would be a very crowded place.*

It was the last time he visited Bal Kirith.

What the city was like now he could hardly imagine. A place of death and ruin. It was an ill omen that the jungle sought to herd them there.

*Enemies all around, closing in . . . .*

Lezarius seized Mikhail's arm, dirty fingers digging into the cords of muscle. "If I die, you must raise an army and march on Jalghuth. You must quench the darkness that festers there before it spreads. Swear it!"

Mikhail's blue eyes burned. He touched the Raven on his neck.

Lezarius exhaled, fingers trembling. "Good. Now, you must know what we face. I told you before that Balaur lives. That he must be the one who did this to me."

The Keef kept his visions at bay, but Lezarius still shivered at the memory. An octagonal tower that stabbed the sky like a spike of black ice. Swirling snow and mocking laughter. His last moments of sanity.

"I kept him in a cell at the top of Sinjali's Lance, every centimeter of his cell Warded so he could not touch the ley. The others would have executed him. He . . . tortured me. But what is our faith but the renunciation of violence? I thought the ley had presented me with a final test. Would I succumb to the thirst for vengeance, or would I show mercy? He was the Pontifex of Bal Agnar! We'd known each other since we were novices. Do you understand?"

Mikhail nodded. Greylight leapt into his lap and began to groom herself. A gentle hand scratched her chin, eliciting a deep purr.

"I visited often to speak with him. I hoped to find some shred of humanity that might be redeemed." Lezarius sighed. "There was none. Yet I could not bring myself to kill him in cold blood. Not even to sever him from the ley. The amputation of hands is a barbaric practice."

He read the question in Mikhail's eyes.

"How did he break free after so long? That I do not know. I cannot remember! But only a handful of others knew he was at Jalghuth. My most trusted knights and two close advisers, both cardinals. Jagat and Vinaya. Remember those names. It must be one of them who betrayed me."

Lezarius picked up a twig and drew a circle in the dirt. "The Arx at Jalghuth." Outside the circle, he drew a sharp spire. "Sinjali's Lance. It sits at the foot of Mount Ogo, the tallest peak in the Sundar Kush. The tower must have been built by the Praefators, though archaeologists believe it predates the Arx itself by centuries. It is a mighty and strange construction, Mikhail. No one has ever been able to discern the original purpose. Later, it was named for one of the ancient Pontifexes, but it is older than her. Far older."

He tapped the tower with the twig. "The power is very strong there. It seemed the safest place to hold Balaur in secret. When I returned from my own imprisonment at Bal Agnar, I moved my rooms from the Pontifex's Palace to the Lance." A small smile. "I said I wished for solitude to ponder the mysteries of the ley. But my chambers were only three levels below Balaur's cell. I could personally ensure no one saw him without my authorization. Then I added Wards to the tower, inside and out. As long as Balaur couldn't touch the ley, he could not touch the world."

Mikhail scraped the last of the oily fish from the tin and set it down for the cat to lick. His expression was thoughtful.

"His food would be brought by knights, or by myself. My occupancy provided an excuse for the tower to be closely guarded." Lezarius shut his eyes against a sudden image of bloody, broken bodies in a stone corridor. They wore the blue tabards of the Northern Flame. "For nearly thirty years, I hid him away. We grew old together. I resolved that if I ever became ill, I would end him. He is poison!

"Balaur must have forged an alliance with Jagat or Vinaya. They were the only ones who visited him. I don't know why they didn't just kill me. Perhaps because those I had Marked would succumb to the sickness and all would know I was dead." Lezarius scraped a bare foot across the circle and tower, obliterating them both. "It was a mistake," he said grimly. "One they will sorely regret."

Mikhail lifted the drowsy kitten in one large hand. He glanced at the canopy, then at Lezarius.

"I know. It will be dark soon." He rose to his feet, knees protesting. "When we reach Kvengard, I will seek an audience with Luk. He knows my Marks. He knows *me*. We were like brothers. I doubt he will agree to send knights. Luk will not break his oaths—not even to forestall the worst. But he won't deny us aid. Perhaps even a ship. And then . . . ." Lezarius shook his head. "I still have power over the ley. I will banish it from Jalghuth. It is not possible that all the clergy believe Balaur's masquerade. When they realize who I am, they will rise against him."

Lezarius clenched his fists. "This time, he will face justice! If the death of one means the lives of thousands more, it is not a violation of the *Meliora*."

He tucked the cat into his pack. Mikhail shouldered his own

burden. Even without the sun, Lezarius had an innate compass. He directed their route as they pushed onward, the Morho fighting them for every meter of ground. Branches tore at his face like claws. Sticky webs snared his hair. Ahead, Mikhail doggedly carved a path, hacking through vines as thick as his wrist. The light faded. A chorus of nocturnal insects chittered and hummed. Something larger crashed through the undergrowth, stalking their rear. One of the tawny cats, perhaps?

Or another monstrosity yet unseen?

Lezarius was starting to lose hope that they'd ever escape when the forest's grip loosened. The great trees thinned. The ground rose and fell in rolling downs. They moved faster, until finally a river came into view, a shimmering ribbon in the moonlight.

Lezarius let out a wordless cry of triumph. They had reached the Mistrelle, which ran swift and deep all the way to Kvengard. The channel cut through a narrow gorge, forcing the flow into whitewater that frothed and crashed between giant boulders that divided the current.

"We are close to Kvengard," he said with a smile. "Half a day at most."

The ruins of a town sat on the far bank. Moonlight glinted on shattered windows. Once, the river had been a great trade artery, but those days ended with the civil war. Mikhail looked southward toward the barren headland of the peninsula.

"The ancestors of the Kvens cut all the trees down," Lezarius said. "The walking will be easy along the river."

He clambered down the bank and let the water run over his weary feet. The Mistrelle started high in the mountains and was shockingly cold, even after its long journey through the Morho.

"You can drink," he said. "It's clean here."

Mikhail walked to the edge and cupped his hands, splashing it on his face and beard.

Lezarius released the kitten from his pack. It scampered to

the edge, tail crooked, one paw cautiously batting at the shallows. He stripped off his shirt and waded in, gooseflesh rising on his belly. "We must make ourselves presentable before we reach the Arx. I do not wish to arrive filthy."

Lezarius pressed a palm to the inverted Mark on his chest. The roaring Lion of the North. The blue flame of light and law. Wielder of the ley unlike any other who walked the earth.

A gift of blood.

Mother a full mage, father an Unmarked. Only Lezarius was privy to the secret of his birth, though he suspected it was the same with Luk and Clavis. Feizah, too, may she find peace. They all possessed unique powers. A quirk of half-bloods.

He felt perfectly lucid, but he knew the madness was there, lurking beneath the surface. It whispered to trust no one ever again, not even Mikhail. Lezarius knew it lied. The knight was true.

He looked back over his shoulder. Mikhail had shed the white cotton tunic and pants of the Institute, both now a dingy gray. He stood naked on the bank, sword in hand. He seemed loathe to put it down.

"Come, bathe yourself." Lezarius ventured deeper. The current swirled around his knees. "It is bracing."

The inland waterways teemed with freshwater crocodilians that lurked just below the surface so only their knobby snouts poked up. They weren't as dangerous as their saltwater cousins, but Lezarius had not thought it wise to attempt a swim.

"Do not fear. The beasts prefer stagnant pools," he said. "The Mistrelle flows too swiftly for their taste."

Mikhail set the sword at the very edge of the water and waded in, Marks livid against his pale skin. As a former captain, he'd been given more than most. Each was deeply personal, a reflection of his psyche filtered through the power of the ley. All but one was imagery from the *Meliora*. Gentle, pastoral scenes that evoked a feeling of harmony.

Lezarius averted his gaze from the Nightmark. He dug his toes into the slippery, pebbled bed of the river. The current was strong.

Mikhail gasped as he waded to his waist. He cast a wry look at Lezarius, then began to splash the frigid water over his body, washing off days of sweat and mud. Lezarius studied the river's flow, wondering if they might construct a raft. It would widen further downstream, becoming a lazier and easily navigable channel. How nice it would be to sit back and give his tired feet a rest—

"Move and you both die."

Lezarius stiffened. They both spun around.

Six figures in red cloaks stood on the bank, arrows nocked to bows. Their leader threw her hood back and stepped forward.

"You thought you'd slipped the net," she said with a chill smile. "But we've been watching. I am Bishop Dantarion of Bal Kirith. You are both under arrest by order of the Reverend Mother Beleth."

"She is no true Pontifex," Lezarius snarled.

The mage laughed. "She's more of one than you are, Lezarius the Mad."

Beside him, Mikhail tensed. His eyes fixed on the sword at the edge of the water. Lezarius knew he would fight them, and he would die.

"What do you want with me?" he demanded.

"No more talk." Her face hardened. "Come out of the river."

Lezarius laid a hand on Mikhail's arm. "I must do as they say," he said quietly.

Mikhail shook his head, desperate, panicked. An arrow sailed past his ear with a deadly buzz.

"Move!" the mage barked.

Lezarius took a step forward, then turned and gave Mikhail a mighty shove. The knight lost his footing on the slick stones. They stood at the brink of a deep depression in the riverbed. He fell back with a splash. An instant later, the current seized him.

A flurry of arrows pierced the water. Lezarius's breath caught, then released as Mikhail's head bobbed up, heading for the center of the rapids. The woman cursed and waded in, grabbing Lezarius's arm. The other mages nocked fresh arrows and took aim.

"Hold!" Dantarion raised a fist.

"You're letting him escape?" one asked in disbelief.

Cold blue eyes turned to the bank. "Didn't you see his Mark? He's the property of Cardinal Malach."

"But Malach turned him—"

"It matters not. No mage may kill another's slave." She hauled Lezarius to the edge and gazed down the river at the flailing form fast diminishing in the distance. "If the rapids don't finish him, Malach will. But that is his right."

The mages lowered their bows. Lezarius felt a small surge of triumph, though it faded as his hands were bound behind his back. The mage named Dantarion quickly searched their packs. Finding no weapons, she gestured at the others to carry them along. How young and innocent she looked! Auburn hair tied back in a horsetail, a scattering of freckles across her upturned nose. But the Broken Chain around her slender neck made his skin crawl.

"Sister Alemeth," she said to the one who'd spoken of Mikhail's inverted Mark. "Run back to the Arx and tell the Reverend Mother our mission was successful. We will make camp and march for Bal Kirith at first light."

Alemeth, dark-haired with a faint white scar across her upper lip, nodded. "Yes, Your Grace." She shouldered her pack and trotted back towards the Morho.

Dantarion's cool eyes flicked over Lezarius, then sharpened. "What have we here?"

He followed her gaze. A shard of ice lodged in his chest.

The kitten watched warily from the shadow of a boulder upstream. Dantarion crouched and held out a hand. It shied away.

"Is it yours?" she asked softly.

"No."

Dantarion smiled. "Liar. It's your pet, isn't it?"

He was about to scream at Greylight to run away when a hand clamped across his mouth. Lezarius struggled as Dantarion produced a scrap of dried meat from one of the packs. She did not try to approach, merely set the meat on the ground and sat cross-legged, speaking in a kind, coaxing voice as the little cat slowly crept forward. When it came within reach, a slim white hand darted out and seized it. "What a darling!"

Greylight struggled wildly, but Dantarion stroked her ears and whispered in a soothing tone. Then she set the cat next to the scrap of meat. Greylight quickly devoured the morsel. Lezarius's heart sank as the cat allowed her to pick it up again. She flicked a finger. The muffling palm fell away.

"Don't hurt her," Lezarius gasped. "Please!"

"You think I'm a monster." Dantarion smiled innocently. "But I like cats. Beleth does, too."

Greylight curled up in her red-robed lap as two of the mages made a small fire in a ring of river stones. The other three shouldered their bows and slunk into the darkness.

"They must hunt for dinner if we want fresh meat," Dantarion said.

"You'll never break me," Lezarius said, stomach churning as he watched her idly stroke the little cat. "Never!"

"We shall see." Pink lips curled in a smile. "We shall see."

---

A SHORT TIME LATER, the nihilim returned with several of the ring-tailed animals that screeched from the trees. They roasted them on a spit, tossing Lezarius the gristle.

"I thought the man who made the Void would look more impressive," Dantarion said, gnawing the last scraps of meat from a bone.

"My face is different, mage."

"Well, I wouldn't know, old man. They took all the paintings away."

Lezarius frowned.

"To the victors go the spoils of war," Dantarion explained with a wolfish smile. "Your knights plundered everything of value from our Arx, down to the last bauble. The Reverend Mother says it's displayed in museums for people to gawk at."

"I had no part of that," he muttered.

"No?" She tilted her head. "Ah, yes, you only divested our city of the ley. Stripped us of our birthright. Indeed, you are blameless as far as the looting goes."

He stared into the flames. "Who are your parents?"

"Why does that matter?"

"I might have known them."

"The Void is my mother." Dantarion spat out a bit of sinew. Greylight leapt to devour it.

"How many of you remain?"

"I'll ask the questions. Who was the skeleton?"

It took him a moment to realize she meant Mikhail.

"A friend from the place where I was kept."

"The crazy-house?" Her eyes narrowed. "He bears my cousin's Mark. Why?"

"I don't know. He cannot speak."

Her head tilted. "Why did you save him and not yourself?"

"Because if I had gone into the river, you would have followed and caught us."

Bone cracked. She sucked out the marrow. "How noble."

"If you think I will give you back the ley," he said, "you are mistaken."

The mage studied him. "Who rules in Jalghuth?"

"I cannot remember anything from before the Institute. I have tried."

"Perhaps you need to try harder."

"Torture me if you wish." He shrugged, though his mouth went dry.

"I could torture your pet instead." She stroked its throat. "Poor little thing, to have a master such as you."

He cast his eyes down. "It would do no good. Whoever did this erased my memory."

"So you say."

"How far to Bal Kirith?" he asked, hoping to distract her.

"A day's march." She tossed a meaty haunch at his feet. "Eat and be merry while you can, Lezarius."

He gave half to Greylight, but his empty stomach demanded *something*. Lezarius chewed the stringy flesh, eyeing the Mark of a Broken Chain around her neck with disgust. "You follow the Via Libertas. Is Beleth still penning her obscene manifestos?"

"She's prolific. Soon all the world will be reading her works."

"Have you?"

Dantarion laughed. "Read them? I have no time for such things."

"Then how can you be sure you agree with her?"

"Because it is the natural order," she said confidently. "One who cannot defend their own rights is unfit to enjoy them. It is a universal truth that requires no defense. Take you, Lezarius. Neither of us is right or wrong. We only want different things. If you were stronger than me, you would act to change your situation. Perhaps kill me. But you are the weaker party and therefore I will have my way whether you like it or not."

White teeth gleamed in the choking darkness. The jungle closed around him like a fist. Lezarius eyed his pack.

"May I smoke?"

Dantarion shrugged. "You don't need my permission."

He crawled to the pack and fumbled for the dwindling package of Keefs. Lezarius lit one from a burning twig and drew deep on the smoke. A wave of calm washed over him.

"You espouse extreme individualism," he said, "yet the mages work together."

"Towards a mutually agreeable end, yes."

"Which is?"

"Simply to return the world to its natural state. Every creature must compete to survive, from the lowliest lichen to the apex predators. I see wisdom in being the latter." She leaned back on her forearms, gazing up at the stars. "In the end, you will do anything to save your own life. That I can promise you."

"I disagree."

"Your opinion is irrelevant."

He smoked in silence until Dantarion finally stood and walked away. Lezarius watched her disappear into the darkness. The others were drinking wine and paid him little attention, but the knew there would be no escaping. The forest would never let him go a second time.

He could try to drown himself, but he was not ready to die. In that, the mage was right. Not until he destroyed the terrible malignancy he'd unleashed on the world.

Lezarius let out a deranged cackle that drew a few amused glances.

He could pretend to be hopelessly insane. A gabbling, incoherent lunatic. It might buy him some time once they reached Beleth.

But it's not a pretense, is it? A voice whispered. You *are* mad.

Lezarius curled up on his pack, Greylight snugged in the

cradle of his arms. The fire burned low. The whispering rush of the Mistrelle chased him into restless sleep.

He dreamed of stelae, thousands of them stretching across a vast white plain, broken stone shards poking from the earth like the supplicating fingers of the dead.

# Chapter Five

Alexei ate a bowl of porridge with dried fruit in the mess hall, organizing his plan of attack for the day. He'd managed to steal a few hours of sleep and felt clearer. They had two families left to interview. Then he could follow up on the missing pet angle. It felt weak, but there must be a pattern if only he could see it. And the search of the Burwald would get underway once they received approval from the community's representatives.

By eight bells, he was at his office. Morvana's door was closed. He found her secretary, a dour little man with a clipped manner of speech who always seemed to be drowning in paperwork.

"Is she in yet?" he asked.

"The Nuncio is in a meeting and cannot be disturbed," Fra Becker said firmly, stamping a sheet of parchment with the bishop's seal and sliding it into a folder on another tottering stack.

"With whom?"

"That is the business of the Nuncio." *Stamp and file.*

"Can you tell me how long she'll be?"

"I've no idea."

Alexei stood there for a minute more, but the man didn't look up.

"Tell the Nuncio I've gone out and I'll be back later."

"Where shall I say you've gone?"

"That is the business of her aide," Alexei said with a bland smile.

*Stamp and file.* "I shall convey the message."

He couldn't interview the families without her. Morvana would be furious, and he didn't speak enough Kven anyway. But he refused to sit in his office staring at the walls.

Alexei strode off to the stables and ordered a mount from the young novice on duty. Then he rode out through the Gate of Saint Freyjus. Where Novostopol conveyed the impression of a stately metropolis, with wide tree-lined boulevards, Kvenmark was akin to a sprawling village. Speckled chickens roamed the streets, dodging slat-sided carts laden with produce. There was no central market, just a hundred little stands that sprouted each morning like mushrooms after a rain. Men in short sleeveless jerkins unloaded barrels of ale in front of the ubiquitous beer gardens that were the primary social gathering place. He'd seen none of the public drunkenness of Novo. Entire extended families would commandeer the long wooden tables, eating and clapping to the nasal wheeze of an accordion.

Children were cherished and multiple generations often lived under the same roof. Family was the city's foundation, which made the crimes even more inexplicable.

Perhaps it was someone who had lost a child and seethed with resentment at the happiness of others. Who wanted to see them suffer as he had suffered. Alexei made a mental note to look into any deaths of children prior to the first abduction. Such a thing would be rare, but accidents happened. Illness. He never expected to have a child himself, but he imagined that such a tragedy might drive someone mad. Alexei knew all too well that some emotions were too primal and potent to be soothed over by Marks.

When he'd first arrived, the tangle of streets had seemed a hopeless labyrinth. But after a week, he'd fixed certain landmarks in his mind. The tall spire of the Vengenkirche meditation chapel. The ancient, winding Kessian Wall that used to mark the boundary of the inner city. The teeming stalls of Brandsburg Biergarden. Alexei rode into a quieter area of small, thatched cottages. He reined up in front of Sofie Arnault's house. The site of the most recent abduction.

He and Morvana had spoken to the parents yesterday. Sofie had been playing in the yard. They kept ducks and the area was enclosed by a wooden fence about two meters high. It had no gate. The only way into the yard was through the house. Her mother, aware of the other disappearances, had kept a close eye on the child as she prepared supper. She had two other children and one had fallen, skinning a knee. She went to comfort him and clean the blood off. A matter of perhaps five minutes. When next she glanced out the window, Sofie was gone.

The mother swore that no one had passed through the house. She'd been in the kitchen the entire time, which had the only door to the yard.

She immediately sent a neighbor to summon the Polizei. By that point, they were under intense pressure and the report appeared to be very thorough. Officers had quarantined the area in a two-kilometer radius, searching every carriage and cart. The family was too poor to have a picture, but they went door to door, describing her. Others walked a circuit of the fence. No footprints were found on either side. The neighbors had seen nothing, including the family on the other side of the fence, who were home at the time.

The child had never cried out. The mother insisted she would have heard.

A five-minute window in which Sofie was there and gone.

How was she taken?

If he could only discover that piece of the puzzle, he might have some idea how to protect the next one.

Five days now.

Alexei dismounted and walked the length of the fence from the opposite side. Slender wooden pickets that might have been scaled with a ladder, but again, a ladder would have left impressions in the earth.

He studied the house. It looked just like every other.

Yet his gut told him it wasn't. The Polizei believed it was a crime of opportunity, that he'd seen the girl playing and decided to take her. The mother had shown them where Sofie had been sitting in the dirt next to the wooden tub of water they kept for the ducks. Even on horseback, the fence was too high to see her from the street. He'd known she was there.

The nape of his neck prickled. Alexei looked around, but there was no one except for a woman milking a goat two yards down. The houses on the street had only one story. No high vantage points.

Yet as he rode back to the Arx, the sensation of being watched grew stronger. He kept turning back. No sinister carriages or mysterious riders, but the feeling persisted. After seven tours of duty in the Void, he'd learned to trust his instincts. He took a circuitous route back to the Freyjus Gate, venturing into tight alleys with the hope of luring his pursuer into the open. After a time the prickly feeling faded.

Alexei's head whirled with names, places, dates. He knew he had a tendency to push too hard. A faint smile touched his lips. If Spassov had been here, he'd tell Alexei to back off.

You think too hard, Alyosha. Even a crocodilian breaks its teeth on stone. You must find the soft underbelly, *da*?

How he missed Patryk Spassov. His partner in the Interfectorem for three years and one true friend. Alexei hoped he hadn't resigned his post. For all of Patryk's toughness, he needed the job. It was the only thing holding him together.

Just as the hunt for Malach had kept Alexei from the brink.

Instead of returning to the office, he decided to spend an hour in quiet meditation. At the Arx in Novo, he would often seek solace at the Iveron Chapel. It was the smallest and least used. On those days when he'd gone without sleep for too long, stumbling through his duties in a fog, even a few minutes kneeling in the sanctuary would give him the strength to go on.

Every Arx was laid out in the same pattern, so he followed the usual route past the Pontifex's Palace and was pleased to find a chapel, more pleased to discover it empty. Alexei left his mount outside and entered the clerestory. A hundred votive candles illuminated the stained glass triptych above the altar. No Lezarius banishing the ley as in the Iveron Chapel. This one depicted Luk and the first Markhound he'd created, lying at his feet and gazing up adoringly. The mother of all the rest. Her name was Adalheida.

The second panel, a knight in a Wolf tabard astride a shadowy Marksteed. He carried no weapon. The third, Luk again, this time with a Markhawk perched on his gauntleted fist.

Alexei sank to his knees.

Prayer to an omnipotent deity was not part of his faith, but he sometimes spoke to the Saints. It gave focus to his intention.

He took a glove off and pressed his palm to the stone floor, drawing ley into his Marks. Blue fire traced the Maiden on his chest, the Towers on his back. Along his left calf, a skeleton gripped a jeweled sword, point driven into the ground. On his torso, a path snaked between jagged cliffs. There were others, nineteen altogether, stitching his skin with light.

Alexei emptied his mind of everything but a single thought.

*Help me find this man. Help me stop him.*

Rage bubbled to the surface and his Marks flared, blindingly bright, pushing it back into the depths of his unconscious.

He saw little Sofie playing in the dirt with her ducks. Willem, school satchel slung over one shoulder, laughing as he said goodbye to his friends. Noach Beitz, chasing a red ball that rolled into an alley. Wandy Keller, who was kissed goodnight in his bed and never seen again.

*Help me find them.*

*Let them be alive.*

He had to believe they were. Had to—

Alexei's eyes flew open. The votive candles flickered as if a faint breeze swept through the sanctuary.

*Flowers*. Flowers, and a hint of foul decay.

Like an offal heap doused with some strong perfume.

He looked around, heart racing. Just a whiff, but he'd smelled it.

Alexei leapt to his feet, tugging off his other glove. He stalked around, sniffing. The smell was gone, but he *knew* it had been there. He searched the benches and the altar, poked into every nook and cranny of the clerestory. Nothing.

It maddened him.

He'd smelled exactly the same peculiar odor at Willem's house. It came from the cloak hanging in the hall. If the stench was from a tannery, there was one way to confirm it. He strode outside, tugging on his gloves. Was the odor a sending from the ley to nudge him in the right direction? He'd never experienced such a thing before, but that didn't mean it wasn't possible.

Alexei's steps quickened as he hurried to the stables.

# Chapter Six

Kasia woke in the small hours of the night. Her gown was damp and tangled around her legs. The covers had been thrown to the floor.

She sat up, head pounding. The iron tang of adrenaline lingered on her tongue. Moonlight spilled through the casements as she poured water from a jug, rinsing her mouth and spitting into the privy.

Kasia often had vivid dreams. Some were carnal, others mundane, but they were usually pleasant. She'd never in her life had a dream of the sort her clients sometimes described. Prisoned in their own bodies, unable to move, as some faceless monster approached. Standing naked before a roomful of strangers. Falling from a great height or being tossed about by waves the size of mountains.

In other words, nightmares.

Had she had just experienced one?

Disjointed images lodged like splinters in her mind. A man in white robes. A stone room with a tall, narrow window and flurries of snow in the darkness beyond. He had asked her questions, though she couldn't remember what they were. Only the residue of dread he left behind.

Within moments, the images faded. Her heart slowed.

A nightmare.

Perhaps it wasn't so strange. She *was* in danger. They all were.

Kasia went to close the window when she perceived something moving across the lawn below. A pale shape flitting from shadow to shadow. The dregs of her fear drained away. Natalya must have snuck out to pee in the bushes. It would be just like her to commit such a petty act of rebellion.

She eased open the door between their rooms. The hinges muttered a soft protest.

Natalya slept peacefully in her bed, covers drawn to her chin.

Kasia hurried back to the window. The figure was gone.

She lit the candles, fully awake now, and found her deck. Kasia drew a single card, laying it face down.

Some cartomancers posed a specific question before seeking the guidance of the ley. They claimed it was dangerous *not* to because you opened a door without knowing what waited on the other side. Kasia trusted her cards. They always spoke the truth even if she only understood the full message in hindsight. She often took an open-ended approach, but now she formed a query in her mind.

*What's out there?*

She turned the card over.

A woman in red robes stood before an archway, fire cupped in her hands, halo like a golden sun behind her head.

The Saint of Flames.

A bringer of justice and protector of the weak.

The suit of Flames for the city of Jalghuth, whose motto was Lux et lex. *Light and Law*.

Kasia knew every card intimately. The robe was supposed to be blue. Natalya would never, ever have painted a red robe in such a context. That could be considered heresy. It made no sense!

She hesitated, then touched the card with a fingertip.

*Show me more.*

Lines of blue flame ignited the image. The saint's halo glowed bright.

She yanked her hand back. The light died.

A strong sense of danger—but not for her. For the pale thing.

Kasia blew out the candles and crept to the door. The corridor was silent. She made her way down the main staircase and through the entry hall to the front door, a massive thing of dark timbers. She shot the bolt open and stepped into the night.

A full, bloated moon hung over the lawn. The forest was a solid dark mass on either side.

She stopped on the threshold. It was stupid to wander the grounds alone. She should wake Tessaria—

Kasia tensed at a flash of white in the distance where the formal gardens began. She sensed a terrible, desperate loneliness. It pulled her across the dew-soaked grass. A breeze stirred her hair. Damp earth filled her nose.

*The Saints watch over me,* she thought. *Watch over us both.*

Another glimpse of furtive movement. Kasia followed a meandering path. It led through mulched beds with decorative rock borders. Somewhere in the forest an owl hooted, three eerie cries that sounded like mad laughter.

The gardens fell behind and hedges rose on either side, all sharp angles and fantastical shapes. Paths intersected each other, paved with gravel. It hurt her feet so she walked on the grassy verge. Her limbs were heavy and sluggish as if she waded through deep water. She knew she ought to turn back, but the ley tugged her inexorably onward.

Tattered shreds of cloud scudded across the face of the moon. Ley swirled in complex currents around her footsteps, blue-green like burning phosphorus. She scanned the shifting pools of light and dark, hoping to find the poor thing that had drawn her from her bed. A wounded animal?

A twig cracked. Kasia's head turned. In the shadows beneath the pines, she sensed a new presence. A deeper pool of darkness beyond the edge of the moonlight. The weight of its gaze was palpable. Was that the faint outline of a hood?

Her flesh prickled as the current of ley changed from blue to a deep, bruised purple bordering on black. Tendrils snaked towards her like rivulets of ink.

Suddenly, Kasia came back to herself. Standing alone far from the main house in the middle of the night. Too far to summon help. She turned away from the forest and started to run, but she'd found her way into a place with tall hedges that twisted and turned until she lost sight of the lawn completely.

She had not brought her cards.

*Idiot!*

She paused to listen, breath rasping like a saw.

The night was quiet, but she felt the watcher nearby.

Then: running feet on the other side of the hedge, light and fleet. She sensed panicky fear and something else. Dark amusement.

Predator and prey?

The sounds on the other side of the hedge faded as the footsteps veered into a side path leading away. Kasia hurried towards a juncture, hoping to intercept. This was no animal being hunted. This was a person. She had to find them! Had to save them before—

The air left her lungs as she slammed into a hard body. Kasia fell back, landing on the gravel.

"Domina Novak?"

She looked up into the startled face of Jule Danziger.

"What are you doing here?" she asked warily, ignoring his offered hand and brushing herself off.

He laughed softly. "I live here, remember? I came outside for a cigarette. My aunt's a dragon about it if I indulge in the house." He leaned closer, eyes twinkling. "Do you want to smell my breath?"

She caught a whiff of tobacco. "I believe you."

"What are *you* doing here?" His gaze prowled the length of her thin nightgown.

"I couldn't sleep." She paused, disoriented and annoyed. What had just happened? It blurred like a half-remembered dream. "I . . . I thought I saw something."

Jule frowned. "An animal?"

"I don't know. It was white."

He frowned. "That rules out deer or boar. A loose sheep?"

"I suppose it could have been," she said slowly.

Yet she had not forgotten that hooded figure, nor the black ley.

"Come, I'll escort you back to the house." Jule held his hands up. Ungloved, she noticed. "Or you can escort me, if that's preferable."

They fell into stride together. The exit from the hedges wasn't far off and soon they were walking up the drive toward the house.

Jule jammed his hands into his pockets. "Aren't you cold?"

"A touch."

"Take my coat."

He still wore formal evening dress. She allowed him to drape the fine wool coat around her shoulders.

A hooded figure. She'd seen it. She *had.*

"Tell the truth," she said with a smile. "It's the wee hours and you're fully dressed."

"I came from the city. My aunt and uncle lead a quiet life out here. Too quiet, if you know what I mean."

"I didn't think Kvengard had a nightlife."

He smiled. "Not by the standards of Novo. But I have friends. Just because we keep to the old ways doesn't mean we don't know how to have fun."

"Does that include walking the gardens in the middle of the night?"

"I could ask you the same," he said levelly. "Why did you come out here?"

"I had a bad dream. I hoped some fresh air might help me shake it off."

"Did it?"

"Perfectly."

"Because you were running like the devil was chasing you, Domina Novak."

She looked at him sharply. "I couldn't find my way out and got a bit panicked. I didn't hurt you, I hope?"

"Besides the broken heart that you're leaving us tomorrow? Not at all."

She winced. "That's an awful line. Not even Natalya would stoop so low."

Jule grinned. "The shoe-thrower? I'll have to watch my step around her."

"She's very talented."

He arched a thick blonde eyebrow.

"With a paintbrush," Kasia added with a laugh.

The ley had returned to a placid blue, the house loomed ahead, and she found herself relaxing.

"I'd commission a portrait if you stayed for a few days. Are you sure Tessaria won't relent?"

"Not a chance."

He kicked a pebble. "So be it."

They reached the front door. She wondered if Jule would try to persuade her to come back to his room, but he said goodnight with an amiable smile and headed for the kitchen. When Kasia reached her room, she immediately went next door and woke Natalya, relating all that had transpired.

"Are you sure you weren't sleepwalking?" Natalya asked.

"Fairly. It was no sheep. It looked like . . . ." Kasia thought hard, trying to recall what she'd seen from the window. Her memory was usually impeccable, but an odd mist veiled the encounter. The figure had been small, but it walked upright. "Like it might have been a child, Nashka."

"A servant's kid?"

"Maybe. But the other one was unsettling." She shook her head. "I got the distinct impression that Cloak was stalking Rabbit and I walked into the middle of it."

"Cloak and Rabbit, eh? Did Rabbit get away?"

"I don't know. Saints, I hope so."

"Should we wake Tess?"

Kasia shook her head. "It'll be dawn in a few hours. We'll be gone from this place soon enough. I didn't tell Jule what I saw."

"Do you suspect him?"

"Not really, but who knows?" She hugged her knees. "Would you sleep with me? I'd rather not be alone."

"Of course." Natalya chuckled. "I've been waiting years for an invitation."

Kasia tweaked her chin. They crawled into bed and pulled the covers up. Kasia was grateful for the warm body beside her.

Cloak and Rabbit.

A strange and terrible dream?

Her eyes drifted shut.

---

Kasia slept deeply. When she finally woke, Natalya was already up and gone, which came as a surprise. She generally stayed in bed until the last possible moment and then flew into a coffee-fueled frenzy to get to her appointments on time.

In the light of day, Kasia's unease from the night before seemed distant. The nightgown had grass stains so that much was real. As for the rest . . . Soon they would all be on a ship to Nantwich. If ghosts haunted the Danziger estate, Kasia would be glad to put them at her back.

She rang for a servant and was pleased to learn the new clothes were ready. Hot water was fetched, a tub filled, and she had a luxurious, mindless soak, all too aware that it would be her last for the next week.

The dress from Amelie fit perfectly. Deep blue velvet with a high neck, long, tight pointed sleeves and voluminous skirts that fell to her calves. She'd even stitched embroidery along the bodice and hem in the Kven fashion, tiny, intricate vines of forest green. As requested, the skirt had hidden pockets where she could stash her cards. A fresh pair of stockings and matching velvet gloves completed the ensemble.

Kasia combed out her long raven hair and twisted it into a loose chignon. She followed the smell of coffee to a southern-facing glass room adjacent to the kitchen. Bright morning sun streamed through the walls, turning the beads of condensation to glittering jewels. A sideboard held a coffee urn, a crock of honeyed yoghurt, and fresh berries.

Natalya sat at a long wooden table, half of which was given over to seedling trays on wire racks with new shoots poking out. Each tray bore a tag with neat, precise script. It was a pleasantly messy room, strewn with bags of compost, dirt-stained gardening gloves and bins of seed packets organized by name. The air smelled of sun-warmed soil.

"You look tired," Kasia said, pouring a cup of coffee and spooning yoghurt into a bowl.

Natalya gave a wan smile. She wore a smart silk blouse in creamy taupe that flattered her dark complexion, but her eyes were puffy and dull.

"I didn't sleep well," she grumbled. "You snore."

"I do not!"

"Like a drunken fishwife."

"Where's Tess?"

"In a pique," she said glumly. "Fra Spassov arrived ten

minutes ago. The *Moonbeam* must have sailed on the midnight tide because it was gone by dawn."

"Oh, no!" Kasia set her cup down, appetite curdling.

"We're stuck here until Tess arranges for another ship." Natalya covered a yawn. Beyond her shoulder, a fly beat helplessly against the glass panes.

"I don't want to stay another night!"

"Nor do I, but I don't see any alternative."

"There must be something we can do. Where are they?"

Natalya nodded at a pair of doors. "Just follow the strident voice."

Kasia went outside. Anise, feverfew, rue, yarrow and other flowering herbs she didn't know bloomed in pots on a flagstone patio. In the kitchen garden beyond, tall wooden frames held a riot of climbing plants—tomatoes, cucumbers, squash, peppers, and zucchini—along with hanging baskets of strawberries. Spassov stood next to a tangle of glossy eggplants, gazing straight ahead while Tessaria paced up and down. Her wide pinstriped trousers swished with each step.

"One task! That's all I asked of you."

He shrugged, unmoved by her wrath. "I watched the ship until eleven or so. The captain went belowdecks. The steam funnels were cold. No smoke. So I went to an alehouse and ordered a beer. When I went back outside, the *Moonbeam* was gone. They must have left under sail."

"One beer?"

"Maybe two."

Her scowl deepened. "And you're just telling me this now?"

"Do you see any telephones? Any taxis? It took me two hours to walk out here. I kept getting lost and that was in broad daylight, Sor Foy."

"Still, if I had known—"

"It's not his fault," Kasia interrupted, stepping into view.

"No doubt the captain was waiting for a chance to slip away like a cutpurse in the night."

Tessaria let out a long breath through her nose. She gave a grudging nod. "But this complicates things. Most of the ships from Kvengard sail the southern routes. It might take some time to find a northbound vessel."

"Is there no other way?" Kasia asked. "What about a carriage?"

"Through the Void?" Tess replied. "I wouldn't even dare risk it in a fast car. It's not like the route from Novo to Kvengard. That's relatively safe. But the roads to Nantwich pass through the Morho Sarpanitum. A treacherous journey even for knight-guarded convoys."

Spassov nodded. "She's right."

"What about the Danzigers? Don't they own a fleet?"

"I'll speak to them," Tess said.

"Speak to us about what?"

Hanne Danziger came around the corner of the house. She was dressed for gardening, with a floppy sun hat and pruning shears. When she saw Patryk Spassov, she stopped dead. Her eyes locked on the inverted trident embroidered on his wrinkled cassock. "Why is the Interfectorem here?" Her voice was cold.

"Oh!" Tessaria smiled reassuringly. "Fra Spassov accompanied us from Novostopol. There's a . . . committee meeting of the Order in Nantwich. We thought we'd travel together. One can't be too careful these days."

Relief flooded her face. "Saints," she said softly, shaking her head. "I thought . . . never mind." Hanne Danziger smiled, though it seemed forced. "It is a pleasure to meet you, Father."

Spassov nodded, his own expression neutral.

"We've had a problem with the ship," Tess said lightly. "It appears to have sailed without us."

"No!" Hanne exclaimed. "First the luggage and now this?

I'll file a complaint on your behalf with the customs office. It's outrageous—"

"That won't be necessary," Tessaria said quickly. "But my commission for the Reverend Father cannot wait. Perhaps you could make an inquiry with the dock master?"

"Of course, I'd be happy to." She brushed dirt from her gloves. "Just permit me to change. Come, we'll sort this out right away."

The women went back into the house, talking quietly together. Kasia smiled at Spassov. "Two beers?"

"Maybe three. But the rest is all true." He looked guilty. "I'm sorry, Domina Novak—"

"Please, it's Kasia. Did you manage to find a room?"

His heavy shoulders twitched. "I slept on the pier. It seemed easiest."

"Have you eaten?"

Another tiny shrug.

"There's yoghurt in the glass house," she said. "And coffee."

"Thank you, but I'm not hungry."

She glanced into the conservatory. Natalya was gone.

"Would you walk with me then?"

Shrewd brown eyes weighed her as he withdrew a crumpled hand-rolled cigarette. "Where?"

"How about the gardens?"

They set off, Patryk smoking in silence. Kasia retraced her path from the night before. It was a world away from the landscape of flitting moon-shadows and phantasmagorical shapes. Gardeners knelt among the flowerbeds, weeding and laying mulch. Color abounded, day-lilies and daffodils, snapdragons, phlox and asters. Bees whirred from blossom to blossom, purring in contented diligence. Yet when her gaze turned to the forest, unease tightened her chest.

"I think I saw someone last night." She pointed to the

stand of pines. "Just over there. They ran off, but there was something decidedly sinister about them."

Patryk rubbed his three-day beard. "Did this person trouble you?"

"No, I think they were hunting something else." She told him about the pale figure she'd spotted from the window and the sudden arrival of Jule Danziger.

"Could it have been him you saw in the woods?"

"Maybe." Kasia hadn't mentioned the part about the ley changing color. As an Unmarked, she shouldn't have been able to see it at all. But she wondered what might have happened if those black tendrils had touched her.

Spassov ground the cigarette beneath his boot. "I don't like this place," he muttered.

"Neither do I."

"Have you told Sor Foy?"

"I just woke up," Kasia admitted. "Natalya knows. She doesn't seem herself this morning."

One of the gardeners, a large, muscular man with short white-blond hair and sharp cheekbones, turned from his raking to stare at them. His expression was suspicious and hostile as if they were trespassers rather than invited guests. Spassov stared back, immovable as an old stump. The man finally dropped his eyes and went back to his work.

"Most of the servants are like that," Kasia muttered as they moved on. "They act as if they don't want us here."

"What about the Danzigers?"

"Perfectly kind," she conceded. "The husband, Jann, was maimed in Bal Agnar. Tortured, Tess said."

"Sor Foy knows them from the war?"

"She was there, too, during Balaur's reign as Pontifex. She was a spy."

It occurred to Kasia that she knew very little about Patryk Spassov other than the fact that he had turned up just in time to save them from Bishop Maria Karolo and her minions.

They had only his word that the *Moonbeam* had sailed without them. He claimed he'd slept on the dock, but he could have been anywhere.

Perhaps even in the woods, watching her.

"Did you fight in the Void?" she asked as they wandered into the hedge garden.

"Mounted cavalry. Two tours."

"Where?"

He glanced down at her. "Not inside the cities, like Alyosha. That was the worst deployment. My unit patrolled the stretch between the Forts of Saint Agnes and Saint Ludolf, along the southern Morho."

"What was it like?"

"We had good days and bad days," he replied vaguely.

"Have you ever heard of the Order of the Black Sun?"

Spassov stiffened. "Where did you hear that name?"

"They're after me."

He stopped walking and turned to her. "After *you*?"

"So you do know of it."

Kasia watched him closely, but his face was guarded, giving little away. She took the deck from her pocket and fanned it out. "Pick a card, Patryk," she said coldly.

His thick brows lowered. "Is this a joke?"

"Not at all. Pick a card or I walk away and never speak to you again."

He stared at her for a long moment, gaze flat. "All right, Domina Novak."

A meaty hand reached out and plucked a card from the deck. Her heart thumped.

"Which is it?" she asked.

He peered down at the card. "I don't know. It's a man in a cloak . . . ."

"What else?" she demanded hoarsely.

"He carries a bolt of lightning in one hand and a staff in the other."

She smiled, tension draining away. "It's not a cloak. It's a cassock. The Priest of Storms."

His gaze was searching. "What does it mean?"

"That I trust you, Patryk."

He eyed her uncertainly. "Why?"

She took the card from his gloved hand. "The Priest of Storms is associated with Novostopol, of course. It signifies past turmoil, even significant missteps." His cheeks colored. "But the path he walks now is a true one. He has paid for his errors and is loyal to the death."

"I'm flattered," he said dryly. "But do you really trust me based on a random card?"

She gazed at the image. One of Natalya's, of course. Neither had met him when she painted the card, yet it looked uncannily like Spassov. Bull neck, shaven head, battered, melancholy face with a cleft chin. Some women would find him frightening, she thought, bemused, others extremely attractive.

"Nothing is random where the ley is concerned," she said.

Their gazes locked. Spassov nodded slowly. "I would never hurt you, Domina Novak."

"I know. So tell me what you know about the Order."

"Only what I've heard around the Arx. Rumors, mainly. They were a splinter group that escaped Bal Agnar after Balaur was taken. They fled to the other cities and created new identities for themselves, but they still adhered to his twisted philosophy. This was all thirty years ago. I never took it seriously."

"Well, the rumors are true. They exist. Those men in the alley, Tess thinks they're the Order of the Black Sun."

"Did they say so?"

"Well, no. But one told me his master wants to meet me."

"Why?"

She could have invented any number of lies, but Kasia sensed that it was a test. The Priest of Storms didn't give his allegiance lightly. He carried old wounds and was slow to trust—although once he did, he would be a champion for the ages.

"Because I can wield the ley without Marks," she said.

Something flickered in his eyes. He didn't seem surprised.

"You already knew," she said.

"Bishop Karolo called you a sorceress. I'm not a complete fool."

"I don't think you're a fool at all," Kasia replied. "Yet you still chose to help us."

He looked away. "It was the right thing. Now, why don't you show me where you saw this person?"

They followed a path that circled near the wood and crossed a grassy verge into the forest. Kasia led him to the area where she'd sensed the watcher. Spassov prowled through the trees. There was little underbrush, just a carpet of fragrant pine needles.

She moved a ways apart, studying the ground. No footprints, but she noticed several distinct lines of dead grass where the forest met the lawns of the estate. It wasn't blackened as though by fire, just withered and dry. She thought again of those dark, reaching tendrils.

"No sign of anyone," Spassov said, coming up behind. "I'm going to the Arx. If Alyosha is there, he needs to know about all this." His gruff voice softened. "He cares for you very much, you know."

"And I for him. But he's had so many troubles. I don't want to involve him—"

Spassov laughed. "Her would murder me if I didn't tell him." His face grew worried. "Besides which, I can't leave without knowing for certain that they granted him sanctuary."

Her gut tightened. "Could they have refused him?"

"I honestly don't know. But I intend to find out."

"We need to come up with a story for Tessaria. She'll never agree to let you go."

"She has no authority over me," he said sardonically. "But I would prefer not to antagonize her. What do you suggest?"

"We'll say you prefer to wait at the docks. I doubt she'll argue."

He nodded and they strolled back to the house together. Kasia was glad to see the unpleasant blond gardener had disappeared. The other groundkeepers paid them little attention. They found Tessaria with Hanne Danziger in a small study on the second floor. Hanne stood at the window, a large bird with a hooked beak perched on her arm. Luminous blue eyes settled on Kasia as she entered. Its feathers shone a deep ebony, but its form was oddly misty at the edges.

"Good news," Tessaria said, beaming. "It's likely we'll be able to set sail tonight."

Hanne whispered in the bird's ear. Shadowy wings spread wide and it soared out the window like a trail of smoke.

"A Markhawk," Spassov said. "I've never seen one before."

"We use them for messages," Hanne said. "They are very swift. It will return within the hour."

"She's lending us one of her ships." Tessaria said. "A fast clipper."

Kasia shared a quick look with Spassov. "That's very generous."

"It is no trouble," Hanne said. "Most of our trade takes the southern route, but there are always goods of value to be exchanged in Nantwich. We'll turn a profit either way."

"I was hoping for one last favor. Fra Spassov must settle his bill for last night's board. Can he borrow one of your horses to ride into the city?"

"Of course," Hanne said quickly. She seemed relieved to be rid of the priest from the Interfectorem. "The stables are just behind the house. Tell the boy he may choose any mount he wishes."

"Don't be long," Tessaria cautioned. "We depart on the eventide."

"Should I just meet you at the port?" Spassov asked.

Tessaria and Hanne exchanged a glance. "The ship isn't leaving from the port," Tess said. "It would take too long to get approval from the Kven customs officials. There's a cove not far off. The crew will row us out in a longboat."

And thus avoid any watching eyes on the docks, Kasia thought. She wondered how much Tess had told her friend.

"We leave at nine," Tessaria continued. "If you miss the ship—"

"He won't," Kasia said.

Patryk promised to return within a few hours. Kasia walked him to the stables. Dust motes danced in shafts of sunlight. It smelled of manure and sweet hay and the pungent aroma of the animals. A dark-haired youth of about thirteen was mucking out the stalls. The Danzigers kept a dozen horses, all regular stock. Spassov looked them over, then asked for a piebald mare who nosed his hand in a friendly way. The boy threw a blanket across her back and Spassov buckled on the harness, swinging nimbly into the saddle.

"I haven't ridden in years," he said with a boyish smile.

"You seem quite experienced," Kasia replied, admiring his easy way with the mount.

"I spent most of my twenties in the saddle. I guess it never goes away. " He glanced at the stableboy, who had moved off to resume his work. "Take care while I'm gone."

She nodded. "Tell Fra Bryce . . . ."

The horse whickered impatiently, stamping its feet.

"Just send him my regards." Her cheeks flushed and she cursed herself for a fool.

Spassov grinned. She watched him gallop down the long drive, dark blue cassock billowing behind.

Alexei Vladimir Bryce. Weary blue eyes, as though he'd carried a burden for so long he'd forgotten it was even there. Yet he'd come back to life in her arms.

Kasia wondered if he'd been sleeping.

If he dreamed, and whether it was of her.

"He's still a Marked priest," she muttered, annoyed with herself. "And I am . . . ."

What was she, exactly?

*There is a block in your mind, either placed there or self-imposed, but I will break through it.*

The Reverend Mother Feizah's cold voice echoed in her thoughts. The Pontifex had rifled through her memories. Whatever she found, she hadn't liked it. If Lezarius and Mikhail Bryce hadn't killed her, Kasia would be locked up in the Arx like some kind of experimental animal while Feizah turned her mind inside out.

Her childhood *was* blurry, but surely the same was true for most people. She'd often gotten into trouble. Just stupid things, but Kasia knew even at a young age that she was not a good, obedient daughter. She was punished often, both at school and at home, though it never bothered her much. She did as she pleased, the consequences be damned. Kasia hadn't been surprised when she failed the tests. If not for Tessaria Foy, Kasia had no idea where she would be.

Scrubbing floors in the Arx, perhaps, like that char she met the night the ley surged.

Nikola Thorn.

A striking woman. Tall and dark like Natalya, but with a tougher edge. She carried her head high, not like the others. Kasia felt a tremor of anger at the Curia. She rarely bemoaned her own position. Thanks to Tess, she had the luxury of passing for Marked. But for that twist of fate, she would be in the same underclass as Domina Thorn. Reviled and whispered about.

Kasia shook off her black mood. They would be leaving tonight. She set off to find Natalya. The news would cheer her up.

The house was quiet as she climbed the stairs to the third floor and knocked at Natalya's door. No answer. She went to her own room next door. Nashka lay atop the coverlet. Sweat beaded her brow. One fist was clenched, the other open, the fingers curled into a claw. Her eyes moved rapidly behind the lids. A moan escaped her lips.

Kasia sat down on the bed and gently touched her arm. Nashka's eyes flew wide. Her breath came in sharp bursts.

"It's me," Kasia said, alarmed. "Don't fret."

Natalya stared at her unblinking for a long moment. Then her head fell back on the pillow.

"Flay me," she whispered hoarsely.

"A nightmare?" Kasia smoothed the hair from her brow.

"I don't know . . . I . . ." She looked puzzled. "I came in to look for you. I didn't mean to lie down, I just felt so tired. The coffee didn't help."

"What did you dream of?"

She slowly shook her head. "It's gone now." Nashka gave a weak laugh. "Your ghost, perhaps."

"I told Spassov. We looked in the woods but didn't find anything. Listen, the Danzigers are arranging for a ship. We leave tonight."

"Thank the Saints." Natalya sat up. "I wish we could go somewhere right now. I don't want to be here."

Kasia smiled. "I have an idea. Let's go find Tess."

# Chapter Seven

Alexei left the chapel, riding hard for the tannery.

It sat on the east bank of the Mistrelle River. Men scraped flesh and hair from hides laid out on wooden racks. More stacks of hides sat out in the sun, or steeped in huge vats of lime. They'd been sprinkled with urine and pigeon droppings to facilitate the curing. The smell was indescribable.

Yet it was not the same as the one at the chapel. Or Willem's house.

Alexei tucked his face into his cowl, breathing shallowly.

Kvengard was a city of potent aromas. Horseshit, first and foremost. Then the sweet cedar smoke of the bokang burning in the braziers of street hawkers selling hot cheese pies. The dry scent of the rushes that covered the wooden boards of the beer gardens and the yeasty smell of the breweries. Far worse were the wagons that disposed of human waste, though they mercifully made the rounds at dawn.

Then there were the inhabitants themselves. The lack of plumbing instilled a lackadaisical approach to personal hygiene. People weren't filthy, but nor were they exactly clean. They relied more on scented rosewater than soap, and the apothecaries did a brisk business in perfumes to smother body odor.

He rode until he saw a sign with a mortar and pestle. Dried bunches of flowers hung in the shop window. Alexei dismounted and went inside. Stoppered bottles of every shape and size crammed the shelves. Vessels for oils and elixirs, resins and pastes. It smelled of musty roots. Somewhere in a back room, he heard the dull thud of a knife against a chopping block.

The proprietor was an older bearded man with a comfortable belly and thick grey brows. He stood at a long counter, crushing dry seed pods between his fingers and dropping them into a bowl.

"Sprichst du Osterlish?" Alexei asked hopefully.

"Ja," the man said.

It was taught alongside Kven since Osterlish was the primary tongue of both Nantwich and Novostopol. Most people retained little after grammar school, but shopkeepers tended to be more fluent since they conducted trade with the other Curia cities.

"I'm trying to identify a smell." Alexei struggled to describe it as precisely as he could. "Putrefaction, but with an overlay of sweetness. Like flowers." He knitted his hands. "Both together at once."

The man eyed the Raven Mark on Alexei's neck. "There is no such compound."

"Are you certain? You must be familiar with them all. Perhaps a combination?"

The apothecary shook his head.

Alexei leaned in and dropped his voice. "I'm a personal aide to Bishop Morvana, the Nuncio. You understand?"

A stony look.

"I swear I won't give your name or mention this conversation." He touched the Raven. "On my honor. But you've heard about the missing children, *ja*?"

The man's shaggy brows lifted in surprise. "Of course. It is terrible."

"This smell, it might be related to the case. If I can discover what it is, it's possible I can save others. Maybe even find the ones that are gone. Please, will you help me?"

Alexei held the man's troubled gaze. The apothecary nodded again, this time more firmly. He looked around. A woman with a basket over one arm was studying a shelf of tonics in the rear of the shop, but not close enough to overhear.

"What you describe . . . . The old alchemical texts say there are two prime smells. The stench of graves and one of flowers. Symbol of . . . . " He scratched his head. "To be born again?"

"Rebirth?"

"Yes, that is it." He gave a nervous laugh. "Alchemy is *verboten*, of course, but that is what comes to mind, you know?"

"Do you have any texts I might consult?"

He looked alarmed. "Oh, no. I don't keep such things. But as an apprentice, I hear about it. That's all."

Alexei believed him. "Thank you," he said. "The Curia is grateful."

The apothecary glanced at the woman. "I have other customers. I'm sorry . . . ."

Alexei could see he was eager to be rid of the foreign priest. "Of course. Again, thank you."

He left the shop boiling with new energy and a hundred questions. Alexei had delved deeply into arcane knowledge in the search for a cure for his brother. After devouring everything in the archives, he'd gone further, obtaining copies of banned books from Novo's black market. Alchemy was not a subject he'd spent much time on, but he still remembered a few names. Pre-Dark Age mystics who dabbled in the esoteric arts.

The apothecary might not have their writings, but he was willing to bet the Arx did.

An hour later, he sat at a table in the archives, a stack of books at his elbow. Only four, and three were biographies of recent vintage that held little of use. The last was a reprint of an original work by Angelus Silesius called *Der Cherubinischer Wandersmann*.

It was a strange tome, comprised of epigrams in the form of couplets. Much of the language was philosophical musings on the meaning of existence.

By the will art thou lost,
by the will art thou found,
by the will art thou free, captive, and bound.

It wasn't so different from the Via Sancta. He rubbed his eyes and carefully flipped through the pages. A very old book, bound in dark crimson leather. What the archivist called an illuminated codex. There were several full-page etchings rendered in vivid color. He paused at a picture of a three-headed beast in a glass vial. Alexei's heart thumped as he scanned the text.

Thrice Forty Nights she lay in grievous Plight.
As many Dais in Mourning sate upright,
The King Revived was in Forty more,
His Birth was fragrant as the Primrose Flower.

Forty nights.

*Forty*.

Alexei had no idea what it meant, but he sensed a connection. His first genuine lead in the case.

But . . . alchemy?

That was akin to magic. Which didn't exist.

He didn't think of the ley as magic. It was a natural force like the ocean tides.

Alexei's gaze roved over the shelves. What if it was a Nightmage? Bending the abyssal ley to lure the children away? At the end of the war, it was rumored that Balaur had sought alchemical knowledge. He was dead, but others might have been involved.

The King Revived . . . .

He quickly scanned the next few pages. The book was too big to fit into his sleeve. Alexei hoisted up his cassock and tucked it into the waist of his pants, then let the cassock fall. He returned the other books to the shelves and slipped out before the archivist caught him. No doubt someone would notice the theft, but Bishop Morvana could smooth any ruffled feathers.

He hurried to her office. She still wasn't there.

"When will she be back?" he demanded of her sour-faced secretary.

"I have no idea."

It was the man's favorite phrase.

"Please tell her I was here?"

He nodded without looking up. "Ja."

Alexei went back outside. Where to start?

*Alice.*

He'd take her to Willem's house and gauge her reaction to the cloak. If she erupted in a frenzy of barking, as he fully expected she would, he'd have an excuse to haul the parents to the Arx for questioning and a full physical examination. Morvana had warned that they were important people in Kvengard, but he'd take the fallout. What more could they do to him?

He stopped in his rooms to slip the book under his mattress, then jogged to the kennels. To his surprise, Alexei found the Markhound already standing outside, hackles raised.

"What is it?" he asked.

Alice bounded over. She nosed at his pocket and growled.

He crouched down and took out Mikhail's copy of the *Meliora*. "This?"

Alice tipped her dark muzzle to the heavens. She let out a mournful howl.

Alexei stared at her, heart thumping.

"*Venari*," he whispered. *Hunt.*

She spun in a circle, then took off running for the Gate of Saint Freyjus. After a moment of stunned disbelief, he leapt to his feet and gave chase.

# Chapter Eight

Oto Valek despised Kvengard.

The streets were filthy, the people more so. Their guttural language grated against his ears. He greatly missed Novostopol and his comfortable job as an orderly at the Batavia Institute. It had been easy to pilfer medication and sell it on the side for a hefty profit. The Curia had already paid him a generous salary—no one wanted to work with Invertido—and he'd also received a private stipend from Archbishop Kireyev to keep an eye on Doctor Ferran Massot.

All that in addition to the incentives from his true masters, who were the only ones Valek truly feared.

When the Wards broke, he had fled. Kireyev blamed him for failing to report Massot's excesses with the patients, but that wasn't what had made him drive all night, risking rutted tracks through the Morho to avoid the knights of Saint Ludolf.

No, it was the fact that Lezarius was loose.

The mad pontifex was Oto's main charge and he had failed.

When he had learned of Kireyev's plans to kill Lezarius and make Mikhail Bryce take the fall for it, he had deliberately skipped Bryce's morning and afternoon medication, hoping he might be alert enough to stop it. The plan had worked—too well. Oto had not been able to prevent their escape from the Institute.

He wasn't sure what his masters would do to him, but the continent wasn't big enough to hide from them so he'd gambled that bringing them news of the debacle might buy him mercy. Valek hugged his coat tighter against the bitter wind. Saints, let it be so.

He'd known the guard to ask for at Kvengard's main gate, whispering another name. The man had given him a flat look but waived the nearly-impossible-to-obtain permit to enter the city with a motorized vehicle. Oto's car drew so many stares, he finally parked and set off on on foot to the address the guard had given him. It was a mere three streets later that he spotted the knight.

In truth, Oto was so miserable, he wouldn't have noticed if it wasn't for the small crowd. After stepping in various sorts of shit, he'd kept his eyes firmly on the cobblestones. But the low mutter of disapproving voices caught his attention. He elbowed his way through.

A man slept beneath a tree in one of the market squares. He was naked and so thin, Oto could count his ribs. The man's chest was covered in Marks. That wasn't unusual except for the fact that one was inverted—and clearly a Nightmark. The crowd pointed and stared in morbid fascination.

Oto didn't speak Kven, but he knew the word Polizei. They'd already been summoned, or would be soon.

He froze, hardly believing his luck.

If he brought his masters a new prize, it might allay his failure. Mikhail Bryce might know where Lezarius went. But how much did he remember? Oto had unlocked his room and stood by as Kireyev's assassins prodded him to his feet. He'd had no choice, but Bryce might not see it that way.

Oto hesitated. The knight hadn't uttered a single word in

four years. At the Institute, he'd stared blankly when spoken to, giving no sign he understood. He'd never made any trouble, like some of the others. And Oto had always been nice to him—until he sold Mikhail like a pig for slaughter.

Valek thought back to the night the ley surged. The knight had moved like a sleepwalker. How much did he remember?

A gore-spattered room flashed before Valek's eyes.

Bryce had roused from his stupor when the Wards broke. That much was certain.

If Oto guessed wrong, he could end up like the two priests.

The thought of his masters sent him scurrying forward. He knelt down and shook Bryce's shoulder. Deep-set blue eyes flew open. He looked bewildered.

"It's me," Oto said with a toothy smile. "Your friend from the Institute."

Bryce jerked away. Oto raised his palms.

"Hey. I'm not here to bring you back. I'm alone, see?" His beady gaze flicked over the crowd. "But those people want to take you away again. Back to your little room."

Oto had no clue how Bryce had gotten inside the walls. His chest was a welter of bruises and scrapes, as if he'd been in a fight.

"Look, I'll help you, okay? I have a car."

People were calling out in Kven. Probably warning him to keep away from the lunatic. Mikhail stared at him so long, Oto started to sweat. Then the knight clambered to his feet.

Saints, the man was trusting.

Oto turned to the crowd. "Friend, ja?" he declared, grinning broadly. "Too much beer."

They weren't buying it. Not with that inverted Mark. A sea of suspicious eyes regarded him, but the Kvens were a docile folk and no one tried to follow as he tugged Bryce's hand, leading him down the street.

"This way," Oto said, adopting the calm, soothing tone he'd honed at the Institute. "Just a little further."

When they reached the car, he fumbled to unlock it with unsteady hands. Mikhail was looking back in the direction they'd come from, as though he was having second thoughts. Oto reached into the glove box and thumbed the cap from a glass syringe. It was already loaded with Somnium. Not the horse-sized dose they'd given Bryce at the Institute, but enough to keep him quiet for a while. Oto had planned to sell it—though now that he'd seen the rustics of Kvengard, straw in their hair and dumb bovine faces, he doubted he could find a market.

"I'll drive!" he said brightly, pretending to turn a steering wheel as if he were addressing a four-year-old.

Something flickered in Bryce's eyes. A new, dangerous awareness. Oto jabbed the syringe into his thigh and depressed the plunger. A heartbeat later, fingers gripped Oto's throat, lifting him off his feet. He kicked and writhed. How could Bryce be so strong? He was all sinew and bone.

Black mist gnawed the edges of Oto's vision. Then the vise loosened. He collapsed to the ground. Bryce swayed. He tried to brace himself on the hood.

Panting, Oto yanked the rear door open. He threw his weight against the knight's broad back, catching him under the arms as his knees gave out. Oto lived a soft life and it took all his strength to maneuver Bryce's bulk into the back seat.

A whistle sounded near the square. Oto threw the car into gear and floored the accelerator. He sped down the cobbled street, nearly hitting a wagon rounding the corner, and spun the wheel.

# Chapter Nine

By the time Alexei reached the Gate of Saint Freyjus, Alice had vanished into the city. He followed the glowing paw prints she left in the ley, wishing he had a horse.

Could Misha have walked all the way from Novo? It had been nearly two weeks since he escaped from the Institute. What if he was with Lezarius?

They must be very near the Arx if she'd caught Misha's scent. What if they sought revenge on Luk, just as they had on Feizah?

The dire thought spurred him to a sprint.

The prints led to a narrow side street just a few minutes away. He found her sniffing around, whining through her nose. Two men were unloading a wagon, hoisting kegs of beer to their broad shoulders and carrying them through the rear entrance of a hostel. They cast him an uncurious glance and resumed their task.

No Misha.

Alexei stood, panting and crestfallen. Alice looked at him and barked once.

He wondered if she hadn't been confused, though Alice

had never muddled a scent before. "Veni," he said, patting his thigh. *Come.*

He walked her around the block, slowly widening the search outward. She kept her snout to the earth, but gave no signs of catching the trail. Frustration mounted. He finally returned to the place they'd lost it. Near a low stone wall, he found a faint tire track.

A car? They were rare, but foreign dignitaries were permitted to drive within the walls.

Alexei spent another fruitless hour searching the nearby streets.

What on earth would he do if he did find them? They'd have to leave the city right away. Have to steal horses and run—

A small boy with a cap of dark curls passed, holding tight to his mother's hand. The child gave a shy smile. Alexei smiled back, though his face felt wooden. Merry laughter assailed him as a gang of slightly older kids dashed by, schoolbags slung over their shoulders.

In the park across the street, another group had gathered to watch a puppet show. The pageants were one of the quaint Kven traditions he'd found amusing when he first arrived. Strings danced as Balaur and Lezarius did battle against a paper cut-out of the Arx at Bal Agnar. The children gasped as streamers of blue cloth suddenly shot from Lezarius's hands.

No one walked to school alone anymore. The children sitting cross-legged on the ground to watch the puppets were watched closely by their parents.

But it would do no good, he knew. No good at all.

Who would be next? The little blond girl, laughing and clapping her hands as Balaur toppled from the battlements? Or the chubby, freckled boy tossing a coin into the puppeteer's hat?

Saints! He couldn't go anywhere before he told Morvana everything he'd discovered.

The shadows lengthened as Alexei walked back to the kennels, Alice heeling close behind, her ears drooping. When they arrived, she pressed her tail between her legs, brown eyes anxious.

"You tried," he said, rubbing her scarred flank. "It's not your fault."

One of the handlers came out with a bowl of chopped meat and set about feeding the hounds. Alice shot him a last guilty look before wolfing down her dinner.

Alexei's shoulders slumped as he left the kennels. Priests and vestals moved along the walkways, hands tucked into their sleeves. A bell tolled in Fallbach Tower, signaling the hour of meditation before dinner. To think Mikhail had been so close. Had he, too, been spirited away? And for what purpose?

The weight of an invisible force pressed down on him. His Marks flickered, trying to soothe the rage and despair. What was he doing here? Why did the ley toy with him, giving him hope and then snatching it away?

He had always believed the power was fundamentally a force for good. This was the foundation of his faith. But what if the ley didn't care what hand wielded it? He stared at the ancient stone buildings with a new bitterness. The Praefators themselves had been nihilim. Falke as much as admitted it. What if the power itself had corrupted them—

*Pull yourself together*, he thought angrily, when the blue light bleeding from his sleeves drew a sharp glance from one of the other priests. If there are mages in this city, you will hunt them down, just as you always have. Hunt them and destroy them.

Alexei was turning for Morvana's office when he saw a man walking down a path in the distance. He didn't wear the cassock of a priest and something in the way he kept glancing around suggested furtiveness. He seemed familiar.

Alexei stopped dead.

Oto Valek from the Batavia Institute?

Impossible. Yet as the man veered down a crossing path,

Alexei caught a clear glimpse of his face. Red hair with a goatee and slug-pale skin. It was indeed Oto Valek. And he was headed toward the chapel where Alexei had gone that morning.

Alexei walked swiftly behind, but Valek never looked back. A minute later, he disappeared through the doors.

"What are you up to?" Alexei muttered, breaking into a jog.

The sound of the bells faded. The pathways emptied. His brothers and sisters would all be sitting quietly in their rooms or the communal meditation halls, chanting the sutras. With a last look around, he slipped inside the chapel.

Oto had vanished. Dim light filtered through the stained glass triptych. Alexei walked down the center aisle of the clerestory, scanning the pews to either side. There didn't seem to be any other exit.

"Come out, Valek," he said loudly, tugging his gloves off.

The votive candles flickered. A putrid aroma hit him.

Alexei spun as a hooded shape silently rose up from the shadows behind the altar. The edge of a short sword caught the light. He barely managed to duck. Air whistled above his head. He lashed out and caught a forearm, snapping it backwards at the elbow. A scream and the blade dropped. Alexei dove for it as two more figures loomed behind the fallen man. He raised the sword just in time to block a powerful downstroke. A blank white face leered down at him. Alexei rolled back as one swiped at him. Cloth ripped. He gained his feet and retreated, glancing down in disbelief. Four razor-thin lines shredded the breast of his cassock.

Alexei gripped the short sword with both hands. He backed away as the two men closed in. Both wore featureless masks, the eyes black holes. Burning embers shone in the depths.

One held a long blade. The other flexed yellowed claws that curved like talons. Its arms were . . . too long for a man.

And its form was strangely insubstantial, merging with the shadows beyond.

"Shit," he muttered, filling with dread.

Alexei feinted, then attacked. Steel rang. The swordsman forced him back, blade flickering, as the second circled his flank. Sweat rolled down his spine. He fought one-handed, the other groping for something, anything solid. His right parried a crushing blow just as his left met the wood of the altar.

The one with a broken arm seized the hem of his cassock. Alexei kicked out with a boot, hitting him squarely in the face. A conduit opened through his palm and he drew deeper, deeper. It purified him, searing away the last remnants of doubt and confusion.

*I am a priest of the Via Sancta. A servant of the righteous ley.*

Blue light shot from his sleeves, strobing through the sanctuary like sheet lightning. The swordsman cried out as the tip of Alexei's blade sliced his throat. The backswing severed one of those monstrous hands. Then the thing was on him, driving him to the ground. Claws stabbed into his side. Alexei tore the mask away. A face from nightmare. His hand scrabbled on the stone as a pointed black tongue emerged from . . . not a mouth. A fleshy sort of beak.

Laughter spilled out. It sounded all too human.

"Die, priest," a voice grated.

Alexei's reaching fingers closed around a hilt. He drove the blade deep. His attacker convulsed, its claws a hair's breadth from his eyes. He shoved it off, gasping, and rolled away. Trembling fingers probed his side, expecting to find a mortal wound. There was no pain, but that meant nothing. More likely he was going into shock.

Yet he found no hot wetness. A weak laugh escaped him. The cloth was torn, the book deeply gouged, but the *Meliora* in his pocket had saved him.

Alexei rose shakily to his feet. The swordsman was dead. Alexei tugged his mask off. A human face, clean-shaven and unremarkable. Not Oto Valek, though he didn't expect it to be. The orderly had led him into a trap, but he was no fighter.

He inspected the body for Nightmarks, finding none. It came as a vast relief that he did not find any Wolf Marks, either. The man wasn't ordained. He did have two Civil Marks, though. And a third with a small circle inside a triangle, inside a square, inside a larger circle. It looked vaguely familiar, though he couldn't say from where. One of the books from the archives perhaps?

By the time he turned back to the thing with a beak, it had shriveled into a blackened, flaky heap, like old meat charred over a fire. The severed hand lay a meter away in similar condition.

"Saints," he whispered, poking it with a toe. "What fresh evil is this?"

Alexei coughed at the smell. There was no hint of the sweet floral scent, just foulness. He regarded the husk in worried disgust for a long moment. Something forged with ley, perhaps alchemy as well. But never had he seen such vile putrefaction. When a Markhound died, it held its natural form, like any living, breathing creature. But this . . . .

"It had one foot in the grave already," he said softly.

Then, another unpleasant discovery. The one he'd kicked by the altar had vanished.

He examined the altar itself carefully, pressing on various wooden panels. None produced a secret passage. Yet how else had the man escaped? And Valek as well? Alexei tugged his gloves back on. He left the bodies where they lay and hurried to Morvana's office.

"She's in," the secretary informed him smugly. "And not in a good humor."

The bishop looked up from the papers spread across her desk, green eyes flashing in irritation. "Where have you been, Bryce? We had an appointment to meet the Messners two bells ago." She eyed his shredded cassock. "What happened to you?"

"I was attacked," he said grimly. "On the grounds of the Arx."

She frowned. "By whom?"

"They wore masks. One is . . . you have to see it."

Morvana rose to her feet. "We must summon the pontifex's guards!"

"After. Just come."

A brow arched. "Why?"

"Because the Reverend Father will want to keep this quiet. Trust me."

She grabbed her exorason from a peg. "I'm sorry I was occupied this morning. My secretary told me you were here."

"Twice," he clarified. "I've made an important discovery."

"Regarding the case?" she asked as they hurried down the corridor.

"Yes. And clearly, someone found out."

She shot him a doubtful look, but followed through the grounds in silence. Alexei threw open the doors. Morvana stepped cautiously into the clerestory. "What am I looking for?"

"I killed two of them." He rubbed the back of his closely shorn scalp. "Right here!"

The bodies were gone. A cone of incense burned on the altar, filling the sanctuary with the woody scent of sandalwood.

Morvana turned to him. "I'd say it's a bad joke, but you're not the type."

Alexei touched the Raven on his neck. "I swear it happened. Someone must have cleaned it up." He strode down the aisle. The stone was unblemished.

"Someone," she repeated slowly. "And why do you think these men attacked you?"

"Because I found a lead, Your Grace."

"Go on."

"The smell at Willem's house. It wasn't from the father's tannery. I rode by this morning. So I got to thinking that perhaps an apothecary could help me identify it." He drew a breath. "There's a connection to alchemy."

She looked skeptical.

"The arcana lists two prime odors. Putrefaction and purity, represented by flowers. I did some reading. Forty is a significant number."

"For what?"

"Rebirth of some kind."

"You're implying Willem's parents are involved?" she said unhappily.

"They must be."

"But we checked them both out. I can't arrest people based on a *smell*, Bryce."

"Then watch them." He bent down and ran a hand along the underside of one of the pews. When he raised his glove, the index finger shone with dark liquid. He sniffed it.

"Blood," he said with satisfaction. "They missed a spot."

She strode over and examined the glove. "Saints. All right, Bryce. I'll look into it." She shot him a look. "Don't tell anyone about this."

"Who would I tell?" He looked around. "There's something else. I think the attackers came from a hidden passage."

She laughed. "This conspiracy just keeps growing."

"Listen to me. Each Arx is nearly identical with the others, *ja*?"

She nodded.

"What's the name of this place?"

"The Chapel of Saint Ydilia."

"In Novostopol, it's called the Chapel of Saint Iveron. I know for a fact that it has a hidden door leading to tunnels below because I've been through them."

She frowned. "I've never heard of such a thing."

"Neither had I, until I . . . ." *Ended up in a cell.* "Had cause to explore them," he finished lamely.

"Where was this hidden door?"

"Over there." He pointed to a blank wall. "I already looked. If there is one here, it's someplace else. But it would explain how they disposed of the bodies and cleaned it up so quickly."

Alexei bent and wiped the droplet of blood on the stone floor.

"This is madness, Bryce," she muttered.

"I came here to meditate this morning. That's when I noticed the same smell. Rotten and sweet at the same time. It led me to the tannery. I wondered if it was the ley pushing me in the right direction. I had used my Marks to . . . seek guidance in the case. But now I wonder if I didn't smell it in truth. Through the passage. They might have been watching even then."

"And why did you come the second time?"

He hesitated. "I thought I saw someone I knew from Novostopol. I followed him here."

"I suppose he vanished, as well?"

Alexei nodded.

She eyed the red smear on the floor. "If it weren't for that, I'd put you on medical leave. But you don't seem to have a scratch. Except for . . . ." She pointed to his cassock, a question on her face. "It looks like an animal."

Alexei suspected it would push his luck too far to mention the bird-man.

"One had a knife," he said.

Morvana shook her head with a heavy sigh. "Alchemists. Well, we have nothing else to go on. I suggest you return to your rooms and change before someone sees you."

"Yes, Your Grace."

"We'll visit the Messners first thing in the morning. And I

suppose we'll have to interview the families a third time to ask if any of them noticed this mysterious smell."

"Did anything turn up on missing pets?"

"Willem's dog was the only one. Another dead end, it seems." She sighed. "I'm still waiting for approval from the head of the Polizei to conduct a search of the Burwald."

Alexei knew now that it would be a colossal waste of time.

"Which makes this new angle even more important," he said. "You'll have his parents watched? We're running out of time."

"I'm aware of that. Yes, I'll do it. Very discreetly."

"Good."

"And Bryce?"

"Yes?"

"I know you're lying about *something*. Don't come to my office until you're ready to unburden your conscience."

Bishop Morvana strode from the chapel.

Alexei watched her go. He spent another half hour fruitlessly searching for a hidden door, then headed for his rooms. Bells tolled the dinner hour and he realized he hadn't eaten since breakfast. He made a quick stop in the mess hall, where he snagged a loaf of bread and chunk of cheese. Alexei ate them on the way back to the kennels, barely tasting the food. A sharp whistle in the yard summoned the Markhound to his side, red tongue lolling. He ruffled her ears. She fell into step with him as he strode for his rooms.

He would keep Alice with him in his rooms from now on. If they came for him again, she would give warning.

Oto Valek. Alexei had always suspected the man was a snake. His presence meant a connection with the Institute. With Misha, who had also vanished into thin air. Alexei felt certain now that Alice had indeed caught his brother's scent, but someone had taken him. Maybe only minutes before Alexei arrived. The thought was an icy hand around his heart.

If it was all of a piece, then finding Misha might mean finding the children, too.

Could alchemy transform a human being into the monster he'd seen in the chapel?

He glanced down at Alice, a slim shadow trotting by his side.

It seemed impossible, but Luk had done it with the ley. Marked dog and horses to enhance their natural abilities. Why not with a human being?

That thought made him even sicker.

He pounded up the winding stairs of the tower, pausing when he reached his rooms. The door was slightly ajar. Alexei's pulse quickened as he nudged it with his boot. A strong odor assailed him—but not the stench of the grave.

Cheap tobacco.

He peered into the room. The ember of a cigarette burned in the darkness. A hulking figure stood silhouetted at the window. Alice gave a single sharp bark and bounded into the room. The figure spun as she leapt up, flattening her paws on its broad chest.

Alexei stepped through the door with an uncertain grin, hardly daring to believe it.

"Patryk?" he said.

# Chapter Ten

"Do I have to?"

Nikola eyed herself in the cracked standing mirror. Her breasts ached beneath the green cloak. Everything was bloated and tender, though the heavy garment concealed her growing curves.

"Beleth insisted that we both dine with her tonight," Malach replied. "I can tell her you're ill—"

"She'll get suspicious."

He walked up behind her and laid a hand on her belly. She stared at his milky reflection, black hair against pale skin.

"I hate this," she muttered.

"Which part?" Malach tried to nuzzle her neck and she stepped back.

"All of it," Nikola retorted savagely. "I think you've gotten the easier end of this bargain by far!"

"I never disputed that," he replied mildly.

"You didn't even bring me here! *I* did all the driving. And now look at me." She shook his hand off and began to pace the stone floor. "How much longer, Malach?"

"I told you, just one more day—"

"Not before I can leave." She hated the tremor in her voice. "How long before this . . . *thing* . . . comes out of me?"

His eyes darkened to tarnished bronze. "That thing is our child."

"*Your* child! Not mine."

He expelled a breath through his nose. "Fair enough. My child. About three more weeks, I think."

"You think? How can you not know?"

"Because no human woman has borne a mage in my memory."

"Will it kill me?" Her voice sounded devoid of emotion, though she was seething inside.

"Tash won't let that happen—"

She rounded on him. "Does he know?"

Malach threw his hands up. "No! No one knows, I swear it. But if it comes sooner, I'll make sure you survive the birth. You have my oath."

She laughed bitterly. "And if the child tears my womb apart, how will you fix that, Malach? How will a *veterinarian* patch me back together in the Void?" His silence enraged her further. "If it came down to saving one of us, which would you choose, eh?"

"You," he said without hesitation. There was a strangely intent quality to his gaze. "I would choose you, Nikola."

"Would you?" she whispered.

"Yes," he snapped, closing the space between them. "I would choose you a thousand times!"

Then he was kissing her, and despite herself she kissed him back, clinging to his broad shoulders like a lifeline. When Nikola finally pulled away, her lips were swollen and raw. Malach's eyes were dark with desire. She hated him then, and hated herself more for wanting him anyway.

"Let's get this over with," she muttered, striding to the door on unsteady legs.

Malach caught up to her in the corridor. Neither spoke as

they descended the grand marble staircase to the dining hall. Just ahead of the arched doorway, he caught her arm.

"You don't have to—"

"Yes," she said, shaking him off. "I do."

Nikola braced herself and stepped into the hall. Long velvet curtains in deep scarlet covered the windows. Three chandeliers with tiers of crimson candles hung on chains from a high vaulted ceiling. A dozen elderly mages sat around the long table, all bewigged and powdered, wearing robes of a similar bloody hue.

Only Tashtemir Kelevan rose when she entered. In his dark coat with frilled sleeves spilling from the cuffs and a mournful face devoid of paint, he looked like he'd wandered into the wrong party. Tashtemir gave them both a friendly nod. Nikola was glad to find him there. She didn't count him an ally exactly, but he was the only other outsider at Bal Kirith—and the only one besides Malach who'd shown her kindness.

Beleth's icy gaze followed as Malach held Nikola's chair, then sat down stiffly at his aunt's left hand.

"I'm pleased you could join us," Beleth said to Nikola. "I feared you might be indisposed again."

The mages tittered. Everyone knew she'd run into the corridor to retch the night she arrived.

"Domina Thorn is perfectly well," Malach said. The laughter died under his flat gaze.

"Well, I hope you brought an appetite." Thin red lips parted in a triumphant smile. "The cook prepared something special."

A masked servant stepped forward with a platter and swept the lid off with a flourish. The head of some antlered beast stared up at Nikola with glassy eyes. She studied it for a long moment. Her dinner companions leaned forward in cruel anticipation. A faint hiss of air signaled Malach's displeasure.

Nikola deliberately met Beleth's cold regard. Then she

picked up her fork and plucked out one of the eyes, using her knife to sever the tough ropes of ganglia. She popped it in her mouth and chewed thoughtfully. The sensation was akin to eating a fleshy grape.

"It's delicious, Reverend Mother," she pronounced with an answering smile. "What a treat!"

Malach prodded the head with his own fork. "Not much meat," he remarked.

Beneath the crimson cloth, his hand settled on her thigh, giving it a gentle squeeze.

Beleth looked disappointed. She clapped her hands. "Bring in the rest," she said curtly.

"Where are the children?" Malach looked around for Tristhus and Sydonie, who were conspicuously absent.

"Being punished," Beleth replied. "No dinner."

"What did they do this time?" he asked in amusement.

"I caught the girl prancing about in my robes."

"The gall," Malach murmured. Nikola managed to keep a straight face, though it wasn't easy.

"I beat her with a switch and she laughed! Then her wretched brother kicked my shin. They go too far. You must take them in hand, Malach," Beleth said sternly.

"I try my best, though they've yet to learn it's unwise to bite it." He tucked his scarlet napkin on his lap. "Ah, supper!"

A roast haunch was hauled in and carved on a sideboard. The meat was so rare Nikola half expected it to bleat in protest, but the instant the bloody plate was set before her, her stomach rumbled in ravenous hunger. Wine was poured. Nikola took a small sip to prove she could—the heavy, sour vintage had been her undoing last time—and dug into the haunch. She could hardly chew fast enough to fill the gaping hole in her belly. Beleth watched from the head of the table with a considering expression, fan tapping, and Nikola forced herself to slow down. She turned to Tashtemir, who sat at her right.

"I can't quite place your accent," she said.

His voice was low and musical, with a slight slurring of the consonants.

"I hail from Paravai." He swallowed his wine and signaled to a servant to refill his cup. Tashtemir had barely touched his food. She resisted the urge to spear a chunk of meat from his plate.

"The lands of the Golden Imperator?" she said in surprise. "You're a long way from home."

Nikola glanced at Beleth, but the Pontifex had ceased her scrutiny and was deep in conversation with Malach.

"Indeed I am," Tashtemir said with a wry grin. "The Morho is a far cry from court life—not that I lack appreciation for its charms."

"Court life?" she echoed. "And here I thought you were a humble animal doctor."

"Ah, I am that." He winked. "But once I was more, Domina Thorn. The Imperator keeps a bestiary. I cared for the exotic pets."

Nikola sopped up pink gravy with a chunk of bread. "That sounds like a comfortable position."

"It was." He dropped his voice. "Unfortunately, I was young and headstrong and offended the Imperator rather unforgivably."

That piqued her interest. Nikola paused in her gluttony. "How so?"

He sighed. "I bedded her wife."

Nikola laughed. "I suppose that is unforgivable."

"It is my own stupidity in getting caught that I referred to, but yes, she was most incensed. I was forced to depart the court in rather a hurry."

She pushed her plate away, feeling lightheaded. "I assumed Malach must have Marked you."

Tashtemir laughed. "Oh, no. We do not hold by such things in the south. I met him in Novostopol. The Imperator, she placed a generous bounty on my head. Some mercenaries found me in a tavern at the docks. I was on the verge of being hooded and trussed like a pheasant when the mage happened across us." He glanced at Malach. Their eyes caught for a moment. Malach smiled slightly, then turned back to his aunt.

"He intervened, more out of curiosity than kindness, I suspect."

"Oh, you can be certain of it," Nikola muttered. "Then what?"

Tashtemir shrugged. "I explained my predicament." He cleared his throat. "I might have claimed greater expertise than I actually had. The mages needed a doctor. I needed sanctuary in the Void. It was the only place I could be certain they wouldn't find me. A bargain was struck."

"Yes, he's a great one for bargains." She swirled the dregs of her wine. "What happened when he found out you were a vet and not a surgeon?"

"He laughed."

"That's all?"

Tashtemir stroked his long black mustaches. "That's all."

She frowned, studying the back of Malach's head as he gestured animatedly. Every time she thought she had him figured out, some new puzzle piece fell into her lap that wouldn't fit. He was selfish and thoughtless. Arrogant, too. Yet he wasn't entirely unredeemable. Her pulse skipped. What if he actually meant what he said? That he would choose her over the child? What if—

The table talk cut off as a young mage ran into the hall. She wore forest greens and her boots left muddy footprints from the door. Beleth's white-powdered face went slack as she whispered in the Pontifex's ear. Her knuckles clenched white around the fan.

The pleasant sleepiness induced by her repast vanished. Nikola tensed with sudden foreboding as Beleth rose to her feet. Her gaze swept the assembled nihilim.

"They have him," she said. "Dantarion has captured Lezarius."

Nikola shared a quick glance with Tashtemir. His expression was hard to read, but the others erupted in jubilation. Malach pounded the table with a wondering laugh.

"Tell the tale!" he cried.

The young mage grinned. "We caught them at the Mistrelle, Your Grace. There were two. One held your Mark."

"Mine?" Malach frowned. "Are you certain?"

"Yes, Your Grace. The Mark was inverted."

"Ahhhh. Mikhail Bryce." Malach still looked a bit flummoxed and Nikola wondered who they were talking about. "Is he dead?"

"The river took him." Her mouth twisted. "I could have finished him with an arrow, but Bishop Dantarion forbade it. She said—"

"The other doesn't matter," Beleth snapped. "What about Lezarius? Did he fight?"

"He gave us no trouble. It was already dark when we found them. Bishop Dantarion sent me to carry the message. She expects to arrive tomorrow."

"We should send a party to meet them," Malach said, rising to his feet.

"And steal Dante's victory from her?" Beleth said. "No, she earned the right to bring him through the gates of the Arx." A satisfied smile. "I will make her a cardinal for this."

His mouth set. "We can't take a chance—"

*"Cannot?"* Beleth's stare would have made most men quiver in their boots, but Malach only stared back. The rest of the table watched them as the silence lengthened, taut as a bowstring.

"Should not," he amended at last. "It's a foolish risk!"

"Do you doubt her abilities?" Beleth demanded softly.

"No, but—"

"Then you will hold your peace, Malach." She turned

away, dismissing him, and raised her goblet. "A toast! To the rise of Bal Kirith!"

Servants hurried to refill glasses. Malach gave a small shake of his head, but lifted his own and drank deeply. The hubbub made Nikola's head pound. She stood and touched his sleeve.

"I think I'll retire," she said. "I'm sure you have much to discuss."

"Are you well?" he whispered.

"Fine." She wiped a sheen of sweat from her brow. The cloak weighed on her shoulders like a waterlogged blanket.

"I'm seeing Domina Thorn to her room," Malach shouted over the din of more toasts and harsh laughter.

Their leering, powder-caked faces and greasy lips suddenly looked even more monstrous, like a gathering of imps in some lower circle of Hell. The whole room smelled of blood. How had she not noticed before?

"As you will," Beleth said. "But I expect you to return."

He gave her a brief nod and steered Nikola to the door. In the corridor, she drew a steadying breath, glancing sidelong at him as they ascended the stairs. Malach's cheeks were flushed, his eyes too bright.

"This changes everything," he said feverishly. "Everything!"

She cast him a dubious look. "Not in my book."

"Don't you see? With Lezarius, we can smash open the Void! The only reason we're living like *this*"—his gaze flicked over the mildewed plaster and cracked floor tiles—"is because the Curia hoards the ley. But they're weaker than we are! Far, far weaker. And there are more of us still alive than they suspect. Scattered throughout the Morho. But once the ley is restored, they will return. Bal Kirith will be a great city again. Let them challenge us then—"

Nikola tuned out the monologue. Once inside his chamber, she threw the cloak off and sat down on Malach's bed. It was wide enough for four people to sleep comfortably, with sharp finial posts at each corner and grotesque sea creatures carved on the footboard.

"You don't have to run anymore, Nikola," he said. "I can protect you now."

"It's not what we agreed—"

He sank to his knees in front of her, hands loose on her knees. "Please, just listen. I don't want you to go away."

"I can't stay—"

"Why not?" He slipped one of her shoes off. "Why can't you?"

Thumbs pressed into her arch. Nikola stifled a sigh of pleasure. "Because I can't!"

"I'll give you anything you want," he purred. "Anything. Just name it."

"Malach—"

"When I'm finished, you won't want to leave," he said stubbornly. "You'll never, ever want to leave." His hand slid up her leg, massaging the calf.

"You just can't stand someone saying no to you."

"What will it take?" Her other shoe came off. "Tell me what it is you really want."

"To be free!" The words spilled out in a rush. "That's all I've ever wanted."

"Then freedom you will have, Nikola Thorn." The hem of her dress was somehow around her hips. "You'll answer to no one, ever." Warms hands stroked her bare thigh. "I'll make no demands on you. Only that you stay with me."

His cheek nuzzled her breast. Nikola cupped his face. Then he was kissing her and the dress lifted over her head.

"Your injury," she murmured helplessly.

His scarlet robe was flung across the room, nothing underneath but pale Marked muscle and a jagged pink scar. Nikola realized that he'd been lying to her for days, he wasn't half as hurt as he'd claimed, but she was beyond caring. She wanted the length of him pressed against her, smoothing all her tender aches. One last time. He whispered to her as they tangled together in the sheets. Promises he could never keep.

Nikola whispered false promises of her own, because that's what they were to each other. Selfish liars, both of them.

Yet it was different this time. *He* was different. Malach always delighted in driving her wild with desire before giving away a single bit of himself. He was obviously a very practiced lover with a boundless imagination. She'd assumed his manipulative nature took pleasure from stripping her defensive layers away, one by one, until she could no longer think straight. If he had been schooled by his cousin, Nikola reluctantly gave Dantarion credit. Malach was a virtuoso in the arts of love. Or more accurately, *lust*.

Yet he handled her with infinite tenderness tonight, asking again and again if he was hurting her, if she liked *this* and *that*. Nikola could feel his own aching need, heat tightly in check. When she told him *yes, yes, yes*, he finally grew bolder, taking her with an agonizing slowness that left them both locked together and shaking uncontrollably.

After, she watched him sleep. His face was still, his breath shallow, almost deathly, as though he'd spent every ounce of himself. The calm after the storm.

But the storm was only beginning.

A mad pontifex was on his way to Bal Kirith. She had no idea whether Beleth's scheme would work, but Nikola did not share Malach's delight at seeing the nihilim regain power. Nor did she believe Dantarion wouldn't deem her a threat. Malach saw only what he wanted to see.

He cared for her in his own twisted way. That much was obvious. But his moods were changeable as the clouds. He would tire of her one day. Or she would tire of him.

Rain pattered against the windowsill as she studied his face. She knew better. So why did it hurt so much?

Nikola's breath caught at a sudden quickening. She pressed a hand to her belly.

No, it couldn't be, not yet—

The movement came again, undeniably a *kick*.

Malach stirred in his sleep, throwing a heavy arm across her side. Nikola froze until his breathing evened out again. She carefully inched out from beneath his weight. He didn't stir again.

The reality of her situation hit home at that moment.

The child was no longer an abstract. It was there, alive. It had limbs.

She felt no maternal instinct. Only the urge to run as far and fast as she could before it arrived in the world.

And then . . . .

Saints help us all, she thought grimly, unsure why but certain it was true.

Nikola quietly packed her Kaldurite stones. She dressed and donned the green cloak, a castoff of Sydonie's. When her gaze fell on the lacquered box, she hesitated, then threw it into the bag.

Malach let out a faint snore. How young he looked in the candlelight—young but not soft. Beleth had carved the softness from him, sliver by sliver, if it had ever been there at all.

Nikola wanted to kiss him goodbye, but didn't dare.

"Just don't make me shoot you, Malach," she whispered, and hurried to the door.

---

She crept down the stairs. Raucous voices drifted along the corridor below. The celebration in the hall was still going full swing. Nikola hesitated. She was already hungry again.

The child would devour her alive if she didn't bring something to eat.

No one suspects, she reminded herself. Just go ask.

She left her bag in a starkly bare chamber—of which there were dozens—and circled around the hall through a labyrinth of narrow passageways. The kitchens were one level down in the cool recesses beneath the palace. She'd gone there once to forage when the hunger woke her like gnawing rats in the night. They were a far cry from the gleaming kitchens of the Castel Saint Agathe in Novostopol, with its neat rows of copper pans, fragrant herbs hanging in bunches, flour-dusted kneading tables and the mouth-watering aromas of baking at all hours of the day and night.

Nikola had furtively gobbled some nuts and whatever else she could lay hands on, which wasn't much. The filthy state of the place and rustles of vermin had dampened her cravings. She'd slunk back to bed.

She didn't blame the servants at Bal Kirith for not giving a damn. Why should they when their masters didn't seem to?

A few wrong turns later, she followed the stench of old grease to an open door. Three enormous ovens sat cold and empty. Casks were stacked against one wall, along with messy heaps of firewood. A bloodied wooden table, buzzing with flies, must have been where they butchered the stag. Her wary gaze flicked across dirty cookpots hanging on hooks and wooden trestles with a few meager baskets of fruit from the orchard.

The Arx had once fed and housed hundreds, perhaps thousands, but that number had dwindled to a few dozen, including the servants.

She saw no one and ventured inside. A soft but distinct moan of copulation made her pause. Nikola skirted the bloody butcher's block and peered into one of the pantries.

"Well, that's an appetite killer," she murmured under her breath, stifling a shocked laugh.

The bony arse of some aged cardinal was pumping away on a mound of sacks. Other figures writhed in the shadows—footmen? chambermaids? the mighty Pontifex herself?—and she sent a prayer of thanks for the dim lighting. Nikola turned away with a grimace and rifled through the next, happily unoccupied, pantry.

She filled her pockets with apples and pears, a round of cheese, and a jar of pickled things she hoped were eggs. Nikola was struggling out the door with her burdens when Tashtemir rounded the corner.

"Domina Thorn!" he said in surprise. "I thought you'd retired for the evening."

She donned a friendly smile. "You caught me. I'm afraid I'm plundering the pantry."

He eyed her bulging cloak. "Quite an appetite you have."

"Malach sent me. We both fancied a midnight snack."

He nodded slowly. "I came down for some wine. All the servants seem to have vanished."

She frowned. "How peculiar."

From the wry look on his face, she suspected he knew exactly what they were up to.

"Well, I must bid you goodnight," she said. "There's certain to be an even more lavish celebration tomorrow. I'm sure we'll see each other then." She moved to pass.

"Is it his?" Tashtemir asked softly as she brushed by.

Nikola briefly closed her eyes. She turned back with a confused expression.

"Pardon me?"

"The child. Is it his?"

"You're mistaken, Domine Kelevan," she said evenly.

"Am I? I've never seen Malach quite so . . . protective of anyone. It's most unusual. And your face is changing." He studied her. "You have the glow."

She laughed, even as ice flooded her veins. *What did he want?*

"I'll take it as a compliment, though I'm afraid it's simply an excess of rich food."

"Hmmm." Tashtemir stood aside. She disliked the calculating look in his eyes. "Goodnight then, Domina Thorn."

Nikola walked swiftly down the corridor, glancing back once to make sure he hadn't followed, but Tashtemir was gone.

The encounter only hardened her resolve. If he'd guessed the truth, it wouldn't be long before the others did. She thought Malach could handle most of them, but Beleth . . . . She's the one who scared Nikola the most. If the Pontifex decided to kill her—or something worse, she thought vaguely—not even Malach could stop her.

*He would try*, a small voice said. *And he would die, too.*

Her steps hastened as she retrieved the bundle of valuables and slipped out a side door into the rainy night. Pinpricks of light glittered in the stone walls, eerily beautiful. The park was a dark mass before her. She glanced up at the candle burning in Malach's bedchamber.

I'm sorry, she thought. So very sorry.

But her heart sung with relief as she raised her hood and hurried around the corner of the vast building, cutting across the park to the other side. The horses were stabled inside an old chapel behind the basilica. An old man was supposed to guard them, but he was often drunk. She crept up to the rain-streaked window. He lay curled on his side, an overturned jug near one hand.

Nikola eased the door open. Straw was scattered across the floor. She moved the lantern away from his foot so he wouldn't kick it over and burn the whole place down. Hooks had been driven into the rich wood paneling, each holding bridles and tack. The animals stood placidly near the water trough, dozing. They whinnied at her sudden approach, stamping their feet.

"Shhhh," she admonished, casting a glance at the unconscious groom. Nikola rummaged in her pocket and shared out two of the precious apples.

The man was a drunk but he seemed to like horses, for the stables were in far better condition than the kitchen. Relatively clean and with the sacks of feed stored in metal bins where the hordes of mice couldn't get at them. The heat of the animals made it quite warm inside. She pushed her hood back, gently fending off the velvety muzzles that nosed at her pockets for more treats.

Nikola found her horse—yes, it was hers now—and tried to saddle him. She hadn't done it herself before. She cursed quietly, fumbling with the buckles and straps. The other horses watched with liquid, dark eyes, giving an occasional encouraging whicker. In the end, she wasn't sure she'd done it correctly, but it *seemed* right.

Sweat trickled down her back as she led her mount outside, each plodding step seeming loud as thunder against the floorboards. The groom mumbled something. She looked around frantically, wondering if she'd have to whack him with a shovel, but he fell back into a doze.

Once outside, she wedged a foot into the stirrup and hauled herself up, tucking the bag in front of her. His tail swished at her ungainly efforts. She dug her knees in and urged the horse to a trot across the park. The paths were overgrown and wet branches, hidden in the dark, slapped at her arms and face.

There would be sentries farther out. She'd have to elude them, or . . . Her gaze dropped to the bundle. Well, she could always shoot them.

*With a gun.*

A strange laugh escaped her. It was like something out of a Second Dark Age novel.

But she would only the bullets to defend against Perditae. Not people—not even nihilim.

Nikola's luck held as the rain thickened. It would cover her trail and help hide her from searching eyes in the night. She reached the main thoroughfare and was just passing a cluster of roofless stone buildings when a faint sound came from ahead, just audible over the steady downpour. Nikola veered off the road and took shelter behind one of the tumbled-down walls. She dismounted, clutching the reins.

The ran hissed down. In the depths of the building, a bullfrog gave a lonely croak. Nikola shifted, nerves tingling. Had she imagined it? She was just getting ready to mount and ride on when she saw a flicker of movement in the road ahead.

Seconds later, a company of knights came into view. They were clad in black cloaks and must not have been wearing plate armor because the soft creak of their leather gambesons was the only sound. About two hundred, otherwise marching in perfect silence. Here and there, steel glinted in the darkness.

Nikola knew she wouldn't meet any sentries. They were already dead.

She pressed back against the wall. Her horse shook its head, eyes rolling at the smell of so many men, and she stroked its neck with a shaking hand. *Hush now. Don't make a sound* . . . .

The marching feet faded up the road. Nikola used a series of slippery, moss-covered handholds to clamber to the top of the ruined wall. She crouched down, gazing back through the trees at the palace. The astrum in the walls made it shine like a beacon.

Everywhere, shadows moved.

More than one company of knights, then. They were closing a noose around the Arx. If she'd been two minutes later, she would have been trapped inside it.

"Damn you, Malach," she whispered.

There was no point in returning. She'd never beat them to the palace. And she could think of only one fate worse than Beleth and her demented mirror-image of the Curia.

Being dragged back to Novostopol.

Nikola didn't give a fig for the other nihilim. Syd and Trist, maybe. Against her better judgment, she'd grown to like them.

But Malach. . . .

"I ought to let them have you!" she muttered angrily.

A unwanted image of him sprawled naked in bed intruded on her rage, dissipating it in an instant. A deep, drugged sleep. He'd wake to a blade at his throat.

"Ah, if only you hadn't rubbed my feet."

Nikola slid down the wall, landing gracefully—if not quite as lightly as she would have a month before. She fumbled the bag open, lifting his gift from its lacquered box. It was heavy and cold.

*An evil thing.*

She gripped it awkwardly, pointed it at the sky, and fired.

A deafening crack. The gun leapt in her hand. She nearly dropped it.

"Shit!" Nikola turned her face away and fired twice more. This time she squeezed the handle with both hands and the gun held steady, though it still jerked. An instant later, distant shouts.

Nikola threw the gun into the bag. She scrambled onto her horse, driving her heels into his flanks. "Run," she urged him. "*Run!*"

# Chapter Eleven

He dreamed of their child.

A boy with golden-brown skin and curly chestnut hair. His eyes were hazel like Malach's but a shade darker, like rich, mellow wood.

He was clever and beautiful and strong, just like his mother.

Malach felt a tenderness he'd never known before. Boundless and all-consuming. What a novel sensation it was! He wanted nothing but to keep them safe. To see them happy. It brought a feeling of peace to want only such simple things.

They walked across a meadow. The boy's small hand was in Malach's, nestled like a warm animal snug in its den. Nikola walked a few steps ahead, the swish of her dress raising motes of pollen from the high grass.

"Slow down," Malach called with a laugh. "There's no hurry!"

She glanced over her shoulder with a silver-toothed smile, but she didn't slow down, she walked faster, and the boy at his side was struggling to keep up now.

"You have to catch me!" she cried, lifting her skirts.

"Wait!" he shouted, as she ran for the line of dark trees ahead.

Malach swept the boy into his arms and gave chase, but no matter how fast he ran, she kept drawing ahead. And then he heard it, the low whine of a shell, followed by a percussive blast—

He sat up, breathing hard, the sound ringing in his ears.

The candle burned low, leaving the room in shadow. He twisted, reaching desperately for Nikola. The bed was cold. Rain billowed the half-open drapes.

A ragged breath escaped him. *Where was she?*

Two sharp pops in quick succession. Outside somewhere.

The sound was so peculiar, so alien, it took a moment to register.

He growled an oath and leapt to his feet. Malach was reaching for the red robes he'd thrown on the floor when a soft creak drew his eyes to the door, which was slowly swinging open.

He moved on the pads of his feet, heart thumping, and stood against the wall just behind it. For a few long moments, the heavy oak obscured his view. Then two tall figures appeared, silently approaching the bed. The were clad in black leather. No steel armor to give them away. It hid bloodstains nicely, too. The single candle flame flickered on long daggers.

One of Falke's death squads.

"He's gone," one said, just as Malach exploded from his hiding place and seized the man's head, snapping his neck with a single vicious twist. The limp body fell away. He leaned back from the slashing blade of the knight's partner and kicked out with a bare foot. He'd aimed for the man's balls, but Malach was off-balance and hit his thigh. The knife blurred. A line of fire streaked his ribs. A boot caught him in the chest and he winced in pain, one hand clutching the half-healed scar.

Malach dove for the fallen dagger. He caught it in his fist and rolled away as the boot lashed out again, just missing his head. Malach grabbed the foot and twisted. The knight toppled. Then they were rolling across the stone floor, tangled together in a parody of lovers, Malach's naked thighs clamped around his waist, each gripping the other's knife hand. The knight's teeth bared in a wordless snarl. The edge of his dagger inched closer to Malach's cheek. With a grunt, he smashed his forehead into the hawk nose. Bone crunched. The knight screamed. An instant later, Malach drove his own blade home.

He rolled to his back, panting. When he touched his side, his fingers met sticky wetness.

"Fuck," he muttered weakly.

Did they already have Nikola?

The tumult of battle in the corridor got him moving.

He examined his ribs. Just a scratch, really. It would stop bleeding eventually. He eased the red robe over his head and pulled on his boots. He yanked the dagger from the knight's throat and wiped it on the leather cuirass.

Malach found Bishops Lewen and Mandellyn outside, lying not far from the door, along with three dead knights. He'd never liked either of them, but he was proud to see they hadn't gone down easily. Malach jogged to the junction of a crossing corridor. He peered around the corner. Seven more knights were halfway down, going door-to-door. He waited until five went inside rooms, then darted across the gap. No one pursued.

His thoughts raced as he passed the main staircase and took a smaller one down. How had they mobilized so quickly? The Cold Truce had held for four years. The Pontifex Feizeh was notoriously slow to change course. But he'd miscalculated—terribly, unforgivably. Never again would he underestimate them.

Falke was behind it, that much he knew for certain.

Rage scoured his veins. If they'd taken Nikola . . . .

At the foot of the stairs, Malach drew up short. Blades clashed just beyond. He stepped into the anteroom of the Pontifex's audience hall.

It was a stark chamber like all the others. Gone were the tapestries and solid gold fixtures. Even the throne had been wrested free of its mooring, leaving a naked stone dais. Beleth stood on it, wide-legged, fighting three fully armored laqueos. Five more lay dead. The powdered wig was gone and her long gray hair swayed around her white face. As he watched, she parried a heavy blow.

Their eyes met.

"Malach!" she cried.

The thud of approaching boots came down the opposite corridor.

A knight moved to flank her on the left. Beleth spun to meet his thrust, batting it aside, but he could see she was tiring. The knights weren't stupid. They didn't take their eyes from her, just continued to circle like a pack of hounds ringing an injured wolf.

"Stand with me! Stand with Bal Kirith!"

He took a step forward.

*Will I die here?*

Once, he might have chosen it willingly. Beleth was like a mother to him, the only one he'd ever known. Bal Kirith was his home. His kin's last refuge. Nothing else mattered.

But things had changed.

*I do not love you,* he thought in confusion. *Respect, yes. Fear—most certainly. But not . . . the other.*

"Malach!"

A harsh note of betrayal now.

From an open archway to the right of the dais, a dozen knights boiled into the chamber. Beleth gave him a final icy glare, then threw herself into the fray. Twisting like an eel, she skewered one of the attackers at the juncture of his gorget.

The last he saw of her before he turned on his heel was the red flash of her sword.

Malach ran.

He ran headlong and heedless, wending ever downward. Bodies littered his path, knights and mages both—though far more of the latter. Servants, too, cut down where they stood. He hardly spared them a glance. His mind was a perfect blank.

Stone walls blurred past. Breath rasped harshly in his ears.

He thought he heard the barking of dogs, but couldn't be sure.

The corridors grew narrower. He seized a torch from a bracket and ran on, into the cramped, secret places he'd explored as a child. Gradually, the sounds of pursuit faded.

At last he found himself in the oldest wine cellars deep below the palace. Rack upon empty rack filled the low, vaulted chamber. Malach stopped, bracing a hand on his knees. His temples throbbed. So did the wound in his side. Besides his own winded panting, the silence was absolute.

Smoke from the torch stung his eyes. He wedged it into an empty sconce. Thick cobwebs curled upward in the heat of the flames.

*Nikola . . . .*

A few dusty bottles remained. Malach pulled one out, staring stupidly at the cork. Then he remembered the dagger in his boot. He used the tip to pry an edge up and his teeth to tear it out the rest of the way. Malach drank deep. The buzzing in his head quieted. He wiped his mouth with the back of his hand.

The thick stone walls suddenly felt like a tomb, and he its final denizen. The last of the mighty lucifers.

Malach started to laugh. It echoed back at him like a crowd of raucous ghosts, which only made him laugh harder.

We almost won, he thought. Almost—but not quite.

He wiped his streaming eyes and slugged from the bottle.

I'll drink my way through the cellar, toasting the dead as I go. So many names . . . .

A tiny, furtive sound. His head cocked. It came from the pool of darkness at the far end of the cellar.

The palace was full of mice. Little mounds of their droppings lay everywhere.

Malach's fingers slowly closed around the hilt of the dagger. He listened, ears straining.

A hitching breath, quickly stifled.

*Not a mouse.*

Malach crept forward, lithe as a jungle cat, the torchlight reflecting from his eyes.

The shadow of a crouching silhouette stirred behind one of the casks. It lurched into sudden movement. He sprang forward, dagger raised—

"By the Alsakhan, it's me, Malach!"

A man stepped into the light. Malach let the dagger fall, the bitter taste of adrenaline in his mouth.

"Tash?"

"I was looking for more wine." Dust streaked Tashtemir's doublet. One sleeve had a ragged tear. He pointed and Malach noticed a pair of boots sticking out from one of the alcoves, pinned beneath an overturned rack. "The bastard chased me all the way down here."

Malach crouched over the knight's body. Young, with the barest fuzz of red beard. He wore a puzzled expression, as though he pondered the answer to some enigmatic riddle.

"I hid and pushed it over on him. Then I took his sword and . . . . I finished him." Tash sounded shaken. "I thought you were one of them at first."

Malach drew the sword from the knight's breast. He was one of the leather-clad killers.

"Where's Nikola?"

Malach looked up. Tashtemir recoiled at the look on his face.

"They took her," he said, voice cold and distant. "Or killed her. I don't know which."

Tash was silent for a moment. "Maybe not," he said softly.

"You saw her?" Malach resisted the urge to grab his tattered doublet and shake the answer free.

"In the kitchens. Minutes before that goat-fucker caught me. She was loaded with food. She claimed you'd sent her."

Malach stared past his shoulder at the shadows playing on the rough walls, his gaze unfocused. The gun. Why would she have been carrying the gun? He knew she didn't like it.

"What was she wearing?"

"Boots. A green cloak. The pockets were bulging."

A foolish grin spread across his face. "She ran," he whispered.

"I'm sorry, it did seem a little suspicious." Tash's long face set in anxious lines. "I should have told you, Malach."

"How long before the knights came? Think!"

Tash seemed rattled. "Ah . . . twenty minutes?"

"Time enough to saddle a horse," he muttered. "Maybe time enough to break through the cordon."

The shots troubled him. He felt sure now that Nikola had planned to leave. It didn't surprise him. He'd been an idiot to expect she'd listen. Which meant they were either fired in self-defense or . . . as a warning?

Would Nikola Thorn truly risk herself for him?

Oh, how Malach wanted to believe she would. But he wasn't certain. Not at all.

She'd saved him once already and he got the strong impression she regretted it. Rightfully so. Still, it was the only slender hope he had.

He remembered the dream-Nikola, silver tooth winking at him.

*You'll have to catch me . . . .*

"What do we do?" Tash asked, an edge in his voice. "They'll find their way down here eventually."

"They will," Malach agreed. "And we'll be long gone when they do."

He handed Tash the dagger, keeping the sword for himself. He doubted the soft southerner knew how to use it anyway—not against an opponent who fought back.

"What about the others?" Tash stared at the dagger in his hand. It still bore traces of the knight's blood.

"Dead."

"I'm sorry."

"Not your fault. It's mine."

Tash had no reply to that.

Malach led him through the honeycomb of rough tunnels to an iron-strapped door. Drops of moisture dotted the stonework around it. The wood had warped and the door didn't budge when Malach tried to shoulder it open.

"Help me," he said.

They threw their combined weight against it and the door finally gave with a reluctant groan. Malach raised the torch. A dank tunnel lay beyond.

"Where does it lead?" Tashtemir asked.

"Out," he replied.

"Truly?" A note of optimism.

"I think so." He paused. "It's been twenty years at least since I was down here."

They walked single-file, Malach leading with the torch. Water dripped down the walls. The floor of the tunnel was slick with black moss. Tash gave a muffled curse as his feet slid.

"Do you know what these shoes cost, Malach?" he muttered.

"No, and neither do you."

His foppish wardrobe was Tashtmir's only requirement at Bal Kirith. He hardly seemed to eat. Other than a dalliance or two, he never joined in the boisterous orgies of the clergy. Since the Cold Truce, he rarely had serious wounds to tend.

Venereal diseases, mostly, and the occasional stomach ulcer. But every time Malach ventured into Novostopol, Tash gave him a shopping list. Velvet coats and lace-frilled shirts. Tight breeches and buckled slippers. None of it was in style anymore—hadn't been for a century or so—and Malach was forced to haunt second-hand costume shops to procure the necessary items. It amused him to see Tash's long face light up when he returned.

The tunnel sloped downward, then almost imperceptibly up again. They sloshed along in silence for the most part, Malach lost in dark thoughts. Was it remorse he felt? The notion was hard to fathom. Beleth had taught him to look out for himself above all others—her included. She could hardly blame him for saving his own hide. Joining her on that dais with nothing but a dagger would have been suicide.

*Stand with me! Stand with Bal Kirith!*

Maybe he would have, Malach thought bleakly, if there had been anything left to save.

The torch sputtered, nearly spent.

"Pah, it's cold," Tash said in a doleful voice. "How much longer?"

"Who knows?" Malach snapped. The weight of the sword made his arm ache.

"Not that I lack gratitude," Tash added hastily. "But I'm starting to feel like we're stuck in the constipated bowels of some ice-wyrm and it'll never shi—"

"Quiet!"

A low hiss of sound came from ahead. Malach paused, then lurched forward. The heavy blackness of the tunnel began to lighten. A short time later they stood before a grating. It was still raining and a gray dawn brightened the sky. On the other side of the bars, the Ascalon rushed on its merry way towards the sea.

"Why does it dead end?" Tash groaned. "What was the gods-forsaken purpose?"

"I don't know. I never came this far." He studied the grate, then handed Tash the torch.

Malach backed up a step, then slammed his heel into the plaster around the bars. It was sodden with mildew. A few fractured chunks fell away. Malach kicked it again, wincing at the sudden heat in his side.

"Stop!" Tash grabbed his arm, thick brows drawing together. "I know you're an ape, but you can think like a man when you want to. If you tear yourself open again, all my hard work will be in vain and you'll never find her."

Malach cast him a black look.

"I'll do it," Tash said loftily, pushing his filthy sleeves up.

Malach folded his arms and lounged against the tunnel wall while Tash went into a frenzy of kicking, punctuated by curses. His suede shoes took quite a beating, but the wall held.

"Give me the sword," he gasped.

Malach handed it over. Tash slipped it between the bars and gave a mighty heave. With a sudden dire crack, an enormous chunk of plaster fell outward, taking the blade—caught between two of the iron bars—along with it. Tashtemir himself would have followed had Malach's hand not shot out and seized the back of his doublet. Together they watched the sword spin end over end, vanishing into the churning waters.

"Well, it worked," Tash said.

"Like a charm," Malach replied wryly.

The tunnel was set into the bank about six meters above the level of the water. They abandoned the dying torch and used jutting rocks and tree roots to clamber down to the pebbled shore.

"There really ought to be a boat tied up on the bank," Tash panted. "It would be most convenient."

Malach studied the dark silhouette of the bridge upstream. "That's sure to be guarded. But there's a place we can ford the river farther down."

Tashtemir pointed up the hill in the direction they'd just come from. "Isn't that west?"

Malach followed his gaze. "Yes."

"So why is dawn breaking over *there*?" Tashtemir sounded annoyed, as if this sudden willfulness on the part of the sun was a personal affront.

Malach stared at the red glow in the sky for a long moment. "It's not," he said softly. "The Arx is burning."

Even during the long civil war, when the fighting had been hot and brutal on both sides, Falke had spared the Arx from total destruction. He'd shelled the city itself and some of the open spaces, but never the buildings themselves. Most were over a thousand years old.

Tashtemir tugged at his sleeve. Daylight was coming swiftly now. Color bloomed in the jungle on the opposite bank, shifting from grey to a hundred subtle shades of green. A dark smudge of smoke stood against the pink-tinged clouds.

"We have to go," Tash said gently.

Malach gave a brusque nod and turned away from the sight, jaw tight. He did not look back.

# Chapter Twelve

Thick mud sucked at Lezarius's bare toes as he slogged behind Dantarion. She seemed unbothered by it, leaping lightly between the clumps of sawgrass that dotted the mire, but after a full day's march he could scarcely put one foot in front of the other, let alone hop like a toad.

At first the going had been easy. The Morho embraced their passage and they'd traveled swiftly, covering twice as much as ground as he had with Mikhail. But there was no avoiding the boglands south of Bal Kirith. Loamy jungle gave way to papyrus reeds nodding on slender stalks. Waterlilies and bright green duckweed floated on shallow, stagnant pools where long-legged gray birds stood sentinel, sharp eyes hunting for frogs and snakes.

To his surprise, the mage had given him back his cat—likely because she knew she could take it away from him again whenever she chose. Greylight was still small enough to fit in his coat pocket, a warm ball of fur that lent him strength. Abandoning the helpless creature in the Morho would be a death sentence. In the depths of his fear, Lezarius had considered quickly snapping her neck, but he couldn't bring himself to do it.

Only if I must, he thought, to spare her.

She was the only one he trusted now that Mikhail was gone.

Lezarius swatted wearily at the cloud of hovering damselflies. They didn't bite, but oh, how they pestered him! Dancing at his eyes and nose. He had accidentally swallowed enough of the irritating insects to make a meal.

"We are nearing the gates, old man," Dantarion called over her shoulder. "Chin up!"

He stared sullenly at her feral grin. "That is cold comfort, mage," he replied.

Dusk fell, though it did little to lessen the oppressive heat. Another red-cloaked nihilim, youthful and flaxen-haired with the angelic features they all seemed to share, walked behind him. The rest scouted ahead.

"Ah, you will be received with the welcome you deserve," Dantarion replied, in high spirits. "As for me, I plan to drink and fuck the night away. It's been a tedious two weeks hunting your trail. Someone's going to pay for it, eh?"

The boy splashing at his heels barked a laugh. "Perhaps Cardinal Malach will oblige."

"No, he's too stoic." The grin widened. "I crave the taste of tears this evening."

"Do such excesses truly make you happy?" Lezarius grumbled.

"Sex without pain is like wine without taste," she shot back merrily. "See? I *have* perused my mother's books."

Saints, she was Beleth's offspring.

"Better you were illiterate then."

Dantarion only laughed louder at that.

It started to rain, lightly at first but soon turning to a deluge. Lights glimmered in the far distance, appearing and disappearing like fireflies. He longed for a Keef.

They gained high ground for a blessed ten meters, then

descended into the bog again. The raindrops made overlapping circles on the sheet of dark, still water. Lezarius used a long stick to prod at the ground ahead. The water had risen to his knees and he didn't want to give Greylight a soaking if he lost his footing. In the dying light, every half-submerged log resembled a lurking crocodilian. Dantarion fell silent, scanning the swamp. A dense ground mist rose around them, swallowing the hem of her red cloak.

"We are nearly through," she said softly.

Every now and then, Lezarius heard a soft plop as a turtle slid into the water. He squinted into the rain. Solid ground lay ahead, girded by a bank of enormous twisting roots. Not simply another hummock but the edge of the mire. Lezarius tested his stick and pressed on. Dry feet! Even knowing what awaited, his spirits lifted.

Then he tensed at a sudden splash in the murk. Dantarion rushed forward as one of the scouts appeared. Blood streaked the girl's face. Her knees gave out and Dantarion caught an arm. "Margaris! What—"

"The Arx has fallen," the nihilim whispered hoarsely. "You must . . . ."

Black-clad figures slipped through the trees ahead. They were almost invisible in the downpour, obscuring the lights beyond like clouds passing before the moon.

"Retreat!" Dantarion cried, one arm still slung around her comrade.

The jungle was suddenly alive with shouts and torches. Lezarius spun to find more closing in behind. Three waded through the water holding longswords. Dantarion dropped the injured mage and unshouldered her bow in a smooth motion, reaching for an arrow in the quiver at her back.

"Surrender, mage!" one of them cried, and now Lezarius could see the Raven Marks on their necks. They wore no helms or armor, only leather gauntlets and heavy gambraces.

Dantarion loosed an arrow. It took the first knight in the throat. He toppled and then the other two were on top of her. Steel flashed. The nihilim behind him reached for Lezarius and he lunged away, wading for a gap in the lines. A chance! But he feared the knights almost as much as his captors. They would take him back! Prison him in the little room again!

Breath rasped in his throat as he glanced over his shoulder. The flaxen-haired mage was a pace behind, face set in grim determination. Lightning strobed, once, twice. Something rose up from the bog. A wide, plated tail lashed, swamping Lezarius to the thighs. Jaws clamped around the nihilim's torso, dragging him under the mire. The water turned to roiling froth as more crocodilians surfaced, excited by the scent of blood. Everywhere, Lezarius heard the screams of dying men.

He staggered through the swamp, mind blank with terror. A knobbed snout popped up before him and Lezarius cracked it hard with his stick. The creature hissed and submerged again. He nearly fell as it bumped his hip, but a flailing knight drew the beast's attention and it slithered away, the massive length taking a full six seconds to pass him.

He dug into the muddy bottom, driven by raw adrenaline, and set off for the far bank, away from the bobbing torches. Slippery roots bruised his feet. Flashes of lightning revealed a nightmare of pale, rolling bellies and ancient, pitiless eyes. He pressed a hand to his ear, trying to silence the terrible frenzy. At any moment, he anticipated the agony of razored teeth crushing his legs.

Then he was scrambling from the bog and running headlong through the jungle. He spilled out on a dirt track and fell to his knees, overcome with exhaustion and panic.

"The Morho will kill us all," he whispered between ragged pants. "It seeks revenge for the wrong I have done!"

Visions spun through his head. Mikhail swept away by the

river, the wintry black sky above Sinjai's Lance, the sickening sensation of vertigo as an ungloved hand touched his Mark . . . .

A pathetic mewl from his pocket brought Lezarius to his senses.

"Stop," he growled, gripping his head. "No more. No more!"

He took the sodden black kitten from his pocket with shaking hands and pressed her to his breast.

"There now," he gasped. "There. We are safe you see—"

The roar of an engine jerked his head up. A heavy transport rounded the bend, spearing him in the headlights. It jolted to a stop. Boots thumped into the mud as four knights in chainmail exited the doors.

Lezarius tried to rise, to run again, and found he had nothing left. He felt empty as a discarded sack. The ley was clearly punishing him and there was little point in defying it any longer. He threw a palm up, turning away from the light. "Please," he called. "I will not resist if you promise to spare my friend. She is young and has done no wrong to the Curia."

"What friend?" A hard voice demanded as they approached. "I see no one else."

"Greylight." He still sheltered the cat from the driving rain.

"Show us your hands, Reverend Father," the knight said in a more kindly tone.

"I can't. I'm holding her."

They seemed to glance at each other, though he could barely make out the faces backlit by the powerful high beams.

"He's harmless," one said.

"That's what the others believed," the second responded.

A blade rasped from its scabbard. "It's a cat."

"We'll take it, Reverend Father," the first knight said cheerfully. "Don't worry."

Lezarius stared at the gauntleted hand. "Promise me you won't hurt my companion."

"I promise, Reverend Father." He stepped forward. "Now—"

The man gargled, clutching at his eye, where a black-fletched arrow protruded. A heartbeat later, the one next to him fell in similar fashion. The last two dropped to a crouch. One took an arrow in the thigh, rolling away with a grimace. Then Dantarion was flying out of the dense undergrowth, a long dagger in each hand. She parried an overhand blow from the last knight standing and stabbed him in the chest with the other. The slender poniard slipped right through the links in his chainmail. He staggered back, surprise on his face. Dantarion kicked him in the knee and he went down on top of his brothers with a muffled thud.

She was covered in mud, eyes wide and haunted, but her reflexes were still sharp and Lezarius didn't make it more than two steps before a strong hand seized him by the arm, spinning him around.

"Not so fast, old man," she snarled. "Did you know about this?"

"How could I?" he demanded. "Besides which, they are my enemies now as much as yours."

"We shall see." She hauled him over to the knight who lay hamstrung on the ground. The man tried to crawl away and she planted a boot on his back.

"How many companies were deployed?" she demanded.

"May the ley bless you, sister," he croaked into the dirt.

Dantarion bent down and twisted the arrow in his leg. He screamed.

"How many companies?"

"Six!"

"That's nearly a full legion," she muttered. "What of Feizah's Cold Truce?"

"Feizah is dead," Lezarius said.

Dantarion frowned. "Dead?" She gave the knight a kick. "Who ordered this?"

"The Pontifex Dmitry," he gasped.

"So Falke wears the ring. What were your orders? Speak, or I will flay your hide in strips and make you eat them."

The calm tone seemed to frighten him more than any shouted threat.

"To seize the city and find Malach. He's to be taken alive. No . . . shelling."

"What else?"

The knight hesitated. Dantarion gave the arrow another vicious twist.

"To find Lezarius!" he gasped, face ashen.

"And then?"

"To kill him."

She laughed. "You see?" she said to Lezarius. "I am more merciful than your own brothers."

He looked away, sickened, as she bent down and slit the knight's throat. A moment later, the tip of the poniard pressed against his own heart. "Break the stelae," she hissed. "Now!"

"No," he said. "I will not."

The dagger drew a spot of blood. He simply stared at her.

Dantarion gave a sudden wince, one hand pressing to her belly. He wondered if she had taken a mortal wound after all. *Please, let it be so.* But a moment later her face hardened.

"Give me back my power!" she hissed.

"Kill me if you must. But it will accomplish nothing."

She growled in frustration. The blade withdrew. Dantarion dragged him to the transport, shoved him into the passenger side, and started the engine. Greylight mewed anxiously. Lezarius kissed her head, tucking her inside his damp pocket. A red glow lit the trees.

"Where are we going?" he asked.

"Shut up!" Dantarion fumbled with the stick and threw

the transport into gear. They lurched forward, bumping over the bodies that lay in the road.

"You have no plan, do you?" he said. "Take me to Jalghuth."

She slammed on the brakes and he skidded forward. "Why? Why would I go north?"

Lezarius felt serene now. All was unfolding as it was meant to. A grand design only he could see.

"Balaur is there," he said. "He stole my face and my name, but it is the monster's fell hand who rules the city."

Dantarion gave a weary shake of her head. "Has he risen from the dead? Never mind, I suppose you are used to conversing with ghosts." A hint of a smile. "Perhaps he dines with Feizah tonight."

"It's true. Balaur was my captive for nearly three decades." He opened his shirt, exposing the inverted Mark. "Who do you think did this? If you doubt, take the sweven from me. I offer it freely."

"I need ley for that, you old fool." Her eyes narrowed. "You said you couldn't remember anything."

He smiled. "I lied."

"Just as you are lying now?" Rain beat down and she searched for the wipers, her muddied, bloodied face glowing an eerie green in the dashboard lights.

He looked away. "Do what you will, mage. I only offer a suggestion."

She sat in silence for a time, the heavy engine idling. Somewhere in the rear, a radio crackled. "If what you say is true, why would you want to go back?"

Lezarius drew himself up. "To defeat Balaur once and for all!"

Dantarion stared at him. Then she chuckled. It turned to full-throated laughter. "You *are* mad!"

"Take me there," he urged. "If you are the stronger one, as you claim, then you bring him a great prize. If I am the stronger one . . . ." Lezarius shrugged. "Well, we'll leave it to the natural order, mage. Or do you doubt your own credo?"

"I doubt nothing," she said.

"Alternatively, we can sit here until they find us. Let me know what you decide."

Lezarius leaned back and closed his eyes. The ley willed it and she had no other choice. Nowhere else to run.

"The roads are shit," she said at last. "But I know the back ways."

A heavy foot depressed the accelerator. They jounced down the rutted road. After a minute, Dantarion veered off into an overgrown track so narrow the tree branches clawed at the windows. It quickly became apparent that she was a terrible driver, alternately hitting the accelerator and brakes until his stomach churned.

"Please," he begged. "Let me drive."

She shot him a glare. "And when was the last time *you* took the wheel?"

In truth, Lezarius had never operated a motor vehicle in his life. "Only a few years ago."

"Well, Malach taught me how. It was broken, but he showed me the pedals. You don't even know where to turn."

"You could tell me—"

"Quiet." Her face was intent. "I can do it."

He endured another stretch of nauseating spurts of speed followed by sudden braking, but the mage was a quick study. Soon their forward motion grew smoother. The storm raged outside, but Lezarius found a switch for the heater. Warmth flooded the cab. His filthy clothes dried. For a wonder, Greylight began to purr. It was a more pleasant mode of travel by far than what he'd grown accustomed to.

He knew that if the Morho had wished, their heavy transport would become trapped in the mud, or discovered by another patrol, but the sentient jungle was with him now. The red glow in the sky faded behind.

"I thought you were dead," he murmured, eyes sliding shut.

Dantarion chuckled. "A few crocodilians are hardly sufficient to trouble us."

His curiosity snagged for a moment on that *us*, but then sleep pulled an exhausted Lezarius into its quiet depths.

# Chapter Thirteen

"Alyosha!"

Huge arms swept Alexei into a bone-crushing hug. He patted Spassov's broad back, laughing. "What are you doing in Kvengard?"

Patryk held him at arm's length. "You look good. Better than the last time I saw you. They took your Marks, eh?"

"Bishop Morvana Ziegler," Alexei confirmed.

"Well, don't piss her off." Alice jumped up again, nosing at his face. He fended her off with an indulgent grin. "Your Markhound is here?"

"She followed me from the Arx."

Spassov gave her a rough pat. Then his gaze lit on Alexei's shredded cassock. "Still finding trouble, I see."

"It finds me," Alexei said grimly. "Come, sit."

He lit a candle and started gathering the heaps of files piled about the room. Spassov perched on the edge of the bed while Alexei took the armchair. His partner looked like he'd been sleeping rough for days. A scruffy beard covered his face, but his eyes were alert.

"I came with someone," Spassov said casually.

"Oh?"

"Kasia Novak."

The name lit a fire in him. Alexei leaned forward, stunned. "Here?"

"Natalya Anderle and Tessaria Foy, as well. We had to leave Novo in a hurry. Bishop Karolo thinks they had something to do with the Reverend Mother's death. She managed to get an arrest warrant."

"Saints! Couldn't Falke intervene?"

"He did—by packing them off to Nantwich. We arrived last night. The captain insisted on stopping. Then the bastard took off. But we're headed onward tonight."

*So soon.* Alexei's hopes of seeing her fell. "But . . . how on earth did you end up with them?"

"I did as you asked. Kept an eye out. It all went bad on Saviors' Eve. The day of Falke's first audience."

Patryk related how he'd tried to follow the two women, lost them, and followed Tessaria Foy instead. When he described his glimpse of masked men in an alley of Ash Court, Alexei gripped the arms of his chair.

"What kind of masks?" he asked.

"I only caught a quick look. They were white. Like mummers."

Alexei swore. "I just killed two men in the same masks."

Patryk's eyebrow twitched. "You've been busy."

"It was here, in one of the sanctuaries. I saw Oto Valek go inside. I think he let me see him deliberately so I'd follow and walk right into their trap."

"Oto Valek?" Spassov exclaimed. "That little shit from the Institute? I'm certain he's the one who let those killers from the O.G.D. inside. I asked around and found out he'd disappeared."

The Office of the General Directorate, headed by Archbishop Casimir Kireyev, wielded greater power than any other organ in the Church. It answered only to the Pontifex, with zero public oversight. That the O.G.D. would be involved with

Valek didn't come as a surprise. But the orderly had more than one master.

"Valek is more than Kireyev's lackey. Much more, I'm afraid." Alexei kneaded his forehead. "I'm glad you're here, Patryk. I need someone to talk to."

Alexei told him about the case he'd been working. Patryk's jaw ratcheted tighter with each word. "Nine children? I'll break his spine."

"I'm still not sure of the connection, but Valek vanished right under my nose. I think he used one of the tunnels under the Arx—which means a possible tie to the clergy. The bodies vanished, too. Twenty minutes I was gone, to fetch the Nuncio. When we returned, the whole place had been sanitized."

"Do you trust Morvana?"

"No. But I don't trust anybody."

"Except for me, I hope."

"That goes without saying. But these people are bad news, Patryk. One of them was *mutated*."

His partner took out a flask and offered it to Alexei, who shook his head. Spassov had a nip, then returned it to his pocket. "Mutated," he repeated softly. "Saints preserve us. How?"

"Talons. A beak. Like some giant . . . man-bird."

Spassov was quiet for a moment. "Have you been getting enough sleep, Alyosha?" he asked.

"No, but I didn't hallucinate it."

"Okay. Sure you don't want a drink?"

"Ah, give it to me." Alexei took a bracing swig of vodka. "I'm worried about Kasia."

"I think the women are safe for now. They're staying outside the city. Old friends of Sor Foy's. The Danzigers. They're giving us one of their ships."

A warning tingle run up Alexei's spine. "Danziger? They live in a manor on the Vlederstrasse."

Spassov looked confused. "No, I just came from the house. It's in the country. About half an hour's ride."

Alexei frowned. "The fifth missing child. That's his surname. I've met the parents."

"These people are old."

"Grandparents, then?"

"Or a different family altogether."

"How common is the name?"

Spassov shrugged. "Not a clue."

"Let's have a look." Alexei went straight to the Danziger file. He leafed through it until he found the list of Willem's next of kin. He was an only child with one much older cousin, Jule Danziger, and paternal grandparents who owned a shipping firm.

"Hanne and Jann?" he asked, pronouncing the names *Han* and *Yon* in Kven fashion.

Spassov nodded. "That's them."

"It sounds like a puppet duo," Alexei muttered, flipping the page.

"I don't know much about them except that they're rich and Tessaria seems to trust them."

He looked up from the file. "I don't like this, Patryk. I've reason to believe Willem's parents might be involved in his disappearance."

Alexei rose and felt under the mattress for the stolen book from the archives. It was still there. Patryk came over and watched over his shoulder as he carefully turned the yellowed parchment.

"What is this?"

"*Der Cherubinischer Wandersmann*. It was written by one of the old pre-Dark Age mystics. Angelus Silesius."

"Okay."

Alexei turned the page. "There!" He stabbed a finger down in satisfaction. "You see that symbol? One of the men who attacked me was Marked with it."

Spassov studied the nested geometric forms—circle, square, triangle—all enclosed within a larger sphere.

"What is it?"

"I don't know. Some alchemical sign."

A grunt. "Shit."

Alexei caught his eye. "What do you know, Patryk?"

"Kasia thinks she's being chased by alchemists. The Order of the Black Sun. I wasn't sure I believed her, but now . . . ."

"Order of the Black Sun?"

"Maybe you're too young to remember. No one mentions that name anymore. Personally, I figured they were all dead. A bunch of crazies who insisted Balaur would return one day."

Puzzle pieces starting falling into place. The picture they formed was not a pretty one.

"Well, they're not dead." He closed the book. "I think I just met three of them in the Chapel of Saint Ydilia."

Alice wandered over, looking up at them both with worried eyes. She sensed the sudden tension in the room.

"Most people," Spassov said slowly, "would be telling the Polizei everything right now. The Nuncio, too."

"Most people would," Alexei agreed.

A sigh. "But we're not going to."

"No." He had to trust *someone*, and Spassov needed to know all of it. "I think the Order has my brother."

Spassov lit a cigarette and shook out the match. "Do I want to know why?"

"Probably not, but I'll tell you anyway. Do you remember what I said at the Institute that night? About Patient 9?"

"The old man?" Spassov drew deeply. "Yeah, you said they came to kill him because he was the Pontifex of the Northern Curia." He closed his eyes with a sigh. "That again?"

"It's true, Patryk. Doctor Massot figured it out. Imagine an Invertido with the power to break the Void. Tell me, what do you think Falke and Kireyev would do when Massot told them who he was?"

"Shit," Patryk muttered.

"Shit is right. They sent Gerlach and Brodzsky to get rid of him, but they bungled it. Lezarius escaped with my brother. They ran into the Morho, but Alice caught Mikhail's scent just a few hours ago. He's here. Or he *was* here. I found a tire track. Someone grabbed him. Maybe both of them."

Patryk exhaled a stream of smoke, face unreadable. "What will you do if you find him?"

"I don't know. If I can get him to Malach—"

"The Nightmage who killed the Reverend Mother? Who nearly killed *you* the last time you saw him? Listen to yourself, Alyosha."

"I have no choice. I won't let my brother die!"

Spassov held his palms up. "I don't mean to be callous. I know it's been hard for you—"

"Mikhail took the Nightmark to protect me," Alexei admitted wearily. "That was the bargain. Oh, he was also spying for Falke. A double agent. But there's always a deal involved in a Nightmark. A quid pro quo. That's what he wanted from Malach. For my life to be spared." He looked away. "I always wondered why I never took a scratch in combat that last year. I thought it was dumb luck."

Spassov watched him sadly.

"If Malach can't remove the Nightmark, at the very least I can take care of Misha. Make sure he's comfortable."

"Of course," Spassov murmured. "But first things first. We must warn the women. Will you come out to the house with me?"

Alexei looked up. "Of course. How can you even ask?" He wrapped the book in a pillowcase. "I want to show this to Tessaria Foy. Find out what she knows. Have you met the Danzigers?"

"Only the wife. Kasia told me they were double agents during the war. Stationed in Bal Agnar."

"Maybe they weren't double agents at all," Alexei muttered darkly.

"You think they're Order?" He frowned. "Kasia said the husband was tortured."

"Anything's possible." He pulled the torn cassock over his head and donned a fresh one. "If they are, we'll have to move fast. You get them to safety while I look for my brother."

"Did Morvana give you any weapons?" Spassov asked hopefully.

Alexei gave him a wry look. "She thinks I'm Falke's spy."

"Shit."

He went to his desk and rummaged around. "You can have a letter opener."

"Oh, fantastic." Spassov flicked his butt out the window. "I'll be deadly."

"If you don't want it—"

"Give it to me." Spassov tucked it into his cassock. "What about you?"

"I'll take Alice."

Alexei snuffed the candle and grabbed the pillowcase with the book. "Just a quick stop first."

"For what?"

"I want to show you something."

Wards glowed blue in the darkness as he led Spassov to the chapel. Alice went straight to the spot where the bird-man had fallen. When her nose touched the stone, she recoiled with a frightened yelp. A jet of urine pattered on the floor. Alexei stroked her back and she gave a low, murderous growl to redeem her reputation, but her body quivered beneath his hand.

"You see?" he said. "I didn't imagine it!"

"I never said you did." Spassov eyed the dog with a

worried expression. "I've never seen a Markhound react that way."

Alexei quickly walked him through the fight. "If that smell hadn't given them away, I would have lost my head."

"And they came from over there?" Spassov asked, studying the altar.

"Yes. But I already searched, there's nothing—"

The harsh grinding of stone against stone made his eyes widen. The entire altar had swung away from a hidden recess.

"How did you do that?" he demanded.

"There's a hidden catch underneath." Spassov showed him a faint depression in the wood. "But you must touch it just so to make it work. There's one like it in the Tomb of the Martyrs." He grinned at Alexei's sour expression. "I'm an old dog, but I still know a few tricks."

"Not that old," Alexei muttered.

He picked up one of the votive candles. A trail of dried blood led down a winding staircase. Alice stuck her snout into the recess and backed up, whining.

"Do you smell it?" Alexei asked.

Spassov wrinkled his nose. "Yeah. Saints, it's vile."

Alice barked unhappily at the top as they descended the stairs, refusing to go any further.

"*Sileo!*" Alexei snapped over his shoulder.

She gave him a dark look, then settled down to wait with her nose on her paws.

The stairs led to a low brick tunnel. After fifty paces, their way was barred by a stout oaken door. Alexei tried the handle but it must have been bolted on the other side.

"Given time and a couple of axes, we could break that down and see where it leads," Spassov said. "But time is what we don't have. The ship leaves in less than two hours. I won't let them board until we know what the hell is going on around here."

Alexei gave it a frustrated kick, but nodded in agreement.

They retreated back to the sanctuary. As Patryk returned the altar to its original position, he wondered if Bishop Morvana was truly ignorant of the secret labyrinth beneath the Arx. Someone in the clergy had to be part of it. How else could the Order know?

"You think they're watching?" Spassov asked, reading his thoughts.

"Maybe, but there's nothing to be done about it." He picked up the heavy linen-wrapped book. "So much for your peaceful retirement, eh?"

Patryk grinned. "You said it yourself. I'm too young to retire." He took out his flask, then seemed to think better of it and returned it to his pocket. A few minutes later, they were both riding out through the Gate of Saint Freyjus, Alice trotting behind.

# Chapter Fourteen

Oto Valek followed a rutted dirt track along the cliffs.

A hundred meters below, the sea crashed against smooth black rocks. To his left, the Kven downs rolled out in muted shades of green and lavender. Sheep grazed on the headland, humps of white against the setting sun. A raven took flight from a fencepost as Oto drove past. Its hoarse croak sounded like an accusation.

*Traitor. Heretic.*

He shook off a twinge of superstitious dread.

This was not the Eastern Curia, he reminded himself. The Raven held no sway here.

A bead of sweat stung his eye. Oto rolled the window down, gulping air. He had no clue where he was, only that he must follow the road to the end. He'd seen it in a dream.

A shudder convulsed him as he thought of the master. At first, the dreams had been pleasant. Visions of who he might become—a powerful, respected man like Doctor Ferran Massot. Oto didn't share the doctor's taste for trussed-up women. He had his own peculiar fantasies. Somehow, the master had pried them from the lowest precincts of his soul. Nothing could be hidden from him. It was both terrifying and liberating. But the master did not judge such things. He only punished failure.

After the Wards broke, the dreams had taken a turn. He'd repressed them from conscious memory, but they lay half-buried in his mind like a shallow grave after a hard rain. Oto sensed the bones of monstrous things sticking up from the earth. All he knew was that he could not fail the master again. The work was too important.

He hummed tunelessly to himself, mouth fixed in a parody of a smile.

All would be well. The knight would tell them everything they needed to know. Lezarius would be captured again and Oto would be redeemed.

A small voice whispered that he was nothing, just a fly crawling across the face of the earth, that he should buzz, buzz, buzz away before he was snapped up by something larger and hungrier, but it was too late now.

The road curved around a bend and he saw them.

Six bone-white masks floating above dark robes.

The Order of the Black Sun concealed their identities even from each other. The masks kept them on an even footing, even though some were low in the world and others high.

Very high, indeed.

Surely they would reward him for his service.

They carried torches, the flames dancing in the wind. Oto braked on the verge, his mouth dry as drought. He got out and unlatched the trunk. Mikhail Bryce lay curled on his side, cheeks flushed, sweat dampening his dark hair. Oto had given him a second dose of Somnium to be sure he wouldn't wake too soon. The memory of an iron hand around his throat had not faded.

"I brought you the mad knight, masters," he said, averting his gaze.

Four of them hoisted Bryce from the confines of the trunk. His body was limp and they struggled to bear his weight, despite the knight's gaunt appearance. The other two prodded Oto across the sparse grass to a stone hut. It was a rough structure, built into the hillside and half tumbled down. A cramped staircase loomed at his feet, leading into blackness.

Hands shoved him forward. "Go," a female voice hissed.

Oto grimaced. A smell came from the hole. Sulfurous and foul.

He hesitated.

"Go!"

He stumbled, catching himself on the wall. The stairs wound down into the earth. The smell grew stronger as he went deeper. An ineffable sweetness, masking something else. Something that made him want to weep in despair. The hiss of the torches and the swish of their robes were the only sounds.

The stairs ended at a low-ceilinged corridor. It looked centuries old, perhaps more. Oto followed it to an arched doorway. A large chamber lay beyond. When he saw what the chamber held, Oto stopped. His knees trembled. He could not bring himself to step through.

"Please," he whispered brokenly.

The eyes behind the masks held no pity.

"You are needed, Oto Valek," the woman said. "A final service."

He did weep then, though it did him little good.

He tried not to look at what lay nearby as the masters tied him down to a stone slab. A quick sting and his blood flowed through a tube into a glass phial. Flasks bubbled over black flames that emitted no smoke. The Order moved in silence, adding nameless ingredients to the elixir.

After a time, Oto grew drowsy. The pain vanished and he heard the master's voice. It was sweeter than wine, more lulling than Somnium. His eyes fluttered open as the other shapes began to stir. A figure stood over him, pale and radiant. It raised a flask to its white lips and drank. Before his heavy eyes, the bloodless cheeks grew ruddy with life, though its terrible mirrored eyes never changed.

*In the deep dark*, the master whispered, *the willing man alone sees the light.*

"Yes," he mumbled, gripped by the helpless ecstasy of the hare in the falcon's claws. "Yes, it is so."

More ghostly figures crowded around him. Oto fed them all.

# Chapter Fifteen

The man said his name was Willem.

That he was very special.

He asked, "Do you remember?"

Will did, but in the way you remember another person entirely. He felt no connection to the boy who had parents and friends and went to school and loved to run. That person was dead.

In the literal sense.

The man was old and walked with a cane. He never wore a mask.

But there were others. They brought him food he didn't eat. Water he didn't drink.

He couldn't see their faces, but he knew they were evil because he could hear their thoughts.

Will remembered enough about how things worked to know it was very wrong that he didn't require sustenance or rest. When he'd tried to breathe on the spoon they gave him, no mist fogged the silver. He regarded the warped reflection.

No, he looked nothing like that other boy.

One day, the old man had brought a little white dog. The moment it laid eyes on him, it began to bark. Sharp, frantic yaps. Will tried to pet it and the dog peed on the floor, shivering and whimpering. The man looked upset and took the dog away. He never saw it again.

But he knew there were boys and girls like him nearby because he could hear their thoughts, too.

It was disorienting at first. Over time, he learned to sort it all out. The masked ones thought mostly of what they wanted, and what they worried might and might not happen. They pretended to be sure of themselves, but they had never done anything like this before. The Magnum Opus, they called it.

He learned new words, listening.

The *Mortificacio*, for example. That meant the killing.

He recalled it quite clearly, though again, as the death of the boy, not himself.

*Nigredo* was the shadow of the sun. The distillation of matter to its primal state. Thrice forty nights of black fire and the deepest melancholy. It had nearly killed him a second time, but enough remained to reach the next stage, like a butterfly emerging damp and quivering from its chrysalis.

*Albedo*.

The whiteness. A second transmutation of the essence. Arising from the ashes purified and reborn, although as what he could not say.

Will knew he was dead—or if not properly dead, at some threshold between being and non-being. He perceived no color, only black and white and shades of grey. Light shone around everything. He thought it might be the ley.

There was a third and final stage they called the *Rubedo*.

He kept hearing the word, over and over. It meant the redness. He thought it might also mean new life in truth, a heart that beat, blood that pulsed, a chest that rose and fell, although he wasn't sure.

Some of his brothers and sisters had passed through that last gate.

The Masked Ones were afraid of them. Some thought the Reborn were too dangerous to live.

One had escaped. An albedo like Will. He'd heard her desperate mind-pleas for help as she ran through a dark wood. They'd cut off abruptly and he knew she'd been caught.

Like the dog, he never saw her again.

Footsteps. The creak of a hinge.

"Hello, Willem."

He looked up. It was the old man.

"Hello," he said.

The door closed. The old man regarded him. His face looked serene, but his thoughts were a frightened jumble.

*I have to . . . Saints, look at the boy. He smells so sweet, and look at him . . . No time for that!*

What the man said was, "How are you?"

"Well, thank you."

"Do you need anything?"

"No, thank you."

He leaned heavily on the cane. "Are you unhappy?"

"I am . . . well."

How else to describe being dead?

The old man licked his lips. "I thought we might take a walk."

"Is it permitted?"

He glanced at the door. "Yes."

A lie.

"I would like that," Will said.

*We must go quickly. If they discover us . . . Don't think of it. It doesn't bear thinking of.*

The old man smiled. "Good."

*We'll take the tunnel to the house. And then . . . Then I'll figure it out. There must be somewhere we can go. Novosotopol. Anywhere but north . . . . But they won't have him. I can't let them have him. Oh Saints, what were we thinking?*

The old man held out a hand. "Come, we must leave this place."

Will rose from the neatly made bed. "I'm sorry."

"Don't ever say that." He shook his head. "You've done nothing wrong."

"They're coming, grandfather."

The smile slipped. "What?"

The door creaked wide. Masked ones filled the frame. Will watched with a heavy heart as they dragged him away. Such evil in the world.

It was hard to comprehend.

---

Will sat on the bed, trying to ignore the overlapping voices in his head.

Most were the same as always. The masked ones were preoccupied with their Great Work. They wanted to please the King. He had promised them many things. Power and eternal youth. A place at his right hand when he returned.

The old man was no threat at all. Once they'd disposed of him, their thoughts turned to the journey ahead. Will paid little attention, but then he sensed a new presence in the place of stone and black fire. A captive like the Reborn, yet different. He was coiled in bonds of slumber, wandering though a mystical landscape of dream and archetype.

Will saw a Tower encased in frozen waterfalls of ice.

He saw a man of dark skin and light eyes, his chest Marked with an inverted lion. The Martyr. Good, but cursed with a troubled mind.

He saw a fierce Knight, and a High Priestess, beautiful and terrible. He saw a Fool, who was no fool at all but a Wild Card, one foot standing in the light and one in deepest shadow.

The Fool intrigued him. His path would branch, and

branch again, leading to a final fork that might decide a great many fates. Perhaps all of them.

Somewhere in the keep, the dreamer tossed and moaned.

Through a shimmering web of mist, Will saw another man. He wore a mask of living flesh, as false as the blank white faces that brought Will's untouched food.

Evil lurked in the last one. An evil so boundless and profound, it corrupted the ley around him.

With a sudden shock of recognition, Will understood that this was the King.

The dreamer had taken countless lives, but his heart remained pure. He served the ley and the Martyr. The dreamer had been reborn after a fashion, though not in the way of Will's brothers and sisters. His Nigredo had lasted for four long years. It had nearly devoured him, yet he had found the light at the end. Now his soul burned bright and true.

Will listened to the masked ones for a while. They planned to take the Reborn to the place of the icy tower. To the King. All except for Sophie Arnault. She was still alive, but they planned to drown her in the sea, as they had the first eight, and commence the hundred days and twenty of blackest night. If she emerged from it—and not all of the children had—she would be Albedo like Will. Alive, but dead. Then they would be given to the King as his disciples.

All this Will saw in a flash.

Until that moment, he had felt disconnected from the living. He existed behind the veil, in a netherworld devoid of shape or purpose. But the dreamer needed his help. He might be the only one who could stop the King from committing more evil. From bringing the world beneath his dark wing.

Will closed his eyes. Light bathed the cold chamber. He sent an urgent signal.

*Wake!*

# Chapter Sixteen

*Thunk!*

A bone-handled knife jutted from the dead tree, striking two meters above the base.

"Not bad," Tessaria said, walking to the trunk and prying it loose. "Try again."

Natalya drew her arm back and threw. This time, it struck the outer edge of the crude X Tessaria had scratched into the wood.

"Better. Watch the grip, not the point." She retrieved the knife. "Again."

The handle bounced off the bark and tumbled to the ground. Natalya frowned.

"It over-rotated," Tess said. "Back up a little. And don't snap your wrist when you release. It's a bad habit. You'll never be able to do it exactly the same each time and consistency is what we want. "

Natalya adjusted her stance, left foot forward, eye fixed on the target.

"Lock your wrist, but just a bit. Smooth release, darling. You're not throwing the knife, merely letting it slide from your hand."

The knife blurred. It landed a few centimeters from the center of the X.

"You have natural skill," Tessaria said approvingly.

Nashka smiled.

"If we had six months, I might make something of you."

"That long?"

"There's more to it than hurling a blade at a target. You must learn the different grips, which depend on the balance. A knife that is handle-heavy must be gripped from the blade. If the weight is greatest in the blade, you throw from the handle. That's rudimentary. This one is balanced in the middle so it can be thrown from either end."

Tess wound up and released in one fluid motion, hardly pausing to aim. It thunked into the center of the target.

Kasia watched them from a stone bench. They'd eaten a pleasant lunch in the garden with Hanne, though Jann never appeared. Apparently, he was feeling unwell. Nashka's new shoes arrived from the city, stylish ankle boots of soft fawn-colored suede. Hanne had received confirmation by Markhawk that the ship was being readied and they'd depart in a few hours, at high tide.

Now the shadows beneath the pines were lengthening and Spassov had yet to return. Kasia hoped he didn't run into trouble. Maria Karolo knew he'd helped them flee. Could she have sent word to the Arx?

The estate was lovely in the golden afternoon sunlight, yet she was eager to be on her way. When Kasia pressed her, Natalya admitted that her sleep the night before had also been plagued by nightmares, though she couldn't recall them. It was why she'd left their bed so early that morning.

She'd suggested the knife lessons to distract Natalya from her dark mood, and was surprised to discover her friend was actually good at it. Kasia had given up after three attempts that missed the tree completely.

"You haven't lost your edge, Tessaria," Hanne Danziger called out. "Not like the rest of us."

Kasia turned on the bench. Hanne had a strange way of appearing out of nowhere. Now she was making her way across the lawn, plump arms swingingly vigorously like a soldier marching to battle.

"I thought it prudent to keep in practice," Tessaria said, watching the older woman approach.

"You should have seen her thirty-five years ago," Hanne said to Kasia. "She could part your hair from forty paces."

"That's an exaggeration," Tess said modestly. "I'd say thirty paces."

"Can you teach me?" Nashka winked at Kasia. "She'll volunteer."

"Not likely," Kasia grumbled.

"Where is Jann?" Tess asked. "I hoped to see him again before we sail."

Hanne studied the knife in the tree, her voice soft. "I'm sorry he's been absent. His health is very poor these days."

"The old injury?" Tess said with sympathy. "I thought it had healed. Is he experiencing complications?"

"Not exactly." She sighed. "We had a tragedy four months ago. Our grandson disappeared."

"What? Which one?"

"Willem."

"Saints! Why didn't you tell me?"

"We don't speak of it anymore. I suppose we've lost hope."

"I'm sorry," Kasia said, rising from the bench to join them. Natalya murmured condolences, looking stricken. She was fond of children.

"Was he abducted for ransom?" Tessaria asked.

That's what Kasia had assumed, given the Danziger's wealth.

"No."

"Did he run away?"

"He's not the only one." The words came heavily. "Will was the fifth child to vanish. There have been nine so far. Someone is stealing them." She pressed a fist to her mouth. "It's been hell. My son says the Polizei keep coming to the house, asking questions, but they have no leads. Jann even hired a private investigator, but he found nothing." A sob broke from her throat. "He finally gave our money back and said he couldn't help us."

Tessaria put an arm around her. "Hanne, I can't begin to imagine . . . ."

"Some evil has come to this city." She shook her head, tears streaking her face. "I don't know what to do."

A missing child.

"Frau Danziger, I saw something in the garden last night," Kasia said. "A figure in white. It was small. Do you think . . .?"

"Jule already told me," she said wearily. "I don't know. It didn't happen here. Willem was coming home from school. If he somehow found his way . . . why didn't he just come to the door? I had the grounds searched, of course. The gardeners found no sign of him." She sank to the bench. "There have been false sightings before. Each time, our hopes were crushed. The toll on my husband has been great. He loved Willem the best." She flashed a fragile smile. "He would never say so, of course. But I know."

"If there's anything I can do . . . ." Tess squeezed her shoulder. "Well, you've already done all that's possible. What about the others? Were any . . . ."

"Found dead?" Hanne finished hollowly. "No. That is all that keeps us going. If they had, I fear Jann would follow our grandson to the grave within weeks." She knitted her hands. "He wanted to cancel the party yesterday, but it would have caused great offense to the Imperator's delegation. And destroying our business won't bring Willem back. I suppose that sounds callous."

"Of course not. You must stay strong and make the decisions Jann cannot."

"Thank you." She looked up at Tessaria gratefully. "I'm sorry to burden you with all this."

"Don't be ridiculous! I feel as if I know the boy from your letters. My heart weeps for all of you." She hesitated. "Do you need us to stay?"

"And do what?" Hanne waved a hand. "No, you must catch your ship tonight. I hear the nuncio herself is involved in the case. She has a reputation for thoroughness."

"Come," Tess said. "We'll return to the house. Perhaps you'd like to lie down for a while."

"Lie down?" Hanne gave her a sharp look. "I might not be the energetic creature I was thirty years ago, but I don't need a nap."

Tess smiled.

"I came because I thought you might want to walk the grounds with me. View the newest pine nursery. It's on a hilltop with a view of the sea." Her gaze grew distant. "I planted a tree there for Willem."

Natalya turned and sneakily wiped away a tear.

"I'd love to," Tessaria said.

Kasia watched the pair of old friends. Since her strange encounter the night before, Tess had forbidden them to venture out of sight of Danziger Haus. Now, in a stroke, she was heading off on a hike. How could she refuse after Hanne's tragic story? Yet the detached observer lurking in Kasia's heart wondered.

"Won't you come?" Hanne addressed the younger women, blue eyes bird-bright.

"I will," Natalya said. She walked to the tree and retrieved the knife.

"I feel rather tired," Kasia said. "Would you mind terribly if I took a pass?"

"Of course not." Hanne smiled. "We'll be back by supper."

They ambled into the woods, Hanne gesturing with her hands as she talked about the varieties of evergreen they'd planted on the property. Kasia turned back to the house. It was a disturbing tale. She'd never heard of such crimes. That sort of thing was supposed to be part of the distant past, before Marks controlled humanity's basest impulses.

Kasia herself was Unmarked because she'd failed the personality tests. The Curia said she was incapable of empathy or sound moral judgment and couldn't be trusted with the ley. But she did have feelings for the people she cared about. Strong feelings. Her birth parents had abandoned her when they learned of her affliction and she rarely thought of them. But her chosen family meant everything. Natalya and Tess.

And Fra Alexei Bryce. As ill-suited as they were for each other, she still ached to see him again.

Yet she couldn't deny that she was different from other people. The story of the children disturbed her, but she hadn't wept over it like Natalya. And while she knew she should be feeling pity for Hanne, for some reason she just . . . didn't. It had struck her as play-acting. Kasia couldn't say why, precisely, but she was a fluent liar herself, able to summon tears at the drop of a hat, and recognized the quality in another.

Of course, she could be wrong. The story was easily verified with the servants. Most likely Willem really had gone missing.

She got around her own shortcomings through methodical reasoning. Tess had taught her how to do it. One tallied up the costs of various choices and then selected the course that did the least harm. Revealing her suspicion would have caused obvious offense. Allowing the Danziger woman to take them off somewhere was a risk, but Tess had her knives. And the fact that Hanne had allowed Kasia to return to the house implied that she didn't intend anything malicious.

She retreated to her room and did a reading. It was the same spread she'd drawn in the carriage, in exactly the same order.

The Jack of Wolves. The Mage. The Lovers. Death and the Sun.

The ley was speaking to her, if she could only understand.

Kasia flopped down on the bed, clutching the eiderdown pillow to her chest.

*Take them one at a time.*

Who was the Jack? Not Jann Danziger. He was feeble. His wife was clearly the more ambitious one. She could be the Jack. The sexes of the characters depicted in the cards were irrelevant. It was the archetype that mattered. One face to the world, another in private. That might well describe her, if Kasia was right. But the crown was puzzling. The Danzigers were already filthy rich. What more could they be seeking? It implied a great prize, just out of reach.

She rolled to her side, propping an elbow on the mattress.

"Ow." Kasia rubbed her elbow. The tender point had struck something hard. Like a pebble.

She groped around. Yes, a small object was buried deep in the feathers. Her dark brows drew together. She went downstairs to the conservatory and found a pair of gardening shears. It was the lull between lunch and dinner and she didn't encounter any servants. Kasia hurried back to her room. She cut open the linen coverlet and probed with the tip of the shears until she unearthed the object.

A stone, jet black like onyx, shot through with streaks of russet.

Kasia pried it out, careful not to touch it.

*Lithomancy.*

Another method of wielding the ley, practiced by the witches in Dur-Athaara.

And, apparently, by certain respectable merchant families in Kvengard.

She guessed this must be the source of the nightmares.

Kasia had been sleeping on the right side of the large double bed when she woke, slick with sweat. It was closest to the window and the draft had chilled her. Later, Natalya had taken her place.

"Fog it," she whispered. "What are they after?"

That nonsense about searching the grounds . . . She'd been in the breakfast room and within view of the lawns all day. When she'd walked with Spassov, she'd seen no sign of any search.

Kasia gathered the deck and shuffled.

"Speak plain," she muttered. "What am I to do?"

She closed her eyes and drew a card.

The Knight of Storms.

Kasia frowned. "Mikhail Bryce?" she whispered crossly. "That makes no sense!"

She drew another.

The Mage Inverted.

"Him *again*?" Kasia stared at the cards, confounded.

Another card.

The High Priestess.

It referred to herself, of that she had no doubt. Natalya had used her as the model and the resemblance was striking. Raven hair, generous figure, cool, direct gaze.

She swept the cards from the coverlet and tucked the deck into her pocket. It was a strange reading. "One I probably won't understand until it's too fogging late," she muttered. "But there it is."

Kasia remade the bed, using the shears to hide the vile stone among the feathers. She hurried out of her room and ran straight into Jule Danziger. He was just coming up the main staircase. For an instant, his face appeared in profile, one bright blue eye meeting her own. Kasia drew up short.

She suddenly wished she hadn't left the gardening shears behind.

"You're in a lather," he said with a smile.

"I was looking for Tessaria. She's with your aunt."

"I haven't seen them."

"She was upset." Kasia paused. "She told us about Willem."

Jule shook a cigarette from a silver case. "It's been awful. We're only ten years apart. He was more like a little brother to me."

Again, she sensed no real grief. Kasia wondered how many Danzigers they'd have to deal with when the time came to flee.

"Is Jann at home?" she asked casually.

Something flickered across his face. "If you know about Willem, you must know how it's affected my uncle's health. He wasn't strong to begin with. It's destroyed him." He lit the cigarette. "Jann is lying down. He doesn't want to be disturbed."

"I thought you weren't supposed to smoke in the house," Kasia said.

Jule's blue eyes crinkled. He blew a stream of smoke at the ceiling. "Our secret, eh?"

He turned as a servant approached with a silver tray. The woman murmured in Kven. Jule unfolded the note on the tray and scanned the single page.

"Your ship is ready to sail," he said. "Would you care to ride out with me to see it?" His face was guileless. "The view from the cliffs is very pretty at sunset."

She smiled. "I'd better wait for Tessaria."

He nodded at the servant. The woman bobbed her head and retreated down the hall, casting a furtive glance over her shoulder.

"She's protective, isn't she? But you're a grown woman. Surely you don't require her approval."

"It's a tempting invitation, but I promised," Kasia said with an easy laugh. "It's terribly kind of Hanne to handle everything. Tess will be pleased, though I must confess, I've enjoyed our stay. Especially the ghosts!"

Jule Danziger hesitated. His gaze flicked to her pocket as if he knew what lay within. A vein pulsed in his neck as he drew on the cigarette. Swift and agitated.

"It is your choice, of course," he said at last. "But it's best you don't leave the house alone. We still don't know what you saw and it's getting dark."

"I wouldn't dream of it," she said.

Jule turned away.

"What's the name of the ship?" she called after him.

"The Splendor Solis." He smiled. "A swift vessel. You'll reach Nantwich in no time."

Splendor of the Sun.

She returned to her room. Kasia watched through the window as a groom brought Jule's horse around. He galloped down the long drive.

It was all unraveling.

Jule knew about the cards. He'd come within an inch of taking them from her by force, but something had stopped him. Maybe he thought she still didn't suspect. Maybe he wasn't sure what she was capable of. But if they boarded that ship, Kasia doubted they would live to see the dawn.

# Chapter Seventeen

Kasia had no intention of waiting for Jule Danziger to return.

After a few minutes passed, she crept down the servants' stair down to the main floor of the house. She slid the bolt, but the front door had been locked with a key.

She peered through the mullioned windows. The hulking blond gardener who had stared at them earlier was raking the gravel along the beds. He looked up and held her eye until Kasia turned away. She strode through the entrance hall, past the formal dining room and library, to the glass conservatory. A maid appeared so quickly that Kasia knew they'd been spying on her.

"Coffee, please," she said, sitting down at the long wooden table.

The woman curtsied and left. The instant she was gone, Kasia kicked her heels off. She tried the glass doors. Locked. She looked around, gaze settling on a heavy planter with flowering rue. The gardener was nowhere in sight. She hurled the planter at the glass doors. Shouts came from deeper in the house as she stepped carefully over the shards.

The conservatory was about thirty meters from the edge of the woods. She sprinted across the strip of grass. More shouts echoed behind her. Kasia reached the trees and ran until the voices faded.

She had to find Tess and Natalya.

She circled around, aiming for the direction the women had taken earlier that afternoon. Pine needles stuck to her stockinged feet as she moved quietly from shadow to shadow. Memories of the night before assailed her. A small white figure. Another, hooded and watchful. The ley, blackening in a pool around it.

What could do that?

Then she heard the sound of hoofbeats coming through the forest. Kasia hid behind a tree. A horse and rider appeared. The rider's cowl was raised. It moved slowly, the hood sweeping from side to side as if searching. She pulled back, pressed to the bark of the pine.

Snuffling, like an animal. It grew louder.

Surely it would catch her scent. The beast must be a few paces away. She gripped her deck, ready to wield the ley. Hoping that it would cooperate.

The creature passed her hiding place and continued onward. Kasia risked a glance around the bole of the tree.

It was a great hound, black and tan, with pointed ears. The massive triangular head was angled towards the ground. She shifted her gaze slightly and it vanished.

A Markhound.

Could the Danzigers have a pack?

They certainly could. But then she recognized the scar bisecting the creature's haunch. It was the same Markhound that had sat at the gate outside Dr. Massot's house on the night he attacked her.

Kasia stepped from behind the tree. Her pulse had remained slow and steady throughout the ordeal, but now it ticked up a notch.

"Alexei?" she called softly.

The hood fell back as the horseman turned toward her. "Kasia!"

He galloped over and slid from the saddle. Fra Bryce didn't believe in half measures. She'd almost forgotten the fierceness of his gaze. He gave her a thorough looking-over, right down to her unshod feet. The scrutiny warmed her cheeks. Kasia wanted very much to kiss him, but wasn't quite sure where they stood. Besides which, the Danzigers and their minions couldn't be far off.

"Thank the Saints you came," she said at last. "Where's Spassov?"

"At the house looking for *you*." His lips quirked. "The servants didn't want to let him in, but he wouldn't stop pounding on the door."

"What did they say?"

"That you'd gone out with the mistress of the house."

Kasia snorted. "These people aren't what they seem, Bryce."

"I know. Then Alice picked up the scent." He looked somewhat abashed. "I left him to deal with the situation. I'm not sure—"

The Markhound had been snuffling around in circles. Now it lifted its muzzle to the air and gave a low howl.

"She's caught it again," Alexei said in excitement.

Kasia studied the dog. It stood rigid, staring intently through the trees.

"Who is she tracking?"

"My brother. I know it sounds crazy, but he's here."

The Knight of Storms. The Mage Inverted. It all tumbled into place.

"I know," she said.

He frowned. "How—"

"I just read it in the cards," she explained. "Where?"

"He could be with Lezarius, I don't know. But I fear they've caught him."

"The Order of the Black Sun," she said grimly.

"The alchemists, yes."

The hound gave another howl and loped off. Alexei whistled sharply and she reluctantly circled back. "I can't wait, Kasia." He glanced back the way he'd come from. "Patryk will protect you until I return."

"Protect *me*?" she said wryly. "It's him I fear for. The Danzigers are wolves in truth. No, I will go with you, if you don't mind. Perhaps I can be of help."

"I have no idea what we're walking into," he said dubiously.

"Does it involve the missing children?"

He nodded. "I think so."

Cold anger settled over her like a mantle of snow. "Then let me help you."

"What about Tessaria and Natalya?"

"They went off with Hanne. I was looking for them just now, but that is not my path," she said, gazing up at him seriously. "It's with you. I can't explain it, but—"

He held a gloved hand out. She stuck a foot in the stirrup, realizing as she mounted and the creature blurred in her peripheral vision that the horse, too, was bred with ley. Alexei swung into the saddle behind her. His arms came around her and though he held the reins loosely, she sensed the tension in his body. She wasn't the only one who felt the heat between them.

Alexei whistled again, a slightly different pitch. The hound darted off, nose to the ground and occasionally lifting to sniff the air. Kasia settled into the warmth at her back, trying to stifle the memory of his lean, muscled body in her bed, the look in his eyes when he told her that she made him feel again.

Why did this man have such power over her? And always at the worst moments?

They followed the Markhound's luminous prints in the

twilight. She moved haltingly at first, seeming to catch the trail and then lose it again.

"Mikhail did not pass this way," Alexei said. "If he had, the trail would be fresh and strong. But he's somewhere close."

Stars drifted through the branches overhead as they moved through the wood, sometimes doubling back and then galloping onward. At last they reached a dirt road, hardly more than a rutted track. It wound through the gorse. On the left, a cliff dropped away to the sea.

"The ship," Kasia exclaimed, pointing.

Alexei reined up. It sat at anchor in a cove under the huge yellow moon. There were masts fore and aft but also a pair of funnels amidships.

"Hanne claimed she was giving us a clipper," Kasia said, twisting in the saddle so she could look at him. "But it has funnels like a steamer."

Alexei's eyes narrowed as he studied the ship. "Clippers have a narrow beam, making them swift under sail. But look at the rounded hull. If I had to guess, I'd say it was an icebreaker."

She frowned. "Did you travel by sea as a knight?"

"Never. But I spent a year studying maritime law. I still remember some of it. My father hoped I'd pursue a career with one of the big shipping firms in Novo, but it wasn't for me."

"You chose to be a criminal defense attorney."

He looked surprised. "Did Spassov tell you that?"

She shook her head. "Feizah. She said you could have been a diplomat after your service in the knights ended, but you turned her down to join the Interfectorem."

"That's true." A cynical smile. "My father wasn't very happy about it."

"But you did it for Misha."

"Yes." The smile died. He looked sad. "The Order views

Invertidos as little more than beasts. They often used excessive force to subdue them. I hoped to change that."

"Did you?"

"Only Patryk." Alexei laughed. "I was relentless. He finally came around, mostly."

Kasia turned back to the ship. "Jule Danziger said it's named the *Splendor Solis*. They promised to take us to Nantwich."

"I wonder where it's really headed," he said softly.

They rode on. After a few minutes, the Markhound caught a clear scent and sprinted down the dirt road. Alexei spurred the horse to a full gallop. The wind tore at her hair, the cliff a black chasm to their left. At last, they reached a bluff. A shepherd's hut stood there—and a car with a Novostopol license plate. The hound braced her paws on the trunk, barking savagely. Alexei dismounted and ran to the car, unlatching the trunk. It was empty. He rummaged through the glove compartment. Kasia's gaze narrowed as he held out a box of syringes and glass vials. Alexei opened one and sniffed the contents.

"Oto Valek," he muttered.

"Who?"

"An orderly from the Batavia Institute." He held up a hand and helped her clamber from the saddle. "Massot was the head doctor there. Both Lezarius and my brother were patients."

She eyed the vial. "What is that?"

"Somnium. A powerful sedative. They use it to keep the patients docile."

"What's he doing in Kvengard?" she asked, puzzled. "And how could he be connected to the children?"

"Alchemy," Alexei said tensely. "The Order is using them for some diabolical purpose." She sensed his Marks flare beneath his robes. Hollow eyes turned to her. "Is my brother still alive?"

"Yes," she said quickly. "I'm certain he is."

Alexei nodded, visibly relieved.

*Let it be so*, she thought, as he led the horse to a grassy meadow and left it to graze. *He's been through enough. They both have.*

But she did not think the ley would send such a strong signal if Mikhail Bryce was already dead.

Alice abandoned the car and started nosing around the hut, stubby tail wagging in agitation. As soon as Kasia drew near, she caught a dank, unpleasant odor. They surveyed the cramped stairs leading into darkness.

"Kasia," Alexei said heavily, turning to her. "I can't let you go down there."

"Why not?"she demanded. "You are."

"I was a knight. I can defend myself. But if I have to worry for your safety, too—"

"If I show you something," she said, "will you promise not to despise me?"

He looked at her with cautious interest. "Yes."

Kasia took out her deck. She pulled her gloves off and drew a card at random. It spun in a single lazy circle before falling at his feet.

The Wheel. The tenth trump of the Major Arcana.

"My luck has been poor lately," she said with a little smile. "But now it has turned again. Greater forces are at work here. The hand of fate intervenes." Her forehead creased in a frown. "What happens here today will set us both on a new road. And it *must* happen."

"I see," he said with a hint of impatience. "But that doesn't solve our problem. You mean something to me, Kasia. I won't lose you, too. Not even for Mikhail." His jaw set stubbornly. "You're not even wearing shoes!"

She gave him a level look. "I'm not done yet."

Kasia bent and picked up the card, unleashing her anger at being hunted, chased, lied to. She thought of the masked men in the alley, the watcher beneath the trees. Her heartbeat quickened. Lines of violet ley burst forth, tracing the spokes and rim of the mighty Wheel, vivid in the dim light of the hut. It pulsed and ebbed, pulsed and ebbed. Alexei stared at the card in mute surprise.

Kasia let the power fade, feeling satisfied despite her trepidation. This time, she'd had a greater measure of control.

"Saints," he muttered. "How did you do that?"

"I don't know and that is the truth. But I can. And I am not defenseless." She tucked the card away. "It doesn't always work as I intend it to. But it saved us once before."

She told him about the men in the alley, and how she'd brought the fire escape down on their heads.

"Liminal ley is unpredictable," he agreed. A pause. "And abyssal? Do you touch the red, Kasia?"

"No," she said quickly. "Natalya warned me not to. She said it's dangerous."

"It is that." Alexei looked thoughtful. "The Church would not approve. But if the ley has given you this gift . . . ." He shrugged. "I am glad."

Several powerful emotions seized her. Relief that he'd called it a gift rather than a curse. Contempt for the Curia's small-mindedness . . . . And a rush of fondness for this unorthodox priest that quickly became unbridled lust. She seized his cassock and kissed him. He looked startled, but an instant later he was kissing her back with the hunger of a starving man who'd just been thrown a crust of bread.

"I've thought of you often," he breathed in her ear. "Why does it always have to be like this?"

"Stolen moments at the brink of peril?" she laughed. "It's our destiny, Bryce."

"To hell with that." His mouth found her neck. She tipped her head back, encouraging him toward the bodice. Alexei seemed happy to comply. Strong hands gripped her waist, arching her tighter against him. She slid her fingers through the silky brush of his hair. His tongue found hers. She slid a hand into the sleeve of his cassock, stroking the smooth forearm, pulling his hand to her breast. There were too many clothes between them. Now. She wanted him *right now*—

Alice emitted a sharp bark.

"No," Kasia murmured. Her lips were swollen and tender. So was the rest of her.

Another bark.

Alexei groaned and turned his head. Kasia followed his gaze. The Markhound had gathered her courage and was halfway down the stairs, gazing back at her master. She tilted her head quizzically. He released a long, unsteady breath.

Kasia made a wry face and smoothed down the tendrils of raven hair that had escaped their pins. "You see?" she said dryly. "That's why I'm a cat person."

Alexei didn't smile. He cupped her face and kissed her once more, long and lingering.

"Tease," she muttered, stepping back. "But I suppose the dog is right. This is neither the time nor the place."

He stared at her seriously. "Are you sure? I worry what we might find."

He sounded afraid and she understood that it wasn't for himself, or even for her. There was unfathomable evil waiting at the end of that tunnel and the memory of it would taint them both for the rest of their lives.

"I'm sure," she said.

Kasia drew another card. The Sword of Justice. Four runes marked the blade, Raven and Crossed Keys, Flame and Wolf, signaling unity of purpose. Some instinct guided her. Instead of using her anger, she thought of the lost boy. Willem Danziger.

*Let us find him. Let us save him, if he can be saved.*

Blue ley lit the card, illuminating the rough walls. The stone was chill beneath her stocking feet.

"I'll go first," Kasia said.

# Chapter Eighteen

The tunnel ran in a straight line into darkness. Rough brick walls framed an uneven dirt floor, scuffed with overlapping footprints. The Markhound raced ahead until Alexei called her back to heel.

Kasia held the card before her like a torch, although the blue surface ley was not very bright—or more precisely, it failed to illuminate the space around it. She could see her own hand and the faint outline of the walls but little else.

"It's awful down here," she whispered as they ventured into the tunnel.

Some of it she could discern. Salt like a brisk sea wind and the rotten-egg fog of sulphur. But there were other nameless notes that wrinkled her nose.

"It'll get worse," Alexei warned. "We're moving toward the source."

Speaking quietly, he told her what had transpired since his arrival in Kvengard, including the visit to the apothecary and his discovery of the book. The fight in the chapel, and the bizarre creature that had putrified before his eyes.

In turn, Kasia told him about the nightmares. The stone

she found inside her mattress and the pale thing that had drawn her into the gardens.

"I wish I knew how many of them there are," Alexei said. "If we can accomplish our misson with stealth, it would be . . . easier."

"Than killing them all? Most certainly. But I will not balk at that."

Alexei gave a quiet laugh.

"What?"

"You would have made a good knight. You have no fear, do you?"

His tone made her uneasy. "I only speak the truth. What does fear have to do with it?"

"I'm not accusing you of anything. You're just different from most people. I like you for it."

"Thank you," she said, somewhat mollified. "Maybe it's because I don't have Marks to stuff everything away. I can't control what I feel." Her voice hardened. "And I wish them dead."

Alexei was silent for a minute. "I experienced that in the Void. There's no ley, you see. My Marks don't work. I despised it."

"Why?"

He seemed surprised she would ask. "Because it's wrong to feel such hatred for the nihilim."

"I don't understand. Weren't they trying to kill you?"

"They're our enemies, yes. But we must have compassion for them."

She stopped. "You've lost me, Bryce. Didn't the Curia *shell* their cities?"

The bluish light washed the color from his face. "We had no choice. They were a threat. But it wasn't done in anger."

It was Kasia's turn to laugh. "I don't suppose that made much difference to them."

"Maybe not, but it makes all the difference to us. Falke

promised it would be the last war. Ever. Imagine it, Kasia! A world without violence."

"I'm all for it," she said. "But I'm not sure Marks are the right way. The mind is a convoluted maze. Ferran Massot told me that and he was right. The Curia would build walls against the monsters, but it doesn't make them go away. They're part of us whether we like it or not. And it's better to face them than to lock them up. Even the strongest chains will snap under pressure."

He opened his mouth as if to argue, then closed it again.

"You can't sleep, can you?" she persisted. "I told Feizah she gave you too many Marks. That it messed you up."

To her surprise, he looked amused. "What did she say?"

*I don't know who you really are, girl, but I intend to find out.*

"That it was none of her doing. But it was!" Kasia shrugged. "She didn't like me, nor I her. She tried to hurt your brother. I think she would have killed him if Lezarius had not intervened."

His eyes widened slightly. "I didn't know that."

"Now you do." She sighed. "I understand that your Marks can never be removed, nor would you want them to be. But these people must know we're coming. They tried to kill you and failed. They know I escaped the house. I expect they'll be on guard."

He nodded. "We'll do what we have to."

They resumed walking in silence. Alice stayed close, her hackles raised. The tunnel began to curve. When a glimmer of light appeared ahead, Kasia released the ley. Darkness pressed in again. After a moment, she sensed that Alexei had halted. Kasia groped her way back to him.

"It's the smell," he whispered dreamily. "Flowers and decay."

She'd noticed it too. A sweetness in the air like the first day of spring. Or a garden after a rainstorm. Yet that wasn't quite it, either. The smell made her think of a newborn animal. Something fresh and clean, still unsullied by the harsh world.

Yet beneath it lurked the stench of death. Worse. An indescribable smell that evoked cold, empty rooms and lightless places that had never heard the sound of laughter. It seemed impossible that the two odors could coexist. Kasia gripped his hand. Alexei squeezed back. He'd taken off his gloves and the rough warmth of his palm gave her strength.

"Saints preserve us," he said quietly.

They walked around the curve together, Alice a dim shadow ahead. An archway waited at the end of the tunnel. Pitch-soaked torches burned on either side.

"*Sileo*," Alexei cautioned softly. Lips peeled back from her sharp teeth, but Alice obeyed her master, padding in perfect silence to the archway. He gestured at Kasia to wait, then crept forward, inching along the wall. When he reached the door, his back stiffened. She drew a card, expecting one of the alchemists to be inside, but after a moment Alexei stepped through and waved her forward.

The smells grew stronger as she approached. It was a spacious chamber, made of brick like the tunnel. Plants hung in bunches from the ceiling. Kasia glimpsed glass jars and crucibles, bubbling iron pots and smoking vials. A case held thick leather-bound tomes embossed in gold leaf. Scrolls covered with arcane symbols lay on a table, their edges pinned down with tongs and other iron implements. More torches flared in brackets. A complex astrolabe with gears and weights ticked away the hours. All this she absorbed in an instant.

Yet it was the four stone slabs in the center of the room that riveted her.

One held a thin red-haired man. A tube ran from his arm, but it wasn't attached to anything and his blood dripped in a steady flow, adding to a dark pool on the stone floor. His eyes were open and glazed in death.

*Valek*, Alexei mouthed.

The other three held children. Deathly pale, they lay with their arms folded across their chests, wearing pretty silks. Two were girls and someone had tied ribbons in their hair. A parody of tender care.

Alexei crossed to the room in four strides. He pressed his fingers to the wrist of the nearest child, then shook his head bleakly and tried the next one. A vein throbbed in his temple, leylight pouring from his sleeves as his Marks tried to tamp down a wave of despair.

It must have just happened because the bodies had no visible decay. Nor were there any wounds, though they appeared bloodless. Kasia touched a cold cheek, furious tears spilling over. *Dead. All dead.*

"We must hide," Alexei hissed. "Someone's coming."

She looked down at the card in her hand. The Sun. A naked cherub frolicking in a field of yellow flowers.

The irony stoked her anger to a boil. It foretold good fortune and happiness, but the ley held nothing but pain for these children. At least they were at peace—

The card burst into flame. Kasia dropped it with a muffled yelp. It burned to ash before it touched the ground. The black matter bubbling in the glass vials flared with blinding white light. She heard Alice's frenzied barking and the sound of running footsteps, but all she saw was the afterimage of a huge, consuming black disk shimmering in the air.

For a moment, all was tumult and blurred shadows. Then three masked figures filled the opposite archway. Alice leapt forward, a snarling arrow of fang and lithe muscle. One of the figures fell, the hound at its throat. Alexei swept up a pair of heavy tongs. Steel rang against iron as he parried a blade. The third lunged at her. Kasia grabbed one of the beakers and hurled its contents at the white mask. It hissed and smoked. The cloaked figure tore at its face. It stumbled into a wall of glass shelving and fell to its knees, gurgling.

She spun in time to see Alexei duck a wild stab and crash

the tongs down on his attacker's head. He brought the weapon down again, and again, though the figure already lay motionless on the ground. Kasia ran over and seized his arm.

"They're dead," she hissed. "Stop!"

He looked up at her with reddened eyes.

"They're dead," she said again, more gently.

Alice trotted over, her muzzle red. Alexei drew a shuddering breath. He tore the mask away. "Filius canis," he muttered. "I know her."

Kasia studied the woman's face. An ordinary face of middle years, though it should have been monstrous.

"Sofie Arneth's mother," he said in disgust. "I interviewed her two days ago. Let's check the others."

The one Kasia had killed was impossible to identify. The mask had melted into the skin. But he recognized the third member of the Order. Wandy Keller's father.

"More will be coming," Kasia said. "We must search for Mikhail."

He nodded wearily and picked up the fallen blade. "Can you do a reading? Figure out where he is?"

"I can try, though it doesn't usually work like that—"

A faint scraping sound raised the hair on her neck. Kasia turned.

The three children stood shoulder to shoulder, silently watching. The foul odor was gone. She smelled only flowers now. They radiated purity and innocence. Yet they were . . . *wrong*. Still pale as death and with milk-white hair now. The eyes . . . One was a silver mirror, the other a pit to nothingness.

The eldest boy cocked his head. "What is this place?"

The voice was hoarse, as though rusted from disuse.

Beside her, Alexei stood frozen. Alice whined nervously, shuffling back a step. But she did not bark or raise her hackles.

They were not evil. Merely used and abandoned. Kasia knew what that felt like. She hurried forward and grasped the child's icy hand. "We will take care of you, all of you," she said seriously. "What is your name?"

A long pause. "I don't know." The mirrored eye clouded. "Our brother calls."

"Who is your brother?"

"Will."

"Willem Danziger," Alexei said behind her. "Saints, did you do this, Kasia?"

"Bring them back?" She shook her head. "If so, it was the ley, not I."

"Splendor Solis," the child said, his voice a sweet soprano now. "We walked through the long dark, but you summoned the light."

In a flash, Kasia understood the juxtaposition of the Sun and Death from that first reading in the carriage with Natalya when they arrived at the house. The accuracy of it sent a chill down her spine.

"Where are the others?" Alexei asked. "Where's Willem?"

The child studied him. "You serve the ley, as we do."

Alexei touched the Raven on his neck, bravely meeting those fey eyes, though Kasia sensed his deep unease. The children's chests did not rise and fall, nor breath enter their lungs.

"I am a priest of the Eastern Curia," he clarified.

"Can you use the ley?" Kasia asked. "Did they Mark you?"

"We serve the ley," the child repeated. "That is all."

She exchanged a look with Alexei and they stepped a little way apart. The children waited placidly. To her surprise, Alice abandoned her master and slunk over to the children, lying down at their feet with her ears perked.

"What do we do with them?" she asked.

"Take them along. There's no choice." He lowered his voice. "Do you think it can be . . . reversed?"

"I've no idea." She glanced around the laboratory. The

flasks were empty now, the black flames extinguished. "This is way beyond my comprehension, Bryce."

He blew out a breath. "And any sane person's. They are dead, but not. If we can take one of these bastards alive, maybe we'll get some answers."

Kasia returned to the children. She suspected it was one of them she'd seen in the gardens that night. They were luminous, as if they channeled every hue of the ley through a reverse prism. Dead, but animated in some way. Was that the alchemists' intent? And for what final purpose?

"We must find Willem," she said. "But we can't leave you here. Will you come with us?"

The boy nodded. The girls hadn't spoken, but they seemed fully aware. More than that. She sensed hard-earned wisdom in their mismatched eyes.

*We walked through the long dark.*

"Do you know where your brother is?" she asked.

"He is here."

"But where exactly?"

The child stared at her, puzzled.

"Never mind. Come, we will look for him together."

Alexei went first through the second archway, blade ready. The children followed behind with Kasia and the Markhound at the rear. They found a flight of stairs leading down and took it to a second, lower level.

Another stone tunnel lit by torches. And a thing, skittering toward them on all fours, white mask a blur. Alexei shouted a warning as more shadows appeared in the corridor. Kasia pushed the children behind her. She tore a card from her deck. It sliced the air as she hurled it down. A violet flash. One of the torches toppled free of its bracket, setting a black cloak alight. Taloned hands beat at the flames with a screech.

Alexei kicked it aside and drove his blade into something with long, oddly jointed limbs. Smoke filled the corridor as the first creature rolled on the ground, batting at the flames.

Claws reached for her ankle. She stepped back, glimpsing a deformed face with frighteningly human eyes. Alexei's blade flashed and hacked. Alice charged into the fray with savage glee, lips skinned back and saliva frothing her muzzle. Black cloth tore, as did flesh. Kasia spared a glance for the children, but they simply stood there, emotionless observers to the carnage.

At last the screams faded. Alexei stomped out the fire, grimacing at the putrid heaps that littered the corridor. Two had fallen to his blade, but within seconds they shrank to blackened husks. Kasia retrieved her card, happily intact. The Nine of Flames.

Alexei used a sleeve to scrub dark blood from his face. He was winded, but seemed unhurt.

"What the fog *were* they?" she demanded.

"I think the alchemists have been . . ." he paused for breath, "experimenting on themselves."

She muttered an oath. He smiled at her, though his face was grim.

"We make a good pair though, don't we?"

Somehow, despite the unending horror of it all, Kasia found an answering grin.

"Yes, Bryce," she agreed. "We do."

"The sword and the ley," he muttered, bracing a hand against the wall. "Saints, but it's easier not to wield them both alone. What about the children?"

She looked them over. They stared back with those eerie eyes. She was about to say *fine*, but thought better of it. "Are . . . the same."

He bent to pat Alice's head. "I think they did not expect me to have a Markhound."

Alice's broad head swung in Kasia's direction, quizzically following Alexei's gaze. Once, Kasia had disliked the dogs almost as much as their masters. The hound could barely sense her presence, she knew. It was bred to hunt Marks and she had none. But occasionally, as now, the hound seemed to notice her—and not know quite what to make of her.

"Don't be afraid," the boy said to Kasia. "She will not harm you."

Kasia frowned down at him. "How did you—"

"*Zey haff ze keys,*" a voice muffled called out in heavily accented Osterlish.

Alexei spun, blade up again in an instant. Kasia palmed another card. It was not the voice of a child, but a man. And oddly familiar. He signaled her to wait and moved down the tunnel. About halfway down, Alexei stopped.

"There's a door," he called back. Then, "Who's in there?"

"Jann Danziger," came the faint reply. "Who is out there?"

Kasia ushered the children past the ghastly corpses. Then she returned and, stifling her revulsion, poked through the remains until she found a heavy ring of keys. She wiped it clean on a scrap of black cloak and returned to Alexei. Jann must have heard the jingle of the keys, for he pounded on the door.

"If you let me out, I will help you. Please!"

Alexei frowned. "I don't like this," he whispered.

"Neither do I. He must have known."

"Where's Willem?" Alexei demanded.

"I will show you. I tried to help him escape and they caught me. Please!" His voice broke. "I know I am a wicked man. But I also know this place. I can guide you."

Alexei hesitated. Kasia, too, was torn by indecision. Who knew how deep this labyrinth went? Or how many more of the alchemists were here? Jann might answer both questions. And she had not forgotten her friends—a word that now firmly included Patryk Spassov. They were all in grave danger.

Alice bumped her leg, then jerked back in obvious surprise at the invisible obstacle in her path. Kasia regarded the Mark-hound. She'd never displayed a jot of fear toward the creature, but the boy had known. And even before Alexei identified himself as a priest, the child had called him a servant of the ley.

She turned to the boy. "Does he speak the truth?"

The mirror eye grew dim. "I hear him," the child replied after a moment. "He is both a wicked man and one who speaks truth."

*Saints and Martyrs!* I must guard my thoughts.

Kasia began trying the keys. Alexei rubbed a palm across his scalp, eyeing the children with new wariness. The fourth key shifted the tumblers. Kasia swung the heavy door wide.

Jann Danziger winced at the sudden torchlight. His silver mane was mussed and stubble covered his cheeks. "They took away my cane," he said weakly, leaning against the wall.

The boy brushed past. Her nose filled with the scent of primroses on a warm summer's evening. "Take my arm," he said in a kind voice.

Jann burst into tears at that, though Kasia had scant pity for him.

"A man was brought here," Alexei said coldly. "Where is he?"

Jann squinted like a badger dragged from its earthen den. "I know nothing of that. I have been locked up for hours. But most likely he would be with others. The cells are not far."

"What are these children's names?" Kasia asked.

Alexei answered. "Noach Beitz," he said heavily, glancing at the boy. "Eddi Haass. Ursula Fellbach. I saw sketches of them."

"How many more are here?"

"Five," Jann replied.

Alexei's eyes narrowed. "There were nine altogether."

The old man flinched under his stare. "The first was . . . not a success. We had to adjust the formulae."

Alexei looked ready to punch him.

"One escaped, didn't they?" Kasia asked.

Jann gave a reluctant nod. "Wandy Keller. He woke earlier than expected."

Her gut tightened. "What happened to him?"

"He was caught and brought back."

"By Jule?"

"The boy was not harmed," Jann said quickly. "He must be rubedo by now."

"Not harmed?" Alexei echoed in disbelief. "You're out of your fucking mind!"

"Is your wife part of it?" Kasia asked, already sure of the reply.

Jann gave another brief nod. "It was her botanical knowledge that guided us on this path."

"What of Tessaria and Natalya? What is planned for them?"

Jann hesitated. Alice gave a loud, vicious bark.

"A ship will take the children to Jalghuth," he stammered. "They mean to put you all on it."

"And what awaits them there?" Alexei growled.

Jann Danziger turned his face away. His throat clenched convulsively, as though some vile thing lodged inside him. A choked sound emerged that might have been sobs or laughter, she couldn't tell which. In the end, it was the boy who answered.

"The King," he replied, torchlight reflecting on a single basilisk eye. "The Red King Reborn."

---

*Who are you?*

The dreamer gazed out a large, square window, a game of chess in progress on a low table at his knees. Blurry, rain-soaked lawns stretched beyond. The white-haired man with the lion Mark sat across from him, staring intently at the board. Will understood that he was only a memory. The Martyr himself was somewhere else—too far for Will to hear.

The dreamer turned as Will approached. He wore a loose white tunic and pants. Bruises darkened his arms, and the pricks of needles.

*Who are you*? he repeated.

I am Will.

*Go away*. He looked down at the board, lips tight.

You must wake now, Will said.

*I cannot.*

Faint voices approached in the corridor. The pastel watercolors hanging on the walls faded and he glimpsed naked stone beneath. Smoking torches replaced the soft wall sconces. Then the dream-place solidified again. Grey carpets and doors with small windows set at eye level.

You must, Will said, more urgently. They're coming for you.

The Martyr captured a rook with his pawn. Will's grandmother had taught him to play. The dreamer would be checkmated in three moves.

*I'm safe here. Go away.*

The voices grew louder. Will could make them out now. They carried cruel implements of iron. Pincers and tongs. Elixirs to force the truth. But the dreamer could only speak in this place. He could not tell them what they wanted to know.

Others stood outside Will's cell. He heard the sharp click of a key in the lock.

Will swept the pieces from the board. The dreamer let out an animal howl as they rolled across the carpet. Will dropped to hands and knees, fingers closing around a black knight. He pressed it into the dreamer's left hand.

"Remember," he cried. "Wake and remember!"

Will's eyes flew open as the door crashed wide and rebounded against the wall. Masked Ones poured into his cell. He did not resist as they dragged him into the corridor.

Beyond the hood of a black cloak, Will saw other doors opening. His brothers and sisters. And, at the far end, a tall man with dark hair and a beard. Gloved hands gripped the dreamer's arms. One of the Masked Ones pressed a blade to his throat. Another grabbed his hair, lifting his chin.

*Help us!* Will sent.

Vivid blue eyes met his with a shock of recognition.

That's when the screaming began.

# Chapter Nineteen

Natalya trailed behind Hanne and Tessaria as they walked back from the pine nursery, following a winding path through the woods.

It had been a pretty spot. She thought she might try painting a landscape when they reached Nantwich. She would have sketched it if she'd had her charcoals, but all her supplies had been left behind in the flat. Years of saving every spare *fide* to buy the finest horsehair brushes and card stock, not to mention all her pencils, pastels, canvases and tools. It was worth a fogging fortune. Now she'd be starting from scratch again.

She rubbed her eyes in weariness. What had seemed a grand adventure at first was wearing thin. She'd barely slept and now they were leaving again. But even if she *could* go home, she would never abandon Kasia. In many ways, they were opposites. Kasia rarely went out while Natalya enjoyed a busy social life. But most of those relationships were shallow. Natalya despised other people's drama and tended to simply walk away when they irritated her. She'd never had her heart broken by anyone, not even close, and sometimes wondered if there was something wrong with her, something missing. Kasia warned her that it would happen someday, but Natalya wasn't so sure. She was passionate about her work—and her lovers, until she tired of them. It felt like enough. Romantic love was for people who couldn't stand to be alone with themselves.

But she did love Kasia. Oh, she could be a flake about the rent, and messy, but these were petty crimes. Kasia disliked drama, too, and although she could lie more convincingly than anyone Natalya had ever met, she never lied to her best friend. She was witty and smart, and tried so hard to do the right thing despite her disability. Sometimes Natalya would see her trying to work through some thorny ethical dilemma, dark brows drawn together in thought, spiked heel tapping the carpet.

Natalya found Kasia's lack of Marks fascinating. Part of her was oddly jealous. She knew it was heretical, but she didn't care for the way her own Mark—a golden-maned dragon on her left arm that wound from biceps to wrist—smothered her feelings. The Marks also enhanced her talent, so it was a tradeoff. Still, she hadn't been given a choice, had she? Anyone who passed the test had to take one. But Kasia was free of such constraints. She did as she pleased.

Though it hadn't worked out very well with the Reverend Mother.

Saints, what a mess *that* was!

*Well*, she thought, *we'll be safe in Nantwich. A fresh start.*

The Danziger house came into view, a dark-timbered bulk in the falling dusk, and as tired as she was, Natalya felt a surge of relief at leaving Kvengard behind. She did not want to spend another night under their roof. The nightmare had faded, but it left an oily residue behind. She pulled off a glove and wiped a sweaty palm on her pant leg, annoyed at herself for dredging it up, but the dream was already surfacing in disjointed fragments.

A man, old and infirm. His surprise and rage were palpable.

*Who are you? Why do you trespass here?*

He made her feel so small. So worthless. Like an insect to be crushed under his boot heel.

*Let me in.*

Chill fingers, prying at her mind.

*Let me in!*

A tear trickled down her cheek. She quickly wiped it away and donned a false smile as Hanne Danziger looked back.

"You must be starved!" she called. "Don't worry, we'll have a nice supper before the carriage comes." Hanne extended a plump arm and Natalya jogged to catch up.

She hated to appear weak, but she decided to confess everything to Kasia on the ship. Her friend was an expert on archetypes and symbolism. Maybe the dream signified a deep-seated fear of male authority figures. The only one with real power over her was Cardinal Falke—the Reverend Father, now—and Natalya had always admired him, so that didn't really make sense. Besides which, he'd helped them to get away. So who did it represent?

Her own father? He'd quarreled constantly with her mother, but they'd both been sweet to Natalya. And they'd mostly let her do whatever she wanted . . . .

She pushed the trail of thought aside and fell into step with them. "Sorry, I must have been wool-gathering."

"This visit has been far too brief!" A strong gloved hand closed around her own. "I'm sure I can coax Jann down to say goodbye. It's done him good to have you both here."

"I've hardly seen him," Tessaria pointed out dryly. "But I do hope he can join us."

It felt awkward, holding the woman's hand like a child. Natalya gave it a squeeze and pulled away. The lawns stretched out like an emerald carpet in the setting sun. She longed to kick her boots off and go barefoot. But then Tess would scowl at her and—

Hanne halted as they approached the front door. A

heavyset blond gardener was sweeping up broken glass in front of the conservatory patio.

"What happened?" she asked.

He responded in some rapid guttural language. Hanne's lips tightened. Something flashed across her face. Anger?

"A bird flew into the glass," she said. "I feared this would happen! Poor little creature. I told them to place adhesives on the windows, but they haven't gotten around to it yet."

"It must have been a large bird," Natalya murmured, eyeing the quantity of glass.

"What tongue was that?" Tess asked as they entered the house. "I speak fair Kven, but I didn't understand a word."

"A dialect of the hill country," Hanne replied. Her face looked flushed. "Let's share a glass of wine and then we'll wash up for dinner."

Before either woman could reply, Hanne steered them into an elegant drawing room. She went to a sideboard and unstoppered a crystal decanter.

Natalya perched on a long velvet sofa, while Tessaria chose a straight-backed Wolf-carved wooden chair that looked spectacularly uncomfortable. "Shall I fetch Kasia?"

"That's what servants are for, dear," Hanne replied absently, her back turned as she filled three glasses. "I'll send one up to her room."

She passed out the wine, then tugged on a bell pull. A uniformed maid appeared.

"Please inform Domina Novak that we're in the salon."

The girl curtsied and hurried from the room. Natalya sipped her wine. It was sweeter than the vintage from the previous night, but her taut nerves began to unwind.

"To the Reverend Father Dmitry," Hanne said, lifting her glass. "May his reign be long and peaceful."

They toasted and drank. Hanne glanced at a gilt clock. The hands stood at seven-thirty. "I wonder where Fra Spassov is. You must depart soon."

"I'm sure he'll turn up," Tessaria said sardonically. "He always does."

Hanne chuckled. "It was lucky for you, *ja*? To encounter a big, strong priest from the Interfectorem."

There was a fraught silence.

"What do you mean?" Tess's voice was careful.

Hanne shrugged. "Only that these are perilous times. Especially for women traveling alone."

Tessaria set her glass down. It was half empty. Natalya glanced at her own glass, clutched in her lap. The ruby-red liquid was nearly sloshing over the edge. She clumsily righted the stem, fingers tingling with odd pins and needles.

Tess scowled. "What do you know, Hanne?"

"Only that you lied to me, old friend." The Danziger woman's blue eyes no longer looked grandmotherly. "You are running. Luckily for all, you ran to the right place."

Tessaria rose. "Where's Kasia?"

Hanne took a sip of wine, then laid her glass on the windowsill.

Natalya groped for Tess's throwing knife. It was small, about the length from her wrist to the tip of her middle finger. She'd tucked it into her belt after pulling it out of the tree, thinking she might practice some more, and Tess had never asked for it back.

"*Where is my ward*?" Tessaria growled. She took a step and stumbled, bracing herself on the back of the chair.

Hanne Danziger studied her speculatively. "I wondered if you might be turned. Back in Bal Agnar, I mean. Jann and I argued about it. I thought you had the ambition to join us. The *fire* to be someone extraordinary, to stand apart from the herd. But he said you were a true believer in the Via Sancta. That you would die first."

Tessaria grimaced. She suddenly looked every one of her seventy-six years. "Shit," she slurred.

Through the fog of whatever Hanne had put in their wine,

Natalya blinked in surprise. She'd never heard Tessaria swear once in ten years.

"Your ward has been causing some trouble, but Jule will settle her down."

The door opened and the blond gardener entered. He walked over to Natalya and eased Tess's knife from her limp hand.

# Chapter Twenty

*The Red King Reborn.*

Alexei grabbed Jann Danziger by the collar. A low, warning rumble came from the Markhound and the boy laid a soothing palm on her head.

"Who rules Jalghuth?" Alexei demanded. "I know it isn't Lezarius!"

Jann Danziger swayed limply as Alexei gave him a shake.

"He speaks of Balaur," Kasia said. "It's the only thing that makes sense."

"It makes *no* sense," Alexei grated, clinging to a last shred of denial. "That monster has been dead for thirty years!"

"I thought so, too," Jann gasped. "But he lives. He came to me in dreams."

A shiver danced across her skin. "You put a stone in my mattress. What was it?"

"Chorazite. It . . . makes a doorway."

"You *bastard*. Natalya slept there, too!" She itched to slap him, but the boy was gazing at her reproachfully as if he knew what she was thinking.

Not as if, she reminded herself. He did know.

Alexei turned to her, skin waxy and pale as curd. "Did you dream of him, Kasia?"

"Yes, I think so. It's all a haze. There was a room. Somewhere high up, I think. I saw snow through the windows." She drew a breath. "And . . . a man, asking me questions."

Rage darkened his features. He slammed Jann against the wall. "What have you done?" Alexei's Marks flared, with little discernible effect. "You let the Beast of Bal Agnar into her head? I should kill you where you stand—"

Kasia touched his sword arm. "Not yet," she said. "He will tell all he knows first."

"Yes!" Jann squeaked. "I will tell you everything!"

Alexei released him and stepped back, his face icily calm now. "Is the connection permanent?"

"I don't know! I swear it!" He licked chapped lips. "We who have long served him require no such aid. He comes to us whenever he chooses. But . . . I imagine the lady was unwilling. Without the stone, he may have trouble finding her."

"But he could?" Alexei persisted.

"I . . . I am not sure. The lithomancy was Hanne's idea."

"I'll find out soon enough," Kasia said grimly. "Now, the children. What have you done to them? Speak quickly!"

"It is called the Magnum Opus," he stammered. "The Great Work. A passage from death to new life. The first stage is the nigredo. The blackening. It speaks with the voice of the raven. The soul is captured at the moment of death and . . . distilled. The process takes—"

"Thrice forty nights," Alexei interrupted softly.

Jann's silver-maned head bobbed assent. "If they emerge from the long dark, they are albedo. All aspects of the soul unified in harmony."

"Like them," Kasia said, glancing at the ghostly pale trio who listened in silence.

"Yes." Jann frowned. "Though they are weeks early to awaken. How could it be?"

"Never mind," she snapped. "What happens next?"

"The final stage is the rubedo. The redness. Only then will their bodies return to true life."

"How is it done?"

"With blood." A flutter of his fingers. "And other ingredients."

"But what's the point?" Alexei exploded. "Why kill them only to bring them back?"

Jann stared at him with a hint of condescension. "You misunderstand, priest. It is not simply life but *eternal* life. Once the rubedo is achieved, they cannot die again. In theory, at least. We have not tried to test it yet." He gazed at the children in awe. "Do you smell the sweetness? They are purified! The shadow is gone as a separate entity, fully absorbed into the psyche."

"You unholy scum. . . ." Alexei trailed off, jaw tight. "How did you kill them?"

"In the sea," one of the girls said calmly. "They died in the sea."

*Drowned.* It was the reason their small bodies bore no marks of violence.

Kasia crouched down and drew the child to her breast, stroking the silky blond hair. "I'm sorry," she whispered.

*You did not do it. And we are not them. We are the Reborn.*

The sending came in a flash. Kasia blinked in astonishment.

*Does Jann know you can talk this way?*

*He does not know. He is an evil man. The priest is a good man.*

*And what am I?*

There was a long pause. Kasia's own face reflected back in the mirrored eye.

*You are both. And neither.*

She heard Alexei ordering Jann Danziger to guide them to the cells, but it was a minute before her knees were willing to lift her up again.

They took the corridor to the end, then climbed another flight of stairs, Noach Beitz supporting his tormentor. The boy seemed to hold no grudge for what had been done to him.

*We are not them.*

What, she wondered, had the Order of the Black Sun created?

This thought was immediately followed by the thought that she shouldn't think anything at all because they could read her mind—which is a thing easier said than done. She finally started humming a pop song, gaze fixed on the back of Alexei's shorn head.

Other passages crossed at intervals, and other stairways. Alice padded ahead, though she returned every now and then to nose protectively at the children and snarl at Jann.

"Did you build this place?" Kasia asked him.

"It was already here, though in disrepair. It belonged to a cult of ancient alchemists. A very, very long time ago. They were persecuted by the Church and forced to carry out their experiments in secret."

"Rightfully so," Alexei remarked hotly over his shoulder.

"I thought I would be giving Willem a gift," Jann murmured. "Never to grow old. Never to suffer."

Kasia snorted.

"But then I had . . . second thoughts. I did not want to hand him over to the mas—to Balaur. I thought I could spirit him away."

"You brought Willem the dog, didn't you?" Alexei said. "The one from the portrait?"

"I thought it might cheer him up," Jann replied wretchedly.

"*Futuere!*" Alexei muttered.

Kasia didn't know what the word meant, but it was clearly a vile oath in the Old Tongue. Jann Danziger lapsed into sullen silence.

They found the first bodies not long after. Two men and a

woman, the masks torn from their faces. Kasia quickly led the children past, skirting the pools of blood. Jann seemed surprised but not especially sorry to find his co-conspirators dead.

"Are there more of you here?" he asked.

Alexei ignored the question, though he looked troubled. "How much farther?"

"Just there." Jann pointed at a crossing corridor. They warily approached a row of thick wooden doors, all standing open. The rhythmic pulse of the sea came through small barred windows set high in the brick walls. Every room was empty save for the last. Kasia heard a tiny muffled sound. She crouched down and peered under the bed.

"I found one!" Kasia called. Alexei hurried to kneel beside her.

"Sofie Arneth," Jann said from the doorway. "The nigredo was to commence at midnight."

Alexei glanced back. "So she is . . . ?"

"Alive and untouched, yes."

"Thank the Saints," he muttered.

The child eyed them in mute fear. Kasia held out a hand. "Come," she said with a smile. "I won't harm you."

Sofie inched backwards, a wild creature caught in a hunter's snare.

"She probably understands only Kven," Kasia muttered.

"I've picked up some." Alexei spoke a few halting words. The girl started to cry.

A sudden waft of dew-damp flowers and Noach Beitz was kneeling before the bed. Kasia thought his fey appearance would terrify the girl, but the moment she saw him, she relaxed and crawled out. A wee, scrawny thing with tangled black hair. Like the others, she wore a pretty silk dress with a sash around the waist, though it was filthy with dust and cobwebs.

"The dreamer has woken," Noach said. "He is with our brothers and sisters."

"Where?" Alexei demanded.

Noach glanced up at the low ceiling. "They are leaving. We must join them."

"What's the closest way out of this place?" Alexei asked Jann, hoisting Sofie Arneth to his hip. The child wrapped her arms around his neck, pressing her cheek to Alexei's cassock.

"There's a stairway," Jann replied. "But who is this dreamer?"

"My brother." Alexei's eyes glinted with excitement. "Now, show us the way up."

Kasia had moved to keep a watch on the corridor. For all his bloody handiwork, Mikhail Bryce might have missed a few of the alchemists. She stiffened as a black-robed figure strode around the corner. The white mask dangled from one finger. A handsome face, capped with thick, wavy blond hair.

They noticed each other at the same instant. Jule Danziger froze in mid-step, a slow smile curling his lips. Then Alexei came up beside her. Sofie Arneth saw the black cloak and let out a piercing scream. Jule's eyes flicked to the blade in Alexei's hand. He turned and ran back down the corridor.

"He means to kill them," Noach said. The boy's expression was burdened with a terrible sadness. "The Red King never wanted the others, only you."

"Kill who?" Alexei asked.

"The ones she loves."

Kasia rounded on Jann. "You bastard!"

"I didn't know!" he cried. "I didn't know!"

Alexei stared at her, the child sobbing in his arms. "Kasia, wait—"

She shook her head. "I can't. I'll find you!"

His shouts chased her into darkness.

# Chapter Twenty-One

Alexei unleashed a last furious oath as he watched Kasia vanish around a corner.

"Who was that?" he demanded.

"My nephew," Jann admitted. "He's the one who caught me. Jule is Hanne's creature entirely."

Alexei ignored the man's attempts to distance himself from what they'd done. Everything was his wife's idea, but Alexei wasn't buying it. Who knew why the others had locked him up? Alexei resolved to watch him closely.

"Where's he going?" He touched the tip of the sword to Jann's throat. "Speak truth! Are the women captives here?"

Jann's eyes slid to Noach Beitz. "Hanne wouldn't bother moving them so far from the house. She plans to take them to the ship in a carriage."

"So they're back at the house?"

Jann nodded. Alexei blew out a frustrated breath.

Kasia can use the ley, he reminded himself. And one of them had to stay with the children. "Move," he snapped. "Lead us out of here."

"Yes, of course," Jann said, a tremor in his voice. "I promise you, Father, I would have told you if I'd known—"

"Shut up!"

Jann ducked his head, hobbling to the stairwell on Noach's arm. Up and up they climbed, Alexei's breath coming in harsh pants. The child had been light as a bit of dandelion fluff when he first picked her up, but now his arm trembled. He considered putting her down, but she clung to him like a barnacle and he couldn't bring himself to do it.

I saved one at least, he thought angrily. *Only one!*

Jann fell behind, but Alexei didn't stop to wait. Chance had brought his brother here and he wouldn't lose him again. The boy said the dreamer had woken. Could he mean that Mikhail would be able to speak again? The prospect kindled a spark of hope. Even if he was still mad, Alexei longed to hear his voice. Four long years Misha had stayed silent, trapped inside some never-ending nightmare. If it was so, Alexei would give up his quest to find Malach. Part of him knew it was pointless. The mage would never help—even if he could.

He paused on a landing and leaned back against the wall, chest heaving. Sofie touched the Raven Mark on his neck, fingers light as a dragonfly. She gazed at him solemnly. "*Rabe*," she whispered, then pressed her face to his shoulder again.

And what of Kasia? The faction in Kvengard might be broken, but others in the Order would be hunting her. They knew about her ability and sought to use her.

*Balaur is alive.*

Alexei quelled the thought. There would be time later to decide on a course of action. He adjusted the child on his hip and started climbing again.

At last, he staggered into the tumbled-down shepherd's hut. Alexei ducked beneath the low stone lintel, drawing fresh air into his burning lungs. Stars blanketed the sky above. His horse was still grazing on the hill. Wind sighed across the moor. Waves thundered at the foot of the cliff. A knot in his chest loosened at being free of the alchemists' fetid lair.

He eased Sofie Arneth to the ground. The child clung to

his waist with surprising strength. Alexei propped the sword against the stone doorway. He couldn't remember the Kven word for *wait*, so he tried the Old Tongue command.

"*Mane*," he said, gesturing with a palm that she should stay. Sofie gave a brief, reluctant nod. Alice's ears swiveled at the command. She tipped her head to the sky and howled. A tall figure stood at the edge of the cliff, silhouetted in the moonlight. The hound darted forward, snapping her jaws. She could smell the inverted Mark.

"*Cessa!*" Alexei shouted desperately. Stop!

The barking grew louder.

"*Veni!*" He slapped his thigh. "*Veni nunc!*" Come now!

The Markhound shot him a confused look but trotted back and sat down at his feet. He ordered her to stay and guard the child. Alexei crossed the rocky ground, heart drumming. Mikhail wore one of the long black robes, the hood thrown back. For a horrible moment, he wondered if his brother was one of them.

"Misha?" he said cautiously.

Blue eyes regarded him. No longer empty but burning with ferocity.

Three children stood behind him. Two were ruddy-cheeked and full of vitality. The last radiated ethereal white light. *Like a Ward*, Alexei thought in wonderment.

"Do you remember me?" he asked softly.

The moment stretched out, drawing his hopes tight as a tripwire.

"Brother," the pale child said with a smile.

Alexei's cheeks were damp as he ran forward and pulled Misha into an embrace. How thin he felt! All sinew and bone. Yet there was none of the sickness, the wasted frailty, of the Institute. Powerful hands gripped Alexei's arms and gently separated them. A beard covered Mikhail's cheeks. His dark hair had grown long, curling over the tips of his ears.

"Come with us," the child said.

Alexei turned. The boy's eyelashes were the frosty white of winter, his lips bloodless. One eye was dark as the sea beyond, the other a silvery mirror. Yet Alexei knew him from the portrait.

"Willem Danziger," he said. "You speak for my brother?"

A silent look passed between Willem and Mikhail. The boy nodded. A wave of unreality washed over Alexei, but he'd seen too many strange and terrible things to doubt it.

He eyed the black robe. "And my brother . . . saved you?"

"He was naked when they brought him here," the boy replied to Alexei's unasked question. "Come with us."

"Where?"

The boy's gaze moved west, where the lights of the ship bobbed at anchor. "To Jalghuth."

Alexei frowned. "What? No!"

Will's voice changed. Grew deeper. "They are the ones I have sought. The Saint's army."

Alexei took a step back. "They're *children*. Not soldiers! You can't just take them away. Are you—" *Mad?* He bit off the word.

"We are the Reborn."

"I don't care what you call yourselves!" he exclaimed. "You will not be given to Balaur!"

"What is happening?" Jann Danziger hobbled over with the other three children.

Alexei fumbled in his pocket. He thrust the corax toward Misha. "You were a knight! Sworn to protect the innocent! Please, you must see—"

Mikhail's face hardened. He snatched the coin and hurled it over the edge of the cliff. As it vanished into the foaming waves, a piece of Alexei died. Four long years he'd kept Mikhail's corax, imagining the day his brother would be whole again. But this . . . He was *worse.* Truly, unredeemably insane.

Hope turned to ashes. Then to a hot, acid surge of rage.

"If you will not come with us," Willem said, "then stand aside."

"No!" Alexei squared his shoulders. "You're not taking them."

The children watched, expressionless.

"Who would you give them to, Alyosha?" Willem asked. "They have no one left. Nothing but the purpose for which the ley made them. The Saint bade me to raise an army and march on Jalghuth."

"And where is your saint now?" Alexei asked bitterly.

His brother's face twisted in anguish. "Taken by nihilim in the Morho," Willem said.

The news dealt another hard blow. "Then we must rescue him. But this is evil! You'd be making a terrible mistake!"

"It is too late. I must carry out his will."

"Lezarius is insane!" Alexei cried in exasperation. "And he never meant—"

The fist caught him square in the jaw. He stumbled back, tasting blood.

"Don't make me hurt you, brother," Willem said, his voice low and intense.

With a wordless roar, Alexei hurled himself at Misha. They tumbled into the sparse grasses at the edge of the cliff. From the corner of his eye, Alexei saw a steep path twisting down. Mikhail drove an elbow into his ribs. The Markhound was a nipping, lunging shadow as Alexei rolled away, gasping. Mikhail stood and Alexei grabbed his bare foot, giving a vicious twist. Mikhail toppled again.

The children began to climb single-file down the path. Alexei caught a glimpse of Jann Danziger's pale face, following, and then his brother was astride him, fists swinging. Alexei felt like an anvil hammered by some monstrous smith. His head throbbed with a high-pitched whine. He tried to call Alice, but the words were silenced by another mighty blow. Alexei threw an arm up to shield himself. With his other hand, he drew ley through the earth. It fought him, wild and uncontrollable. A whirlpool of red chaos yawned open beneath him. The primal lizard at the core of his mind opened slitted eyes.

*No!*

Alexei tore his palm from the earth, wracked by a convulsive shudder. Then the crushing weight was gone. Through one slitted eye, he saw Willem Danziger crouching over him. A pale hand touched his brow.

"You are both good men." The voice was Willem's own, a boy on the cusp of manhood but heavy with sorrow beyond his years. "Be well, Father Bryce."

Then he was gone. Alexei turned his head and spat blood. Alice squatted not far off, shivering violently. She gave a pitiful whine, then bounded over and licked his face. The boy did something to her. She would have died to protect him. *And Misha . . . would he have killed me?*

He had no honest answer to that. It chilled him to the bone.

Alexei gingerly prodded his nose. It felt broken, but he still had all his teeth. Misha's knuckles must be a bloody mess.

They'd fought before, many times. But never like this.

He'd barely landed a single punch—and not for lack of trying.

Alexei crawled to the edge of the cliff, fingers gripping the clumps of grass. The group had made it to the bottom. A longboat waited in a narrow inlet where the swell was calmer. He watched in despair as an oarsman rowed them out to the ship. Straight into the lion's jaws.

*No*, he amended with a caustic laugh that made his ribs ache. *Not the Lion.*

*The Red King.*

Small hands helped him to his feet. Sofie Arneth reached up and gave him a pat on the shoulder, her eyes tight but resolute. A brave child not to run when she had the chance. She tugged at his hand, unbalancing him. His head spun.

"Yes," he muttered. "I will take you away. Just give me a moment."

She pulled his hand again, more urgently. Then he heard it.

The staccato thunder of hooves.

---

A SWIRL of black cloak vanished into a side tunnel. By the time Kasia reached it, Jule Danziger had vanished.

She drew a card, catching her breath. The Jack of Wolves—no surprise there. The image shone with blue leylight, giving the single eye an even more sinister aspect.

Fresh bootprints in the dust.

Kasia held the card before her, illuminating a faint space, and plunged into the darkness. The prints moved in a straight line, visible more strongly in the toe and spaced far apart.

Jule Danziger was running.

Fantasies of what she would do to him when she found him spun through her head.

Kasia could never bear children of her own. At her last examination, the doctor had told her she was barren. Something called uterine fibroids. They were benign, but prevented her from ever becoming pregnant. The woman obviously expected her to be devastated, but Kasia had secretly felt relief. She didn't want to be a mother. Sorting out her own problems was hard enough.

Yet seeing what had been done to those children enraged her beyond all measure.

Brutally murdered and brought back to serve as deathless slaves to a Nightmage—and not just any mage. The worst of them ever to walk the earth.

Why, she wondered, can't people just leave each other alone?

Why must they eternally grasp for more, more, more?

If she had a motto, it would be *mind your own fogging business*.

Natalya and Tess must still be alive. Spassov, too. The boy, Noach, said Jule planned to kill them, not that he'd done it. Her teeth flashed in the dark.

Jule Danziger was in for a surprise.

The footprints took other turnings, then entered a long tunnel. This one had torches spaced at intervals along the walls. She ran faster, confident now that he couldn't lie in wait and ambush her.

The footprints slowed and grew closer together. Then, inexplicably, she found his boots. Kasia drew up short. New prints led away around a curve in the tunnel. She bent to examine them.

"Fog me," she muttered.

Distinct pads with elongated toes and a faint detached line at the end. It took her a moment to realize what they signified.

Claws.

Kasia's skin tingled. "Oh, you bastard."

She ran. The tunnel went on and on. A kilometer at least. They must be far from the laboratory by now. At last it dead-ended at a locked door. Kasia pressed her ear to the wood. Muffled voices came from the other side.

She drew a card, pulling on the liminal violet ley. The voices sharpened.

". . . this happen? A disaster! You utter fool!"

"We can make more. I know the formulae." Jule's voice, though it sounded strange.

"And what of the cartomancer?"

"There were too many of them to take her. The priest had a sword. It was a massacre."

"Jann will pay for his treachery." A note of hysteria. "All of them will! Where are the Reborn now?"

"I don't know."

"*You don't know?!*"

"They can't have gone far. But we must kill these three quickly and dispose of the bodies. No one knows they were ever here. Then I'll find the Novak woman. She'll tell us where the Reborn went. We can still salvage—"

Kasia stood back, anger boiling over.

*Open for me*, she commanded. *Open for the High Priestess!*

The card glimmered brightly for an instant. Then it flickered and died. She gritted her teeth, bending the ley to her will, but it was as if a sheen of frozen oil floated on top. Black tendrils snaked outward. She stared at her hand in queasy fascination as the veins darkened. Saints, it was running through her! Kasia tried to jerk away. The poisonous coils tightened, winding up her arm. Her pulse fluttered weakly.

She felt her very essence withering. Oh, the pain! It was death-ley, she understood that now, some taint cloaking the Danzigers like a protective shroud. In desperation, she pushed back, her mind battering against the icy black walls. She heard the dry croak of the raven. The rattle of leafless limbs in a shadowed wood. Dissolution and decay.

And the faint echo of a man's laughter.

*He is the devouring black fire.*

*One must be at home in the darkness of suffering, Kasia.*

Breath plumed white in the tunnel as she drew deeper of that chill power, and deeper still.

*I am stronger than you*, she thought furiously. *I am stronger—*

A blinding flash and the barrier burst like a lanced wound. Abyssal ley the color of fresh blood gushed forth. It swept her up in a river. Life pulsed through her veins, raw and hot and screaming like a newborn.

The heavy wood cracked, falling under the onslaught of crimson light.

Kasia stepped into the room beyond.

Hanne Danziger held one of Tess's knives. A scaled thing with folded leathery wings stood erect at her side. Death-ley pooled around them, but Kasia had no fear of it now. With a contemptuous flick, she tossed the card at their feet. The dark ley hissed and jumped like oil on a hot pan. Jule gave an incoherent screech as the red abyss touched him.

Patches of blond hair still clung to a grayish scalp. The deep-set blue eyes were the same, but his face was more skull than living man. A nub of cartilage served as a nose and a wide fleshless gash for a mouth. He turned to his cowering aunt. Long talons flashed, disemboweling her in a single sweep. A second slash and she collapsed, throat gaping from ear to ear.

"Now *you*," Kasia spat, trembling with righteous rage.

Jule plunged the talons deep into his own chest. He sank to his knees, eyes blinking rapidly.

She picked up the knife and ran across the drawing room. Tessaria kept her blades razor-sharp. A few quick jerks through the ropes and she was free. Tess stared glassily as Kasia sawed through Natalya's bonds. Her friend slumped like an unstrung puppet when Kasia let go.

"Wake up!" she cried, slapping Natalya's face. Brown eyes blinked.

"Kiska?" she slurred.

Kasia glanced over her shoulder. Jule Danziger lay face-down in a spreading pool of blood.

She hurried to Patryk Spassov, who lay tied up next to the window. One eye was swollen shut, but the other was open and he looked more alert than the others.

"Hang on," she muttered, slicing through the ropes around his feet.

"The wine," he gasped. "Hanne drugged them."

"Fog it! We have to get out of here." She moved to his wrists even as a small voice warned her that something was wrong. *Something…*

Kasia paused. The putrefaction. Why had Jule not decayed like the others?

She spun to find him crouching. Tessaria faced him with

another knife. Kasia fumbled for the deck in her pocket as Jule sprang, one wing enfolding Tessaria in a foul embrace. Red ley pulsed around them. Kasia realized that she had no clue how to rein it back in. A sickening crunch as he flung Tessaria away like a broken doll.

Jule Danziger rounded on her with maddened eyes.

Dying, yes. But not quite yet.

She glanced down at the card in her shaking hand.

The Wheel, Inverted this time.

Round and round it goes, she thought as he came for her.

And where it will stop . . . .

# Chapter Twenty-Two

Horses pounded down the opposite slope. Torches bobbed in the darkness.

Alexei counted seven riders.

He watched them come with bone-deep weariness. He could hardly breathe through his nose, which was still bleeding. His whole face throbbed. Alexei doubted he'd offer much of a fight, but Sofie's frightened whimper spurred him into motion. He took her hand and limped back to the shepherd's hut. The sword was where he'd left it, leaning against the doorway. He pushed her inside and raised the blade as the lead rider appeared, dark cloak trailing out behind.

An instant later, three Markhounds crested the hill. Alice sprang to meet them. She was larger than the newcomers, but his gut tightened as they ringed her in a circle, barking ferociously.

"*Platz!*" a woman's voice snapped.

The hounds peeled away and returned to the riders. Alice stood her ground, growling low in her throat. The torch of the first rider grew closer. It glinted on short golden hair.

"Bryce!" Bishop Morvana Ziegler reined up. Her gaze

swept across Sofie Arneth, who peeked around the edge of the doorway. "You found them. Are the rest inside?"

A wave of relief washed over him. Not cloaks. Cassocks.

"A ship took them away, Your Grace. I couldn't stop it."

It came out muffled, like he had a bad head cold.

"A ship?"

He pointed and she galloped to the edge of the cliff. After a long moment, she returned.

"I see nothing, Bryce."

"They must have doused the running lights."

"How did you find them?" Morvana demanded.

"How did *you* find *me*?" he retorted with sudden suspicion.

"When you vanished without a word, I gave the dogs your scent." She studied his battered face. "What happened here?"

Alexei lowered his sword. "It was the parents."

Blond brows drew together. "Which? The Danzigers?"

He stared at her. "All of them. Every single one."

Morvana shook her head. "That's not possible," she said. "We interviewed them ourselves. The stories checked out—"

"They had to report the children missing, but every other word they told us about the disappearances was a lie designed to sow confusion." Alexei paused, gauging her reaction. "I was right about the alchemy. They're members of the Order of the Black Sun."

Something flickered in her gaze. Morvana dismounted. She lowered her voice, glancing at the other riders. "That is quite an accusation, Bryce."

He pointed at the hut. "Follow those stairs. You'll find a laboratory. They were . . . conducting experiments."

Her gaze sharpened. "What sort of experiments?"

"They call it the Magnum Opus. A passage from death to rebirth." He glanced at Sofie. "She's not hurt. Not physically, at least. But the others . . . I'm not sure what they are now."

Morvana regarded him without expression. Then she turned to her companions and gestured at the hut. The men dismounted. They *were* priests. He could see the Wolf Marks on their necks, just below the left ear. Yet Alexei trusted no one anymore. His grip on the sword tightened as they brushed past him. He watched their torches vanish down the winding stairs.

Morvana was speaking to Sofie in Kven, a torrent of words too rapid for him to make out. At first the girl refused to answer. Morvana pressed her. Sofie broke into a sob and whispered a few halting phrases.

The bishop's face darkened. "She confirms some of what you claim. I will take her back to the Arx and give her to the vestals. The Reverend Father will want to speak with her when she is able."

Another exchange. The girl vehemently shook her head. She gripped Alexei's hand, gazing up at him in desperation.

*I killed her mother*, he thought. *She's an orphan now. What will become of her? But I can't take her with me.*

He crouched down and looked Sofie in the eye. "It's all right," he whispered, forcing a smile.

She cast him a look of betrayal that cut to the quick.

"I can't. . . ." Alexei hardened his voice. "You must go with Bishop Zeigler now."

She might not have understood his words, but she grasped the tone. Her lips thinned. She angrily dropped his hand and walked to Morvana's side, the wind lifting her long black hair.

"How exactly did you find this place?" the bishop asked him. "And why did you come alone? You could have been killed!" Her gaze turned to the sea. "As it was, you apparently lost the rest."

"The Markhound followed the smell from the chapel. I wasn't sure what I would find," he replied vaguely, holding up a hand to forestall further questions. "The parents may not all be dead, but they do bear an identical Mark. Nested geometrical figures. You'll arrest them?"

There was a long beat before Morvana replied. "And where will you be, Bryce?"

Inspiration struck. "Some of them got away. They ran into the woods."

She glared at him. "Why didn't you say so? We must get reinforcements and sweep the area."

Alexei whistled for his horse. "There's no time. I'll start the search."

"Wait! What of this ship? Who does it belong to?"

"The Danzigers." His horse trotted up and Alexei seized the reins. To his relief, the saddlebag with the stolen book was intact. "The grandfather is aboard."

She looked skeptical. "He did that to you?"

"He had others."

"Who?"

"They were masked. I never saw their faces."

Morvana scowled deeply. "You will give me a full report later!"

"Of course." He mounted with a grimace. Everything hurt. "But Your Grace should see the laboratory for herself first. It corroborates all I've told you."

"What about the automobile?" She stabbed a finger at Oto Valek's sporty yellow Legende. "Who owns *that*?"

He thought of her fussy secretary's favorite phrase.

"I've no idea!" Alexei wheeled the horse around and galloped off down the road, Alice a shadowy streak at his side.

---

BLACK ICHOR STAINED his mouth as he moved to block the door to the secret tunnel. It was cunningly hidden in the wooden paneling next to the hearth. The Danzigers' private passage to their vile laboratory.

"*You little bitch*," Jule spat. The bony membranes on his back trembled. "The Black Sun cannot die. It rises again in all its glory, brighter than ever before! You are nothing to its radiance! He will bend you until you break, then mold you in his image—"

Something flashed past Kasia's ear. The hilt of a knife jutted from his throat. Clawed hands scrabbled at the blade. Blue eyes dimmed. This time, the decay was shockingly swift. Within seconds, Jule Danziger dissolved into a putrid heap. And with that, the abyssal ley sank back into the earth, its purpose expended.

Kasia turned to see Natalya swaying on her feet.

"I hit the fucker," she muttered in disbelief, then fell over, landing in Patryk Spassov's broad arms.

Under other circumstances, Kasia would have laughed. The swoon was executed so perfectly Nashka might have planned it. But her friend was not the swooning type. And Kasia's only thought was for Tessaria Foy.

She rushed over and knelt down. When she saw the wounds, her chest went cold.

"Darling." Tessaria looked up at her. "Did they hurt you?"

"I'm fine." Kasia bit back her tears. Tess wouldn't welcome them. "I'm so sorry."

"Don't be." The words were slurred.

From the wine, Kasia told herself, though she knew better. *Just the wine.*

"You did . . . what you had . . . to do."

"But—"

"Quiet!" The old snap of authority silenced her protestations. "Listen to me . . . closely now. You must go . . . to Nantwich." Tess paused, gasping for air. A pinkish bubble burst on her lips. Kasia gripped her hand. "Clavis . . . she holds the keys."

"What keys?"

Tessaria's eyes slid shut. She was silent for so long that Kasia feared the worst. But then she seemed to rally. "To . . . all your questions. She *knows*."

"Knows what, auntie? Just tell me!"

"Not here." A faint smile. "I love you, girl. Remember . . . you . . . can choose." Her hand tightened. "No one can take that from you!"

The tears spilled free then. "I don't understand. Please, don't leave me."

"Promise you will go to Nantwich!" Sudden strength seemed to fill her. Kasia's hand hurt from the iron grip, but she didn't pull away.

"I promise," she whispered.

Tessaria's gaze moved beyond her shoulder. The smile widened, strangely knowing.

"Ah, the priest is here. He will see you there safely."

She turned, expecting Spassov, but it was Alexei who stood over her. His nose was a crooked mess, his face solemn and full of helpless pity.

When she looked back, Tessaria Foy was gone. Kasia knew it instantly.

The proud, high-cheeked face was set in fixed lines. Never to laugh or scold again. Her dark eyes were slightly open, staring at something distant and unreachable. Yet there was a measure of peace in her features—even satisfaction—as if she had won some small victory at the end.

Kasia sat in numb silence, still holding Tess's hand. It seemed impossible. Just a few hours ago, she'd been full of life. Tessaria should have had years yet. She might be approaching eighty, but there was nothing old or frail about her. She was supposed to be indestructible.

The Order had taken Kasia's home and livelihood. Those, she could live without. But to lose the only true mother she'd ever known . . . .

"I'll kill them," she said at last, her voice a monotone. "Every last one. Until I get to Balaur. Him . . . ." Her jaw clenched. "Him I will make suffer as he has never suffered before."

Alexei's hand fell on her shoulder. "We must leave," he said gently.

Kasia heard Natalya's quiet weeping. The murmur of voices as Patryk and Alexei spoke. But these things were distant. Not even the stench of Jule's body made her want to abandon her solitary vigil.

Tessaria had taken her in when her own family renounced her. She could be harsh, but she'd raised Kasia to never fear the judgment of others. To be her own person. A bitter smile twisted Kasia's mouth. Even in death the woman hoarded her secrets! Well, she'd promised to go to Clavis and there was no backing out now.

But she meant every word she'd said. If the Reverend Mother would not give her revenge, she'd take it herself.

She rose and gathered Tess's knives. The cloth she kept them wrapped in was on a side table. Hanne must have taken it when she searched the women. It held six sleeves, each for blades of different sizes. Kasia rolled up the bundle and pressed it into Natalya's hands, her eyes dry now.

"She would want you to have them," Kasia said.

Natalya gave her a tight nod. "I'm sorry, I . . . ." She clamped a hand over her mouth and ran to the window, throwing it wide just in time to vomit noisily in the bushes. When the retching subsided, she scrubbed a hand across her mouth. "Gah, this is worse than a brandy hangover. My brain is splitting."

Alexei sniffed a jug on the sideboard. "It smells like water."

Natalya nodded weakly. "Please."

He poured a cup and brought it over. Natalya drank it down, then refilled it and drank that, too. "Thank you."

He nodded. "Can you walk?"

"Yes, I'm better now." She shut the window with a grimace. "Where are the servants? They're part of it, too."

"I saw no one when I rode up," Alexei said. "They must have fled."

Kasia picked up The Wheel. It just a card now. Just a piece of waxed cardboard. She tore it in half and threw the pieces into the cold hearth. *I will make my own fate from now on*, she vowed. *This deck is cursed.*

On sudden impulse, she returned to Tess's body and felt in a pocket of her jacket. The letter from Falke was there, giving the bearer safe passage. After a moment's reflection, Kasia took it. Tess would want her to. If it was found on her body, the Reverend Father would be implicated in this whole mess. But the letter was not what she sought. Kasia tried the other pocket. Her fingers closed around a slim metal tube.

"I knew you'd have it," she said, smiling. "You always did."

She twisted the tube. Bright red lipstick. The color was banned, but Tess had a source. Her one small act of heresy. There was a mirror above the fireplace mantel. A pale face stared back, the eyes dark hollows. Kasia pressed the tube to her mouth, carefully applying it.

"That's better," she murmured.

Spassov's reflection swam in the glass beside her. His expression held a new wariness—and not just because she was wearing a dead woman's makeup. He knew what she'd done.

"I'm sorry," he said gravely. "They jumped me in the entry hall. Someone bashed me in the head. I tried to fight them—"

"I can see that," she replied, pocketing the lipstick. "This is no fault of yours."

He glanced at Tessaria, then quickly away. "It is a great loss for the Curia. Her wisdom and courage will be sorely missed."

Alexei knelt next to the body. His eyes were shut, swollen lips moving as he quietly recited the benediction for the dead. They all gathered around, the names of the saints and martyrs filling the silence. Most of it was in the Old Tongue, which Kasia knew little of, but the words soothed her. When it was done, he passed a hand across Tessaria's eyes, sealing them forever.

"Be free, Sor Foy," he said, rising wearily to his feet.

Kasia studied his face. It looked worse than Spassov's. "Who—"

"Later," he said. "I'll tell you everything later, but there's no time. The Polizei will be here any minute. They're already at the lab. If they find us, we'll never get out of the Arx."

"We need horses," Patryk said. "And food."

"There are mounts in the stables," Natalya put in. "It's not far. I'll gather some supplies from the kitchen."

Kasia strode to the drapes. She gave a hard yank and the rod tumbled down. In a moment, she held a length of heavy maroon velvet. She laid it over Tessaria, taking a final look at the smooth brown skin, the high sloping forehead and determined chin. Something was already absent, like an empty house with the lights left burning.

Kasia hoped she wouldn't remember her that way, yet the image was seared into her mind as she followed the others outside, stopping on the way to scoop up her pumps from the glasshouse. Besides the cartomancy deck, the shoes were the last piece of her old life. Faux snakeskin with spiked heels. She couldn't ride in them, but she'd be damned if she left them behind.

Alexei's hound waited for them outside. He had his own Marksteed, as did Patryk. Two regular horses for the women were quickly saddled at the stables. As they galloped north, Kasia turned in the saddle. Danziger Haus was a dark hulk against the sky. She wished they'd burned it to the ground.

*I will bring you all war and strife like you've never imagined*, she thought. *This … This is just the beginning.*

# Chapter Twenty-Three

The transport finally ran out of charge in the northern reaches of the Morho Sarpanitum.

Lezarius had watched the charge needle dip deeper into the red for hours. Dantarion swore as the armored vehicle ground to a halt somewhere between Nantwich and the ruins of Bal Agnar. Sparse pines gave way to the great snow plain that girded Khotang Lake.

"We walk from here, old man," she said, opening the door.

Chill air raised gooseflesh on his arms. Lezarius gazed through the windscreen at the gray wall of the Sundar Kush rising in the distance. Sawtoothed peaks wreathed in mist, their shoulders giving way to green, fertile valleys. Jalghuth itself would not be visible until they reached the shores of the lake, yet he could see Mount Ogo, the tallest of their number, and a faint dark smudge that must be Sinjali's Lance.

"You cannot go barefoot," she said, rummaging through the rear of the transport.

They'd survived on the knights' emergency rations for the last two days, which would have been enough except that the mage ate most of it. Lezarius had hoarded some tins of milk and a block of hard cheese for Greylight.

Dantarion showed no interest in his pet anymore, though she'd grown increasingly grouchy and ill-tempered. Perhaps she had caught some foul humor in the swamp, for he woke to hear her retching that morning. She had returned, whey-faced, and erupted in rage when he asked her what was wrong.

Since then, they'd spoken little. When she slept—a rare occurrence—she manacled him to the steering wheel, refusing to believe that he would not try to run at the first chance.

But Lezarius had no thought of escape. Only justice.

"Bind your feet," she said, tossing him lengths of cloth she'd cut from a cloak one of the knights had left behind. "I have no wish to carry you, frail though you are."

The kitten scampered across the snow, leaping up to bat wildly at the crystals that flurried in little eddies. It was a whole new world to her! Lezarius marveled that they were both alive and together after so many adventures. He laughed as she hopped sideways, back arching. Dantarion cast him a doubtful look.

"Greylight is glad to stretch her legs," he said, grinning.

"So am I." She shaded her eyes with a hand, peering through the trees. "Where do the stelae begin?"

"Near the lake."

He had already agreed to shatter enough of the Ward-stones so the mage could pass through them safely. Of course, she would have the ley herself then. But what could she do to him? He was already Invertido. When the time came, he would banish the ley from the entire city. Then he could begin to undo whatever damage Balaur had wrought in his absence.

An icy gust whipped her red cloak. "If Balaur is alive, why has he not made his presence known?"

"Ask him yourself."

Lezarius expected her to round on him in a fury, but she just nodded. "I will." Green eyes caught his. "I believe you now. I have had . . . dreams. Will we reach the walls today?"

The sun still sat high overhead. He nodded. "By nightfall if we don't tarry."

"Then we will carry nothing." Two poniards hung at her belt, the bow and quiver over one shoulder. She'd washed the mud from her hair in one of the Morho's streams. It hung in shining auburn waves. The cold air pinked her cheeks and Lezarius was again struck by how fair and youthful-seeming the mage appeared. How could such corruption not show in her face?

He caught Greylight and they set off for the distant mountains. Sunlight dazzled on the snow, the sky a deep, bottomless blue save for a few wispy, streaking clouds. Lezarius wore only the tweed coat Nurse Jeyna had given him so long ago, yet he relished the frigid air. It swept the last traces of the Morho from his lungs.

"Beleth is your mother," he said. "But who is your father?"

Dantarion shrugged. "I don't know. She never told me."

"How old are you?"

"How old are *you*?"

"Seventy-four."

She blew on her fingers. "I am six and thirty."

He blinked in surprise. "I thought you were younger."

"It must be my soft life," she replied with a grin.

Lezarius spotted a stout branch beneath one of the trees and used it as a walking stick. His legs felt stiff from so much sitting. "Who is this Malach you spoke of? The knight mentioned him, too."

"My cousin."

"Why does Falke want him so badly?"

Dantarion glanced over. Frost rimed her lashes. "Here's a question for *you*. Why were you so stupid as to hold Balaur captive instead of killing him?"

Lezarius opened his mouth and she cut him off. "Let me guess. Your honor forbade it. And what rewards your mercy has reaped, Lezarius!" Dantarion tipped her head back to laugh. He caught a quick flash of the dark links circling her throat, broken at the collarbone. The Broken Chain of Beleth's demented Via Libertas.

The words echoed his own sentiments too closely. He scowled. "You would have anarchy rule the world! How is that progress?"

"It is too cold for philosophical debate," she muttered. "I will say only this. Morality, religion, law—they are false constructs designed to inhibit our natural impulses. The only truth is the pursuit of pleasure."

"Yet here you are suffering for a cause," he pointed out.

"Not a cause. My own interests."

Her infantile reasoning disgusted him. "You descend from greatness! The first Praefators were light-bringers in the literal sense, mage. They ended the Second Dark Age. They gave us a roadmap for peace and prosperity. How many times much we learn the same lessons?"

"Peace?" she snorted. "Only for those who agree with you. All we ever wanted was our freedom, but the Curia saw no contradiction in violating its own precepts to drag us back into the fold."

"Freedom for who?" he shot back. "The masses who starved while your favorites lived like kings? The women forced into prostitution to feed their families? Or perhaps the serfs working off the debts of their mothers and fathers? Do not speak to me of freedom! The Via Libertas is anything but that."

She winced and he thought he'd hit home, but then Dantarion pressed a hand to her belly.

"Are you still sick?" he asked in a milder tone. "We can rest—"

"I am fine, old man. No more talk. You twist everything to suit your hypocritical ideals."

*I could say the same*, he thought, but fell silent.

The glacier began to slope gently upward. His eyes stung

in the bitter wind. Greylight had wiggled indignantly when he returned her to his shirt, but now she snuggled against him, grateful for their shared warmth. The kitten had been a gift from Dr. Ferran Massot. A vile man, yet without his interference Lezarius would still be at the Batavia Institute. Feizeh must have been in league with Balaur, though why they'd risked tampering with his mind Lezarius didn't know. Perhaps it was all part of the ley's grand design.

The trees grew thin and stunted. They topped a rise and the first stelae came into view. The monoliths stood in long rows spaced a few meters apart. They marked the northern boundary of the Void and Jalghuth's first defense against a mage assault. When he'd trekked through the Morho with Mikhail, the stelae there had shown signs of decay. Tiny pits in the stone, as if they had been pierced with molten-hot needles. But this . . . .

Lezarius stumbled forward, breath shallow. Even from a distance, he could sense the taint. Dantarion chased after him with a muffled oath.

A web of fine cracks marred the outer Wardstones. The Blue Flame of Jalghuth was so eroded they might have stood on the plain for a millennia instead of three decades. Lezarius traced the stone sigil with a fingertip, drawing a faint line of blue light. Just enough power remained to keep the ley from spilling into the Void, but no more than that.

"His very presence has done this," Lezarius whispered, leaning heavily on his staff. "The dam will not hold much longer. Saints preserve us—"

The tip of a poniard pressed against his neck just below the ear. "Disable it," Dantarion hissed. He could hear the strain in her voice to stand so close. Yet the stela should have rendered her violently ill. Incapable of approaching at all.

Lezarius exerted the smallest push. The ley slid away. The blue light winked out.

"Now the next," she said.

The second row was in even worse shape. Shards of stone had flaked away, leaving little piles of snow-covered rubble beneath. He cautiously cleared a path through the Wardstones, allowing them to reignite again behind them. Dantarion kept the poniard to his throat the entire time. It took the better part of an hour to get through, mainly because he was terrified that he might shatter them all for good. The innermost rings closest to Jalghuth were fragile as eggshells—yet somehow they were holding.

Once the last of the stelae fell behind, Dantarion sheathed the blade. The Broken Chain around her neck glimmered redly.

"It is good to feel the ley again," she grinned. "You were a fool to come here, Lezarius."

He was starting to wonder if she wasn't right. Power swirled at their feet, but the surface ley was only a thin veneer. Beneath that, he sensed the deep, raging torrent of the abyss—far stronger than it should have been. It made his Marks itch. How he longed for a Keef!

"I am fulfilling my destiny," he said.

"Well put," she replied cheerfully. "Since it is your destiny to restore us to our rightful place."

"Never!"

Dantarion reached for him and Lezarius's teeth bared in a snarl. "Touch me and I will banish it all this very instant."

"I had no ill intentions." The hand withdrew. "You are bleeding, old man."

"What?" He wiped his nose with the back of a hand. It came away smeared with blood. "Only the cold," he muttered.

The rags around his feet were a poor barrier against the ice. Already he had lost feeling in his toes.

"Then let us get someplace warmer," she said. "Is it safe to cut across or must we go around?"

Lake Khotang stretched ahead, a frozen expanse nestled

in the mountains' bosom. Settlements dotted the valley on the far side. A winding track led steeply up towards Jalghuth. Carts climbed the road, though fewer than usual.

"The ice will be half a meter thick in the center," he said. "Perhaps a bit less at the edges. But yes, I have seen heavy transports cross it."

The mage tested it with a boot. A thin layer of snow covered the ice, blurring the boundary between lake and shoreline. Farther out, though, the wind had swept it clean and the surface was riven with seams where plates of ice fused together.

"Feels solid enough," she muttered.

Dantarion started across the ice as Lezarius bent down to check his feet for signs of frostbite. She'd gone about two dozen steps when a sudden crack echoed in the silence. He looked up. The sheet Dantarion stood on was tilting at a crazy angle.

Her eyes went wide. "Oh, sh—"

Then she was gone, swallowed beneath the dark waters of the lake.

# Chapter Twenty-Four

"We must stop to rest."

"I told you," Malach snapped. "I can go on—"

A hand pressed against his brow. Malach batted it away.

"You're burning with fever!" Tashtemir said. "Show me the wound."

Malach scowled at the southerner's belligerent expression. He knew Tash wouldn't stop nagging until he gave in.

"Fine." Malach lifted the crimson robe. He wore nothing underneath and despite the warmth of the air, his skin tightened with a sudden chill. Tashtemir prodded the half-healed scar just below his navel.

"That looks all right." The robe was unceremoniously yanked higher. Tashtemir's lips tightened. "But this doesn't. There's a bad slash along your ribs. It looks inflamed. Why didn't you tell me you were hurt?"

"Because it's nothing."

"It *was* nothing," Tash replied in disgust. "Now it's something."

Malach let the robe fall. "It'll have to wait."

"Let that fester and you'll be dead in two days. I need to

clean it, at least." He glanced around. "Is there any way to make a fire?"

They had followed the Ascalon west for the last day. It cut a winding swathe through the jungles of the Morho, emptying into the Bight of Balmora and the Parnassian Sea. Nikola had a head start. She was also riding. Malach didn't want to waste a single minute, but his side throbbed with every step. He wondered if the knight's blade had been coated with something nasty.

"Forget the fire," he said. "It's too damp."

Tash had already abandoned his wool coat. Now he peeled his frilly shirt off and tore it into strips. "I hate to use this water without boiling it first," he muttered. "But we need to bind that."

Malach sat on a boulder while Tashtemir dampened the strips in the river. Wiry black hair covered his pale chest, which was bare of Marks. The little Malach knew about the Masdar League all came from Tashtemir. They believed in one god called the Alsakhan. Twice a day, at dawn and dusk, Tash insisted on stopping so he could bow down and pray in the direction of his homeland. He claimed that if they angered the Alsakhan, the ley would cease to flow. Superstitious nonsense, but Malach had no choice but to tolerate it or leave him behind.

"There might be some dragon's claw in the forest," Tashtemir said. "That would help with the swelling."

"We don't have time to forage!" Malach grunted as the makeshift bandage wound around his middle.

"Ten minutes." He stood back. "Maybe a fat rabbit will cross my path."

"And how would you catch it?"

"A hungry man is a fast man."

"Perhaps you can harangue it to death," Malach grumbled.

"You'll thank me when we're dining on roasted . . . raw hare. Ah, doesn't have the same appeal, does it?"

Tash entered the jungle. Within seconds, the dense vegetation swallowed him whole.

Malach rubbed the day-old beard on his face with a sour grimace. Bal Kirith gone. Beleth almost certainly dead. He'd seen no sign of Tristhus or Sydonie. They'd been sent to their rooms, but he very much doubted they had obeyed his aunt's command to stay put. The children often hunted at night. Maybe they'd gotten away.

And what of Dantarion and Lezarius? Was there still hope or should he just face the truth?

We lost the war a second time. All because he didn't expect Feizah to move so quickly.

He remembered a quote from one of Falke's books. *Give them just enough rope to hang themselves. Make them believe they know your tactics. Then upend their expectations. The shock and terror will be all the greater.*

"You nailed that one, you old bastard," Malach muttered.

Long minutes passed. He should go look for Tash, but the hot sun and gentle murmur of the river lulled him into a delirious trance. They were up in the tree, Nikola stroking his hair, and this time Malach didn't resist when she unbuckled his belt—

A cracking twig snapped his eyes open. Malach turned, expecting to see Tashtemir.

Eight Perditae slipped out of the jungle. They wore in ragged garments, part spun cloth, part animal skins, and held crude spears. Nightmarks covered every visible bit of flesh, a landscape of macabre imagery. Malach leapt to his feet and grabbed a heavy rock from the bank. The Perditae eyed him warily, half-crouched. He raised the rock. The motion sent a jolt of heat along his ribs.

"No!" Tashtemir came blundering out of the jungle, three more at his heels.

"What do you mean, *no*?" Malach snarled. "They'll eat us!"

The largest male readied his spear. He had a wild beard and broad shoulders, but he seemed scrawny. If Malach could get the spear, he might stand a chance, though the odds were still poor. Perditae were quick. And stronger than they looked.

"They haven't attacked me, have they?" Tash held his palms out. "I talked to them. They understand. They're not like the others."

Malach's only experience with the Perditae was when the ley flooded. It drove them out of the depths of the Morho like worms wriggling from rain-soaked earth. They would attack anything that moved. Some were foolhardy enough to seek meat at Bal Kirith, though those that did never lived long.

Malach studied the motley group. They *were* different. It was the eyes. They didn't have the slitted, goat-like pupils.

"One of their tribe was hurt by the knights. She got away but lies gravely injured. I told them I'm a healer."

"For fuck's sake, why?" Malach demanded wearily.

The leader lowered his spear. Malach followed suit, though he kept the rock in his hand.

"Because there was a sharp flint at my throat and it seemed like the thing to do." Tash turned to the oldest woman. She had long, unkempt hair, but it looked clean. " How far is the village?"

"Near," she said. "Short walking." Her voice had the same clipped accent as Beleth.

Malach was momentarily stunned into silence. He'd never heard one speak before.

"We help you and you help us, yes?" Tashtemir said with an oily smile.

She glanced at the leader. He nodded. "But if you lie, you die," he added gruffly.

*See?* Malach mouthed.

"I'm not lying," Tashtemir said quickly. "Take us there."

Malach considered refusing. He could keep going down the river and let Tash catch up if he survived. That would be the logical choice. If this Perditae was mortally wounded, they'd both be finished. Then Malach's gaze fell on the bundle of spiky leaves in Tash's fist. He'd found the dragon's claw.

Unwillingly, he heard Nikola's wry voice in his head.

*If that idiot hadn't been trying to save your life, neither of you would be in this mess.*

"Cardinal?" Tash called. "Are you coming?"

Malach sighed. He dropped the rock and fell into step behind the shirtless veterinarian. "This is a bad idea," he said softly.

They walked single-file, three Perditae behind them, three ahead with the leader.

"I know what you're thinking. The other kind is *rahib*." Tashtemir shuddered. "Most unpleasant. But they're just people."

Malach shook his head. "Most of those Marks came from dead mages. The sickness just hasn't finished them yet because we're in the Void. They could snap at any moment, you understand?"

Tash paled a little at that. He stroked his black mustache but said nothing more.

They followed a muddy trail through the forest. After a few minutes, Malach caught a whiff of smoke. He pushed through a clump of ferns and emerged into a natural clearing beneath one of the great regnum trees. Again, he was surprised at the Perditae's ingenuity. Sturdy huts were arranged in three concentric circles around the massive trunk. Tightly woven vines draped the hide roofs, adding a second layer of protection against the rains and camouflaging the encampment so that it was invisible until you were beneath the spreading canopy of the regnum. Naked children ran about, and even a few dogs. Leaf-wrapped parcels steamed in the coals of a dozen cook fires. The smell of food made his stomach rumble.

He'd always assumed the Lost Ones lived like animals. That the "village" would be some filthy den, rank with gnawed bones. But this was a place of intelligent beings, making do with what they had. Malach thought of the sport the mages had with their maddened cousins and felt that queasy sensation in his chest again. *Guilt.*

He didn't like it.

The Perditae paid little attention to Tashtemir, but they stared at Malach's red robes with fear. The mothers quickly gathered their offspring, herding them away from him. One approached the leader of the scouting band and muttered some angry words Malach couldn't make out, but he made a pacifying gesture and glanced at one of the huts. She looked at Tashtemir, then at Malach, and gave a tight nod.

The leader came over. "My wife," he said. "She does not trust you."

"Perfectly understandable," Tashtemir said. "But I will do no harm, I swear."

A bleak look crossed the man's face. He rubbed the Mark on his arm, a chimera with the head of a snake and body of a lion. "Come, healer," he said roughly. "Before she changes her mind."

They walked to the hut. He lifted a flap, beckoning for them to enter. They family had scavenged a wooden chair and some chipped crockery. A pallet lay against the far wall, with what looked like a bundle of rags on top. As Malach drew near, he saw it was a child. Her eyes were closed, face drawn with pain.

"Hello," Tashtemir said quietly. "I must examine you, dear one, but I will try not to hurt you, yes?"

She didn't answer, though her dark eyes opened. The child seemed beyond fear. She gazed at him dumbly. Malach tensed as Tashtemir carefully drew the rags aside, fearing some terrible suppurating wound from a sword. But her chest and abdomen were unblemished. Tash let out a hiss at the bone jutting from her thigh. He studied the break closely and seemed relieved.

"I can set that," he said. "It's not a compound fracture. But I will need certain items."

Her father's relief was evident. "Anything. Tell me what you need."

Malach stepped back as Tash barked orders and set to work. Water was boiled and splints prepared from green saplings. He listed the plants he required to stave off infection. The Perditae looked confused at first. They called them by other names. Tash described the leaves in detail and explained where they could be found. One by running water, another in the shade of the lingnut tree, a third where the moss grew thickest. The villagers finally seemed to understand.

The child cried out when he joined the bones together, but it was a weak protest. He brewed an elixir that smelled like dirt and urged her to drink it down. By the time the sun was setting, she rested easier, color returning to her cheeks.

Malach had been of little use. One of the women finally took him aside and gave him a plate of mashed tubers, a crumbly cake that tasted of nuts, and mild-flavored meat he suspected was frog. She watched him eat with a friendly smile that only tightened the hard knot in his chest.

"Good?" she asked.

"Good," he mumbled, avoiding her eyes. "Thank you."

When Tash emerged from the hut, Malach pushed to his feet. He felt light-headed and overly warm, though his brow was dry. "Can we go now?" he demanded. "This little excursion has cost us hours."

"We saved a child's life," Tash said mildly.

"You did." He glanced at the hut, expression softening. "And I am glad. But I'm not spending the night here. I have ground to make up."

"After you drink this." Tashtemir held out a cup with an evil smile. "I saved you some."

Malach eyed the cup. "Fine." He sniffed it and tipped it back. "Tastes like dirt, too," he said, when the cup was drained.

"It will lessen your fever."

"Wonderful. Now—"

"And I have a surprise for you, you cranky *hemar.*" Tash turned as the girl's father approached. "Brew the elixir every day for a week," he said. "And you must keep the bone splinted for at least four moon cycles."

"You mean months?" his wife asked, joining them. She smiled sardonically. "It will be as you advise, healer."

Two of the men walked them back to the river. Even in his feverish state, Malach noticed that it was a different path. Dark thoughts swirled in his head. Maybe it hadn't been frog after all. He was about to voice his suspicions when he heard the liquid murmur of the Escalon and they emerged onto a sandy bank. Three rafts had been shoved up onto the shore, along with several long poles.

"You see?" Tashtemir said happily. "No more walking."

Malach eyed the crude-looking bamboo crafts, which were lashed together with vines. "Do you know how to steer?"

"How hard can it be?" Tash replied carelessly. He turned to their guides with an elaborate bow. "Many thanks, my friends. May the Alsakhan bless all your endeavors!"

The Perditae dragged one of the rafts partway into the water and held it steady while they climbed aboard. Tash used a pole to push them off the bank. The raft swung around, tilting alarmingly. Malach scrambled for the center and spread his legs to even out the weight.

"Don't worry!" Tash cried, fumbling with the pole. "It's all under—"

The current seized them. Muffled laughter came from the men on the bank, who stood leaning on their spears as the raft hurtled downstream. One tried to shout instructions but his words were snatched away by the roar of the river.

The raft spun around again. Then Tash found bottom with the pole. He pushed and they drifted sideways. A wave soaked Malach to the knees. They spun twice more and then Tash managed to shove them out to the center of the current. The raft righted itself, surging forward. Steering seemed to be a nominal concept. The river would carry them at its own pace and the pole was only useful to keep them from running aground.

Malach knelt at the front, calling out when he saw an obstacle ahead. He learned to watch for telltale ripples that signified a rock or sunken tree limb. Twice Tashtemir was too slow to correct their course and the raft got stuck, but the river was shallow and they were able to jump out and free it. Despite its flimsy appearance, the craft was well-constructed. It survived several brutal batterings and Malach's conviction that they would both drown began to fade. By the time the sun was setting, the banks had widened. The current grew calmer and salt marshes replaced the thick jungle on either side.

At last, Tashtemir announced that it was too dark to continue. He poled them to the shore and they both dragged the raft to a hummock of dry land. Tashtemir performed his evening ritual, facing southward with thumbs and forefingers forming two circles. Then he bowed seven times, murmuring in the thick tongue of the Masdaris.

"We're close to the Bight," Malach said, lying back on the raft.

Tashtemir sat next to him, resting his arms on his knees. "What will you do if she's not there?"

He closed his eyes. "She'll be there."

Tash was silent for a minute. "She's carrying your child, isn't she? That's why you want her back so badly."

Malach covered his surprise. It was easy to forget how clever and observant Tashtemir was—especially since he did his best to convey the impression of a shallow courtier. But he'd lived among the clergy for four years without being killed or Marked, which was a considerable accomplishment.

"Yes," Malach said softly, "and no."

When he didn't elaborate, the southerner let the matter drop. He knew Malach's moods well enough by now. "I suppose I must serve out my exile someplace else." A heavy sigh. "Why must you have so many enemies? Bal Kirith was the perfect hideaway."

"I'll make sure you're taken care of, Tash."

"What will *you* do?"

An excellent question.

"I'll tell you when I know."

Tash slapped at a mosquito. "My shoes are ruined," he said sadly.

Perhaps they didn't like the taste of Malach's blood, for the biting insects left him alone. He listened to Tashtemir's muttered invocations to his god, presumably begging for mercy, calling down retribution, or both at once. The wound felt better. And he was sweating again, a good sign. Tash's elixir had done its work. Malach drifted off to the southerner's faint snores and the monotonous *chonk-chonk* of a nightjar.

An aching bladder roused him at first light. Malach was pissing in the mudflats a few meters from the raft when he saw something that made him whoop aloud.

"What?" Tashtemir was sitting up on the raft, hair and eyes wild. "Are we under attack?"

"I found a hoof print!" He let the robe drop, grinning like a fool.

Tashtemir scratched at a bite on his chest and gave a jaw-cracking yawn. "Oh."

"*Oh?* Don't you see? Nikola came through here. Not long ago. A day at most, else the rains would have washed it away."

"How do you know it's not another horse?"

Malach gave him a level look. "How many riders do you see around here?"

"A fair point." Tash rose and stretched. Malach grabbed the pole.

"We have to leave."

An incredulous look. "*You* got to piss, Cardinal. What about me? Or must I aim over the edge while I'm steering?"

"Make it quick."

Tashtemir grumbled but hastened some distance away. Malach stared down the river, burning with impatience. He could smell the salt of the sea. Judging by the dried mud on the banks, the tide was on its way out. It would be a swift journey to the river's mouth.

When Tash returned, Malach clapped him on the shoulder. "We came thrice as far as we would have on foot. I owe you, brother."

Tashtemir looked startled, then pleased. "If we are indeed brothers, there is no debt."

Malach's smile died. "Other than the three years of faithful service that remain under our bargain, you mean?"

"Of course!" Tash frowned. "Other than that, ah, Your Grace."

"I'm joking. You are free to do as you will." Malach handed him the pole. "But the slavers often sail with the morning tide. We'd better hurry."

They launched the raft again and poled out to the center. The ebb tide pulled them along in a smooth, even current. Malach trailed one hand in the brown water. Here and there, stelae rose from the marsh flats. None were close enough to cause discomfort other than a faint warning buzz in the back of his mind.

"I know what you sell the mercenaries," Tashtemir said. "What do you get in exchange?"

"Oh, various contraband items. Weapons. Cinnabar. Parchment and ink for Beleth."

"She was always scribbling away," Tash said with a trace of nostalgia, though Malach knew he detested her. "A woman of letters, the Reverend Mother was."

Malach laughed, lighter of heart since the night he'd woken up with a death squad rattling the doorknob. "If you mean four letters, yes. She went through reams of vellum. I wonder if Falke burned all her books."

"That would be . . . ." Tash cleared his throat. "A great loss."

Malach had only read her work on those occasions when Beleth demanded his editorial opinion. The parts that weren't pornographic were incomprehensible. As much as Malach loathed Falke, at least the man knew how to make a clear point.

"You mentioned cinnabar," Tash said. "That comes from *my* homeland."

"Which is why it's so expensive."

The powdered mineral was used to dye the mages' vermilion robes. For the last three decades, it had been banned by law in the Via Sancta.

"So the ships do take the southern route," Tashtemir said thoughtfully.

"Sometimes. Do you want to return?"

"More than anything. But if the Imperator finds me, she'll cut my manhood off and feed it to her pets. I hold the eunuchs in great esteem, of course, but have no desire to join their numbers."

"Rough justice," Malach observed cheerfully.

"Oh, that's just the first part." Tash gave a languid shove with the pole. "The Golden Imperator is both wise and creative. She's had three long years to devise my punishment. I imagine it will be lengthy and elaborate. Fire ants, most certainly. A lashing with the horsehide *sawt*. The Cage of Forty-Seven Agonies—*that* goes without saying. The only mystery is the precise order of events . . . ."

---

The Ascalon emptied into the Bight of Balmora, a deep curve in the continent's western coastline that sheltered hundreds of small islands. The waters of the Bight were shallow and rife with rocky outcrops. Countless wrecks littered the seabed, adding to the underwater hazards. The Bight was also well beyond the usual shipping lanes of the Via Sancta, making it an ideal location for smugglers.

As they neared the mouth of the river, the marshes gave way to scrubby dunes with stunted, wind-bent pine trees. And at last, a wide white beach, girded by the last of the stelae. The edge of the Void. Open ocean lay beyond, where the ley would be too deep to touch.

They abandoned the raft on a sandy spit where the cross-currents of the river and ocean joined. A large schooner was anchored a short distance offshore. A slave pen held a few dozen disconsolate Perditae, guarded by a group of women with the tanned skin and sinewy muscles of a ship's crew. They glanced at Malach as he approached.

"Trade is closed for the day, mage."

"I'm not here to trade. I'm looking for someone. A woman seeking passage to the isles."

The sailor jerked her head toward a wooden building on stilts. "She's in the post with Captain Aemlyn."

It was a simple thatched-roof structure with two windows on the ocean-facing side. They had peeling white shutters that could be sealed against poor weather, but it was a fine morning and the windows stood open. Low voices came from inside as he climbed the rickety stairs. Then the raucous sound of Nikola's laughter. She had several kinds in her repertoire. A dry chuckle. A snort of disbelief. And a full-throated belly laugh that sounded like a wounded hyena, reserved for remarks she found especially amusing. When the last one erupted, it was impossible not to join her, even when you weren't sure what was funny.

Malach paused, heart suddenly racing. What if she didn't want to see him? She'd run from him, after all. Left without even a goodbye. Never had he felt so full of doubt. He paused on the landing, paralyzed, as light footsteps approached. Before he could turn away, the door opened. Nikola stood before him. She had shed the heavy green cloak and wore one of her cheap flower-print dresses from Novostopol, straining across the middle now. Their eyes met. She quickly pulled the door closed behind her. Emotions flitted across her mobile face, too swift to decipher. Nikola ran down the stairs, grabbed his hand, and pulled him into the dunes behind the trading post.

"What are you doing here?" she hissed, so close he could count the grains of sand caught in her hair.

Malach opened his mouth to reply and Nicola scowled deeply. Then she kissed him, a long, passionate kiss that left him breathless and burning for more. "Idiot! So you got away, did you?" Another violent, lingering kiss. "Saints, I feared you were dead!"

"Not yet," he murmured, still drunk from the taste of her on his lips. Her nearness made him half-mad. He leaned forward, fist closing on the dress to drag her against him, and Nikola pushed him away. She looked angry, though he couldn't tell if was directed at him or herself.

"I'm not going back," she growled. "My passage is paid. It's done, Malach."

He released a long breath, mastering himself with an effort. "I'm not here to bring you back. Only to see you one last time."

Her delicate brows knit. "You came all this way just for that?"

"I thought you might need my help, but I see you've

arranged things already." He glanced down the beach. "Tash came with me."

Nikola smiled at the southerner, who waded in the surf. He was the only other male in sight besides the Perditae. The witches would not do business with men, so all the mercenary crews were women down to the lowest deck swab.

"I'm glad. What about the children?"

"I don't know where they are."

Her smile faded. "I tried to give you warning. It was the best I could do."

He closed his eyes, a feeling of peace settling over him. "I hoped it was so."

"Malach—"

He touched her mouth, silencing her. What could he say that she would believe? Not the truth—that he was madly, recklessly in love with her. She would take it for some ruse. He wouldn't speak those words until he had proven himself. So Malach settled for another truth, one she could accept.

"I wish you the best of all things, Nikola Thorn," he said softly. "I wish you freedom."

She stared at him as if he were a riddle she couldn't quite unravel. "Thank you."

"I'll keep my promise. Someone will come for the child."

"The Mother's Rest. I haven't forgotten." She paused. "Just don't sent your cousin, eh?"

He laughed. "Not Dante, I swear."

A hand fell to her swollen belly. "What of Bal Kirith?"

His amusement faded. "It's Feizah's now."

"I'm sorry."

Malach watched as two longboats rowed out from the ship. The sailors opened the pens and herded the fresh slaves towards the spit of sand to meet them.

"We'll take it back," he said.

"You sound so confident."

"I am. Our child will break them. It's her destiny."

Nikola tilted her head. He longed to tug the scarf from her hair, to touch her, kiss her again, but restrained himself. Malach settled for twining his fingers with hers.

"How do you know it isn't a boy?"

"Because I want a daughter." He smiled. "And I usually get what I want."

She returned the smile. It was bittersweet. "But not always?"

"No, Domina Thorn." He looked at her seriously. "Not always."

The door of the trading post banged open and a woman with the silver bars of a captain on her blue coat strode down the steps. A short, curved blade rode at one slim hip. She was in her late thirties, tall and lanky, boots polished to a high gleam. Malach knew her. They'd done business a few years before. She glanced at him without recognition, but mages were a common enough site at the Bight. No doubt she'd just purchased a hold's worth of Perditae from one of his distant cousins.

"How many stones did you pay for passage?" Malach asked in a low voice.

"Just one." A fierce grin. "I told her it was all I had."

He nodded. "Good. That more than covers it."

The longboats landed on the beach and eight crew disembarked. The benches of one were swiftly filled with the slaves.

"It is time, Domina," Captain Aemlyn called.

"I'll walk you down," Malach said to Nikola.

A weight pressed down on his chest, but it was different from the hot prick of remorse. Joy and sorrow mixed together. Malach had never experienced anything quite like it.

*I will still have a piece of her*, he told himself. *And I will love our child as they both deserve.*

Tashtemir walked over as they reached the spit. He gave Nikola a bow.

"May the Alsakhan bless you with calm seas and steady winds," he said.

"Thank you, Domine Kelevan. May your path lead home someday."

He stroked his black mustache. "I believe it will."

Nikola turned to Malach and embraced him tightly. He breathed in the scent of her, the warmth of her belly pressed against him. "I'll curse your name when our child is born," she whispered in his ear. "But I will never forget it."

*Our child.*

He grinned, though his heart cracked to splinters that he knew would never be whole again.

"I will find a way to you," he said hoarsely, fingers touching the Broken Chain around his neck. "That is a solemn oath."

Her eyes shone. *Tears?* he wondered in shock. But then Nikola was turning away, the longboat with its Perditae cargo rowing out to sea, the last one awaiting her and the captain. Malach studied the remaining crew. A motley bunch, hailing from many different lands. Two were brown-skinned and lithe, with dozens of tiny gold hoops adorning their ears. The third was freckled and sunburnt. The last consulted a logbook as she approached, long brown hair hanging over her face.

"A pleasant morning for a journey, eh, mage?" Captain Aemlyn remarked at his side.

Malach studied Nikola's elegant, sharp-lipped profile. "Treat her well," he said brusquely. "If you don't, I'll hear of it."

Aemlyn laughed. "Is that a threat?"

"Merely an observation."

"Well, you needn't concern yourself. She has nothing to fear from us."

The slight emphasis on *she* made him frown just as the sailor with the logbook came up. Her gaze fixed on his right hand. It was Marked with a dagger. Most of the blade ran up his forearm and was concealed within the sleeve of his robe, but the tip brushed his knuckles. She looked up, eyes locking with Malach's. Pewter eyes the color of ash and smoke. Every muscle in his body went rigid.

"Run!" he shouted.

The woman raised a fist. Her fingers sprang open as though she offered him a gift. Something small glimmered in her palm.

Malach drew a ragged breath. "It's a fucking wit—"

An invisible force rocked him. Malach landed on his back, dazed. He felt like he'd just run headlong into a brick wall. Or the wall had run into *him.*

"Go!" he gasped, staring up at Nikola's shocked face. "Just go!"

The witch spat another stone into her palm. She closed her eyes. He sensed power gathering. Ley concentrated in a way he'd never seen before.

"RUN!" Malach bellowed as a second shockwave sent him tumbling end over end like a pebble in an avalanche. He finished on his belly, spitting sand.

The next few seconds blurred together. Tashtemir, arms waving, and the captain's fist knocking him flat. A boot catching Malach's ribs. The roar of the surf, too loud. Shouted orders and the rattle of chains. He bit and clawed, feeling satisfaction that he'd drawn blood, but then those pewter eyes were staring down at him. Pain everywhere. Beyond belief.

Malach went limp. Hands trussed him in cold iron.

"Get him aboard."

"What about the other?"

"Him, too."

Sunlight blinded him. The world tilted, swayed.

A longboat.

He found breath again. "You fucking bit—"

A lance of pain. Then blessed darkness.

# Chapter Twenty-Five

"Run!" Malach screamed.

Nikola was striding towards the longboat. She pivoted around. Before she could see what was wrong, he flew backwards through the air and crashed down at the edge of the water.

"Go! Just go!"

One of the sailors was staring at him intently. She spit in her hand and made a strange gesture. The sand rippled. Malach was swept away as briskly as if he'd been caught in the bristles of a giant broom. Captain Aemlyn backhanded Tashtemir as the other women swarmed over to Malach.

Nikola locked eyes with the sailor. The woman spat into her palm. Fingers flicked wide, this time aimed at Nikola. Again, the sand rippled. A hot wind blew around her, Nikola sensed its passage, but whatever force drove it didn't touch her. The woman scowled and pulled a chunky ring from her finger. Its blue gem began to pulse with an eerie light.

"Run!" Malach sputtered again. Nikola needed no urging. She took off down the beach, adrenaline lighting a fire in her legs. Malach's muffled curses chased her down the beach. She glanced over a shoulder and saw him being dragged to the longboat. Part of her wanted to turn back, but she couldn't fight five of them. Not when at least one was a fogging witch!

Nikola veered into the dunes. Fine, dry sand crumbled beneath her boots and she grabbed at clumps of grass to keep from sliding back down. Beyond lay scrub and low, wind-bent trees. She ran until she couldn't run anymore, then sank to one knee, gasping. There was no sign of pursuit.

She hadn't suspected a thing. The captain haggled hard over the price of passage. She couldn't possibly have known Malach was coming, could she? Not when Nikola didn't even know it herself. Aemlyn hadn't asked about mages once. Nikola said she'd escaped Novostopol alone and come straight up the coast, walking until she found the cove. She claimed the same black market dealer who'd converted her savings into kaldurite told her about it. The captain seemed to accept the story. And the smugglers traded with the nihilim themselves! She'd seen them pay one for the group of Perditae.

Nikola drew a deep breath, heart still pounding hard.

For some reason, they wanted *him*.

If Malach hadn't followed, would she be on board that ship right now?

"Motherfucker," she muttered, but there was no real anger. Only fear.

What would they do to him?

Her fists balled.

Two weeks before the baby was born. Maybe less. All her hopes rested on getting to Dur-Athaara. "I can't go back to Novo," she muttered. "Nantwich?"

It was clear across the Morho Sarpanitum. She'd have to pass Bal Kirith again. And what would she do when she got to Nantwich? They'd search her for Marks before letting her in. Nikola would be back where she started, a gray-clad char, except this time she'd also be a single mother. To a nihilim, no less.

Every option was worse than the last.

She rose and retraced her steps until she reached the dunes, peering cautiously over the top. The shore was empty now. The longboat had reached the ship and was being winched aboard. She watched the sails go up. A few minutes later, the bow came about and pointed into the wind, heading east. Nikola waited until the schooner had dwindled to a speck on the horizon.

She made her way back down the beach, numb and despairing. The tide was coming in, erasing any signs of a scuffle—save for a single dark pebble half-hidden in the sand. Nikola picked it up, holding it in her palm. It looked the same as any other bit of stone. She let her fingers spring open, imitating the witch's gesture. Not surprisingly, nothing happened.

Did the witch leave it behind because its power was expended? Or had she overlooked it? Nikola slipped the stone into the bag with her remaining kaldurite. Her own stones had blocked the spell, she realized. They didn't know she had more.

"I'll find you someday," she whispered, though it felt like an empty threat.

She walked up to the trading shack. One of the shutters banged in the wind. The room held a table and two rickety chairs. Nikola sank down in one, back aching. She could wait for another ship to come and try her luck again. But who knew when that might be?

There's no choice, she thought. The Morho on foot would be certain death. She'd given her horse to a band of mages who were just leaving when she arrived at the cove. And the gun was at the bottom of the river. She hadn't dared to keep it in case the slavers searched her.

Hindsight sure was a bitch.

Nikola wondered if she would have had the courage to use the gun, had she kept it. She thought she would—but more likely the witch would have kicked the shit out of her, too.

A hand cradled her swollen belly. *Why did you have to come after me, Malach? Why?*

She knew him well enough by now. He thought he was so smooth, but she could tell when he was lying or trying to manipulate her. Even when he behaved like a perfect gentleman there was always an ulterior motive. Yet she'd detected no guile when he said he wished her freedom. Malach had nothing to gain by finding her—and everything to lose.

A confusing welter of emotions made her eyes brim. Nikola wiped her face. *I haven't cried since I was a kid. What's wrong with me?* She blew out a long breath. The tears ceased as quickly as they'd come. Then the wind banged the shutter again. She leapt to her feet, suddenly furious, and secured it with a latch. "Shut up!"

She kicked the door shut, a wave of exhaustion dragging her down. Just a quick rest. Nikola curled up on the floor in her cloak. She listened to the roar of the surf and tried to ignore the hollow ache in her stomach.

No food for either of us, she thought savagely, so go ahead and eat me if you want.

---

*Bang.*

Nikola's eyes opened, itchy with sand. The shack was dim and cool. How long had she slept?

"Fogging shutter," she murmured.

A sharp movement in her belly made her wince. The baby was kicking again.

*Bang, bang.*

Her gaze drifted blearily to the window. The shutter was still secured by the latch.

Not the wind.

Nikola scrambled back as heavy boots pounded up the

stairs. The door flew open. The knight's visor was up. Brown eyes fixed on her with surprise. He drew his sword. "Got one!" he yelled over his shoulder.

Another jolt of pain speared her womb. Nikola curled into a ball, panting. Deep male voices filled the doorway.

" . . .a nihilim . . . you sure . . . how did she . . ."

The cramps came in waves, curling her toes. She rubbed her stomach. *It's okay, it's okay, it's okay.* A rounded lump slid beneath her hand. It felt like the heel of a tiny foot. Nikola gave it a squeeze. *Not yet. Don't come yet. Please. Oh, please don't.*

In endless increments, the agony subsided.

"I'm . . . not a nihilim," she managed.

Three knights stood over her. Heads shaved to stubble, with beards that were just growing in. They wore plate armor and steel gauntlets over leather gloves.

"You sport their hunting garb," one pointed out, looking at her green cloak.

"They caught me. Held me prisoner."

"She isn't Perditae, Captain."

A wry tone. "I can see that. Search her for weapons."

Nikola eyed them warily. What were Raven-Marked knights doing on the coast?

"If you are not nihilim, we won't hurt you," the captain said, but she disliked the way he glanced at the knight holding the sword.

"And if I was?" she asked.

He didn't reply. Nikola thought of the half-healed scar on Malach's wrist. A wild recklessness seized her. She spat on the captain's boot.

"That's what I think of the Via Sancta," she said.

They grabbed her, gloved hands tearing the cloak away. Nikola kicked and fought as they stripped her dress off. The garment was cheap and the seams tore like paper. There was nothing sexual about it, but her face still burned as the captain scanned her nude body. At least the scrutiny was mercifully brief. His light eyes swept her up and down, and did not linger where they shouldn't have.

"Raise your arms and turn around."

Nikola complied, wanting to get it over with.

"Now show me the soles of your feet," he said briskly.

Nikola's mouth tightened. She braced a hand on the table and lifted each foot in turn.

"She's clean," he said, turning away.

The knights tossed her clothes on the table.

"I apologize, domina," their captain said, his broad back still facing her. "You should have told me you were pregnant."

"Then you'll let me go?" Nikola jerked the torn dress over her head. "I might be Unmarked, but I have the same rights as everyone else."

"Not in the Void, you don't. Curia law is suspended here." He strode to the door. "And you're obviously a sympathizer."

"Captain!" one of the knights called out.

He turned back on the landing.

"I found something." The knight handed him her pouch. It must have fallen on the floor.

He untied the drawstrings and tipped the stones into his palm. "What is this?" he demanded, staring at her.

"My rock collection. Can I have it back?"

The captain slid them back inside the pouch. He did not give it back. "Let's go," he said.

His men prodded her down the stairs. Three large warships anchored off the coast. The pontifex was moving to secure the entire Morho Sarpanitum, not just Bal Kirith.

You've set the continent ablaze, Malach, she thought grimly. *Over a stupid letter!*

More knights erected tents on the beach. A raven banner fluttered in the wind. She wondered if they would row her out to one of the ships, but a prisoner transport roared up behind the dunes, the big wheels spitting sand. Nikola tried to break free and run into the jungle. They caught her in six strides.

"Go easy!" the captain snapped. He was young and stocky like a farmboy. Kven ancestry judging by his light beard and eyes, though his accent was pure working-class Novo.

Nikola could see the knights didn't want to hurt a pregnant woman. They gripped her arms firmly, but without excessive force.

"Think of the child," one of them scolded her. "Are you so corrupted that you care nothing for its welfare?"

She spat a curse that made his eyes widen.

The knights hustled her into the back of the transport and slammed the door. She heard muffled voices. The transport jolted forward. Nikola sat down on one of the side-facing benches. It was that or be tossed around like a pair of dice in a cup.

At least the baby was quiet. Maybe it enjoyed all the excitement.

Nikola barked a harsh laugh. "Well, we're both screwed now. All told, I think your father got the better end of this particular stick."

They drove fast for hours. Rough, unpaved tracks from all the bouncing, though the compartment had no windows to see out. Malach said the Morho was criss-crossed with old roads from the days when there was trade between all six Curia cities. Nikola had to pee badly by the time it stopped and the knights came around to open the door.

She was back at Bal Kirith. A heavy force occupied the Arx. Dozens of transports ringed the palace and patrols moved through the grounds, radios chattering. In the fading light, she saw black scorch marks around the windows of some of the buildings, but they hadn't dropped any shells. No bodies, either. Maybe they were all inside—or they'd already been disposed of.

She hoped the children had escaped. Sydonie and Tristhus were bad seeds by every conceivable measure, but she liked them anyway. They didn't deserve the brutality of severing. No one did.

The knights led her to a large tent erected in the field where she used to practice riding. Two guards stood outside.

"Lux, Veritas, Virtus!" the captain said heartily.

They returned the greeting with stiff salutes.

"Is the cardinal inside?"

One nodded. "I'll tell him you've returned, Captain."

He disappeared into the tent. Nikola turned to the knight next to her, a tall, humorless woman with thin features and a blond ponytail that looked painfully tight.

"Unless you want me to pee on your foot, I suggest you let me have a bathroom break."

The captain nodded. "Take her to the pits."

Nikola did her business in a crude latrine behind the basilica, the female knight watching her every second. By the time they returned, the captain had been cleared to go inside. She entered the tent with her escort. Thick rugs covered the ground and four standing lamps with reservoirs of oil burned brightly. The center held a table covered with topographical maps. Several officers stood over it, contemplating small blocks of painted wood that were arranged in complex patterns across the maps. Troop movements?

At the head of the table was a stooped man in purple robes. Fine, wispy white hair stood out from his head like the down of a chick. Nikola's gut tightened. For the last six years, she'd cleaned Cardinal Sedorov's chambers. He was rarely present—none of them wanted to actually see the chars tidying up. The clergy just wanted their beds made and their linens changed and their clothes washed by invisible little elves. But their paths had crossed several times. They'd even spoken on occasion, about the weather or some other nonsense. The cardinal had been polite and reserved.

Sedorov looked up, dark eyes briefly meeting her own. There wasn't a hint of recognition.

He'd seen only the gray dress, she realized. Not the woman who wore it.

"Captain Komenko," he said. "You took a prisoner?"

"She's Unmarked. We found her at the coast in the slavers' shack." He strode to the table and set her pouch on a corner of the map. "She was carrying this, nothing else."

The cardinal opened the bag and glanced inside.

"I'm from Nantwich," Nikola said quickly.

"You don't sound like it," Sedorov replied, his expression neutral.

"My mother was from Novostopol. Everyone says I have her accent."

The tent had fallen silent, all eyes studying her. She heard the faint squawk of a radio outside. The rising drone of an engine.

"And how did you come to be in the slaver's shack?"

"I ran away," she admitted, casting her eyes down. "I was pregnant and the father would have nothing to do with me." He'd believe that. Unmarked had loose morals. "The mages caught me in the Morho. They were going to sell me to the witches. But I managed to escape when some of the other slaves fought back. I hid in the jungle, Your Eminence. After the ship left, I went back to the shack." A pause as she summoned the proper note of despair. "I had nowhere else to go."

That much was true at least.

"How did you get the kaldurite? Is it stolen?"

"I earned it!" she said fiercely. "Cleaning houses. Ten years I saved up every penny." She lifted her chin. "I was trying to better myself, Your Eminence. When I learned I was pregnant, I decided to convert it to the stones. They were easier to travel with."

He arched a brow. "And the mages didn't take them from you?"

"I hid them in my bodice." Nikola's shoulders slumped.

She sighed and lowered her voice—a reluctant confession. "I thought maybe the witches would take me in. It is not easy being Unmarked in the Via Sancta."

Sedorov didn't speak for a long minute. "It might be as you say, Domina. But that is for others to determine." He turned to Captain Komenko. "Take her back to the Arx in Novostopol. There's a convoy leaving in the morning."

"No!" Nikola cried out. "Please, Your Eminence. I've done nothing wrong."

Komenko's gaze flicked her way. She knew he was thinking about what she said when she spat on his boot. Stupid! Why did I have to provoke them?

To Nikola's surprise, the captain stayed silent.

"It is not a punishment," Sedorov said in a gentler tone. "This is a war zone. I cannot simply turn you loose."

"Then take me back to Nantwich! I'm sure my family would take me in."

He hesitated, then shook his head. "There is no transport going to Nantwich and I cannot spare one just to give you an escort. Novostopol is the only option."

"I could stay here!" she pleaded. "I'll clean, help cook for the knights—"

His voice turned gruff. "The decision is made, domina." He gestured with a finger. "See to it, Captain."

Nikola shook off Komenko's hand, marching out of the tent with a straight back, though angry tears pricked her eyes. Her whole body cringed at the thought of going back. But they couldn't keep her there. She'd find a way to escape. She was just a char. They'd dock her pay, probably fire her, and that would be that.

Captain Komenko hurried to fall into stride with her. He carried his helm under one arm.

"I'm sorry for your misfortunes," he said. "But Novostopol isn't so bad. You might like it there."

She shot him a look. "I'm from Novo."

There was no point denying it now. She'd be recognized the moment they arrived.

Komenko frowned. "So that whole story—"

"A pack of lies, captain. I'm Unmarked, remember? That's what we do."

He shook his head in wonder. "You were very convincing."

She smiled. "Because I have no conscience."

What was it about this farmboy that made her want to jab his soft spots?

He halted. "So you *are* a sympathizer!"

"Not that either." Nikola sighed. "I'm a char at the Arx who ran away. The father is one of the clergy, but you won't get his name from me. And that *is* the truth, captain. Make of it what you will."

He regarded her, pity and indignation mixing. "How do I know that's not just another lie?"

"You don't, but what difference does it make? You're not letting me go either way." Nikola looked around. There must be at least five hundred knights occupying the Arx and more holding a perimeter in the Morho. "Where are we?"

She certainly wasn't going to admit that she'd been here before.

"Bal Kirith." He looked at the palace. "There was a nest of nihilim, but we cleaned them out."

"Well, bully for—" Nikola cut off as a group of soldiers emerged from the main doors. Not regular knights. These wore black leather from head to foot, faces hard as granite. Special forces. They surrounded a lean gray-haired woman in a dark cassock. It took a moment to recognize Beleth without the wig and powder. Her wintry blue eyes gave her away. Nikola would know them anywhere. The soldiers parted for a moment and she saw that Beleth's right arm was in a sling. A thick white bandage swathed the stump of her wrist. The other was encased in a glove with a tight manacle around the wrist. Nikola's gorge rose. She turned away before Beleth spotted her.

"The false pontifex," Captain Komenko said with contempt and a hint of awe. "She killed many brave knights before they captured her. Thirty years she eluded justice. But she will be made an example of."

"What will they do with her?" Nikola wondered.

"That is for the Reverend Father to decide."

His words sunk in. "Reverend Father? Where is the Pontifex Feizah?"

"You don't know?" Captain Komenko seemed surprised. "She's dead. Murdered by a mage." Anger tinged his voice. "Inside her own bedchamber."

A chill gripped her flesh. "Are you certain?"

"It was about three weeks ago. The ley flooded early. He somehow managed to pass the Wards." Komenko watched as Beleth was dragged into the cardinal's tent. "He is her nephew. She must know where he is. If she continues to keep silent, she will lose her other hand, too." He studied Nikola's face and seemed to regret his words. The captain clearly assumed it was the amputation that upset her. "I know it must seem harsh, but if you knew that woman's crimes you would understand the necessity. But I apologize. This is no talk for a woman with child. Come, I'll escort you to the vestal knights."

He took Nikola's arm, steering her towards a row of tents erected around the stela at the end of the field. Her feet followed, but her mind was racing. The massive deployment made sense now. She was only surprised they hadn't invaded sooner.

"Who is the new Reverend Father?" she asked.

Komenko glanced at her. "Dmitry Falke."

Malach's worst enemy. The man who had tried to sever him from the ley. Yet even knowing Malach's penchant for deception, she couldn't untangle the logic. If he'd murdered Feizah, he would have to expect harsh retribution. Whatever his other faults, he wasn't stupid. And Malach had repeatedly spoken of Feizah as if she were still alive—as if *he* didn't know, either.

If he hadn't killed her, that meant it was someone else. Perhaps someone who saw their chance and allowed him to take the blame. Falke? Nikola had no idea, but her problems had just multiplied tenfold. She'd gone missing that same night. Just a faceless char so these men didn't seem to know about it. But once she got back to the Arx, someone would put two and two together.

How was it, she wondered, that Malach kept finding new ways to ruin her life even when he was halfway to Dur-Athaara?

Assuming he wasn't already dead. The thought worsened her mood.

Captain Komenko signaled to Painful Ponytail.

"Give her a cot in one of the tents and some hot food." A pause. "She is to be guarded at all times but not mistreated. Anyone who violates that order will answer to me."

"Yes, Captain."

Nikola watched him stride away. The same man who had ordered her to be stripped naked in front of three male knights was now her chivalrous protector. She shook her head in wonder. The fogging Via Sancta! None of them made a lick of sense.

She was about to start gnawing her own boots by the time they handed her a ready-to-eat foil packet with reconstituted mystery stew, crackers and peanut butter, an orange, creamed corn, a chocolate bar and a piece of yellow cake. She ate it all to the last crumb, washing it down with a cup of hot coffee. That made her have to pee again, but Painful Ponytail just nodded. She looked almost sympathetic.

"My sister had a baby last Caristia," she said, as they walked to the women's latrines with a flashlight. "She said she was going to the bathroom ten times a night by the end."

"Oh, joy," Nikola muttered, hoisting her dress up.

"How far along are you?"

A good question. Nikola tried to work out a reasonable estimate. She knew next to nothing about pregnant people. She'd certainly never expected to be one of them. And her child wasn't even human. "Ah, six and a half months."

"Be glad we found you." Ponytail scanned the dark jungle. "You don't want to have the baby out here."

I don't want to have it *anywhere*, Nikola thought, but she just smiled and nodded. Better to play nice for now.

A hundred campfires burned in the night as they returned to the tent. As she passed the stela, Nikola thought about Tashtemir Kelevan. He'd given her water when the children trapped her at the Wardstone. A decent man. And another of Malach's collateral casualties. She hadn't seen him on the beach. The witches must have taken him, too.

At least they had each other.

Ponytail watched her go inside the tent, then took up a post just outside the flap. Six other female knights were already sleeping in their cots, but one was awake, reading the Meliora with a flashlight. Nikola's minder.

"Goodnight!" Nikola said cheerfully.

The woman gave a brusque nod and turned the page.

Nikola turned to her side on the cot. She used to be a stomach sleeper, but that was out of the question now. For the last two weeks, she'd had Malach to curl up with. Sometimes he sang in his sleep.

"Motherfucker," she whispered, fondly, and passed out.

---

The journey to Novostopol passed far more swiftly than she hoped.

She rode in the same convoy as Beleth, though not the

same vehicle, thank all the Saints. *That* would have been awkward.

But Beleth was a high-value prisoner, Nikola a mere curiosity. They didn't even make her ride in a detainee transport. She got to sit in the backseat of an armored Centurion, which had black-tinted windows. Once they were off the back roads, the convoy picked up speed. The same trip that had taken Nikola all night to drive was a mere four hours in the opposite direction. They rolled through the gates of the Arx sometime in the late afternoon. Captain Komenko sat in the front passenger seat. Other than a terse greeting when she got in, he hadn't spoken to her once.

They must have radioed ahead because a force of knights was waiting in the quad. Beleth's vehicle peeled off into the rain. Ah, of course it was fogging raining! That's all it ever did in Novostopol. In the Morho, it poured in the morning, but then the sun came out.

Not here.

Nikola expected to be brought before the Mistress of Chars, who would confirm that she worked there and initiate some sort of disciplinary proceeding. But they whisked her from the vehicle in front of the Pontifex's Palace. The outside was a pale imitation of the one in Bal Kirith, she knew now. Even scorched by fire, the Arx there had a grandeur that transcended any of the buildings in Novo. She could scarcely imagine what the inside had been like before it was plundered.

"Where are you taking me?" she demanded of Captain Komenko as they approached the great bronze doors.

Rain dripped from his beard. His eyes were guarded. "To see the Reverend Father."

Fear sparked in her heart. "But I'm no one!"

His jaw tightened. He didn't reply.

They strode through the long, high-ceilinged corridors, each more lavish than the last. Nikola barely noticed. A premonition of dread was building inside her. Yet she would not give the knight the satisfaction of dragging her to meet her fate. She might be a deviant, but her pride was all she had left.

At last, she found herself at the door of a large study lined with books. A fire burned in the hearth. Nikola curtsied, not daring to look at the man in white who sat behind a massive oaken desk.

"Did you encounter any trouble, Captain?"

A deep, commanding voice. She wondered if Komenko would kneel and kiss the ring, but Falke didn't seem to expect it.

"The journey was uneventful, Reverend Father."

"Then you may leave us. I would speak with Domina Thorn alone."

The panic ticked up a notch. So he knew her name. Well, of course he would. It meant nothing. Komenko bowed and backed to the door. Nikola heard it close softly behind him.

"Please, you may rise."

She stood erect, grateful that the cloak covered her torn dress. The new Pontifex of the Eastern Curia regarded her. He had a square, handsome face and closely shorn silver hair. She knew he'd fought in the civil war and he still had a martial bearing, back straight and shoulders squared. Cunning as an old fox, the chars had whispered. And those were the ones who liked him.

"Reverend Father," Nikola said contritely, knitting her hands together. "Please, I am deeply ashamed of my behavior. I will atone in any way I can. Running off was reckless and impulsive—"

"Let's drop the pretense. You carry Malach's child, do you not?"

The room tilted. She swallowed hard, but managed to meet his stare. "What? I don't know that name—"

"You showed no sign of pregnancy only a few weeks ago. Now you are heavy with child. Therefore, it must have been fathered by a mage. Only one has been inside the walls of this city." He steepled his fingers. Her eyes drifted to the heavy gold ring.

Nikola suddenly remembered the fight she'd had with Malach. The car was stopped at a crossroads. One way led to Bal Kirith, the other to the coast. He'd been high as a kite on painkillers, so she'd taken his rambling with a large grain of salt. But he'd said something about a deal with Falke. That he'd promised to give the cardinal a baby in exchange for a truce. He said there had been other women. Other failures. She was furious. But in the end, Nikola had chosen Bal Kirith. Malach would have died if she hadn't.

She met Falke's proprietary gaze. Somehow, he knew everything. Her body was no longer her own. It belonged to the Curia.

"You were in league with him from the start, weren't you?" Falke continued. "I know you were in Domina Novak's chambers the night Malach came. I assume you told him where to find her." He sighed. "But I hold no malice. I blame Malach's corrupting influence. He used you. Don't worry, you will be well cared for, Domina Thorn. This is a great gift you bring us."

Fear gave way to anger, sudden and biting. "It's *my* child! You cannot have it!"

"You are the vessel, but it is Malach's child." Falke smiled. "I wish I could see his face when he learns I have custody. But I don't suppose you know where he is, either. I cannot imagine he would have let you go willingly."

A sharp kick made her gasp. "You see?" she shouted. "Even the baby despises you! You cannot take it from me—"

The door flew open. Four knights rushed in. Two placed themselves between her and the pontifex. The other two took her arms.

"Bring her to the chambers that have been prepared. She is to be watched every second of every day. The child must be protected."

From her, Falke meant. He thought she'd attempt suicide. Or try to induce an abortion. But it was the last thing she intended. Nikola gave him a cold stare and let them escort her from the study. Malach's words echoed in her mind.

*Our child will break them. It's her destiny.*

Nikola cradled her roiling womb. She'd give Falke what he wanted.

And Saints help him then.

# Chapter Twenty-Six

Lezarius stared at the dark hole in the ice where Dantarion had fallen through.

He'd prayed to be rid of her. The only reason she'd let him live was because she wanted to use him to break the Void.

She'd threatened to torture his cat.

Beleth's daughter. A killer through and through.

He stepped back as a hand burst up from the depths. White fingers gripped the edge of the ice. Dantarion's head emerged, the hood of her cloak floating around her shoulders like a bloodstain. She sucked in a rasping breath. The ice crumbled beneath her fingers. For an instant, wide green eyes fixed on him. Then the black waters closed over her again.

Lezarius prodded the sheet with his walking stick. He could see air bubbles trapped beneath. It was not as thick as it should have been. He didn't dare take another step, but if he knelt and extended the stick, it would just reach the hole.

*You are an old fool*, he thought. *If she takes hold of it, she'll pull you both down.*

He sank to the snow. His knees ached with cold.

"Mage!" he shouted. "If you can hear me, I am trying to fish you out!"

He poked the stick into the gap, stirring the surface, but no hand came up again to seize it.

A minute passed. Even if she could hold her breath, the chill water would paralyze her.

He reached into his coat. Greylight was a bundle of warmth against his chest.

"It's better this way," he whispered. "If all else fails, she will try to use compulsion on me. I will be forced to banish the ley, which will alert Balaur to our presence. And I cannot allow him to escape again!"

Lezarius stood and brushed the snow from his knees. Then he noticed a fine crack in the ice a few meters away. Seconds later more appeared, radiating out from a central point.

As though a fist pounded from underneath.

Before he could entertain second thoughts, his feet were shuffling over, testing each step. He brought the stick down hard. Once. Twice. The ice cracked and fell inward. An arm thrust from the hole, scrabbling for purchase.

"Grab hold!" he called, tapping lightly on the knuckles.

She seized the stick and suddenly her full weight was tugging him across the ice. Lezarius grunted and clung to the stick. Dantarion's head and shoulders emerged. He gave a mighty heave. She was halfway out when the stick slipped through his fingers. The ice groaned beneath them. Some of it gave way, the sodden cloak dragging her down again. Dantarion found the opposite side of the hole with her heels and kicked. The force pushed her out all the way. He hooked her sleeve and dragged her a few meters to what he hoped was solid ice.

Other than convulsive shivering, the mage didn't move or speak. He knew she would die anyway. He had no way to make a fire. No dry clothes or blankets. Lezarius considered chafing her hands, but he was afraid to touch her. The cloak was already stiff, her auburn hair rimed with frost. He was about to recite the liturgy for the dying, but realized she would not want it.

"If you can use the ley to save yourself, I will not stop you," he said.

Her teeth chattered as she met his eyes. "W-w-w . . ." Tears of frustration froze to her cheeks. "W-w-why?"

"Because you saved me from the knights. Now we are even."

He could see this made no sense to her. If anything, she looked angry. The Broken Chain around her neck glowed like banked coals.

Yet her breath remained shallow and the shivering started to slow. She tried to push herself up, but her movements were clumsy. She slumped back down.

"It will not be long now," he told Greylight. "The ley cannot give heat. Nor can it heal. We have done what we could." He regarded the cat. "What? Don't be ridiculous. I will not give her my own warmth. If I touch her, she will—"

He cut off at movement on the far side of the lake. A sledge, drawn by shaggy white beasts with curling horns. It came on fast, runners slicing through the powdery snow. Lezarius squinted against the glare. The knights wore the livery of the Blue Flame. *His* knights.

The urge to run nearly overwhelmed him. But why had he come here if not to pass through the gates?

Lezarius leaned on his stick as the sledge drew to a halt. The curly-haired beasts snorted, breath steaming from flared nostrils. Three knights jumped out. They gave the broken ice a wide berth. None were so foolish as to wear armor on Lake Khotang, though swords hung at their hips. The lieutenant, slender and dark like Lezarius, eyed him with suspicion.

"What are you doing out here?" he demanded in harsh tones. "The road is on the other side."

"We came from the forest," Lezarius replied, realizing as

he spoke the words that this was not Osterlish but another language—one in which he was apparently fluent.

*Kindu.*

"The city is closed," the knight said with a scowl.

"Please, she's soaked through! I must get her someplace warm."

Dantarion lay still as a corpse now. Her lips had a bluish tinge. The knights regarded her without a trace of pity. Their tabards looked dirty, their swords dull.

"At least help us cross the lake," Lezarius pleaded.

"You will find no succor here," the lieutenant spat. "Go back to the Morho."

Lezarius felt a prick of anger. The Order of the Blue Flame used to be protectors. Sworn to uphold the Five Virtues —compassion, courage, fidelity, honesty, and forgiveness. Compassion came first because without it none of the rest mattered. *How far they have fallen*, he thought.

"Go!" The knight repeated, stabbing a finger in the direction of the forest.

Lezarius considered teaching them a lesson in manners, but he decided to let Dantarion do it. Assuming the mage was still alive.

"Just let me take our purse," he stammered. "My daughter has every coin of our money."

A greedy light entered the man's eyes. "That ought to be enough to compensate us for our wasted time."

"What?" Lezarius feigned dismay. "Please, it's all I have."

The knight brushed him aside and knelt down next to Dantarion. He started rooting through her cloak. "Consider it a tax," he said with an ugly laugh. "And count yourself lucky we don't throw you both back in that hole."

Lezarius let out a wail, sniveling and begging to be spared. The other two knights watched him with grim pleasure. Neither noticed Dantarion's eyes open. A pale hand closed around the would-be thief's wrist. Lezarius sensed abyssal ley lighting her Marks. The lieutenant's unshaven face went slack. She hissed a few words. He blinked and nodded.

"We must take them to the Reverend Father," he said curtly, standing up.

The other knights looked incredulous. "Why?" one ventured. "He never—"

"Because I say so!" the lieutenant roared. "Carry her to the sledge or I'll have you both whipped for insubordination."

They hurried to obey with the frightened expressions of men who knew it was no idle threat. Lezarius was bundled into the center bench, Dantarion next to him. She was shivering again, a good sign, though she did not look at him once. The lieutenant shouted a command to the shaggy beasts—they were called *gauru*, he suddenly remembered—and the sledge skimmed across the ice. The wind picked up in the middle of the lake, sending skirls of dry, powdery snow across the ice. Lezarius tried not to think about the depth of the water beneath them. He listened to the smooth hiss of the runners and the rhythm of the gauru's shaggy hooves.

The settlement on the other side drew closer. Houses two and three stories high with curving, upturned eaves at the roof corners crowded shoulder to shoulder along narrow terraces that hugged the lower slope of the mountain. Carts laden with produce from the valleys wound along the main road leading to Jalghuth. It was a mixture of snow and frozen mud. Two of the knights jumped out and raised the runners, converting the sledge to a wheeled conveyance. They joined the traffic moving towards the Arx.

Lezarius hunched his shoulders. From a distance the town had looked the same, but up close, the changes were obvious. Refuse littered the streets. Beggars huddled in doorways or stood at the side of the road, hands out, entreating passersby for charity. Few seemed to notice them. Those who did spat in the mud and shouted for them to make way. Everywhere, he saw angry, bitter faces. A gang of ragged children surrounded one miserable soul with a growth on his neck and started pelting him with stones. He threw his hands up, trying vainly to shield his face.

"Stop that!" Lezarius shouted, rising from the bench.

The children laughed at him. The beggar lurched toward the cart, a desperate look in his eye.

"I'm starving, grandfather! Spare a coin—"

One of the knights alit and casually backhanded him, knocking him to the mud. The beggar scrambled away on all fours.

"S-s-stay out of it," Dantarion stammered.

Lezarius scowled as the knight jumped back into the moving cart without a word.

They wound ever upward through a series of hairpin turns. The town fell behind them. Then the cart rounded a bend and he saw the gates of the Arx above them.

The Wards on the walls glowed red.

His mouth fell open in dumb shock. How could it be possible? There were hundreds of Wards, inside and out. But it answered the last question—how Balaur had overcome the protective network that circled the Arx. They rolled through the gates. A deep shudder wracked him. Voices whispered at the edge of hearing.

*Now. I must do it now!*

Lezarius tried to banish the ley. It was like standing in the midst of the Mistrelle and attempting to stem the river with his hands. Only blue ley responded to the rational, conscious mind. It was the weakest layer, but shift the surface and the deeper currents followed. He gritted his teeth, but there wasn't enough blue ley to respond to his will. Or the Inverted Marks just didn't work right.

Then the wagon was drawing up before the Pontifex's Palace. The lieutenant jumped out. His knights dragged Lezarius and Dantarion from the bench, pushing them towards the tall bronze doors. More Knights of the Blue

Flame stood guard outside. He barely heard the exchange of words. Every pair of eyes seemed to be staring at him. They *knew*. Inside, they were howling with laughter at his fecklessness.

Lezarius struggled to draw air. His heart raced. He staggered and would have fallen if Dantarion had not gripped his arm.

"S-s-tand t-tall," she whispered. "You are a P-p-p-ontifex."

There was no mockery in her voice. Nor was there any sympathy. But it lent him strength. Whatever else she might be, the mage had courage. Lezarius straightened and walked through the great doors, head high. Dantarion stumbled along beside him. She seemed on her last legs, and he was rather astonished she'd made it this far at all.

A few priests and vestals scurried through the corridors, heads downcast. None of the great hearths were lit and it was deathly cold inside. Faded tapestries covered the stone walls, but Jalghuth was the poorest city and there was none of the gilding or ornamental plasterwork found in greater palaces. Lezarius expected to be brought to the audience chamber, but instead he found himself at the door of his old apartments, the ones he'd occupied before moving to Sinjali's Lance. The lieutenant spoke in hushed tones to the guards outside. They eyed him with stark disbelief.

"No one enters," one replied gruffly. "Those are the standing orders. The Reverend Father is not to be disturbed."

Sweat beaded the lieutenant's brow despite the chill. Yet the compulsion Dantarion had planted in his mind would not allow him to walk away.

"Just relay the message," he begged. "It is of the utmost importance."

The knights drew their swords, faces hardening. At that moment, the door opened. A tall man in purple robes stood on the other side. He looked hollow-eyed and weary.

"Cardinal Jagat," one said in alarm. "We beg forgiveness, but—"

"The Reverend Father will see them," Jagat replied. His gaze flicked to Lezarius with no sign of recognition.

The lieutenant sighed in relief. "Thank you, Your Eminence."

The guards sheathed the blades and returned to their post, allowing the three knights and their captives to enter. Heavy drapes covered the windows, leaving only the dim, flickering light of a few candles. Lezarius perceived a white-clad figure lying on the bed. The lieutenant sank to one knee.

"Reverend Father, I bring you two prisoners. We found them at the far edge of the lake."

A firm hand from one of the other knights pushed Lezarius to his knees. Dantarion had already made the obeisance—or perhaps she had just collapsed.

"And why are they prisoners?" It was a rich, mellow voice, hardly in keeping with the overall impression of a sickroom. "Have they committed some crime?"

The lieutenant stared at the floor. "No, Reverend Father. But they came from the direction of the Morho. It seemed suspicious."

Lezarius looked up. The face above the white robe swam into focus. It was as if he looked into a distorted mirror. Brown skin and bright green eyes with a shock of unruly white hair, yet the features were warped. Warped and . . . horribly familiar.

*I know him. I know him. He is me!*

"Usurper!" he cried, pointing a trembling finger.

Cardinal Jagat leaned over and whispered in Balaur's ear. He flicked a hand dismissively. "I am Lezarius," he said in a reasonable tone. "Who are you?"

"*I am Lezarius!*"

One of the knights cuffed him on the side of the head.

"None of that!" Balaur said sharply. "I share your

concerns, Lieutenant Vashti, but I would question this man myself and I will not see him suffer rough treatment. He must have a disease of the mind."

"I am not mad!"

*Not mad, not mad,* the voices echoed, laughing.

"Bring him to the Lance," Balaur said. "The chamber at the top. I will deal with him later." His gaze turned to Dantarion. "Poor child. She looks half-frozen. See that she's given a hot meal in the kitchens. And dry clothes."

"Yes, Reverend Father."

The walls closed in as Lezarius was hauled to his feet. Then, a soft mew from his shirt.

"What was that?" Balaur demanded.

The knight holding Lezarius frowned. "I don't—"

Greylight! He'd nearly forgotten her. "Hush!" he hissed. "No—" Needle claws sank into his skin. With a yowl, the cat leapt from his shirt.

"Catch that creature!" Balaur bellowed.

Two of the knights leapt to obey. Greylight streaked for the open door. She shot past the startled guards outside and vanished into the corridor.

Balaur had risen from his pillows, face intent. "Search the palace," he commanded. "We mustn't lose this man's beloved pet."

"Yes, Reverend Father," they stammered.

A pang of loss pierced his heart, but Lezarius was glad. Cats were good at squeezing into tight places. And Greylight was just a little thing. Let her hide herself if she could.

Then he was being dragged through the doors and out of the Arx itself to another winding road, this one steep and covered in ice. The runners were lowered and the cart converted back to a sledge. Dark came swiftly as they raced through snowy passes, circling ever closer to Mount Ogo.

A final leg across a narrow stone span and they drew to a halt at the foot of Sinjali's Lance.

The tower loomed like a shard of black ice against the star-strewn sky. It was constructed around a central open column, the outer ring honeycombed with chambers and circular staircases. Lezarius exhausted the last of his strength climbing with the knights to the top. At every step, the voices whispered at him. *You are the usurper. Just a mad old Invertido. That is the truth you cannot face. All a mad dream.*

Lezarius rubbed the scratches across his chest. *No! I have the Mark. I am the Lion of the North! You cannot take that from me. I have the Mark!*

His legs trembled by the time he sank down to a cot in the very same room he had once held Balaur. An intricate pattern of wards covered the walls and ceiling. All glowed a fiery red. Lezarius curled into a tight ball as the knights locked the door behind them.

*He will leave me here to rot, just as I left him.*

Lezarius burrowed beneath the blankets and drifted into an uneasy doze. He woke to the soft echo of footsteps. The door opened.

"I brought you something to eat, old friend," Balaur said, bustling inside with a tray.

He set it down on a wooden table and lit the candles. Seeing Lezarius's own face looking back still disturbed him greatly. There was nothing to indicate the monster that lurked inside save for a tightness around the eyes, as if the mask pained him in some way.

"We are not friends," Lezarius muttered.

"Perhaps not." Balaur smiled. "But I don't hold a grudge."

Lezarius thought this unlikely. Then Balaur tossed something on the bed. A package of Keefs.

"Your companion told me you've acquired the habit."

Lezarius longed to grab them, but the voices warned him of betrayal. "Where did you get this?"

A chuckle. "I have my ways. Go on, indulge yourself. If I

wished to poison you, do you really think I would be so obvious?"

The food tempted him, but not as much as the Keefs. He tore the package open. Balaur offered him a candle. Lezarius lit the cigarette with shaking hands. He drew deep, holding the harsh smoke in his lungs. The voices finally fell silent.

Logs and kindling lay piled in the hearth. Balaur tossed a lit taper inside and soon a fire crackled. He rubbed his hands, holding his palms to the flames. The heavy gold ring of the Pontifex winked on his left hand. The right was missing three fingers. Severed by Dmitry Falke in single combat when the Arx at Bal Agnar fell. Falke had been on the verge of taking Balaur's head when Lezarius intervened.

He must keep it hidden in his sleeve, Lezarius thought. But the transformation was not perfect. And his Marks will be the same. Not even alchemy can alter those.

"How was the journey?" Balaur inquired. "The Morho can be fickle with trespassers."

Lezarius exhaled a stream of smoke, calmer now. "You sound as though you expected me."

"I knew you would come."

"Bal Kirith has fallen to the Curia," Lezarius said, hoping to shake his confidence.

"For now. They will not hold it long."

"You're penned by the outer Wards, aren't you?" It gave him a small degree of satisfaction that not all of his work had been undone.

"In some ways." Balaur studied him. "But I have abilities that reach beyond the Wards."

"Your dream-walking?" Lezarius sniffed dismissively, though he knew just how dangerous that could be.

"Among other things. While you whiled away your days playing chess at the Batavia Institute, I engaged in my own games of strategy. The north is mine. Soon, the west will topple."

"Clavis will never let that happen."

Balaur's green eyes sparkled with amusement. "What do you remember, old friend?"

"Enough. You corrupted my cardinals and stole my face." He tossed the butt of the Keef into the flames. "So you feign illness? Is that how you've avoided discovery?"

"It is not feigned. I grow old." Balaur gave a wry smile. "As do you."

"What food did you bring?"

"Chatar and a lentil zal."

Lezarius lifted a lid. Spices filled his nose. He spooned rice into a bowl and set to. The spicy flavors evoked hazy images of a plump woman with grey hair stirring pots on a woodstove. *My grandmother?* So much of his mind was still damaged.

Balaur uncorked a dark green bottle with no label and poured two cups.

"God drank the Virgin's milk, left us his wine," he murmured, raising his cup. "How human things have humanized divine!"

"You speak in riddles," Lezarius muttered.

"And you never read the old mystics. Angelus Silesius is an unsung poet." He sipped the wine. "It is the missing piece in your faith. Humanity needs a god to worship. One to fear. It is the only thing that separates them from savagery."

"When did you ever care about savagery? I saw the state of the city."

Balaur waved his mangled hand. "I have done nothing to encourage that. Jalghuth merely reverted to its natural state after you left. They are weak." The friendly tone slipped for a moment and contempt tinged his voice. "Weaker than you imagine. Once the Wards reversed, they all drank the abyssal ley with abandon."

"That's nonsense." Lezarius ignored the proffered cup. "But I will be of no use to you, *old friend.* I already tried to banish the ley. I couldn't do it. Which means I cannot break the outer stelae either. So we are both trapped here."

Balaur laughed. "You think so? I don't need you. My disciples are coming. My Magnum Opus!"

Lezarius's eyes narrowed. "Whom do you speak of? The nihilim in the Morho? Bah! I have seen them. They are a sorry lot. And as I already told you, Bal Kirith is occupied."

"Never mind." A thin smile. "You will see for yourself when they arrive. In the meantime, you can tell me what you know about a young woman from Novostopol. Dark-haired and buxom. She is one of the Curia's pariahs. Unmarked."

Lezarius frowned. "I don't know who—"

"You met her in Feizah's chambers," he said with a touch of impatience.

Lezarius remembered the woman now. She liked cats, too.

"How do you know about that?" he demanded.

"We have spoken." A shadow crossed Balaur's face. "But she resists me."

"Is she here?"

"No, but I will find her. What do you know of her?"

"Nothing."

Balaur stared at him, expressionless. The Wards in the room flared. "Speak truth!"

A hot pinprick in his belly. "I know nothing!" Lezarius cried.

He sensed an ocean of pain lapping at his feet. The needles jabbed deeper. Lezarius winced, knocking the empty bowl to the floor. " Katarzynka Nowakowski!" he gasped. "She gave me her name but that's all!"

The pain ceased as suddenly as it arrived.

"You see," Balaur said in a regretful tone. "That is all I wished to know. Ever you were prideful, Lezarius. It is your downfall."

He strode to a small arched door set into the outer wall of the chamber and unlocked it with a key. A strong gust swirled his white robes. The rectangular doorway was black in the darkness, though Lezarius knew what lay beyond. An icy parapet that plunged a hundred meters to the rocks below. Present and past fused. Wind howled as shadowy figures advanced, driving him backwards on the ledge.

*No!* Lezarius pressed his hands to his ears, rocking on the cot. *That is done! I will not live it again and again!* He bit his cheek until he tasted blood. Slowly, the vision faded.

*You must face it—or be forever haunted.*

Sleet stung his cheeks as he followed through the open arch. The craggy, snow-mantled heights of the Sundar Kush glittered in the starlight. Balaur stood at the far edge of the parapet, gazing out over the valley. His back was turned.

Lezarius saw them locked together in a final embrace, two old men tumbling down, down through the snowy night . . . .

*Balaur called you prideful, but it is his own arrogance that brought him down before. Again he underestimates you. Seize your chance! He thinks you haven't the courage—*

Lezarius was poised to lunge forward when something swooped from above and alit on the parapet. At first, his eyes refused to accept what he was seeing, even though he had anticipated the betrayal. "It cannot be," he whispered, chilled to the bone.

Cardinal Vinaya's squarely handsome face was the same —heavy black brows, strong nose, faint pockmarked scars from adolescent acne—but the rest of him was . . . no longer a man. Wings snapped, the thin, veinous membranes buffeted by another gust, then folded against his back. Slits in his crimson robes accommodated the bony protuberances erupting from his shoulder blades. Instead of the Blue Flame, a jagged sun was embroidered on the breast.

A second abomination landed moments later. Cardinal Sabitri. She knelt at Balaur's feet. "Reverend Father," she said. "You summoned us."

Veins of darkness ran down the backs of her hands and up her slender neck.

Lezarius slid deeper into nightmare. He remembered when Sabitri was a novice vestal. Bright-eyed and studious, always asking questions. She'd risen quickly through the ranks. He had Marked her himself.

"Bring me the cartomancer," Balaur said. "She will be traveling with companions." His gaze grew distant. "They're not in Kvengard anymore. Scour the western reaches of the Morho. I want her found!"

Vinaya glanced at Lezarius, who stood in silent shock. The cardinal had been his closest confidante. A shrewd tactician, but full of good humor. Even in their darkest moments, he could make Lezarius laugh. Now his eyes looked cold and dead.

"What of the others?"

"Use them as leverage. Or kill them, if need be."

Vinaya and Sabitri both bowed low. "It will be as you command, Reverend Father."

Wings extended, blotting out the stars. The hunters soared into the frigid darkness.

"What have you done?" Lezarius shouted, trembling with helpless rage. He took a step forward and the abyssal Wards on the tower ignited, driving him to his knees.

"Only what I must." Balaur stepped back from the edge of the parapet. "You experience the mortificacio, old lion. Defeat and failure. The bitter death of the soul. One rarely chooses it willingly, but I will tell you a secret from the *Rosarium Philosophorum*. When you see your matter going black, rejoice." A gentle smile. "For you are at the beginning of the Work."

# Chapter Twenty-Seven

They rode hard for hours. It was too dark to see in the woods, so Alexei insisted they stay on the main road between Kvengard and Nantwich, which was lined with white stone stela that ticked off the kilometers. Every now and then, he galloped back to check for signs of pursuit, Alice loping alongside with her hitching gait. Finally, he signaled the others to rein up.

"We must find a place to camp," he said. "The Marksteeds could go all night, but your mounts need rest."

"*I* need rest," Natalya remarked, swaying in the saddle. "Just point me to a dry patch of ground."

Neither of the women was used to riding. By the time Kasia dismounted, she wondered if she'd ever walk properly again.

"It'll be worse tomorrow," Patryk Spassov warned as they led the horses into a thick stand of trees that concealed them from the road.

"I'm not sure that's possible," Kasia replied, wincing as she sank to the ground.

"At least we're more than halfway there," Alexei said. "I checked the last k-marker. Another day at most."

He parceled out bread and cheese from the Danzigers' kitchen. They ate in silence, Tessaria's death casting a pall over everyone, Kasia most of all. She kept expecting to hear Tess's dry voice barking orders or reassuring her that all would be well. She wished Jule Danziger was still alive so she could kill him again. But even her rage crumbled beneath the heavy stone of grief. She had no desire to do a reading. She wanted only to sleep for days.

Alexei volunteered to take the first watch while the others curled up in a pile of dry leaves. Kasia immediately fell into a deep slumber. If she dreamt, she did not remember it.

At first light, they drank water from a nearby stream and set off again. Alice had vanished, but she soon reappeared, jaws red with the blood of some luckless creature. The road cut through northwestern outskirts of the Morho where the jungle turned to firs and hardwood. Birds sang in the trees and the weather grew cooler, though still pleasant.

They let the horses go at a brisk walk. Kasia spurred her mount forward to ride next to Alexei. In daylight, his face looked even worse. One of his lips was split open and a vicious bruise marked his cheekbone. He'd washed off the dried blood in the stream, but there were still traces on his cassock.

"Who did that to you?" she asked.

He glanced over with a guarded expression. "My brother."

She'd suspected as much. "You still haven't told me what happened to the children."

Alexei's fingers tightened around the reins. "He took them on the ship to Jalghuth."

Kasia stared at him in amazement. "To Balaur?"

"Yes." A bitter smile. "He thinks they're his own personal army."

"Saints," she whispered.

"He left Sofie Arneth. I gave her to Bishop Morvana Zeigler."

"Do you trust this woman?"

Alexei was silent for a long minute. "No, I don't. Which makes me a monster, I suppose." He turned to her. "But I had no choice! I had to find you and I couldn't take the child back to the house with me. I had no idea what was waiting there."

"You did the only thing you could," she said reassuringly. "I'm sure she'll be cared for."

He gave a tight nod. "Morvana came with other priests. If they were all in on it, they would have killed me then and there. I sent them into the lab. Morvana promised to round up any of the parents who weren't there. But there's a connection to the Arx. I have no idea how far up it goes."

She absorbed this. "Then how can we be sure we won't find the same thing in Nantwich?"

"We can't."

Kasia released a long breath. "I promised her, Alexei. I have to go."

"I know. But we must be very careful."

They both turned as Alice started to bark. Spassov came up at a gallop, waving frantically. "Get off the road!" he hissed.

They hastened into the trees and dismounted. Alexei handed the reins to Kasia and crept back. After a moment, she gave them over to Natalya and followed. He lay on his belly, peering through the underbrush. Kasia wiggled up beside him, propped on her elbows. They watched as a company of riders came into view.

"The Kvens," he mouthed.

She caught a brief flash of blue tabards. They seemed to float in midair above their shadowy steeds. Kasia counted a dozen knights. They galloped past, hoofbeats fading into the distance.

"Well, they're ahead of us now," he said grimly.

They waited for another few minutes. No more appeared, but Alexei looked uneasy.

"Why didn't Morvana send hounds?" he wondered. "They would never have missed us."

"Can they track in the Void?"

"By scent only, not Marks, but yes."

"Maybe she couldn't spare them?"

"The kennels hold two dozen. Luk breeds them. It makes no sense."

"Or she doesn't really want to catch you."

"That makes no sense either. She's a hard woman. Whether or not she's in league with the Order, I imagine she's royally pissed right now."

Kasia rose to her feet, brushing the leaves from her dress. "Well, it's an unanswerable question, Bryce. I'm just glad they passed us by."

Alexei nodded, though she could see it troubled him.

"At least we know where our pursuers are," Spassov said when they returned. "If we cut through the forest, we might beat them to the gates."

"Didn't you say the forest was dangerous?" Kasia asked.

"No more so than the road is now." He shrugged. "Take your pick."

"The forest," Natalya said firmly. "If it's shorter, that's all I need to know."

Patryk and Alexei exchanged a look. "There's a place we can camp," Patryk said, though he sounded oddly reluctant. "If we make good time, we'll reach it by dusk."

Both men had served in the long, grinding conflict that followed the creation of the Void. The Curia had glossed over the casualties, casting it as a victorious occupation, but Kasia knew better now. They'd never broken the mages—not really. The Morho was simply too big and too wild to be tamed.

Kasia hauled herself back into the saddle with a repressed groan. She cast a last look at the road, then turned her horse toward the deep woods.

---

THE SUN WAS SLANTING low through the branches by the time they forded a shallow river and scrambled up the muddy bank on the opposite side. Patryk held up a hand.

"It's just ahead," he said.

The land beyond the river sloped downward to a grassy plain. Sparse stands of trees dotted the landscape. In the near distance, a tumble of boulders thrust up from the earth. Kasia squinted, shading her eyes. Some of them looked too regular to be natural formations, with sharp, squared corners.

"Are those stelae?" she asked.

Spassov shook his head. "Older. Ruins from the Second Dark Age."

She studied the ground ahead and saw a grassy depression that might have been the remains of a road. "What was it called?"

"I've no idea. But there's another stream there and some of the buildings are intact. We're still half a day from Nantwich. Rough shelter is better than none." His voice sounded gruff, but it didn't seem directed at her.

Alexei's sharp gaze swept the plain. The skies to the west were clear, but thunderheads mounded to the east, promising a wet night. He spurred his mount to a trot. The others followed. In a few minutes, they'd reached the ruins. The outer perimeter was composed of weather-worn marble blocks surrounded by dead clumps of grass. They held traces of inscriptions, too faint to tell what language it had been written in. Kasia rode past a pitted staircase that led to nowhere. Dead leaves drifted against roofless buildings, now fractured by meandering tree roots. She paused next to a headless statue pockmarked with tiny craters.

"Bullet holes," Alexei said softly beside her. He pointed to a large patch of blackened, melted stone. "That's a blast mark."

"What kind of weapon could do that?"

"Not a shell. Something bigger."

She suppressed a shudder. "People were horrible back then."

His gaze looked hollow. "Worse than us?"

"Yes, worse than us! Tessaria says—" She cut off, lips tight. Alexei touched her arm.

"I'm sorry. What does she say?"

Kasia drew a deep breath. "Tess told me that we used to be beasts. That the mages forced us to fight, but it would be the last war. She said we have no choice but to serve the Via Sancta because the alternative is barbarity. I . . . I was so angry at her. I just wanted to be left alone. I never really believed any of it." She held his eyes, defiant. "But I do now. And you can't take that away from me!"

Alexei rubbed a hand across his scalp. "I don't want to take it away." He laughed, and for a moment the deep bitterness dissipated. "I *am* a priest, as you might recall. I haven't renounced my faith. I just—"

"Over here!"

They turned to Patryk, who was waving at them.

"We'll continue our theological debate later?" Alexei said with a hopeful grin that made her pulse speed up.

Kasia nodded. "I'd like that," she said.

They rode deeper into the ruins, Alice ranging ahead, her nose to the earth. Patryk and Natalya had found a structure that was mostly standing. Part of the roof had fallen in and the tiled floor was covered with more dead leaves, but it offered shelter from the rain. They unsaddled the horses, who seemed grateful for the respite from two days of hard travel.

Patryk handed them two small apples apiece. "I found them in the orchard. The deer got most of them, but there were a few higher up."

Kasia bit into the apple. It was tart, but juicy.

"Can we have a fire?" Natalya asked, rubbing her hands.

Patryk lit a cigarette and tossed her the box of matches. "I'll help you gather some kindling."

"Is it safe?" Kasia wondered.

The ruins sat on a hilltop. Any flame could be seen for kilometers around.

"We'll build it inside the walls. The smoke can vent through the roof. In the rain, it won't be visible." He grinned, though it seemed forced. "I've camped here before on patrol. And we never took stupid chances."

Kasia and Alexei led the horses to a patch of open grass and turned them loose to graze. She sat down on a block of stone, watching storm clouds gather over the plain while Alexei rummaged in his saddlebags.

"I found this in the Arx," he said, sitting down next to her with a large book bound in dark red leather. "I wanted to show it to you before the weather turns. See what you make of it."

She eyed the book with curiosity. "*Der Cherubinischer Wandersmann*. What does it mean?"

"The Wandering Cherub. It's by Angelus Silesius. A work on alchemy."

He opened the cover. The pages looked fragile, ancient. Alexei turned them with great care, showing her a series of vividly rendered illustrations that she immediately recognized as allegory in the same way as her cards, though their meaning was obscure. A white peacock. A three-headed beast roaring in a glass phial. A serpent devouring its own tail.

"The dragon consumes itself, dying to rise again," she said softly.

He cast her a sharp look.

"That's what one of the Order said to me in Novostopol."

"There's more." Alexei's gloved finger traced a passage.

*Thrice Forty Nights she lay in grievous Plight.*
*As many Dais in Mourning sate upright,*

*The King Revived was in Forty more,*
*His Birth was fragrant as the Primrose Flower.*

"The Magnum Opus," he said. "It must be." He shook his head in frustration. "But it's all so cryptic! Does Balaur seek only to use the children? Or does he plan to undergo this process himself? If he does, what will he become? I tried to find other books at the Arx, but there were none."

A drop of rain pattered down and he quickly closed the cover, returning the book to his saddlebags.

"I can give you some names," she said. "Perhaps Clavis will know more. Tess said her archives are extensive."

He frowned. "You've studied alchemy?"

"No, of course not. But I remember the books from the laboratory. I only saw the spines, but I can tell you the authors." Kasia thought for a moment. "Paracelsus and Korakkar. Tris . . .Trismegistus . . . ." She stumbled a little over that one. "Al-Farabi and Magnus. There was one more . . . Llull! Double L's."

"You noticed all that?" He gave an incredulous laugh. "We were attacked moments after we entered the room. And then the children . . . ." He swallowed at the memory of them rising from the stone slabs.

Kasia touched his hand with a laugh. "I remember *everything*, Alexei."

A slight flush crested his cheeks as she gazed at him. "I won't forget that again," he said.

The rain grew heavier and they ran back to the shelter of the building. Spassov had a small fire going under the roof hole. Kasia expected Natalya to be lounging with her boots off, but she'd unwrapped Tess's knives and was hurling them at a rotten log propped in the corner, a determined expression on her face.

"If I nailed that bastard after being drugged, I think I

show promise," she grunted, a knife flying from her hand. It thunked into the log just off center.

The reminder of Jule Danziger erased Kasia's smile. "I just wish you'd killed him slowly," she said.

Nashka strode to the log and yanked out the blade. "Next time," she said, "I'll start at the cock and work my way up."

Spassov blinked. "Remind me to stay on your good side, Domina Anderle."

"I have no good side," she replied dourly. Then she winked at him. "Unless we're drinking buddies. For that, I can make an exception."

Spassov grinned and offered her his flask. "Almost empty, but as long as you save me a drop. . . ."

They shared out the last of the cheese and bread. It was a meager meal, but the light and warmth raised Kasia's spirits. She listened to the rain drumming on the roof and wondered about the people who'd lived here. Had it been a beautiful place once? She wanted to believe so. Records from the Second Dark Age were fragmentary. Perhaps that was on purpose. A period that should be forever erased from human history. But she knew they'd invented things like cars and telephones. The hydro dams that powered Novostopol. Not all of it had been bad. Yet somewhere along the line, society entered a downward spiral. The Praefators had stopped it by building their sanctuaries.

Did the world now stand at another brink?

She shifted, trying to find a comfortable position on the shattered tiles.

"Are you cold?" Alexei knelt down next to her. "You don't even have a cloak."

"It's all right—" Kasia smiled as he wrapped her in his exorason. "Thank you."

"I'll take first watch," Spassov said.

"And I'll take second," Natalya murmured. She'd made a

leafy nest for herself in the corner, though Kasia noticed she kept her knives unrolled and close at hand.

Alexei nodded and sat down by the fire. She studied the lines of his face. The bruise was livid in the firelight.

It must be hard to love someone like Mikhail Bryce, she thought. He's not just mad, he's dangerous. Easier to steel your heart and walk away. But she knew Alexei wouldn't do that. He was too loyal. And he would suffer more for it.

Her hand stole to the cards in her pocket. Would they even work in the Void? Probably not. Either way, she wasn't ready to try it. The last time had been too disastrous.

Kasia's eyes grew heavy. At first, she dreamt of Alexei. They were in an enclosed garden, dappled sunlight filtering through the trees. It was the ruins, restored to their former glory but empty of people other than the two of them. The air smelled of honeysuckle and sex. She lay on her side in the grass while he combed her hair, and she wanted to turn around and touch him, but then he stood up.

"Where are you going?" she said. "Don't leave me!"

He smiled and his form shimmered to mist. She stood up, angry and confused. This wasn't right. This wasn't—

The thought was driven straight out of her head at the sight of another man approaching.

He had white-blonde hair and very blue eyes, but they weren't like Alexei's, warm and teasing. These were shrewd. But she was not afraid of him. He was old. Harmless.

"There are many kinds of power in the world," he said, as if they'd been in the middle of a conversation. "The ley is only one."

"All power comes from the ley," she said. "There is no other."

"You misunderstand. The ley is the tool, but the source is the mind." He tapped his temple. "The will."

Kasia shrugged. "I suppose so."

"You wield it yourself." His gaze sharpened. "How do you do that?"

"I don't know."

"Yet you have a deep understanding of archetypes. Of symbols and their literal truth."

The man wore a dark cassock. Some kind of priest. He waved a hand. He wore a heavy gold ring on the stub of a severed finger. A series of cards appeared in the air between them.

Twenty-two, like the Major Arcana, beautifully rendered in red and gold paint, with ornate borders. One reminded her of The Mage. The figure held a flask, but instead of light, a dark ribbon emerged from the top, bearing words in the Old Tongue that she couldn't read. Kasia's gaze flicked across the images. Seven flasks, each containing a strange beast. A man, his face both beautiful and terrible, brown hair swept to the side as if in a sudden wind. Wings extended from his shoulders, marked with glowing runes. Then, seven keys, each forged from a different base metal. A great three-headed serpent, it's body sundered in pieces. A fiery cauldron with an ashen corpse standing upright, a dove perched on its head. A tower with the sun on one side and the moon on the other. Two more flasks, holding a King in red robes and a Queen in white.

There was a strange coherence to the cards as though they told a story, but the whole meaning eluded her.

"The Splendor Solis," he said. "The path from death to eternal life, as imagined by Salomon Trismosin. Look at the pictures. Can you tell me what they mean?"

She felt a spark of irritation. The garden was for delights, not serious talk.

Kasia swept her own hands through the cards and they vanished. "I do not know. I think it would require long study."

His lips had tightened when she banished the image, but now he smiled. "I have spent thirty years pondering them.

Parts I understand, yet others remain opaque. It would mean much to me to hear the thoughts of an expert."

The tone was obsequious. Flattering. But Kasia cared little for the opinions of others. "I cannot help you," she said coldly.

"Perhaps not." He regarded her. "You have a fierce will. It sets you apart. Just as it sets me apart."

"Apart from whom?" she wondered.

"The common masses." His lip curled. "The followers."

Kasia folded her arms. She disliked this man. "This is my garden. I want you to leave."

His smile died. "And if I say no?"

"I will make you leave."

A small orange salamander skittered past his foot. The man casually crushed it beneath his heel. "We will talk again soon, Katarzynka." He reached for her, a look of intense longing on his face, then let the hand drop. "And you cannot shield yourself then."

Kasia stared at the poor broken creature. When she looked up, her eyes blazed. "You dare?" A hot wind bent the trees. "I will do the same to you—"

She blinked and the man was gone. *He knew my name. How?*

But the thought was lost as Alexei's hand caressed her shoulder. When she looked back, the salamander was whole again. It wiggled away, an orange streak through the emerald grass.

"Kiss me." Hot breath in her ear.

*A dream within a dream.*

Alexei's arms folded around her and she thought no more.

# Chapter Twenty-Eight

"Couldn't sleep, eh?"

Patryk cast him a wry look as Alexei joined him beneath the dripping eaves of the roof. The hound sat at his feet, ears pricked.

"Why don't you go lie down?" Alexei suggested. "I'll finish the watch."

Patryk turned his flask upside down and gave it a sad shake. "No, I'll stay." He shot Alexei a sideways look. "Did your unit ever camp here?"

Alexei shook his head. "The Laqueos were always sent to Bal Agnar or Bal Kirith."

"The hotbeds of dissent." Spassov turned his back and lit a cigarette, heavy shoulders hunched around the flame. "I'm sure it was worse there."

"It was bad everywhere."

"Did you ever do something you regret?"

Alexei laughed mirthlessly. "Is that a serious question?"

In all the years he'd known Spassov, they'd never once talked about the war. It was easier to forget it in the bright lights and crowds of Novostopol. When the memories did surface, his Marks made them go away. But standing in the rainy darkness of the Void, he felt the old ghosts stirring. It must be the same for Patryk. He looked tense, fingers instinctively cupping the ember of his cigarette so it wouldn't be visible.

"I'm not talking about the things you had to do," he said. "I mean a major fucking mistake."

Alexei leaned back against the weathered stone wall. "The last day of my final deployment, we were at the Arx in Bal Kirith inspecting the stela. Scouts found the remains of a campfire in the basilica. Somehow, the mages had slipped through the cordon. We went to investigate. I had a bad feeling and I turned out to be right."

"What happened?"

Every minute of that day was etched into Alexei's mind. He shoved down the sound of an inhuman scream. "They ambushed us. Malach was there. He flipped my brother's Mark. I was wounded." Alexei glanced down at Alice. "She saved my life."

Patryk crushed the cigarette under his boot. "That's not your fault."

"I should have listened to my instincts. Misha spun a story about how we shouldn't pull another unit for backup because we'd be playing into their hands. I let it go, but deep down I knew. I'm sure he did, too. He wanted to confront Malach. To kill him. Misha would have died too from the sickness, but he didn't care anymore. I think he just wanted the Nightmark gone. It had changed him for the worse." Alexei shook his head. "He was willing to sacrifice us all."

"Where is he now?"

"On his way to Jalghuth. Another suicide mission."

"Saints. I'm sorry."

"Yeah." Alexei turned to him. "Go ahead, get it off your chest."

Patryk looked blank. "What?"

"Whatever you did." A slight smile. "I'll take your confession, like the old days. No judgment. Believe me, I've got plenty more myself. It would take hours."

Patryk took out his cigarette case, turning it over in his hands. "Do you remember how tired you used to get? I mean, all the way past exhaustion to a state that was like . . . like living death?"

Alexei stared at him. "What do you think, Patryk? I haven't had a good night's sleep since—" *I passed out in Kasia's bed*. He cleared his throat. "Years."

A barked laugh. "Yeah, okay. You get it. This was a while back. We were escorting a convoy to Nantwich. Some bigwig cardinal. I was a lieutenant captain in charge of the advance party. We were doing sweeps, checking the terrain ahead." He let out a breath. "The fighting was hot back then. We were losing a lot of knights."

Alexei nodded. "I was in law school, but I read about the casualty counts in the papers."

Spassov's face darkened. "What they didn't print was the brutal mutilations. Severing and worse. It was different in the elite units like the Beatus Laqueo, but among the foot soldiers, desertion wasn't uncommon. You'll say they were cowards, but I understood it. The pressure was intense."

Alexei hadn't known that. "Where did they go?" he wondered.

"The Morho. Maybe they're Perditae now, who knows?" He rolled the case over and over in his hands. "Anyway, we were losing guys, women, too, and not just to the mages. So when one of my advance scouts didn't come back, I figured he'd taken off."

"But he hadn't."

"No. I should have sent more scouts to check it out, but I gave the all-clear. The whole convoy rolled straight into a trap." Patryk finally broke down and opened the case, lighting another cigarette. The match trembled slightly. "Only three of us made it out. The cardinal got killed. It was a complete clusterfuck."

Alexei had expected worse. "Look, my whole unit got shelled once when field artillery screwed up the coordinates—"

"It's why Kireyev owned me," Patryk said in a rush. "He wanted eyes in the Interfectorem. Especially after you came. I guess it was because of your brother. They didn't trust you."

Alexei met his eyes. "Ah, shit, Patryk. No."

"Listen to me!" Spassov looked a little wild. "I only reported to him for the first year or so. And there was nothing to tell! You did your job and you did it well. I never told him a fucking thing. And once I got to know you, I decided I was done. It was bullshit!" He touched his Raven Mark. "I swear on the ley I had no idea about Massot or any of that. I didn't even know why they were interested in you. It was a one-way street, Alyosha. Kireyev never shared information. I kept Kasia's name out of it when you asked, didn't I? I got her in to see you in the cells, right? I was sick when they arrested you. I had no idea it was coming."

Alexei's mind raced. He understood now why Patryk always seemed so well-connected.

"I'm sorry, brother. It's been eating away at me. I know you'll probably never speak to me again, but I had to come clean." He eyed Alexei with trepidation. "Say something. Even if it's just to tell me to fuck off and die."

"Did he send you to keep tabs on Kasia and Tessaria?"

"No! I did that because you asked me to. I intended to submit my resignation." He looked away. "I was sick of it all. Kireyev had me by the balls for long enough."

Alexei's anger faded. The Archbishop of Novostopol might look like a friendly gnome, but the man was a ruthless manipulator. He'd ordered Alexei's death to clean up his own mess—and Spassov would never have gone along with that.

"I know Kireyev," he said. "If it wasn't you, it would have been someone else."

"Yeah, but it wasn't." Patryk's shoulders slumped. "Kasia saw it. She made me pick one of her cards. I didn't believe in that crap until she read me like a fucking book."

A smile twitched Alexei's lips. "What did she say?"

"That I'd screwed up badly."

"What else?"

A shrug. "That I'd paid for my mistakes and she trusted me now."

"What was the card?"

"The Priest of Storms."

Alexei remembered sitting on her couch, watching her lay out the cards. The intent look on her face as she studied them. Another rainy night—just before the buzzer sounded and Malach appeared.

"She gave me a reading once," he said.

A spark of curiosity lit Patryk's brown eyes. "What'd you get?"

*The Lovers.*

"I don't remember."

"Yeah, well, I don't know how she does it." He sighed. "Does this mean I'm forgiven? I'll swear on a *Meliora* if you want."

Alexei's hand stole to the damaged book in his pocket. It was all he had left of Misha now.

"Forget it," he said. "We're good. I'm glad you told me though."

Patryk looked immensely relieved. "No more secrets." He shifted. "I need to piss. Will you stand watch?"

"Your turn's almost up anyway." He glanced into the building. Both women were fast asleep. "I'll take the next one. Let them rest."

Spassov nodded and slipped into the darkness. Alexei rubbed his eyes, jaw cracking in a yawn. He always slept better in the Void, even when he was afraid for his life. Whatever connection existed between his Marks and the insomnia, it faded when the ley was gone.

Alice had sunk down, resting her head on her paws.

"How do you feel in the Void, eh?" he asked softly.

She gave a low whine.

"Me, too."

He'd told Kasia he hated losing the ley, but the truth was more complicated. No warm bubble to dull the unpleasantness, yet it did bring a certain clarity. Alexei wondered whether Patryk would still have confessed if his Marks had been functioning. He wondered if he'd been drinking when he made the wrong call.

A question Alexei would never ask.

He squinted into the darkness. Patryk had been gone for too long. Maybe he had a secret stash of vodka he didn't want Natalya to know about—

Alice shot to her feet. A growl rumbled in her throat.

He reached for a blade that wasn't there. He'd left it lying by the fire.

A black shadow swept down through the rain, alighting in front of him. Alice leapt and was batted aside by a leathery wing. He had a moment to register taloned feet digging into the mud on back-jointed legs and then it was on him, slamming him back against the stone wall. He slid down, dazed. It threw its head back and screamed, a piercing birdlike cry from an all too human throat.

He grabbed a fistful of red robes and yanked hard. The thing went off balance for an instant, but the impact had frozen his diaphragm. It shook him off and stepped through the doorway, wings folding down against its back. An aura of intense cold surrounded it. Alexei sucked in a desperate breath. It came out in a spurt of white mist.

A muffled exclamation inside the building. Alexei found his feet. In the dancing light of the fire, Natalya held the creature at bay with a small knife, Kasia behind her. Alexei dove for his sword. A blade flashed past his peripheral vision. The thing shrieked again. A hilt jutted from its shoulder. It spun around and he saw the face. A woman with glossy black hair and large almond eyes. Veins of pulsing darkness corded her neck. A wing unfurled, vast in the enclosed space, and swept Natalya to the ground. She rolled over with a moan. Kasia gripped the cards in her hand, glaring down at them. She looked more furious than afraid.

"Get outside," Alexei rasped, raising his sword. "Run!"

The woman's head swung between them. She judged him a greater threat and crouched to attack. He braced his legs, sword ready, but she twisted at the last moment to spring at Kasia. The leap carried her across the room. She grabbed Kasia by the arm. Kasia's eyes went wide, face twisting in pain. Alexei lunged towards them when a sudden bone-deep chill made him turn. Another one stood in the doorway, a head taller and broad of chest. Male, but not a man. Crimson robes emblazoned with a jagged black sun that seemed to suck all the light into itself. Dead eyes locked on Kasia.

"The King seeks an audience," it said. "Come willingly or we kill them all."

She hesitated, her expression tight. "How do I know you'll spare them?"

"No!" Alexei slashed at the folded wings. It grabbed his blade in a bare hand. The steel cut deep but the thing held on, a thin smile on its lips. No blood dripped from the wound.

"You cannot harm us." It jerked the sword from his grasp. "Bow down, priest. Bow down before your new masters—"

Savage barking and then forty kilos of fang and muscle slammed into its back. The thing stumbled forward just as Alexei brought a knee up to meet its face. Bone crunched. Alice's jaws opened wide and clamped down, locking on the black-throbbing vein in its throat. She seemed gripped by a frenzy of hatred, whipping her muzzle to and fro. Alexei tore the sword from its limp hand. He needed a clean blow to take the head off, but Alice was in the way.

"Mitis!" he snapped. *Stop biting!*

She wouldn't listen. It was still fighting, the wings half unfurled and tipped with nasty-looking curved talons. Alexei finally planted a boot on her side and drove her off long enough to bring the blade down with both hands. Its severed head rolled into the fire. Putrid smoke filled the room.

"Kasia!" he shouted.

She was still struggling in the other one's grasp. Then Natalya loomed behind them. She drove a knife into its eye and kicked it toward the flames. Kasia was nearly dragged along, saved only by Natalya's grip on the back of her dress. The deck went flying, cards scattering across the floor tiles. Her attacker staggered into the campfire. Its red robe went up like dry twigs. A flaming wing spread wide as it screamed. There was a horrible note of despair, like a soul tortured to the brink. Alexei cringed at the sound. He wondered if part of the thing welcomed its own end.

The two women hurried to the door. Natalya seemed equally shaken, but Kasia stopped short on the threshold. "My deck!"

"Leave it, for fog's sake," Natalya growled. "I'll make you another!"

The decapitated one had finally stopped twitching, but the fire was spreading to the leaves drifted against the walls, fanned by a fresh breeze blowing in the doorway. Alexei caught a whiff of putrefaction. At least they were dead—or, more accurately, dead for good. Alice still worried at the headless corpse. Alexei seized the loose skin along her hackles and dragged her off.

"Nulla!" he said sternly.

She curled her upper lip. Then she gave a sharp bark and started rolling in the foul remains, back arched and feet kicking.

"What? No!" He eyed the dog with disgust. "*Cessa*!"

Alice had a last luxurious wriggle and bounced to her feet, tail wagging.

"Are you proud of yourself?" he muttered.

She grinned, tongue lolling, and obediently followed him into the wet night. Clumps of dark matter clung to her coat. He hoped the rain would wash it off.

"I have to find Patryk," he said. "Watch the sky. There could be more."

Kasia grabbed his sleeve. "What happened to Spassov?"

"I relieved him for a minute. He never came back."

Alexei watched her, but there wasn't a hint of suspicion. She did seem to trust Patryk unconditionally.

"Saints," she said, biting her lip. "I'll help you look."

"I'll check on the horses," Natalya said, sheathing the knife in her belt. Like his sword, it was clean of gore, as though the things were already desiccated inside.

"He went this way," Alexei said.

They'd only walked about twenty meters before Alice found him. She let out a low, mournful howl and dropped to her haunches. Kasia rushed over and knelt down. Patryk's eyes were closed, his skin ashen. His hand was icy to the touch. Alexei's mouth dried as he searched for a pulse. It fluttered weakly beneath his fingertip. The knot in his chest loosened.

"He's still alive," Alexei said.

Kasia nodded. Her face was calm, but he sensed the same intense relief. "Where's he hurt? I don't see any blood."

Alexei carefully examined him. The dark cassock had concealed a shallow slash down his left arm, but he couldn't find any other injuries. The cut had already stopped bleeding.

"Doesn't look too bad," he said, puzzled. He'd seen Spassov take worse from Invertido without batting an eyelash. "He's drenched through. If he's in shock, that doesn't help." It was still raining hard. "I'd give him my cassock, but I'm soaked, too."

"We have to get out of here," Kasia said, scanning the thick, low clouds.

"I'll try to rouse him." Alexei gave him a shake, lightly slapping his cheeks. "Wake up, Patryk," he said gently. "You have to ride."

Spassov didn't respond. Alexei shook him harder. His eyes cracked open.

"Patryk. Can you hear me?"

He blinked. "Yeah," he said hoarsely.

"Can you stand?" Alexei glanced up at Kasia. "Help me."

Between the two of them, they managed to haul him up.

"Why'd you have to be such a big bastard?" Alexei muttered, swaying a little under the weight.

"That's what all the women say," Patryk managed.

Natalya's barking laughter rang out. She held the traces of the two regular horses. The Marksteeds followed of their own accord, eyes shining golden in the darkness. "I see you found our hero."

"What happened?" Spassov asked. He was still pale as milk.

"We were attacked." Alexei briefly described the encounter.

Spassov muttered a curse. "The last thing I remember, I was, uh . . . ." He glanced at the women. "Visiting the bushes. The rest is a blank."

"Be glad you missed it," Kasia said, not unkindly. "And that they didn't finish you."

He gave a strange shudder. "I'm fucking useless, aren't I?"

"Not as useless as I am," she replied with sudden anger. "Alexei and his dog got one. Nashka skewered the other. But without my cards, I was—" She bit the words off, staring at the orange glow flickering through the doorway. "Since we literally lit a signal fire, I think it's time to get moving."

It took several attempts to lever Patryk onto his horse.

When they finally did get him settled, he slumped in the saddle, expression tight.

"Half a day," Alexei said. "Then you can lounge around in a feather bed at the Arx while pretty vestals wait on you hand and foot."

"Pretty *knights*," Patryk corrected with a sickly smile. "The armor turns me on."

"Pervert," Natalya said cheerfully.

Alexei swung up to the saddle, marveling at the woman's resiliency. When they first met, he'd taken her for one of Novo's party girls. She was that, but plenty more besides. He knew battle-hardened knights who would have pissed themselves at the sight of those demons.

The robes disturbed him deeply. Cardinals of the Black Sun.

*It rises again.*

He shoved the thought from his mind.

They set off across the plain, Alice ranging ahead. The old wound seemed to pain her, for her gait was stiff. He hoped it was just the damp and not a fresh injury. The downpour remained steady and drenching, but he was grateful for it. If there were more searchers, the poor visibility would hamper them. Alexei rubbed his back. It ached from getting slammed against the wall, but he knew he'd gotten very lucky. Whatever power ran in those things' veins, at least it hadn't touched him.

Patryk was more familiar with this part of the Black Zone, though Alexei had a general idea of which way to go. Nantwich lay to the west on the coast of the Northern Ocean. They were well out of the Morho Sarpanitum now. If they kept going across the plain, eventually they would hit the road again.

Alexei rode in the lead so he didn't realize Patryk had fallen from his saddle until Kasia gave a shout. He turned. His partner lay motionless in the knee-high grass. The riderless mare was spooked and danced a few steps sideways as he rode up. Alexei managed to catch the reins. He quickly looped them around his own saddle horn.

"What happened?" He dismounted and hurried over. Alice had stopped a short distance away. Her hackles rose, though she didn't growl.

"I don't know," Kasia said. "He started shivering like he had a fever. Then he just toppled."

Alexei felt his brow. It was freezing cold. He pushed up the left sleeve and hissed. The wound looked like it had been festering for days. Patryk's whole arm was a dark, mottled purple. Alexei pulled the sleeve down before the women saw it.

"What?" Kasia demanded. Strands of dark hair were plastered to her face.

"We have to get him to Nantwich," Alexei said grimly. "To the Reverend Mother. It's the only chance."

"What's wrong with him?" Natalya asked softly.

"There might have been venom on those talons. Or something else. I don't know. But it's killing him." He eyed Patryk's bulk and dismissed the notion of a litter. They had nothing to make one from anyway. "He'll have to ride with me."

This was easier said than done. Spassov was a dead weight, though he roused now and then to mutter deliriously. They tried laying him across the saddle, but he kept sliding off. Alexei finally mounted and braced his feet in the stirrups while the two women heaved Patryk up under his arms. Between Alexei's pulling and their pushing, they eventually got him astride the horse. Spassov's head lolled back against his shoulder like a broken doll.

The riderless Marksteed had calmed down. Alexei trusted it to follow.

"Stay close," he said. The women nodded. He urged his mount to a gallop, thighs aching from the effort of keeping them both upright. Dawn was still hours away. He gritted his teeth against the chill radiating from Patryk's body. How fast would it consume him? Once the infection reached his heart . . . . Alexei refused to think about it. He dug his heels in, willing the horse to go faster.

Dark hills sped past. Swaying clumps of oak and ash, their branches creaking in the wind. Patryk mumbled incoherently in his arms. Alexei slipped into a waking doze, his muscles taut and aching but his mind floating free. He remembered the day he'd met Spassov for the first time and groaned inwardly that Kireyev had stuck him with a violent, chain-smoking lunatic. They'd immediately gotten into an argument over Invertido. Patryk had called him an overeducated rich boy, among other things. Yet somehow they'd wound up in Spassov's room, drinking and perusing his stack of lurid pulp novels. He claimed they didn't qualify as pornography because the storylines had a moral lesson, which Alexei pointed out was only because Bishop Karolo insisted on it.

"You think she reads them?" Spassov had wondered, flipping through *The Cocky Mage*. "Like, every single one?"

Alexei took a bracing sip of vodka. "It's her solemn duty, Spassov."

Then the dogs had started barking and they'd scrambled down to the kennels. That's when he discovered that Spassov was indeed a competent drunk driver. Alexei been more or less sober by the time they reached the scene. His first Invertido was an old woman whose Marks had flipped during a rancorous game of bridge with her elderly sisters. Patryk burst into the parlor like a battering ram, but once he saw what he was dealing with he'd been surprisingly civilized, coaxing the old woman out from underneath the card table with a pack of cigarettes. They'd whisked her off to the Institute without much trouble. No one was hurt.

"See?" Alexei said as they drove back to the Tower of Saint Dima. "They're not so bad."

Patryk had laughed. "You don't know anything, do you? Just wait."

It turned out to be the easiest case Alexei ever had. They'd still argued frequently, but he sensed Patryk ceding ground—probably out of sheer weariness. After a few weeks, Alexei insisted on doing the driving. Spassov shrugged. "Great," he said amiably, tipping the flask. "Now I can really get lit."

But he never seemed drunk, just permanently hungover. They saved each other's lives many times over. Alexei grew to love him like a brother, though not enough to tell him about Mikhail. Or his hunt for Malach.

*We both lied*, he thought, as the sky began to lighten. *But it doesn't matter.*

Alexei realized that Patryk had stopped mumbling.

"No, you bastard," he said roughly, groping for his icy wrist.

Nothing. Alexei dug deeper, refusing to accept it. A faint flutter.

"Hang on," he said, his throat catching. "Just a little fucking longer. Please."

Dawn streaked the grey clouds. Even the Marksteed was flagging, its head hanging low. Alexei urged it to a trot. He wondered how much farther the poor beast could go before it collapsed from exhaustion.

"Alexei!"

He twisted in the saddle, then followed Natalya's pointing finger. Six dark dots had appeared against the eastern sky. Ten minutes earlier and they would have been invisible in the dark.

"Ride for the trees!" he shouted.

They wheeled around and galloped for a stand of oaks. Water dripped from the branches, though the rain had stopped. The horses huddled together. A thin scream came from the sky above. "Sileo," he hissed at Alice, who stood quivering, her lips curled.

He heard the slow sweep of wings and eased his sword from the saddlebag. The things cast no shadow, but he sensed them passing overhead. Searching. One of the mounts shifted nervously. Ice crackled beneath its hooves. He released a misty breath, suddenly chilled to the bone.

And then they passed by, dwindling to specks over the Morho.

"Will they keep hunting in daylight?" Kasia wondered softly.

"If they do, we're finished," Alexei replied. "But we must go on."

She glanced at Patryk and looked away, her lips tight. They rode out from the cover of the trees. The landscape gradually grew brighter, a high plateau of open grassland broken by occasional granite boulders thrusting up from the earth. The last trees vanished behind. If they were caught out here, there would be no place to hide. The women realized it, too. Without speaking, they all spurred their weary mounts to a gallop again.

A few minutes later, to his great relief, Alexei spotted the road. It was partly hidden by a series of hills, but several of the stelae along the verge were visible, shining white in the morning sun.

"How much farther from here?" Kasia asked.

"I don't know," he said. "Not too much, Saints willing."

They trotted down a long slope, reining up at the first Wardstone. To the right, the road curved away into the hills. To the left, it ran due west towards Nantwich. Alexei was leaning down to read the kilometer number when Alice started barking. He squinted up at the sky, heart pounding. It was clear. "What—"

"Riders," Natalya snapped.

They wheeled around, but it was too late. In an instant, they were surrounded by a dozen knights in blue Wolf tabards. They must have been just around the bend. When Alexei saw who was leading them, he muttered an oath.

The last time he'd seen Kommandant Rademacher, spiders had been crawling out of his mouth.

The kommandant surveyed him coldly. He was a lean man, with blonde hair neatly parted on the side. "It's my old friend Captain Bryce. But no, that was your brother, wasn't it?" Grey eyes turned to Spassov's limp form. "What is wrong with him?" Rademacher demanded.

"He was bit by a viper," Alexei said quickly. "On the arm. The wound requires immediate medical attention."

Rademacher said nothing.

"I'm escorting these women to Nantwich. Just let me see them to the gates and I'll go back to Kvengard with you."

"Fra Bryce," he said crisply. "You already deceived me once. I have no warrant for the others, but Bishop Morvana Ziegler made it quite clear that you are to return to the Arx without further delay."

Kasia rode forward. "You're not taking him," she said calmly.

Rademacher frowned. "And who are you?"

"A citizen of Novostopol." She held up a piece of parchment. "We are acting at the behest of the Reverend Father Dmitry. I have proof. This document gives the bearer safe passage and orders all subjects of the Via Sancta to obey his writ."

The kommandant eyed her with a touch of surprise. "Bring it here."

Alexei glanced at Natalya, who gave a slight nod. Not a forgery then. He wondered how on earth she'd gotten hold of it.

Rademacher scanned the parchment closely. "It bears the Raven seal," he announced.

Alexei held his breath.

"But as you noted yourself, it grants only the bearer safe passage. Had this been given to me by Fra Bryce, I would have no choice but to obey." False regret tinged his tone. "Unfortunately, that was not the case."

Kasia's eyes narrowed. "This is dangerous country. I require

Fra Bryce's aid to reach the city. Without him, I cannot be guaranteed safe passage. Therefore, it must extend to all of us."

Alexei suppressed a smile. She would have made a decent lawyer.

"A technicality," Rademacher said with a chilly smile. "I will send two of my knights to escort you."

"That is not acceptable. The Reverend Father will be furious when he learns—"

"That his spy has been apprehended?" Radamacher spat, his face reddening. "Count yourself fortunate I don't drag you all back. Now, Fra Bryce, since your companion is unable to ride, he will return to the garrison with you."

Alexei stared in disbelief. "He'll die! You must take him to Nantwich."

"We adhere to the restrictions of the *Meliora*," Rademacher said stiffly. "But when force is necessary for the preservation of public order, the knights of Saint Ludolf have latitude. Do not test me, Fra Bryce."

Four of the knights dismounted. They held thick cudgels. Alice started barking.

"My men are trained to deal with Markhounds," Rademacher said. "If yours proves troublesome, it will be dealt with harshly."

One of the knights took out a black metal collar with a hinged joint. When Alice saw it, she gave a low whine and began to tremble.

"What is that?" Alexei demanded. He'd never seen the like.

"A device to sever it from the ley. A failsafe for dogs that cannot be controlled."

"But . . . the ley is woven into her flesh! You cannot—"

"*Sede!*" The knight with the collar snapped.

Alice's rump hit the ground. She lowered her head in submission, tail pressing tight between her legs.

"Leave her alone!" Alexei wanted to run to her side, but he still bore Spassov's weight. At this point another fall might finish him. Natalya saw Alexei's stricken expression and slid from her horse.

"Stop it!" she cried. Two of the knights blocked her way. She gave one a hard shove that knocked him back. "Don't you touch me!"

Natalya started tussling with the knights, Kasia cursing and trying to steer her horse into the fray, as the Kven with the collar approached. Alice turned her face away. She snapped at the dirt, a jet of urine spurting from her hindquarters. His fearless little sister. Rage flooded him.

"Put the dog down," Rademacher said impatiently. "We've wasted enough time."

"*Evanesce!*" Alexei whispered, urging her to vanish. "For Saints' sake, go!"

Alice shivered violently, but her brown eyes were dull. She refused to look at him. Time slowed to a crawl as the hinges of the collar clinked open. The knight suddenly gave a cry of pain as something bounced off his head.

A pointy-toed pump with a vicious spiked heel.

He frowned down at it in confusion. A thin line of blood trickled from his temple.

"Touch that dog," Kasia yelled, brandishing its match, "and I'll shove this right up your—"

"Enough!" Rademacher roared. "Seize them all!"

Alexei was reaching for his sword when the thunder of hooves drew his gaze down the road. Two dozen knights in full armor rounded the bend, yellow tabards bright in the morning sun. A banner with Crossed Keys snapped from a lance at the rear. They galloped up and formed a ring around the Kvens.

One of the knights raised her helm. Steely eyes locked on Rademacher.

"Kommandant," she said loudly. "A little out of your jurisdiction, aren't you?"

He drew himself up. "Captain Anderton. I am merely executing an arrest warrant on behalf of—"

"Run back to Luk!" one of the knights behind her jeered.

Alexei knew the two cities had tepid relations, but he was surprised at the open hostility. Things had worsened. He quietly slid the blade back into his saddlebag.

Rademacher's eyes narrowed. "The Reverend Father of the Southern Curia. You may examine it if you like."

Anderton held up a gauntleted hand. "That won't be necessary. We're taking them all into our custody."

He stared at her, a slight flush creeping toward his white-blond hair. "You will not honor the writ?" he demanded. "This is a serious breach of both custom and law."

"Luk holds no sway here." She glanced up the road. "The Fort of Saint Agnes controls these lands. And I obey the Reverend Mother Clavis." A cheeky smile. "So I'm afraid you're out of luck today, kommandant."

The Wolves and Keys traded glares of mutual enmity. Alexei feared it would end in bloodshed, but the Kvens were outnumbered and the company from Saint Agnes all wore swords at their hips.

"So be it," Rademacher said finally, nodding at his men.

Alexei locked eyes with the knight who held the vile collar. He gave him a thin smile. The man spun without a word and mounted his horse.

"This is not the end of the matter," the kommandant vowed tersely.

Captain Anderton looked untroubled. "You may convey your objections through the usual channels. Have a safe journey back to Saint Ludolf."

Rademacher sawed the reins, jerking his poor horse around and galloping off. The rest of the Wolf knights followed. Captain Anderton turned to two of her men.

"Follow," she said. "At a distance, but let them see you. I won't have him changing his mind."

They saluted and galloped off. Anderton rode up to Alexei. "Your friend looks at death's door—and you not far from it. If you'll allow us, we will take charge of him."

He hesitated, then gave a brief nod of assent. His back was screaming from hours in the saddle with Patryk slumped against him.

Kasia dismounted to collect her shoe. "You'll take us to the Arx?"

The captain nodded, her shrewd gaze studying them all. "The garrison is closer, but I don't think your friend has long."

Three knights eased Patryk from the saddle. They wore gloves but must have felt the wintry chill emanating from him. A young blue-eyed woman cast Alexei a guarded look of pity, then addressed the captain. "He's already dead, sir."

Kasia had gone very pale. She gave a slight shake of head.

"No," Alexei said sharply. "He has a pulse! Look for it!"

The knight tugged a glove off and pressed a finger to the juncture of Patryk's bullish, stubbled neck. Her eyes widened. "I'm sorry, I was wrong . . . but how . . . ." She snatched her hand back.

"We should make haste," Captain Anderton said matter-of-factly. "Who will ride with him?"

No one volunteered. The knights looked at each other. Then an olive-skinned man nearly as big as Spassov took his helm off. "I'll take him."

"Very good, Liebowitz." She signaled the lance corporal and he hoisted the banner. Alexei nudged his horse over to Kasia and Natalya. "Rademacher kept the letter from Falke," he said in a low voice. "There will be fallout from this."

Kasia scowled. "I don't give a rat's arse about that little martinet." She glanced at Spassov's limp form, which was being handed up to Liebowitz. "We'll sort it out later."

Alexei whistled and Alice slunk over. She still had a

forlorn, haunted look he disliked. He leaned down from the saddle, ignoring the curious stares of the knights. "I would never let them do that to you, understand? Never!" He dangled a hand down and she gave it a lick.

Then the knights were forming into two lines. Six fell back to take the rear, hemming Alexei, Kasia and Natalya between them. *Are we guests?* Alexei wondered. *Or prisoners?* Either way, Clavis had clearly been expecting them. The odds of meeting a random patrol would be slim.

As they rode north, he realized that Captain Anderton had never asked how Patryk was injured.

# Chapter Twenty-Nine

The schooner rode up a swell, then slid down the opposite side, trailing a wake of white spindrift. Malach's calves flexed in time with the motion. The coast was a dark line behind him now. Rocky islands poked their heads above the waves, inhabited only by multitudes of squabbling gulls that watched the ship's passage with incurious eyes.

He'd woken with a few bruises but nothing worse. It surprised him—though not as much as the fact that he was still alive at all.

"See anything you like, witch?" Malach asked with a slow smile.

He stood on the deck naked except for his chains while Captain Aemlyn and the witch, whose name was Paarjini, inspected his Marks. The women ignored his taunt. They were speaking in a foreign tongue, apparently debating something.

"Do you understand?" Malach whispered to Tashtemir, who stood next to him, also naked and chained, but with a spectacular black eye to boot.

"Some," Tash whispered back.

"And?"

"Aemlyn is wondering if they should throw you overboard."

"With the chains on?"

"I assume so."

Malach peered into the choppy depths. They were beyond the Void now. There was ley down there somewhere, near the bottom. If he could reach it before he drowned, he might escape his bonds.

The witch turned to him with narrowed gaze as if she'd deduced his train of thought. She was dark-tanned and fierce, with long brown hair worn loose, but it was the pewter eyes that gave her away. On the beach, she'd worn the same garb as the rest of the crew—a dark blue coat over white breeches. Now the wind whipped a black gown slit up the sides, with silver and gold embroidery along the hem. It had oddly wrapped sleeves that left her shoulders and elbows bare. Rings with inset stones gleamed on every finger, even the thumbs. A leather pouch hung at her waist.

Paarjini said something to the captain. She relayed it to four burly sailors who looked like they could give armored knights a run for their *fides*. Malach readied himself as the women approached.

"Oh dear," Tashtemir muttered. "They have the same look Fat Yagbu gets when he fondles his horsewhip."

He started gabbling in the witches' tongue. The sailors pushed past him and wrestled Malach to the deck. He didn't fight as hard as he could have. The possibility of drowning struck him as a reasonable tradeoff considering the other potential outcomes. If he survived, he could swim to one of the islands.

Then hands gripped his face, forcing his mouth open. The witch dropped something on his tongue.

"Swallow, *aingeal dian*," she said in a thick accent.

The women clamped Malach's jaw shut. He shook his head wildly. It tasted bitter and metallic.

"..uk…ooo," he managed, trying desperately to spit it out.

"Swallow. Or ye'll choke."

The stone seemed to swell, slipping back on his tongue. Two of the women pinned his head, the others his arms and legs. Black spots swam before his eyes. In a panic, Malach sucked in a breath of air. He shuddered as the stone slid down his throat. The sailors released him and he sat up, coughing violently. A tingle of power ran through him.

Malach stared up at the witch with reddened eyes. "What," he rasped, "did you just put inside me?"

"The kaldurite stone of your lover. Somethin' to remember her by." An evil grin. "It's bound by spells so ye won't shit it out, aingeal."

Malach spat on the deck and wiped his mouth. It was the only consolation. Nikola had escaped—or maybe they'd let her go. Either way, he was grateful she didn't share his fate.

The witch joined her sisters at the bow. There were three on board the vessel, which was unheard of. They never set foot on the continent. They hated the Via Sancta and the Curia loathed them back. One might think the nihilim would be their natural allies, but the witches despised Malach's kind even more.

Chains rattled as Tashtemir helped him to his feet. "Look on the bright side," he whispered. "They could have stuck it someplace else."

Malach winced as the stone worked its way down. It didn't hurt like a Ward, but it would block him from the ley. His own personal Void.

Even through his rage, Malach felt a glimmer of admiration.

How horribly ingenious of them.

"It's almost as bad as being severed," he muttered, throat still raw. "How will I get rid of it?"

Tash shrugged. "Maybe I can cut it out."

The ship pitched upward, riding another billow.

"After we make port," Malach agreed quickly.

Sailors climbed through the rigging, trimming the sails at the shouted orders of a first mate who stood in the wheelhouse. Captain Aemlyn sauntered over, nimbly skirting the web of taut lines. Six crew loomed behind her, each with a curved dagger at her belt.

"Time to head below," the captain said. "It's your choice whether you go feet first down the hatch or the other way 'round."

Malach spat at her feet. "Go fuck yourself."

Aemlyn shrugged. "So be it."

The crew flexed their muscles and stepped forward.

"Wait!" Tash cried. He turned to Malach. "Haven't you had enough?" he hissed with quiet intensity. "Getting our skulls cracked will accomplish nothing. Save your strength for when you need it!"

Malach released a sharp exhale. The southerner made sense. "Fine."

"No need for violence," Tashtemir told the captain with a smile. "We'll inspect our accommodations now."

Aemlyn arched a brow in amusement, though her face was cold. "Give me any more trouble and you'll pass the journey in the bilges."

They were shoved down a series of ladders to the hold in the belly of the ship. Malach expected abject squalor, but other than the reek of salted fish, it wasn't so bad. One end held sealed barrels and heaps of folded sailcloth weighted with coiled rope. Light came through a series of square portholes just above the waterline. The Perditae huddled together, knees drawn to their chests. They glanced at the newcomers with empty, hopeless eyes.

The hatch closed and a bolt slid into place.

Malach found a spot as far away from them as he could get. Tashtemir sank down next to him. The chains ran from wrists to ankles, anchored by iron manacles, but there was enough slack to allow them to stretch their legs out.

"I don't like those women," Tashtemir said with a sigh. "I imagine they intend to sell us like the others. How did you know Paarjini was a witch?"

"Beleth warned me about the eyes. Practice lithomancy too long and it changes you." Malach glanced over. "I thought you'd know that."

Tashtemir shrugged. "I've never met one myself, though I was taught some of their language. The Masdar League has amicable relations with Dur-Athaara."

"What do you know about their powers?"

"Little. Only that it involves metals, stones and gems. Gifts of the earth, forged by ley. But I have no idea how they harness it."

"We were inside the Void, yet that didn't stop her," Malach said thoughtfully. "The stone itself must hold a reservoir of ley." The idea intrigued him. "Who runs Dur-Athaara?"

"The Mahadeva Sahevis. The witch-queen."

Malach felt a spark of hope. He'd behaved crudely, but that was one small facet of his temperament. He also had considerable skills of persuasion and its warm-blooded sister, seduction. Since the day Cardinal Falke made the mistake of permitting him inside the walls of Novostopol, Malach had struck scores of bargains with its citizenry, some of them quite powerful. Nikola Thorn was his only failure—and that was only because he'd conceded defeat. Given enough time, he could talk his way out of this mess.

"I will request an audience," he said.

Tashtemir laughed. "No one meets with her—not even the Golden Imperator."

"Then I will be the first."

"I'll pray for you, Cardinal." Tash tipped his head back. "Slavery is still an easier life than returning to court. Dur-

Athaara means Isles of the Blessed. It is reputed to be a very beautiful city."

Malach made a retching sound.

"No, really, it is—Ah, you shouldn't . . . Ugh."

Tashtemir winced and turned away as Malach stuck two fingers deeper down his throat. He gagged, stomach clenching, but nothing came up.

"If you can't shit it out, you can't vomit it out," Tashtemir said reasonably. "I tell you, a blade is the only way. Just . . . stop that. It's making me ill watching you."

Malach gave a last dry heave and wiped his mouth. "Worth a try," he said thickly.

"Does the stone pain you?" he asked, pity in his eyes.

"Truthfully, I can't even feel it anymore."

"Then let it go for now."

Tashtemir dozed while Malach prowled the hold, searching for anything he could use as a weapon. He tried to pry open one of the casks, but only succeeded in tearing his fingernails. After a while, the hatch opened and a dozen sailors passed out water and bowls of pottage. Malach ate it all, wiping the bowl clean with a chunk of bread.

"No maggots," Tashtemir observed. "Maybe a weevil or two, but that's only to be expected. I've had worse at your aunt's table."

A few foul buckets sloshed in the corner, but the sailors took them away and brought clean ones back. They handed out blankets and even gave the children pallets to sleep on, treating them with brisk kindness. Only Malach and Tashtemir wore chains. The others were permitted free rein of the hold.

The seas grew rougher at sunset and they spent a miserable night rolling to and fro. Malach tried to rouse the Perditae to mutiny, but they weren't having it.

"One of *you* sold us," a bony middle-aged woman pointed out. "You're worse than they are."

"What was the name?" Malach demanded.

"I have no idea. He caught us in the forest." She glanced at her three children. "Said he'd slit their throats if I didn't do as he said."

"Young or old?"

"Young. Blond beard and a missing hand."

Malach nodded. "Valdrian. I haven't seen him for a while."

The woman stared at him with hatred. "Curse you all," she muttered.

"What about you?" Malach called to a group of men.

They eyed him sullenly and refused to answer.

"Go ask," he urged Tashtemir. "Maybe they'll talk to you."

Tash sighed and crawled across the tilting deck. They watched him come with open hostility, but the southerner had a silver tongue and soon enough they were conversing softly. He returned a few minutes later.

"A small band of mages came upon them digging for crabs in the marshes. The leader had a bloody handprint with an eye in the center." Tashtemir touched his left forearm. "Just here."

"I know them. Rogues from Bal Agnar." Malach braced a hand on the wall as the vessel pitched into a deep trough. "It makes no sense. If the witches were after mages, why aren't any of the others in chains?"

"Maybe they got away."

Malach hadn't forgotten the tremendous force Paarjini used against him. He sensed it wasn't nearly the worst she could do.

"Maybe," he conceded, though he wasn't convinced.

He snatched a few hours of sleep wrapped in one of the blankets. Shortly after dawn, they were given more pottage and water. Rain lashed the portholes, but the seas grew calmer. Malach passed the morning in alternating fantasies about Nikola Thorn and what he would do to the witches if he had the ley. Their power rested in the talismans they carried, but his was boundless. It ran in his blood. Or more accurately, his mind.

"She called me *aingeal dian*," he said to Tashtemir. "What does it mean?"

Tash was trying to scratch the welter of mosquito bites on his ankles, but couldn't quite fit his fingers under the manacle. He finally swore and gave up. "*Aingeal* is what they call the light-bringers. As for *Dian,* the literal translation is fervent or intense. But the idiom has a different significance. Closer to . . . fallen from grace."

Malach grunted. "I weary of the endless comparisons to my ancestors. The Praefators were idealistic fools."

"I don't think the witches like the Praefators, either. They are certainly not worshipped as humanity's saviors, as they are in the Via Sancta." Tash stroked his mustaches. "No, Dur-Athaara dates back to before the Second Dark Age. It is older than the Curia—though not as old as the Masdar League."

"And they really hate all men?"

"*Hate* is incorrect. They think we are too emotional to use the ley. That women are the more rational sex and thus should be in charge."

"Do the men go along with it?"

"They seem to. But I have never asked one."

Malach closed his eyes. "Nikola would have liked it there."

"You know, it's almost funny that you're here in her place, Cardinal," Tashtemir said, attacking the bites again. "Domina Thorn risked everything to secure passage, but it's the last place on earth *you'd* choose to be."

Chains clanked as the ship rolled to port.

"The irony," Malach replied wearily, "is not lost on me."

Hours passed. He heard the thud of boots outside and the hatch opened.

"You." One of the sailors beckoned to Tashtemir. "And you." To Malach. "Get up."

The men glanced at each other. "What for?" Malach asked.

An evil smile. "Get up or we drag you."

He shrugged and rose stiffly to his feet, offering a hand to Tash. They passed through a long, dark companionway and up a steel ladder. It led to a hatch that opened to the deck. Malach flinched at the bright sun. He knew only the Southern Ocean and the Bight, both of which were gray. This sea was a dazzling turquoise. A warm salt breeze caressed his bare skin. He'd stopped noticing the fog of bodies in the hold, but he must stink by now. Tashtemir certainly did.

The three witches stood in a line at the stern with Captain Aemlyn. They all wore similar gowns, long and slitted with strips of silver-threaded cloth wound around their arms. One was short and plump, her hair yellow and pinned with jeweled clips. The second had smooth, blue-black skin and long limbs. Paarjini's rings flashed as she swept a curtain of chestnut hair from her face, tucking it behind one ear. The three women couldn't have been more different, yet there was a sameness to them. More than just the smoke-colored irises. An aura of controlled power.

Malach forced himself to meet their fey eyes. He stared at each in turn, then skimmed the horizon. The dark mass of an island lay ahead. Low, forested mountains thrust up from the interior, with strips of white beach along the coastline.

"Will you give me clothes," he asked tightly, "or must I disembark in this state?"

A dozen crew moved about the deck. The ones who understood Osterlish started laughing. Aemlyn's first mate cracked a jest that made them laugh harder. All he understood was *aingeal álainn.*

He glanced at Tashtemir.

"At least she called you pretty." Tashtemir seemed to be stifling a grin. "You don't want to know the rest of it."

Paarjini stepped forward. "You will be dealt with once the saoradh are off the ship," she said.

Malach guessed she meant the slaves. "Why did you capture us?" He cast a cold eye on the captain. "We have traded with you fairly for years."

Aemlyn looked at Tashtemir. "Your companion is free to go."

"So I won't be saoradh?" Tash asked hopefully.

"If you prove that you can behave in a civilized manner." Her tone conveyed doubts.

"What about me?" Malach wondered.

The yellow-haired witch at Panjinni's side scowled. "You are *aingeal*." She made it sound the vilest thing imaginable. Her eyes flicked to his Marks with a hint of fear. "Never to be trusted," she spat.

Paarjini made a slight quelling gesture. "Enough, Cairness."

"Then why bring me here?" Malach asked tightly.

"Because you are a thorn in the foot of the ley," Cairness hissed. "The flaw that breaks the alloy. You should be—" She cut off and spun away, face flushed.

A knot of panic cinched in his gut. This was no random breach of the peace. If he stepped foot on that white shore, Malach knew he would never leave.

He suddenly doubled over, clutching his stomach. Malach bit his lip and tasted copper. He sank to his knees, retching bloody saliva on the deck. "Ah, please," he groaned, tears springing to his eyes. "It hurts! Like a knife twisting in my guts . . . ."

He curled into a ball, squeezing his eyes shut.

"Help him!" Tash shouted.

Feet pattered across the deck. Calloused hands rolled him over. Malach coughed weakly. Through slitted eyes, he saw

Paarjini bend over him, her expression wary but also worried. "This should not be happening. I imbued the stone with a spell of protection—"

Malach looped his chain around her throat, jerking it tight. In a fluid motion, he rolled away, the witch in his arms, choking and writhing.

"Drop a longboat," he growled. "Or I snap her neck!"

Captain Aemlyn looked furious but not altogether surprised. She let out a stream of curses. Cairness was bright red now. Only the third witch looked calm. Her hand slid inside the leather bag at her waist.

"Do it!" Malach dragged Paarjini to the side of the ship. Her struggles were growing weaker. Yet no one hurried to release a longboat.

Even if they had, the whole thing was stupid. Where would he go?

But he kept flashing back to that night in the Arx, Falke's scalpel at his wrist. The witches meant to sever him. Either by taking his hands or stuffing him full of kaldurite.

He might never get another chance to end it on his own terms.

Malach released Paarjini just as the spell's shockwave hit. It washed over him, deflected by the kaldurite, but he gripped the rail and vaulted over the side. A moment of weightlessness. Then blue-green water closed over his head. The chains dragged him down swiftly. He came to rest on a sandy bottom. Dark shapes slid through the murk.

He released a stream of bubbles, emptying his lungs. Yet Malach couldn't quite convince himself to inhale. The body fought death even when the mind accepted it.

The seabed was not deep and he could see the ship's shadow drifting above him, framed in shafts of sunlight that filtered through the clear water. An anchor slithered down, landing not far from him. Then three splashes at the surface.

He started crawling away, fingers digging into the sand. A

school of bright fish darted past. He'd had some futile hope that he might sense the ley, but the kaldurite blocked it as surely as if he'd been in the Curia's Black Zone. His vision dimmed. When he could stand it no more, he opened his mouth and let the sea rush in. It burned like acid. Then something seized his hair. He lashed out, but a rough hand curled around his ankle. They dragged him up from the depths. Malach was barely conscious as a rope around his waist hauled him back to the deck, aware only of an intense ache in his chest as the water was thumped out of him. He spewed it in a hot stream, coughed, and spewed again.

The stone remained firmly lodged in his gut.

"Cardinal." Tashtemir knelt beside him, expression dour. "That was a foolish thing you did."

Malach shook wet hair from his eyes with a scowl. "Why?"

"Because—" He cut off as the three witches approached.

Paarjini rubbed her neck and regarded him with icy disdain.

"I shall tell the Mahadeva of this," she said hoarsely.

"Go ahead," Malach shot back. "I will try again and again. And eventually I will succeed."

Paarjini shook her head. "What she wants with ye, I canna imagine."

Cairness and the dark-skinned witch exchanged a look of resignation. They turned away, following Paarjini to the bow. A few sailors remained to keep an eye on the prisoners. The rest set to work readying the ship for its entrance into the half-moon harbor.

Malach gazed at the shore. Dur-Athaara was the capital of the north island of Tenethe. A south Island called Yrelle formed a distant green hump. Everyone referred to the witches' domain by their capital since it was the only city of any size. Malach's first impression was of sun-baked white stone and trees with bare trunks and swaying fern-like fronds at the top.

His brain was still waterlogged, but Paarjini's last words finally sunk in.

Malach turned. "Tash, did she just say—"

"That's what I was about to tell you," he replied with asperity. "I heard them talking after you went overboard. They're bringing you to the witch-queen. It was their intent from the first. Drowning yourself was needless." He laughed uncertainly. "Though I would not trade places with you. If any man has met the Mahadeva Sahevis, he did not live to tell of it afterward."

# Chapter Thirty

Nantwich was a grand city, melding new and old in equal measure. The incessant honk of car horns competed with the clatter of wooden carriage wheels and foghorn blasts from the barges plying the Caerfax River. Lamps burned along the main thoroughfares, which teemed with crowds of evening shoppers. The rush hour traffic gave way before Captain Anderton and her knights, two of whom rode ahead with the Crossed Keys banner, bellowing at the various conveyances to clear a path. The knights seemed well-regarded, for Kasia detected no hostility at their passage. Several drivers even doffed their caps and waved in respectful greeting.

The company galloped through a stately district of large limestone buildings in the classical style, which Kasia guessed might be the pre-Dark Age museums Nantwich was famous for. Then they crossed the river on a stone bridge anchored by circular guard posts at both ends. A curtain wall rose ahead, heavily Warded, with torches burning along the parapet. Chains rattled as a portcullis was raised. They rode into a tunnel, perhaps eight meters long, hooves echoing in the dark.

Kasia shared a look with Alexei. The Arx in Novostopol had a wall, but the gates were usually left open and it was more akin to an enclosed park. This one was an unabashed fortress. Perhaps it had to be. Bal Agnar was half a day's drive, if that. Nantwich had almost fallen to Balaur once. Clearly, they weren't taking any chances.

The company emerged from the tunnel into a dirt yard. Thick-walled buildings rose on either side, with armored knights patrolling the rooftops. More banners flew from the tops of cylindrical turrets, whipped by a chill wind from the Northern Ocean. The rattle of wooden practice swords rang through the bailey. A group of soldiers was sparring, watched by a grizzled, heavyset officer who stood with his arms folded. Kasia's gaze was drawn to a pair that seemed sorely mismatched. One was a young boy who looked scarcely old enough to sign the recruiting papers. His opponent was brawny and bearded with the scarred face of a seasoned veteran. They squared off, the boy gripping his practice sword with both hands. He wore light armor over a leather jerkin.

Poor kid, she thought, as the others stopped sparring to watch. Their captain must have it in for him.

The boy grinned at his opponent and lunged forward. They traded a flurry of blows too rapid for Kasia to make out. But when the dust cleared, he stood over the larger man, the tip of his sword touching the Mark on his opponent's throat.

"I cede, Reverend Mother," the knight gasped.

The wooden sword lowered.

"Perhaps next time, Copton."

The youth spoke in the clipped, precise accent of the Nantians. It was also the sweet, throaty voice of a young woman. She offered Copton a hand and pulled him to his feet. Clavis turned and noticed the newcomers for the first time. She strode over, sweat matting dark curls to her forehead. Her armor was dented and scratched from hard use. Perhaps the man hadn't let her win after all.

Clavis ignored the humans, sinking to one knee and holding out a hand to Alice. The Markhound sniffed it. Clavis tussled with her for moment, then slapped her flank in a friendly way.

"This is a fine hound," she said, surveying the company. "Whose is it?"

Alexei slid from the saddle and bowed. "Mine, Reverend Mother."

He didn't seem surprised. Kasia had known she was young—twenty-five now, raised to pontifex at sixteen—but little else. Up close, the high cheekbones and smooth brown skin with no trace of a beard made it clear she was a woman—though she still didn't look a day past fourteen. A knight handed her a white cloak, which she threw carelessly over her shoulders.

"The Wolves rode out from Saint Ludolf, Reverend Mother," Captain Anderton said.

"I hope you sent them back with their tails between their legs," Clavis replied.

Anderton's knights laughed.

"Aye, we did, Reverend Mother. They were sore wroth about it, too."

"I'll deal with Rademacher." Her gaze swept over Kasia and Natalya. "Where is Sor Foy?"

The grief Kasia had refused to face lodged in her throat. She looked away as it brimmed over.

"Murdered in Kvengard," Alexei said. "She commanded us to come to you. It was her dying wish."

Clavis stared at him. "This is dire news," she said softly.

"There is more to tell, Reverend Mother, much more. But our companion is gravely injured." Alexei looked at the knight supporting Spassov. "We must see to him first."

"Of course." She turned to Captain Anderton. "Bring him to the infirmary. I'll find you there."

She strode off without waiting for a response. Two of the knights rode off to fetch the surgeon. The rest dispersed, leaving only Liebowitz and Anderton, who glanced down at Alice.

"We have no Markhounds," she said. "But Clavis keeps hunting hounds. Will yours tolerate them?"

"I've never seen her quarrel with other dogs," Alexei said dubiously. He glanced at Patryk, clearly torn. "But I'd prefer to inspect the kennels myself before handing her over. May she come with us for now?"

Anderton smiled. "The surgeon won't like it, but I have no objection."

They handed over the horses. A litter was brought to carry Spassov. The infirmary wasn't far, a brick building with larger windows than the rest. As they approached, Kasia was struck by the youthful appearance of the clergy moving about the Arx—even the cardinals and bishops. The whole place had an energy and liveliness that reminded her of the Lyceum campus. It lifted her flagging spirits. Whatever darkness was spreading elsewhere, she saw no sign of it here.

The surgeon was waiting in the antechamber of the infirmary with two burly male nurses. He cast a dubious look at the Markhound.

"No animals are permitted inside," he said briskly.

"Wait here," Kasia said to Alexei. "I'll come fetch you when there's news."

He gave a weary nod. Alice flopped down at his feet and rested her muzzle on her paws. Jaws cracked in a loud yawn. The dog had run for a night and a day with barely a pause, Kasia realized. She must be even more exhausted than we are.

The two nurses took charge of the stretcher and carried Spassov through a long open ward. Only a few beds were taken, the occupants sleeping, but they passed straight through the swinging doors at the end and settled Patryk in a private room. The surgeon—who Kasia was glad to see had a few gray hairs—ordered the others to wait outside. She sank down on a wooden bench in the corridor, Natalya next to her. Neither woman said a word. Part of it was sheer numbness.

But Kasia knew they'd both seen Patryk's face as he was brought inside. Cold and still—just like Tessaria.

No more death, she thought. Not so soon.

Long minutes passed. At last, footsteps in the corridor signaled the arrival of Clavis. She was accompanied by a cardinal in purple robes, but she herself still wore light armor and looked just as dusty as before. The only concession to her high office was the gold ring on the third finger of her right hand.

"Any word?" she asked, impatiently gesturing for the women to sit down again.

"Not yet," Natalya replied.

"Give me a moment." Clavis went inside the room.

She came out moments later. "He's been given a dose of antibiotics, but the surgeon says there is little more that can be done. They are . . . trying to make him comfortable."

"What do you mean?" Kasia demanded, adding a belated, "Reverend Mother."

"What happened to him?" Dark eyes dared her to lie, but Kasia had no intention of doing so.

"He was poisoned. Likely by a talon." She described the things that had attacked them, leaving nothing out except for the dream she'd had just before.

"And this happened in the Void?" Clavis asked with a frown.

"Yes. The creatures putrified when they died. I saw it before in Kvengard. They are foul constructs, Reverend Mother."

The young pontifex's gaze caught on Kasia for a moment, but her mind seemed elsewhere. "Then it couldn't have been abyssal ley."

"Something even darker," Kasia said. "Please, can't you . . . Mark him? Use the sanctified ley against it?"

"We're already surrounded by hundreds of Wards," Clavis said gently. "They seem to have no effect. It flows strong within these walls, but the ley cannot save him now, I'm afraid."

Her words struck Kasia's heart like a hammer blow.

"You should go to your quarters," Clavis said, as the surgeon emerged with the two nurses. He did not meet Kasia's eye. "There is no more to be done here and you look half-dead yourself."

"No!" She glanced at Natalya, who gave a grim nod. "We won't leave him."

To her surprise, Clavis took her hand. Neither of them wore gloves and her palm was warm and calloused. "You are a stout friend."

Kasia squeezed her hand. "You'll let us stay?"

"Of course." Something flickered in her eyes. "He is still unconscious, but perhaps he will know you are there and find comfort in it."

Clavis left with her aide, speaking quietly to the surgeon.

They entered the room. A bandage swathed his arm. He lay motionless, lashes fanned against his cheeks. The poison had not aged him. If anything, it had stripped away the cynicism, paring Patryk Spassov down to a ruggedly handsome man of early middle years who slept peacefully. An IV ran into his good arm, connecting to a glass bottle on a stand. Otherwise the room was bare. Natalya took one look and whirled to the door with a choking sob.

"I'm sorry," she muttered. "I can't."

Sharp footsteps echoed down the corridor. Natalya was strong but brittle in places. She hated unpleasantness and the death of a friend went far beyond that. Nashka would come back eventually, after cursing herself for a coward, but Kasia doubted Patryk had that much time left. She touched his chill brow. The Knight of Storms. Lost and damaged, but vitally important. She knew it in her bones.

"We need you," she whispered. "*I* need you."

Kasia withdrew her hand. It automatically went to her

pocket, though she knew there was nothing— Her pulse quickened as she brushed the edge of a card. She drew it out. Not one but two cards stuck together. The lining had torn and they'd slipped down. She hadn't lost her whole deck after all.

Kasia half-turned as Alexei burst through the door, breathing hard as if he'd run the whole way. "Natalya told me they claimed nothing could be done!"

"That is what they said," she agreed.

He joined her at Patryk's bedside. "He doesn't look as bad as before," Alexei said with a more hopeful note. "Maybe the antibiotic—"

"Is useless. Patryk has death ley inside him."

Blue eyes narrowed. "Death ley?"

"Call it what you will. I saw it at Danziger Haus." Kasia knew what had to be done now. "There might be a cure. If the Wards allow it."

"What do you mean?"

"Abyssal ley." She turned to him. "I used it against Jule Danziger."

Alexei stepped back, appalled. "But it corrupts!"

She peeled back the sheet. Black veins mottled Patryk's shoulder like the branches of a monstrous tree.

"More than that?" she asked quietly. "When it reaches his heart, he will die." She drew a deep breath. "So will you stop me?"

Alexei shook his head. "No," he murmured, sudden relief in his eyes.

He'd feared she would ask him to do it.

She turned the cards over, laying them face-up on Patryk's broad chest.

The Mage and the High Priestess. Numbers one and two of the Major Arcana, respectively. The mage wore red, the priestess white. The mage held a vial that shone like the sun. The priestess wore a silver diadem with a crescent moon. But they were kin in power.

She wasn't sure what the juxtaposition meant, though it was significant that the cards had stuck together. One could not be read without the other.

"What's going on?" Natalya was back, looking a bit shame-faced.

"Watch the hallway," Alexei said. "We're . . . trying something."

She gave a terse nod and stationed herself outside.

Kasia laid one hand on the mage, the other on the priestess. Then she opened the door.

The cards flickered with blue light. It leapt to obey her now. She focused on her need, diving deeper to the violet liminal layer. A slight tug of resistance from the Wards, but she easily delved past it.

Into the turbulent red.

The Wards above the window flared. She shifted a finger to Patryk's icy cheek. A parasite coiled around his mind. The thing hissed as the abyssal ley touched it. Tendrils flinched, gripping tighter. Patryk groaned. Kasia pried them loose, one by one. It fed on his will to live, but it feared and hated the red ley. The red burned it. The thing shriveled, but as it weakened, she encountered a new obstacle. Patryk's own sanctified Marks fought her, seeking to repel the abyssal ley.

The two layers warred, red and blue. Patryk cried out. She felt the thing's glee. It started slipping through her grasp. Kasia reached deeper, deeper, into the churning maelstrom. Yet the parasite was winning now, feeding on Spassov's terror. She had to calm him somehow. Had to . . . . Without conscious thought, Kasia wove all three layers together—blue, violet and red—joining them in a blade. It glowed with light. *White* light. She slashed the blade through the gripping tentacles.

Alexei inhaled sharply as dark mist welled up from Patryk's mouth. She tore it apart, hurling the shreds at the

Ward above the window. They dimmed for a moment, then absorbed the shadow.

She drew on the power again and probed Patryk's mind for any remaining hint of the vile thing.

"It's out," she gasped.

The blue and violet ley dissipated easily. But closing the portal against the red wasn't easy. She felt so good! Like she could do *anything*. But Alexei was watching her closely and Kasia remembered what had happened last time when the floodgates remained wide. The thought was enough to damper her enthusiasm and the abyssal ley sank back into the floor.

She was dimly aware of Natalya at her side. Patryk's breathing seemed easier. Other than the edge of a Mark, his bare shoulder looked unblemished.

"He's warm," Alexei said in wonderment.

"Thank the Saints," Kasia muttered. Suddenly, her eyes were sliding shut.

"Catch her!" someone cried.

Distant voices. Hands lifted her up. Then cool sheets and Alexei's face swimming above her. "Sleep, Kiska." A hand stroked her hair. She drifted away.

But there was, it seemed, no rest for the wicked. A blond man chased her through her dreams. She kept turning away, her surroundings melting into her old flat, or Tessaria's house, or any of a dozen mundane places she visited in sleep, but always he found her.

And each time, he drew closer before she managed to escape.

---

She woke in the infirmary early the next morning. A nurse showed her to a bathroom with—Saints be praised!—hot running water. Kasia showered and brushed her velvet gown.

Then she asked to see Patryk. The surgeon was in his room, checking vital signs, as she came in.

"I've never seen anything like it," the surgeon said softly. "He seems to have recovered completely. That wound . . . . It was like nothing I've ever seen before. Perhaps the Wards did purge whatever ill humors infected him."

Kasia made a noise of agreement. "Has he eaten?"

"A little broth about an hour ago. He is still very weak. We should let him rest."

She followed him from the room. "Do you know where my friends are quartered?"

"The knight is in the soldier's barracks. Your female companion would be with the vestals, I expect."

Kasia thanked him and walked outside. It was a bright morning, though noticeably cooler than Kvengard. She'd have to find herself a cloak. She was about to ask for directions to the vestals' quarters when the pontifex's aide approached. Cardinal Gray was a slim man of about thirty, with spectacles and an air of quiet intelligence.

"Domina Novak," he said, catching up to her. "I hear Fra Spassov has turned a corner."

"It seems he has. We are grateful for your care."

"The Reverend Mother would like to see you." A pause. "Right away."

Did Clavis know? The woman was notoriously militant. A close ally of Falke and bane of the nihilim. Kasia wondered what the punishment would be for using abyssal ley within the Arx.

"Is she sparring again?" she asked lightly.

A quick, severe glance. "The Reverend Mother is meditating in the basilica."

"Ah. Has she ever been bested?"

"You're wondering if the soldiers fear to strike her. The opposite is true. If she suspected any of them held back, she would demote them to raw recruits." Cardinal Gray stared straight ahead. "Clavis is an expert swordsman, but that is the least of her talents. The Reverend Mother is a visionary. She sees what others do not."

A warning? Kasia thought hard as they crossed the bailey. Step wrong with Clavis and her last ally might turn against her. Kasia had kept her own secret for so long, lying came as second nature. Perhaps she was more like Tess than she cared to admit. But that time had passed. There was too much at stake now.

The basilica was a rectangular building with a central nave and soaring ceiling supported by two long rows of marble columns. It was a stark, echoing space designed to make those who entered feel small. Light spilled through a glass dome, illuminating a slender figure in a chainmail byrnie who knelt with bowed head before the altar. A white cloak hung from her shoulders. Clavis turned at their footsteps.

"You may leave us, cardinal," she said.

He bowed and retreated, closing the great doors behind him.

"Reverend Mother," Kasia said with a curtsy.

Clavis dropped down on one of the benches, throwing a leg carelessly over the edge. A sword hung at her waist. For the premiere symbol of the Western Curia to openly wear a weapon struck Kasia as revealing. Truly, Nantwich held to the *Meliora* by a thread.

"Sor Foy was a dear friend," she said, patting the bench. "Tell me how it happened."

Kasia sat down. Tess had hinted that Clavis already knew much about her.

*She holds the keys.*

"The story is a long one, Reverend Mother."

"Then start at the beginning."

Kasia drew a deep breath. "It all began a few weeks ago. My friend Natalya was invited to a party. The host was a man named Ferran Massot. A friend of Cardinal Falke."

She related it all except for the part about Mikhail Bryce killing Feizah. Her encounter with Malach. The flooding of the ley. Their flight aboard the *Moonbeam*. The Danzigers. Their discovery of the laboratory and her pursuit of Jule through the tunnel. Jule killing Tessaria and falling to Natalya's blade. The attack at the ruins. She admitted to using ley through the cards, but not abyssal ley.

Clavis listened intently. "I know about Lezarius," she said at last. "Falke already sent a message. And I am aware of the Order of the Black Sun. But it is hardly proof that Balaur lives. Lezarius said he was executed for his crimes. Why would he lie? And Balaur must be an old man by now. More likely Lezarius was deposed in a coup. The northerners are a strange breed."

"I have dreamt of him, Reverend Mother," Kasia admitted.

Her dark eyes sharpened. "Tell me."

Kasia described the blond man. "Jann Danziger believes he lives. So did the children. I don't know how it's possible, but you cannot rule it out."

Clavis was silent for a long minute, studying a mosaic above the altar. It depicted the first Praefators, smiling men and women with ley streaming from their hands. "I was not yet born when Balaur was defeated. All I know about him is second-hand. But when I was thirteen, I led a company of knights into the Arx at Bal Agnar. It was still infested by nihilim. We routed them. It was the first of many campaigns."

Kasia nodded. Clavis's uncanny string of victories was legendary. By the time she finished, Bal Agnar had been thoroughly purged.

"It was during one of those campaigns that I met Cardinal Falke. We were of like minds and grew to be allies. He confided in me."

"I see." Kasia wasn't sure where Clavis was going, but a film of sweat covered her palms.

"He gave me a sweven. I would share it with you now."

Wings fluttered in the dim recesses of the ceiling. The low, sweet coo of a mourning dove drifted down as it settled in the rafters.

"And if I don't want it?"

"Then you may leave. A place will be found for you in Nantwich and I will do my best to protect you. But there are things I have to say that depend on your answer. If you prefer to remain in the dark, we will leave it there."

This is why Tess sent me here. The heart of the matter.

Kasia saw her own reflection in Noach Beitz's silver eye.

*And what am I?*

Not even the child had known. But Clavis did.

Kasia held out her hand, gratified that it remained steady.

"Give me the sweven," she said.

# Chapter Thirty-One

Dust chokes your throat as you enter the council chambers of the Apostolic Signatura at Bal Kirith. The shell took out an exterior wall and bodies lie beneath the rubble, but a man in a crimson robe is rising to his knees. He staggers through a shattered doorframe, running deeper into the building. He cannot be allowed to escape. He is one of the worst. A war criminal and high-priority target.

The moans of the dying fall behind as you follow him through the stone corridors.

You hate this. The colossal waste. The stubborn resistance of the nihilim. You still believe in the sanctity of life, despite everything, despite all you have seen and done, and only the knowledge that there is no other choice saves you from blackest despair. The Last War.

Then Peace Eternal.

It is no pipe dream. It is possible. Once your enemies are vanquished.

The target is injured and you follow the droplets of blood to a small room looking out over the river. He is bending over a cradle when the second shell lands. Not a direct hit or you'd both be dead. But the blast takes out part of the roof. In an instant, he is buried. You stumble backwards, sprayed with shards of stone. One strikes your face. A red film covers one eye.

You raise the visor and see a young child crouching in the corner. Three, perhaps four years old. Dark hair like his father. He is shirtless and a dagger Mark winds down one slim, tanned forearm. A Broken Chain circles his neck. He clutches a rock in his hand.

The boy's gaze moves between the cradle and the blade in your hand, stark terror in his eyes. You don't have the stomach for this. Not even knowing he will grow to be a man someday.

"Run!" you growl. "Run, boy!"

He hesitates. Looks at the cradle once more, then at the rubble pinning his father's body. He hurls the rock. It bounces off your armor. Then he lunges at you, teeth bared. You seize a hank of hair, forcing his head up to meet your eyes. The boy's are greenish-brown flecked with gold. They stare defiance.

"Run! Or I'll skewer you!"

You push the boy away. He spits at your feet and takes off.

If only mages succumbed to Mark sickness like the rest of us, the boy would wither and go mad now that ones who Marked him are dead. But nihilim are immune.

Then, a lusty cry.

With a sinking heart, you approach the cradle. By some miracle, the child within is unharmed. Same eyes as the boy, same raven hair, though it is the silky fluff of an infant. Chubby fists wave in indignation. The child is bright red from screaming.

You open the swaddling blanket, but it has not yet been Nightmarked. Perhaps that was what the father intended when he was killed. The ley flooded and there might have been enough. He must have known the child would die regardless, but he wanted it to die carrying his Mark.

You should just leave it there.

Tainted. The child is tainted.

Yet the ley spared it. Brought you to this very place. Stopped the father from Marking it.

You tell yourself that it must be a sign, but the truth is that you are weary, so very weary, and cannot add this stain to your conscience. Abandoning the child would be crueler than just killing it on the spot.

You tug a glove off and the baby seizes your finger, gripping it tight.

"Come, little girl," you say, lifting her from the cradle. "Let's see what can be done with you."

The instant you pick her up, the child stops crying. She stares at you seriously.

Saints help me, you think.

But it is too late to change your mind now.

---

Kasia tore her hand away. She still smelled dust and blood. Still felt the weight of the armor on her shoulders and the grip of the infant's sticky fingers.

*My* fingers.

"It was so real," she whispered.

Her heart thundered in her breast, partly from her own emotions, partly from Falke's.

"You've never had a sweven before?" Clavis asked with a note of sympathy. "The first time can be overwhelming."

"I gave one." She drew a shaky breath. "Never received."

Kasia wiped her palms on her dress, as if the action could rid herself of the sweven. But she had asked for it. It belonged to her now.

"The rest of the tale is simply told," Clavis said. "Falke claimed you were a servant's child. He drove you back to the Arx inn Novostopol and weaned you with a wet nurse, then paid a family to take you in."

"Did they know?"

The Pontifex shook her head. "No. But they turned out to be ill-chosen. I understand that when you failed the tests, they were unkind."

Kasia thought of her parents. *Foster* parents. Her father had been loving, but he died. And her mother blamed Kasia. Said the shame of it broke his heart.

"You ran away. When Falke learned about it, he was furious. He set Tessaria Foy to find you."

"It was no coincidence then," Kasia said woodenly. "When she took me in. Just a favor for Falke."

"She grew to love you dearly," Clavis said. "Never doubt that. When Falke came to her, second-guessing himself, she was your staunchest supporter. Only the three of us knew. If it ever came out what he'd done, he'd be finished."

"Why didn't he just Mark me himself?" Kasia exclaimed. "To prevent me from . . . ."

"Using abyssal ley? He was afraid to. He thought it might bring your latent abilities to the surface. So he left it to the Probatio to decide."

A suspicion dawned. "Did they rig the tests against me?"

Clavis flashed a quick, humorless smile. "No, you failed them on your own."

Kasia absorbed this. All told, she wasn't shocked at the truth. It explained many things—including Falke's peculiar kindness toward her.

"The Wards didn't prevent me from entering the Arx," she said, brow furrowing. "Not here, nor in Novostopol. How can that be?"

"Because you are not a mage—not as the others are. It stands strongly in your favor that the Wards judged your heart pure enough to pass."

"What do *you* think of me?" Kasia asked, opting for a direct approach.

"Falke did not believe the nihilim were inherently bad,"

Clavis replied, evading the question. She regarded the mosaic of the Praefators. "You descend from our saviors. I do not entirely understand it myself. You are a full-blooded adult mage, yet Unmarked. To my knowledge, you are unique."

"Do all nihilim have peculiar memories? I can recall details of encounters years later, but my early years are foggy."

"That I do not know, although you would have developed much faster than a human child. Since there is no other like you, it is hard to say."

Kasia remembered Feizah's probing. She felt sure the Pontifex had suspected. Given enough time, she would surely have pried out the truth.

"What did Falke plan to do with me?" Kasia shook her head in wonder. "I cannot believe he let me run loose!"

"The Reverend Father is a just man," Clavis said firmly. "He heeded Tessaria's counsel. She said you showed no signs of deviancy. And you had other unforeseen abilities that proved very useful to the Curia."

"The cartomancy."

Clavis inclined her head. "Just so." A pause. "He hoped you might bear children, but this proved a fruitless wish—"

"Is there anything about me you don't know?" Kasia demanded. "Ah, Reverend Mother."

"Plenty," Clavis replied. "The Curia killed your parents. Are you still loyal?"

Kasia stared at her. "I never knew them."

"That is irrelevant." Her gaze hardened. "Some might still want revenge."

"I do not," she said in a quieter tone.

"You've found a way to use your power. Just as you did in the infirmary last night. I felt it." A hand dropped to her sword. Her voice was low and deadly. "Now that you know all, Kasia, how will you wield the ley?"

"For the Via Sancta, Reverend Mother! I have seen myself what their followers do. It sickens me! I despise them and all they stand for. I am not like the others, you must believe me. If I could take your Mark right now, I would!"

Clavis searched her face. Violet ley gathered around them both, flowing in strange patterns Kasia had never seen before. The young pontifex finally nodded.

"The choice is made," she said.

Kasia vented a breath as Clavis's hand moved away from the sword.

"I would charge you with hunting the Order in my city," the pontifex said. "We had a potential informant. He was found yesterday with his throat slit. If they've infiltrated Kvengard, there can be little doubt they are here as well."

"I am at your disposal," Kasia said, blood heating. "In fact, I would relish the chance to bring them low. I will do anything you ask of me."

"Good. But you must accept my conditions. You will not use the ley within these walls."

"Without my cards, I cannot touch it, Reverend Mother."

A frown. "You used it last night."

"That was only to save my friend. He was infected by a dark form of the ley I've never seen before. I think it stems from alchemy. You saw the wound yourself. It was not natural."

Clavis reluctantly nodded. "And you used the blue to heal him, as well. That is unheard of for a full-blooded nihilim. You *are* different from them, Kasia. Yet if you continue to use the red, it will corrupt you in time. This is certain."

"I understand that."

"How does the cartomancy work? Have you always used the ley?"

"Not directly. I simply draw the cards at random. Usually five, though it can be less or more. I do think the ley guides the cards, but it was always . . . passive on my part. The ability to use it actively, to make things happen—that came to me only recently."

"And the foretellings are true?"

"Usually, yes."

"That is a very valuable skill. It could prove critical in hunting the Order. But I must know that you have control over it. That you will never actively use the ley without my permission."

"I give you my word, Reverend Mother," Kasia said. "My deck was lost in the Void. I found two cards that allowed me to use it to help Fra Spassov. But I will need another. Natalya Anderle could make one, if you permit it."

Clavis nodded. "No one will know save for Cardinal Gray. Officially, you will be a cartomancer, nothing more. I want any members of the Order that you ferret out to be kept alive for questioning. We must be careful. Move openly and they will run."

"They are already hunting me, Reverend Mother. I think my very presence will draw them out."

The Pontifex nodded without surprise and Kasia understood that her plan was to dangle the bait and see what swam up from the depths. The knowledge did not bother her. It made sense. And Kasia would do anything to stop them—even if it meant hopping on the hook herself.

"Then there is the matter of the dreams. What does Balaur want from you?"

"I cannot remember much of them," Kasia admitted. "But you believe me?"

"I would be a fool not to. And if he is alive, I will not have him trying to influence you!"

"He could not," Kasia said quickly.

"Still. You will report any further encounters to me immediately."

"Of course, Reverend Mother." She paused. "Will you tell the others?"

"I leave that decision to you."

A good person would tell the truth, whatever the cost. Kasia knew Natalya wouldn't care. But Alexei . . . .

"What of the boy? My brother." She swallowed. "Do you know if he's alive?"

Clavis rose and strode to the altar. A shaft of sunlight bathed her chainmail byrnie.

"You've already met him," she said.

---

NATALYA WAS APPROACHING the basilica with Clavis's aide as Kasia walked out the doors.

"Morning, beautiful!" She drew Kasia aside. "Are you better?"

"I feel fine."

"I hear Spassov is recovering. What did the pontifex say?" Her voice dropped a notch. "Are we in the shit?"

"Later, Nashka."

Her friend frowned. "That bad? Well, I'm up next. Will she grill me? Do we need to get our stories straight?"

"Just tell the truth."

Natalya gave her a strange look. "Very well. That's easy enough."

"Where's Alexei?"

"At the barracks eating breakfast." She pointed. "Over there."

Kasia nodded absently.

"Sure you're well?"

"Fine."

Cardinal Gray cleared his throat. Natalya shot him an apologetic look. "Look, I'll find you later." She fluffed her bleach-blonde hair. "There has to be somewhere around here I can get my roots done. If we don't end up in cells."

Nashka strode confidently into the basilica. Kasia wondered what Clavis wanted with her. The young pontifex seemed to be in a bomb-dropping mood. Maybe Natalya had some deep, ugly secret Kasia had never guessed at.

Ah, Tess, she thought. Why couldn't you just have told me? It would have saved us all a lot of misery.

She found Alexei at a long table eating scrambled eggs. He smiled cheerfully when she walked up. "Hungry? I'm willing to share."

Kasia shook her head. "Is there somewhere we can talk?"

He pushed the plate back. How handsome he looked this morning, despite the battered face. "I actually slept, can you believe it?" The smile died. "You look like you had a rough night. I'm sorry, I sat by the bed, but they finally threw me out." He brightened. "Alice made a friend though! She's taken well to the kennels—"

"I'm glad. But I . . . I need to tell you something before I lose my nerve."

"Sure." He stood up. The complete trust on his face made her wither inside. "We can go to my room."

Alexei led her through the barracks to a tiny bedchamber on the third floor. It was a soldier's room, no frills. Just a single bed and chair. She sat down on the edge of the bed.

"I met with Clavis this morning," she said, heart thumping. "She told me a story."

"Okay." He stood at the narrow window, back to the light. It left his face in shadow. She was glad for that.

"Once, there was a Hierophant. A true believer in the cause of the Via Sancta." She saw the card in her mind's eye. A stern-faced man on a throne. "He was its greatest general. A steadfast keeper of dogma and tradition, but he violated his own precepts to save a life. The Mage."

Alexei nodded uncertainly.

"The Hierophant was tired of death. Tired of killing. He spared her when she was just an infant in the ruins of Bal Kirith. Not yet Marked."

She heard his breath catch. "You speak of Falke," Alexei said. "And. . . ."

"She grew up to become the High Priestess." Kasia swallowed, her throat suddenly dry. "But hers was not the only life he spared that day."

She sensed Alexei's Marks flickering. He said nothing.

"There was another. Only a little boy then. Her brother. The Wheel turned. He grew up to become the Fool. The Hierophant's greatest enemy." The moment stretched out. She stared at the rumpled sheets, unable to meet his gaze. "And yours."

Alexei gripped the stone lintel. The ley pooling at his feet suddenly began to swirl, flickering with rivulets of red and violet. His Marks pulsed, bleeding light from the sleeves of his cassock. Kasia knew they fought to repress whatever was going through his mind.

Then the Marks extinguished, all together. The room seemed to dim.

"You're nihilim." Alexei's voice sounded calm. Detached. Yet he rubbed absently at his forehead as if he felt pain. His pupils had dilated to black discs, only a thin line of blue iris visible at the edges. "You're Malach's sister."

"Yes."

"You look alike. I should have seen it before."

Kasia remembered the moment on the rooftop when Malach seized her wrist. His raven hair and hazel eyes, so remarkably like her own.

"I never knew him," she said desperately. "You must believe me, there are no ties between us. I despise him, too!"

She reached for Alexei's hand. He pulled her to her feet, into his arms. A hard, urgent kiss. Then they were both tumbling back to the bed, his weight on top of her. Alexei tore a glove off and slid his bare hand up her dress, finding her thigh. His eyes held a fey light.

"It's too late for us now," he whispered roughly. "Too late

to go back. I'm yours now, and you're mine. It will never be any other way." The bodice of her dress tore as he tugged at the buttons, cupping a breast with his a gloved hand. The leather was ice-cold against her bare skin. Teeth grazed her shoulder. "Say it," he slurred. "Say you love me—"

Kasia wrenched an arm free and slapped his face.

Alexei blinked rapidly like a man awakening from a dream —or a nightmare. A slow flush crept across his high cheekbones. His pupils shrank as though a torch suddenly shone in his eyes. "Kasia, please—"

"If you want to fuck my brother," she said with icy disdain, "go find him yourself."

She stalked away, slamming the door behind her.

# Chapter Thirty-Two

Alexei rolled to his back, chest heaving. He couldn't breathe.

A kaleidoscope of images flashed past, all tangled together, one after the other. Misha, screaming in psychic agony. Malach's boot and the taste of rain. Kasia pulling off one of her lace gloves. Touching him, making him burn with desire, then wielding ley against the alchemists. Spiders crawling from Rademacher's mouth. Black mist streaming from Patryk's. They spun him round and round like a leaf in an autumn storm.

He sank teeth into his forearm, biting down hard on one of his Marks. Blood flowed, real and warm. The room swam into focus. Suddenly, he hated the ley. Hated the man they'd made him into.

*What have I done?*

*It is no fault of hers.*

*What have I done?*

A brisk rap on the door. He blearily turned his head.

"Fra Bryce? You are summoned to the Reverend Mother."

Alexei wiped his lips on one sleeve. He still tasted the salt of his own blood.

"Fra Bryce?"

He groped for the wall, hoisted himself upright. Found the glove and pulled it on. A red trickle dripped from his sleeve. "Yes, just give me a moment."

He scrubbed his mouth again and put on his lawyer face. *Nothing wrong here, judge.* Alexei opened the door.

"Can we stop at the infirmary?" He held up his arm. "I was wrestling with my dog. She got excited."

The cardinal frowned at the toothmarks. "Of course." A quick, wary glance at the blood-spotted sheets. "We'll go there straightaway. But the Reverend Mother is waiting."

And what story, Alexei wondered bleakly, will she tell *me?*

---

When the audience ended, Alexei began searching for Kasia. He couldn't find her anywhere. He finally ran into Natalya outside the infirmary. She gave him a cool greeting.

"Please, just tell me where she is," he said. "I know I behaved badly. I want only to apologize."

Her face softened a fraction. "She said something about the catacombs."

"How do I find them?"

"There's an entrance at the Tomb of the Martyrs." Natalya eyed him. "But I warn you, she was in a vile mood. I doubt it's improved."

Natalya knew everything, he realized, and no doubt she'd reacted far better. Another jolt of remorse. "I'll take my chances," he muttered.

The open ground beyond the infirmary was a hive of activity. Archers with longbows sent volleys of arrows into targets on earthen butts. Knights marched through the bailey, armor blazoned with the Crossed Keys. Clavis was sending troops into the Morho to join their comrades from Novostopol, though only a token force. She wouldn't leave her own walls undefended, not pinned as she was between

Jalghuth and Bal Agnar. The whole city was on a war footing now. Saints only knew how far it would go.

Alexei relied on his knowledge of the other Arxes to find the Tomb of the Martyrs and descended a wide flight of stone stairs. They leveled out in a labyrinth of low, arched passageways. Yellowed skulls lined the walls, anchored by fragments of bone. It was a ghoulish place. None of the other Arxes kept their dead in this way. The tradition had been started by the first Pontifex of Nantwich, though he didn't know why.

Alexei walked until he heard the slow click of spiked heels. He rounded a corner and saw her, black hair unbound and falling to her waist, one hand trailing along the bones. Kasia turned to face him. She'd painted her lips a vivid, shocking red. It suited her.

"Why are you here, Bryce?"

Her eyes gathered the torchlight like a wolf. Half-tame, he thought, if that. And yet I love her. Love her with all my soul.

"The Reverend Mother is sending me into the Void." He paused. "I welcome it."

Something flitted across her face. Anger? Unhappiness?

"It's not an exile. She asked me to go to Jalghuth and I agreed."

"Why?" Kasia studied him, expressionless. "Because you despise me now?"

"No!" He needed to make her understand. "You were right. I am damaged. But it has nothing to do with you."

"What else did she tell you?"

"She wants to know what's happening in the north. Her visions are murky."

A slight frown. "Does she see the future?"

"She is strong in liminal ley. It's a rare ability. Clavis sees thresholds. Secrets. Boundaries and the in-between places."

Kasia nodded in sudden understanding. "I stand in such a place now. What was is gone forever. What will be is uncertain."

Alexei held her eyes. "I think we all stand in that place every moment of our lives."

"This is different." Her expression grew distant. "A branching in the path that cannot be undone. Some choices weigh more than others. Falke's mercy was impulsive, but it changed everything. I wonder if he regrets it now."

"I don't," Alexei said firmly. "Even if it means Malach is loose. But Falke is marching on the Morho. He's probably at Bal Kirith by now."

She thought about that for a moment. "What will happen to your brother if Malach dies?"

"Misha will die, too. I have to see him one last time."

Alexei expected her to tell him it was a foolish mission, if not suicidal, but Kasia merely nodded. "How soon are you going?"

"Dusk and dawn are potent times for liminal ley. Clavis said I must leave at sunset, when her visions are clearer." He cleared his throat. "I wanted to apologize for . . . mistreating you that way. It was despicable. I know you are not your brother. My feelings for him should not be directed at you."

Kasia approached him warily. "Thank you. I'd say that sums it up."

He longed to reach for her hand but didn't dare. "How can you stand to be down here?"

She shrugged. "I wanted to be alone. It's peaceful. Do the dead trouble you?"

He thought of his years deployed in the Void. The violence on both sides. That time never left him, not really. "I can still smell it," he muttered. "The stench."

"What, here?"

"I know it's in my mind." She stood very close now. "Clavis . . . she told me what my greatest fear was."

"Losing Mikhail?"

Alexei shook his head. "Losing my humanity," he said quietly.

"No one can take that from you."

"But I could. I almost did with you. And that's what scares me."

She touched the Raven on his neck. "You are a priest of the Via Sancta, Alexei. You don't need Marks to know what's right. Just follow your heart."

His pulse beat against her fingers. "That's why I'm with you."

She cupped the back of his neck and pulled him to her mouth. He tasted lipstick. Then her tongue. Heat flooded him. "Wait," he managed. But she was already yanking his cassock up, turning them both so she pressed against the wall. Arms twined around his neck.

"Not here," he panted. Kasia ignored his objections, hooking a thigh over his hip, and Alexei's treacherous hands hoisted her up, fitting her against him. "My gloves—"

"Leave them on," she gasped.

Nails raked his bare back, sending lines of flame along the Towers. He found a silken stocking and tore it down. One of her shoes fell off. The other heel dug painfully into his leg. Hollow eye sockets leered at him and Alexei buried his face in her hair, drowning. This felt wrong, profane, but he didn't care. He'd ached for her for weeks. Here and now in this bleak ossuary they were both alive.

The currents of ley blazed like a bed of hot coals. They lapped at his boots but his leather gloves blocked it from entering his Marks. Alexei could not blame the abyss. All he did, he did willingly, with full awareness. Their bodies joined and he was whole for the first time in weeks, free of his burdens, free of any thought but her and the hopeless wish that the moment could last forever. She screamed his name into the darkness of the catacombs.

If the dead were offended, they gave no sign of it.

The release left him shaking and slick with sweat. He

braced a hand on the dome of a skull, head tipped back. He could hardly stand.

Kasia stepped away. She was trembling, too. Neither of them spoke as she put her shoe back on. Then she kissed him once on the mouth, with infinite tenderness, and straightened her dress.

Alexei listened to her heels ring briskly down the passage.

It felt like a final goodbye.

---

ALEXEI STOOD on the parapet with Clavis at his side, watching the waves beat against the cliff below. It was the outermost curtain wall of the Arx where sea met land.

Another potent boundary.

They watched the sun sink below the waves in a lump of molten gold. She'd insisted on Marking him before he left and his neck now had the Raven of Novostopol on the right and the Crossed Keys of Nantwich on the left.

Twenty Marks. Too many for his mind to accept without shattering itself? But soon he would be in the Void where they meant nothing.

The shadows lengthened and with them rose the liminal ley, a deep violet power that blended the surface and abyssal layers. It coiled around Clavis's greaves, following the etchings in her armor.

"What do you see, Reverend Mother?"

She gazed at the horizon. "The future hinges on many things. More than just the Via Sancta. Other nations will come into play before this is done. Friends and enemies alike. But that is far off yet and I cannot say with any certainty what the outcome will be." She sighed. "For now, I must join Falke to pacify the Morho. He has reports that nihilim are again infesting the ruins of Bal Agnar. They are the immediate threat. If I try to secure the north before the mages have been dealt with, my army will be stretched thin. The Fort of Saint Agnes alone cannot hold the border if the fighting spills over. And my first duty is to the citizens of Nantwich."

"How many nihilim are in the Void?" Alexei asked.

"No one knows for certain. But they've had four years of the Cold Truce to regroup." Clavis sounded unhappy about that. "We must strike hard and fast. Bal Agnar is a potent symbol. I will not see the Black Sun rise there again."

Alexei had been deployed to the city several times. "It is a haunted place," he said quietly.

"And so it shall remain," Clavis replied, her voice firm. "What I need most is intelligence. Without it, any decision is made blindly." She glanced over at him. "Sometimes one man alone, moving swiftly and in secrecy, is the better choice than a company of knights who would only draw unwanted attention."

"That is logical. I told you, Reverend Mother, I am willing."

An albatross soared in a wide arc over the sea, mighty wings extended. It swooped downwind towards the waves, caught something in its beak, then rode an updraft into the darkening sky.

"If you do find Lezarius," Clavis said, "you must ensure he does not break the Void. By any means necessary."

She wanted him to be her assassin.

"I will keep to the *Meliora*, Reverend Mother," he said stiffly.

"The doctrine binds us all," she agreed. "But its words will be ash in the wind if the nihilim rise again. Think on that, Fra Bryce."

She'd gifted him a sword with a silver-chased scabbard. He wore light mail beneath a plain brown cassock. It was expertly crafted and made no sound as he knelt and kissed her ring. Clavis laid a gloved hand on his head. "You are a loyal knight," she said. "I know you will make the correct choice."

The certainty in her voice gave him pause. He could not imagine killing a defenseless old man—well, perhaps not *defenseless*, but a revered Pontifex nonetheless!—yet nor could Alexei deny Clavis's powerful charisma. He would follow this young woman against a thousand nihilim without hesitation.

There had to be another way. He would find it.

"May the ley bless your journey," Clavis said.

He left her on the ramparts, gazing out over the sea. A fresh horse waited in the bailey below, carrying panniers with food and a blanket roll—and the book by Angelus Silesius. Alexei had decided to keep it. Perhaps he could make sense of it on the road.

He had a foot in the stirrup when Natalya came running up, breathless. "Patryk told me you're leaving us," she said with a frown. "So soon."

"It was the Reverend Mother's decision."

"That's bullshit. You could have said no."

"I don't think it's a word she hears very often," he replied with a wry grin.

Natalya laughed. "True. Well, I hate farewells," she said lightly. "So I'll just say . . . see you later."

She surprised him with a warm hug and peck on the cheek. Alice sniffed at her boots. Natalya held out a hand and earned a lick. "Keep an eye out for this pilgrim, eh?"

Then she was striding away, long and lithe with a dancer's grace. If she kept practicing with the knives she would be formidable someday.

He'd already said goodbye to Spassov. Of course, Patryk had wanted to come along. He'd stood at the window, furtively puffing on one of the cigarettes Alexei had smuggled inside the infirmary and trying to argue, but his quivering knees gave him away. Alexei had told him he couldn't afford the delay, but the truth was that he wanted to go alone. He couldn't bear to be around anyone who wasn't Kasia Novak.

She hadn't tried to find him again. What was the point?

They were destined to forever be torn apart. And he wasn't sure she'd entirely forgiven him. Someday, perhaps. When he had fulfilled his duty to Misha and could give her his loyalty without condition—as she deserved.

Alice loped along next to the horse as he rode beneath the portcullis and across the stone span bridging the Caerfax River. From there, it was a short ride to the outer stelae. He reined up at the threshold of the Wardstones. A single road led north, rutted and overgrown with disuse. There had been no traffic with Jalghuth for years. Not since Falke's campaigns in the Morho, which Lezarius heartily disapproved of. He'd shunned them all except for Luk.

"Ready, little sister?" he asked.

Alice gave an enthusiastic bark.

He rode through the stelae. The ley vanished. Alexei had wondered if it would all come down on him like an avalanche—the heartbreak, the anger, the fear and doubt—but he felt no different. He'd reached his own accommodation with the ghosts. A smile touched his lips as he spurred his mount to a gallop towards Jalghuth.

Perhaps he'd left them in the catacombs.

# Chapter Thirty-Three

The icebreaker *Splendor Solis* steamed past Nantwich just as full dark fell. The city sat on a promontory above the ocean and Will could make out the blue Wards glowing along the walls of the Arx. He studied the man standing next to him at the rail. Jann Danziger still called Will *grandson*, or sometimes *Willem*. He could not accept the fact that the other boy was dead. Nor did he seem aware that Will could hear every thought that passed through his mind.

It was an endless monologue of fear and doubt. Now he was worrying about the Pontifex of the Western Curia and whether she posed a threat to Jalghuth. The two cities were not very far apart.

. . . *Does Clavis know? She is the most dangerous. But if she did, she would have invaded already. Oh Saints, I cannot believe we are going to Him. Will He be pleased? Or will He kill us all? The children frighten me. And the mute Invertido . . . what does he want? His eyes follow me everywhere. I wish I had the courage to turn the ship around. It is my ship! But Willem won't allow it. Saints help me, he scares me too—*

Will severed the connection with a slight twitch of the strands of ley that flowed from the man's mind. It joined other threads, weaving a tapestry of such stupefying complexity that

Will could only glimpse a tiny part. A banquet of light. Everything had it. Not just people and animals, but the rocks and trees and water. Each drop of the great ocean shimmered with energy.

Once the boy had struggled through the drudgery and confusion of the day-to-day world. Confined by the prison of the ego. But he was dead and the sunstruck creature who emerged knew the truth—that all was spiritual and eternal. Will was lucid now. In the Old Tongue, the word meant *filled with light.* Like the lucifers of old, until the Fall broke their godhead into fragments.

He puzzled over his own transformation. Why was he here? To serve the ley, yes, but what did that mean?

Will didn't care about the politics the man obsessed over. The names meant nothing to him. But he sensed a dissonance to the north. It was the Red King. His mind was polluting the ley, a poison that tainted all it touched.

That presence searched for him, sending out questing tentacles. He batted them aside. He existed on a different plane, one that saw the ley as a single entity. His own psyche had been distilled and purified. Where others perceived colors, he saw only white light. Part of him understood that this was unnatural. All things held an immutable spark, but it was clothed in living flesh. Evolution occurred over long millennia, a gradual awakening.

His had been compressed into thrice forty nights. Forced through alchemy for a wicked purpose. Did that make him wicked, too? Was the grandfather right to be afraid? So much Will still didn't understand. His brothers and sisters asked the same questions. It comforted him that he was not alone.

Will turned from the rail, meeting the knight's stormy blue eyes.

His body was a battlefield, the Marks on his skin telling the story of a mind divided, each side fighting the other to a bloody stalemate. The Nightmark had corrupted him once. It fed the worst and starved the best. But he had taken the Mark for selfless reasons. It failed to consume him—though it would have in time. The knight knew it, too. He had tried to kill the one who had given it to him. The mage Will knew as the Fool. Then, a reversal, sudden and devastating. A long walk through the nigredo, the knight's essence splintered into a thousand bright shards.

The Martyr had made him whole again—or at least partly so. The knight served the ley through Lezarius. It was Lezarius's command that he stop the Red King. Perhaps that was Will's purpose, too. Yet he had no idea how to accomplish it.

Will did not fear death. He'd already passed through that gate. But he did fear the deep dark. And he knew that if the Red King was left unchecked, one day there would be nothing else left.

---

THE NEXT DAY, the first sea ice appeared. The crew bundled up in fur-lined coats. Will marveled at the way their warm breath made mist in the air, but he kept his distance. They feared the Reborn. He had heard the grandfather arguing with them. Some wanted to turn back, but the promise of more gold finally quelled their thoughts of mutiny. That and the presence of the knight. The crew feared him even more than the children.

The knight wore a fur-lined coat, too. Will had noticed him shaking with cold and asked the grandfather to bring one up from below. Now the knight's lips moved, reciting the sutras of the *Meliora*. He sat cross-legged on the deck, a sword across his lap. It glittered with ice.

*What will you do?* Will sent. *How will you defeat the Red King?*

The knight glanced up. Will knew he had heard. But his whispers never ceased.

". . . From faith stems humility. From ley stems awareness. Follow in the steps of the righteous for evil stems from evil, good from good. Perform charity without expectation of reward for therein lies the wealth of eternal happiness . . . ."

The knight had learned to guard his thoughts, but Will sensed no fear in him. Only single-minded purpose. At the journey's start, he'd given Will his name—Mikhail Semyon Bryce. He had been a captain in the Beatus Laqueo, which was a special unit in Novostopol that fought the fallen lightbringers. His brother, the priest, had served in the same unit. The words were not spoken aloud. They had conversed through the ley. But the closer they came to Jalghuth, the more withdrawn he became. Will feared he was preparing himself to die.

Will's three sisters and four brothers stood with him at the bow, watching a pod of narwhals breach the surface. The backs of the young calfs were a mottled blue-gray. Their elders were almost completely white. Each had a long, pointed tusk. The children stared at them, mesmerized.

Noach sent Will a picture of a stone spear that pierced the heavens.

*Yes*, Will sent back.

The tower called to them all.

A place of great power and importance. Will didn't yet know why, but it tugged at them like iron filings to a magnet.

The coast was riven with deep, icebound fjords, but the *Splendor Solis* had a reinforced iron hull that pushed through the floating bergs. When it reached a wide bay, the ship turned inland. They steamed up a channel until the ice grew too thick. Then the sailors dropped an anchor and rowed them to the shore. It was snowing hard.

"Wait here," the grandfather instructed the captain, but Will knew the captain wouldn't wait and the grandfather knew it, too.

A vast frozen lake sat in the cradle of tall mountains.

Three sledges awaited with shaggy beasts standing placidly in the harnesses. They were driven by knights wearing tabards with a Blue Flame, but Will knew they were not true knights.

"Who is this?" one demanded, staring hard at Mikhail.

"He is Nightmarked," the grandfather said quickly.

"Throw your weapon down!" the knight ordered, stepping back.

Mikhail stared at them. He seemed confused. The knight growled and unsheathed a sword. Will quickly stepped forward. "Wait! He does not understand."

The insight had come to him in a flash. When Will spoke, he was unaware of the sounds, only the meaning. But there were different tongues in the world and most people knew only one or two. The impure knights knew Kindu and some Kven. But Mikhail only knew Osterlish.

Will repeated the command aloud, in the correct language. He feared Mikhail would refuse, but he only nodded, unbuckling the sword and tossing it to the snow. One of the knights ran forward and picked it up.

"Now show us the Mark."

Will translated. Mikhail took his coat off, shivering in the wind, and displayed the Nightmark.

"It's inverted!" the impure knight snarled, raising his own blade again.

"A punishment by the Curia," the grandfather said, licking his lips. "I vouch for him." He drew himself up. "I am a founding member of the Order of the Black Sun! Do you dare to question me?"

The man's eyes narrowed. Suspicion filled his mind, and the sudden urge to spill blood.

*He is loyal,* Will sent in Kindu. *A devout follower and valuable soldier.*

That was the truth—though not the truth the impure knight believed it to be.

He relaxed, unaware the thought was not his own, and

slowly sheathed the blade. "The Invertido may come, but he will wait outside when we present you."

They stepped into the sledges and crossed the lake, runners whispering through the snow.

The tower was near now, a vortex of energy and power, yet Will sensed its wrongness. For the first time in his brief existence, he felt a righteous anger. Mikhail seemed to feel it, too, for he gripped the edge of the sled with white knuckles, his eyes tight.

On the far side of the lake, a town nestled at the foot of the mountains. Will fought to silence thousands of shrieking voices. So much pain and fear. It multiplied the disruption, roiling the ley in powerful currents that circled the source of the taint like filthy water swirling around a sewer drain. The chaos appalled him, though he'd expected it.

The runners of the sledge were converted to wheels and they rumbled up into a winding pass. A citadel lay above, but they bypassed the gates and continued on into the mountains. Will sensed the tower before they rounded a corner and it came into view. Seven chins lifted together as the Reborn followed it to the cloud-wreathed summit.

"Sinjali's Lance," the grandfather whispered.

The knights drew up the sledges. The grandfather was pale and shaking as he got out. Will helped him to the black doors. Mikhail walked next to them, his face calm and at peace. The light was everywhere, burning white-hot. Will paused on the threshold to bathe in its radiance. Then he stepped through, where the deep dark waited.

# Chapter Thirty-Four

"How fare you, old man?"

Lezarius looked up as the door to his aerie opened and Dantarion strode inside. She wore a scarlet robe that set off her auburn hair, which was tied back in a high ponytail. Her cheeks were ruddy, her blue eyes bright. But this rose had hidden thorns that dripped poison. His gaze flicked to her ungloved hands.

"You could knock," he said warily.

She laughed. "I brought you Keefs." She tossed the pack to the bed beside him and looked around. "This is nicer than I expected."

Dirty plates sat in a teetering stack on the floor, next to an overflowing ashtray. Balaur had left several books, all of them blasphemous works on alchemy that sat untouched. A bottle of reddish liquid he claimed was wine, also untouched. It amused Balaur to read him passages from the books, just as Lezarius had done with the *Meliora* when Balaur was the prisoner. Other than those visits, he had seen no one for days.

He tore open the foil package and lit a Keef with trembling hands. They were the only thing that kept him from screaming until his lungs gave out. Balaur had locked the outer door so throwing himself from the tower wasn't an option, but the ocean of abyssal ley lapping at the walls made his madness much worse. Balaur's face changed sometimes when they were alone together. Grew monstrous, as though it were dissolving in potent acid. Balaur did not seem to notice and Lezarius had no idea whether it was real or imagined. The voices pestered him endlessly. He almost welcomed Dantarion's company, unpleasant as she was.

"Have you seen my cat?" he asked.

"No."

"Good. She has more sense than to show herself. Do you think she is old enough to catch mice? I would not like to think of her going hungry."

The mage shrugged and sank into the single chair. He eyed the line of her robes. They swelled at the front. "Are you pregnant?" he asked, wondering if it was another hallucination.

She smiled. "By my cousin. I imagine you don't approve."

"Saints." He exhaled a stream of smoke, then hastily waved it away from her. "You brought me north through the Void heavy with child? And it survived the fall through the ice?"

She patted her belly. "The baby is strong."

"Like its mother," he conceded. "What do you want, Dantarion?"

"For you to stop this foolishness and break the outer Wards."

He scowled. "So Balaur sent you."

She leaned back. "He has started public executions. Ten pyres each day until you agree to his demands."

Nausea churned his stomach. "I told you, I cannot do it! Do you think I would be sitting here if I had any control over the ley? The Wards have twisted the flow!"

"He doesn't believe you."

"Do you?"

She studied him. "I don't know."

"You must put a stop to it!"

He expected her to laugh in his face, but Dantarion only regarded him gravely. "I cannot, Lezarius. He is the Pontifex."

"Not of Jalghuth!"

"Of Bal Agnar, if you prefer. But I will not defy his wishes."

"Then why don't you just compel me?" he demanded. "You will see for yourself that it's impossible. There is no surface ley to work!"

"He wants to you to do it by choice."

"That's perverse!" he spluttered. "It is still compulsion."

"I'm merely conveying the message." Dantarion glanced at the door. "His experiments have arrived."

Lezarius lit another Keef. He wanted to float away, though it didn't seem to have the same effect it once did. Maybe he was smoking too much. "What are you talking about?"

Unwillingly, he remembered Balaur's talk of disciples. Of his Magnum Opus.

"They are children. Or they appear to be so. I saw them enter the Lance." The mage looked uneasy. "They are fey, Lezarius. I think he dabbles in things he does not fully understand."

"Children? From where?"

"Kvengard." She shot to her feet. He shrank back. "Just do as he asks, I beg you! I wish to be gone from this place. And I cannot leave until the outer Wards are broken!"

"I thought he was your Pontifex. Can it be that you are repelled by his actions, mage?"

"I don't care about the fucking executions," she snarled. "But this goes . . . beyond." Dantarion began to pace. A hand stole to her belly. "They are little dead things, yet alive. Some are white and cold-looking."

"You pity them."

"No!" But she sounded unsure. "I believe in the natural

order. This is . . . not natural."

"You are starting to see through the lies." He tossed the Keef into the cold hearth. Then he threw the rest of the pack after them. No more.

"You distort my words," Dantarion said angrily.

"I speak the truth. You know it." He held her gaze. "Get me out of here. Take me to the outer stelae. I will free you. Then I will banish the ley from the city." His fists tightened. "As I should have done when I had the chance."

Dantarion stared at him for a long moment. "End it, Lezarius. Open the floodgates. If you do this, perhaps it will unmake them as well." Her mouth twisted. "It would be a mercy."

"I told you, it is impossible—"

"Your friend is here. The skeleton. I just saw him outside the Lance."

Mikhail lived? An ember of hope flickered to life.

"I said nothing," Dantarion continued grimly. "I decided to come to you first. But if you still refuse me, I will have no choice but to tell Balaur who he is."

"Is he inside the tower?"

"He arrived with the children."

"How could that be?"

"What does it matter?" she asked wearily. "He cannot defeat Balaur alone. A hundred knights guard this place. If you think I could get you past them, you're dreaming, old man."

"You could use the abyssal ley! Compel them—"

Her hand shot out, gripping his wrist. "Like this?"

Red light bathed the chamber as she seized control of his will. A cold command. *Break the Wards. Break them. Break them. Break them!*

He tried—oh, how he tried!—but could find no surface ley to tame the chaos. The blue was the layer of control. Without it, he was powerless.

At last, Dantarion released him. "Shit," she muttered.

She strode to the door without another word. The bolt slid into place behind her. He exhaled a shuddering breath.

Never had he wanted his little cat so badly.

---

THE KNIGHTS TOOK them along a circular corridor to another pair of tall black doors. The taint was palpable here. Will expected Mikhail to put up a struggle, but he meekly allowed them to put him in chains. Will felt his intense blue gaze as the children entered a vast chamber whose far reaches were lost to shadow. Inset floor tiles formed a Black Sun with jagged rays. At the end, cloaked in shadow, sat a dais. It glowed with Wards in the shape of a flame. They cast the only light.

The Red King sat upon a throne carved from the same jet-black substance as the Lance itself. He wore the mask of a pleasant dark-skinned face, but it was slipping. White flesh gleamed through the cracks. When he saw the Reborn, he flinched and turned away as if the sight pained him.

"Do not bring them to me just yet, Jann," he called across the chamber. The voice was calm, powerful, but Will sensed his agitation. "Come forward alone."

The grandfather was so frightened, his thoughts had ceased completely. He motioned the children to wait at the doors and limped to the dais, bowing low.

"These are the diamond ones?" the Red King asked.

He spoke quietly, but Will heard every word.

"Yes, Reverend Father. We came from Kvengard as you commanded."

"Why do they shine so? It pains my eyes." A touch of petulance.

"Indeed, the Reborn are radiant," the grandfather said cautiously. "Do they not please you?"

There was a long pause. "From the living flows death, and

from the dead life. From youth comes old age, and from senility a return to youth. From sleep we awake and from waking, slumber again. The cycle of decay and regeneration never stills. Yet you have accomplished it."

"At your instructions, Reverend Father."

"They have sailed the waters of the Night Sea. What wonders it must hold. We are but wretched creatures beside them."

"As . . . as you say, Reverend Father."

His voice firmed. "I would look upon them." He pointed at Will. "That one." A peremptory command. "Come here."

Will approached the throne. The Red King studied him, his gaze slitted and watery. "What of the eyes? Why is one black and one silver?"

"He is at the second stage of the Great Work." The grandfather was still afraid, but he warmed to the subject. Alchemy was his passion. "The Morning Star has fallen from the heavens to a state of duality. As lead is the metal of nigredo, silver is the metal of albedo, transmuted from lead. He contains them both. Four of the children are in this state."

"And the others?"

"Fully resurrected."

"Why are four in the albedo stage?"

The grandfather began to tremble. "They were awakened early."

"How is it possible?"

"I do not know, Reverend Father."

A clawlike hand emerged from the white sleeve of his robes, beckoning the grandfather within reach. "You know. Give me the sweven."

The grandfather knelt at the Red King's feet. A withered hand tangled in his thin silver hair. His eyes flew wide as the Red King rifled through his memories. A line of spittle trickled from his mouth.

"Where is it?" the Red King grated.

The grandfather cried out, back arching. He was an evil man, but Will felt sickened. "Please, stop. He doesn't know. But we do."

The clawlike fingers opened, releasing him. The grandfather fell to the floor. Will knelt at his side and tried to give comfort.

"Tell me, boy," the Red King commanded brusquely. "Or I will squeeze him dry."

Will's vision dimmed as all the Reborn joined in a sending. The Sun, blinding and brilliant, banishing the deep dark. The High Priestess wielded it like a sword. She was both pure and impure. Will did not trust her, but he wished she were here now.

The Red King stared into space for a long moment. "The cartomancer is one of us," he said softly. "Yet with powers I have not even dreamt of."

The grandfather had received the sending, too. He looked stunned. "I was not there, Reverend Father. You saw! I had no idea who she was."

The Red King smiled. "It doesn't matter. She is already half mine. If she can speed up the process, it would solve many problems." He spoke as if to himself. "The nigredo is a vulnerable phase. To sail the Night Sea for thrice forty days while my own body lay without its soul was unpalatable, to say the least. And this vessel grows old." His lips twisted. "Weak." The cold gaze fell on Will. "But they already have the diamond bodies. I could occupy a fresh vessel." He stood. The clawlike hand reached for Will. "So bright—"

It touched Will's marble flesh. The red King recoiled as if the contact had burned him.

"Feh!" he spat in sudden fury. "What have you made, Jann?"

The grandfather looked up at him, mouth sagging.

"What use are they to me?!"

"They . . . they will fight for you. They cannot be killed."

"Do you serve me?" the Red King demanded of Will. "Your father?"

"We serve the ley."

He sat back on the throne with a look of disgust. The scowl opened fresh cracks in his skin. They did not bleed, but Will caught another glimpse of the pale man beneath. "They are little automatons. Can you not feel the taint? You must destroy them. Return them to the prima materia from whence they came."

The grandfather bowed his head. "Yes, Reverend Father."

"They are impervious to all but the devouring black fire. See that it is done." His tone softened. "Still, I count the effort a success. Done properly, the Great Work will birth a new god to this sorry world. You have proven it is possible. And your rewards will be great, Jann."

All this time, he had spoken with his face averted to the shadows. "Take the boy away. Take them all away! My knights will ensure you have what is needed."

The darkness behind the throne stirred. A woman stood there. A lightbringer like the High Priestess, but far more corrupted. Will perceived two overlapping heartbeats. She carried a child inside her.

The lightbringer stepped forward. "The children came with a man. An Invertido. He was with Lezarius in the Morho. We can use him, Reverend Father."

"An Invertido?" The Red King rounded on the grandfather. "Why did you not tell me of this?"

The grandfather quailed. "He frightens me, Reverend Father! He killed many of the Order in Kvengard. I had no choice. But your knights have him in custody outside. He is no danger to anyone."

The Red King gestured to the light-bringer, who strode to the doors. "Bring him to me."

Mikhail was hauled forward in chains. He did not resist when he was pushed to his knees before the dais. His face was bruised and bloody. The knights had mistreated him. Will could have thrown himself on the Red King. Could have burned him. Hurt him. But the Reborn did not cause harm. It would be a violation of all they were.

"Show me the Mark."

The knights tore Mikhail's coat open, exposing his bare chest. He stared vacantly into the clinging darkness beyond the throne.

"It's is Malach's," the woman light-bringer said. "A mage of Bal Kirith."

"I do not know him," the Red King said ruminatively. "He Marked a priest of Novostopol?"

"A knight," she confirmed with an amused smile.

"*That* is interesting. He must have agreed to it. And he looks strong. In the prime of life, yet his mind is half-gone already. A suitable vessel perhaps, until a better one is found." The Red King glanced at the light-bringer's belly. She didn't seem to notice. "I will keep him for now. Dispose of these *mistakes* and then return to me, Jann. I have need of you."

The grandfather nodded quickly. "Yes, Reverend Father. I am grateful for your mercy. I serve faithfully." He kissed the ring on the king's shriveled stub. "May the Black Sun rise again in all its glory!"

Will helped him walk to the door. A dozen more knights waited outside.

"Take us to the alchemical laboratory," the grandfather said. His voice was cold and decisive. The Reborn followed obediently. His brothers and sisters were serene. Coming here had fulfilled their destiny. It was the heart of the ley. The Root. Only Will felt fear. Not of a return to the prima materia—not even of the devouring black fire that awaited them. But he sensed there was something more the ley wanted them to do, some critical task.

And he still had no idea what it was.

# Chapter Thirty-Five

The corridor circled ever downward in a great spiral. The grandfather had trouble walking without his cane. Noach supported him on one side, Will on the other. The grandfather allowed them to aid him, but he did not look at either of them. With each step, the power of the Root grew stronger, though it was twisted.

At last, the knights brought them to a windowless chamber hewn from the dark walls. Will understood its purpose immediately. It was much the same as the one they had left behind in Kvengard. Books and flasks and stone slabs. Rows of jars holding the various ingredients of alchemical witchcraft. But this one also had a pillar wreathed in black fire. Where the flames danced, the ley ended. A doorway to utter darkness.

Will tore his gaze away. The others were troubled, too. They had heard the Red King's words. They knew what was coming and were powerless to stop it.

The grandfather dismissed the knights. They treated him with more respect now. He had the favor of the Red King. "If only you had called him Father," he muttered. "But it cannot be undone now."

Will stared at him, beseeching. "You don't have to do this. You know it's wrong."

The grandfather's mouth puckered. "Right and wrong mean nothing in this place. I must follow his orders."

"Find a way to free the knight," Will urged him. "It is not too late. He will save us all—"

The grandfather's chilly gaze swept across his brothers and sisters. "Nothing can save them now." His face softened. "But you, Willem." Hands knitted together. "I will hide you away. If I make you rubedo, you will be strong. You can run."

He hobbled to a cabinet and drew out several flasks containing grains that looked like sand. He poured the first in a circle and beckoned one of the sisters forward. Her name was Isild. She was one of the rubedos. Will could hear the steady drumbeat of her heart.

"Come, my dear," he said, not meeting her eyes. "Stand just here."

The child stepped across the line, her face solemn. Will sensed no fear in her, just sad acceptance. The grandfather poured out the second vial, and the third, creating three concentric circles around her. He was smiling, but his thoughts were so terrible Will could not bear to hear them.

"Please, grandfather, I beg you. You condemn yourself by doing this. Evil deeds harm the one who commits them as much as the victim—"

"Be quiet," the grandfather snapped. "I do not wish to hear your platitudes, Willem. You do not understand." He gazed at Isild. "I'm sorry, my dear. You are a beautiful thing, but beauty is temporal. You never chose this. It is for the best." He poured a few grains of the grey substance into his hand. Then he reached into the black flames. The substance sparked and burst into flame. The fire was cold and did not burn his skin, but his jaw grew tight.

"Morere!" he cried, casting the burning salts at her small silk slippers.

The outer circle caught first. Then the next and the next. The black flames leapt higher. Isild's eyes met Will's as the hem of her silk dress began to shrivel.

"No!" he cried, reaching for her.

Isild shone bright as a starburst for an instant and then she was gone. The dress had burned to ash, but nothing else remained. The flames sank back into the stone floor. The grandfather wiped sweat from his brow.

"You see?" he mumbled. "She did not scream. It was swift and painless. She has gone to the ley. All is for the best." He hurried to the cabinet for fresh flasks.

*We must do something to stop him!* Will sent.

*That is not our purpose,* the others sent back.

*But how will we know our purpose if we are destroyed?*

*Have faith, little brother.*

The last sending came from Mikhail.

*Where are you?*

*In a cell.*

*You must help us!*

The grandfather had finished pouring out the circles. Now his eyes flickered across the Reborn as if deciding who would be next. They stood silently awaiting their fate. All but Will. He ran to the door and tested the knob. It was bolted from the outside. In desperation, he placed himself between the grandfather and his brothers and sisters.

"Take me next," he pleaded.

The grandfather looked angry. "I already told you, Willem, you will be spared. Do not make trouble." He waved a hand. "Look at them! They do not care. They are beyond mortal concerns now." He seemed to like the sound of that, for he nodded firmly. "They have already been liberated from suffering. This is merely the final step. It is a blessing!"

"Then why not do it to me?"

"Because . . . because you are a Danziger! Can't you see how different you are? They are sheep. You are the wolf." His eyes shone with pride. "You will be my heir. Deathless and strong! Someday, you will stand at his side. A prince among men! He will see it. He will reward us both once he achieves godhood." A wheedling tone. "But for now you must trust that I know what is best."

"I will never serve him," Will said quietly.

"Many have said the same. Yet in the end they all bend the knee. You will, too." The grandfather's voice hardened. "Now, step aside. I know you cannot harm me. Your nature forbids it. Look away, if you prefer." He tipped the grey salt into his hand. A finger pointed at Noah Beitz. "Step inside the circle. Join the girl in everlasting peace."

"Don't!" Will cried, but Noach did as he was told.

The grandfather was reaching for the black flames when the door flew open, rebounding against the wall. He stared at the newcomer, face a thunderhead. "I cannot be interrupted! Come back later—"

His haughty tone faltered as she crossed the chamber in six long strides. The light-bringer swung a bloody sword, severing the grandfather's head in a stroke. His body remained on its feet for several seconds, then toppled over. The ley pulsing inside it winked out.

Will eyed the woman in shock. He had not heard her coming. Not heard a single thought.

Her cool gaze took in the burnt circles, then settled on the Reborn. She did not squint like the Red King, though her face showed little emotion.

"I am leaving," she said. "You may do the same if you can manage it. The knights guarding the corridor are dead."

"The man we came with," Will said. "Is he freed?"

"Not by me," she replied. "I have done what I could. Do not ask for more." She eyed him speculatively. "Can you break Wards?"

Will shook his head. "I have no power."

"You do not work the ley?"

"No."

She sighed. "Then I will cross the Wards if it kills me. Malach did it once. If he can, I can."

*Malach.* The name resounded through the ley like a gong.

"You speak of The Fool?" Will asked.

She laughed. "Yes, he is a fool. And no doubt a dead one now." Her face darkened. "Balaur covets my child. I will not let him have it." Her gaze fell on the grandfather. "That man was a groveling worm. Whatever you are, you are better than him."

She turned to go. Will hurried after her. "Wait!"

She paused at the door with a look of impatience. "Thank you, light-bringer." He took her hand. She flinched, but not from pain like the Red King.

"You are cold," she whispered. Her nose wrinkled. Wonderment stole across her face. "And you smell of . . . flowers."

"I am albedo."

The light-bringer shook her head. "The world has grown very strange of late." Clear green eyes peered down at him. "Run, child," she said softly. "Run while you can."

Then she was gone, robes sweeping behind her.

*Where will we go?*

The others stared at Will. Somehow, I have become their leader and I do not know—

A small black shadow darted through the door and twined between his legs. Will frowned down at it. "Katze," he said aloud, sorting through the various tongues. "Biralo." The creature flicked its tail. "Cat."

He crouched down. The Reborn gathered around. Will sensed the ghosts inside them stirring. Distant memories of warmth and softness. Six pale hands reached out to pet it. The cat arched its back and streaked down the corridor. After a moment, the children followed.

---

"I HAVE YOUR FRIEND." Balaur tipped the goblet back and drank deeply. A line of blood-dark wine trickled from the corner of his mouth. "He is being brought to the torturers. I have instructed them to keep his body as intact as possible, but flesh can heal."

"There is no point!" Lezarius raged. "I already told you, I cannot shift the ley. Not unless you break your own Wards—"

"And give you free rein?" Balaur laughed and set the goblet down. "No, old friend. That will never happen. But you are holding out on me. I can sense it. So the choice is yours. Perhaps when I bring you what remains of the Invertido, you will change your mind. It is a simple favor I ask—"

Lezarius fell to his knees, clutching Balaur's robes. "Please, I beg you! Take me to the outer stelae! I can do it there!"

"You think I trust you not to run the moment you have the chance? Do not take me for a complete idiot." Balaur shook him off. His face was a fright to behold. It ran like melting wax, a patchwork of raw, pink skin. The wiry black hair was falling out in clumps now. But his physical strength seemed undiminished and he pushed Lezarius away with ease.

"Think on my offer. The torture chamber is only nine levels down. If he screams loudly enough, you should be able to hear it."

He strode to the door. The bolt shot on the outside.

Lezarius hurried over, listening to his footsteps recede down the stairs. Then he ran across the chamber to the outer door. He'd lifted the key from Balaur's pocket. A fierce gust hit him as he unlocked the door and stepped out to the parapet.

If he killed himself, they would have no reason to torture Mikhail. Perhaps the Wards would keep Balaur from marching out to the Morho, but Lezarius suspected they would not last much longer anyway. They were hanging by a thread.

Oh, it had been folly to come here! He walked to the edge, looking out over the Sundar Kush. Why had he been given this power over the ley? It was a burden no one should bear. He had done what he thought right, but what a mess he had made of things.

Lezarius stepped to the brink, feet sliding on the skin of ice. Smoke rose from the pyres in the valley below, a dark smudge against the snowy fields.

How many of his people had Balaur burned? How many had murdered each other? Tears stung his eyes. He should never have turned his back on the other cities. None of them knew what had happened here and that was squarely his own fault. But he knew that Balaur would continued to torture all of Jalghuth until Lezarius complied with his demands. Demands that were impossible! Balaur despised weakness more than anything. It must have driven him mad to be imprisoned here for so long. He would perceive Lezarius's suicide as an act of weakness, but it was not.

In those last moments, his mind cleared. Even if the northern stelae eventually broke, Lezarius felt certain his other work would outlast him. The Void would remain.

Lezarius raised a hand. He had no one to give him the litany for the dying, but he could still do it himself. "Kyrie, eleison," he cried over the howling lament of the wind. "Kyrie, eleison. Sancte Jule. Sancte Dima. Sancta Agathe. Sancte Kwame. Sancta Imani—"

A hand suddenly shot over the edge of the parapet, groping for purchase. Lezarius recognized the Mark on the muscled forearm. A dove with a laurel wreath around its neck. The fingers began to slip. He grabbed the arm, hauling with all his might. The whole tower was slick with ice. He feared they would both go over, but Mikhail must have found some crevice with his toes for he heaved his shoulders above the edge. Lezarius dragged him the rest of the way.

The knight was frozen, his lips nearly the same shade as his eyes.

"How did you escape them?" Lezarius cried.

But of course, he did not answer.

Lezarius peered over the edge. He could see a dark opening far below, at least thirty meters. It seemed unfathomable that Mikhail had scaled the icy tower unclothed, beaten and bloody, yet here he was.

Lezarius helped him inside the chamber. He closed the door, sealing out the frigid wind, and chafed Mikhail's frozen hands.

"I am grateful you came," he said. "But I cannot get down that way."

The knight huddled by the fire. Frost rimed his beard. He looked around the chamber, then dipped a finger in the half-drunk glass of wine Balaur had left behind. He traced a single word in the margin of one of the books.

*No.*

"You did not intend for us to do that," Lezarius said. "But how then?" A distant tumult in the corridor. It quickly grew louder. "They know you are here!"

The knight rose to his full height. Still painfully thin and covered with bruises, yet there was a fierceness to him that gave Lezarius hope, even against impossible odds. Mikhail was something more—and perhaps less—than fully human. Lezarius had seen it when they went after Feizah.

Mikhail gazed calmly at the door, then motioned Lezarius to stand back.

He planned for this, Lezarius realized. Since the moment he arrived.

Lezarius retreated as far as he could get.

The door swung wide.

Swifter than thought, Mikhail grabbed the wrist of the first knight, snapping it. In an instant, he had the man's blade. Lezarius looked away. He heard air whistle against the edge of the sword, screams as it did its work. The thud of bodies and shouts of men in the corridor beyond. It went on and on. At last, all fell silent.

He turned, praying Mikhail was not among the dead, but the knight stood over them, breathing hard. So many. They had been Lezarius's guards once and he would weep for them later, but there was no time now. He stepped forward. Balaur climbed over the bodies clogging the doorway, flanked by two of his batwinged minions. Mikhail raised the blade.

"And so I have you both together," Balaur said softly. "I should have done it from the start."

The blade slashed for his head. Balaur caught Mikhail's forearm. For a moment, they stood locked together. Mikhail's teeth gritted with strain. His Marks glowed a fiery red. Balaur smiled, but the abyssal ley seemed to sink into them without effect. Balaur's smile turned to a rictus of anger. He twisted away and the blade swept over his head.

Balaur looked shocked that his compulsion had been rebuffed, but he recovered quickly.

"Finish it!" he bellowed at the winged abominations.

The light faded. Rivulets of black ley snaked outward, coiling like serpents around Mikhail's feet. The sword slipped from his hand. He sank to his knees, head bowed. Lezarius instinctively cringed away as they moved inside the chamber, seizing Mikhail's arms.

"Do it now," Balaur snarled at him. "Break the stelae!"

He strode to the door to the parapet and opened it. Mikhail writhed in the cardinals' taloned grip as they dragged him outside. Veins of darkness ran up his arms.

"I . . . I will try!" Lezarius stammered.

He could think of nothing else to do. He followed them outside.

"You have the power!" Balaur urged. "Use it!"

Mikhail's mouth was open as though a terrible scream sat trapped in his throat. The sight broke Lezarius's heart. He opened himself to the red chaos, searching for any hint of rationality. There was none.

"I cannot!" he sobbed.

Balaur stepped up to him, white robes whipping. His eyes burned like a pair of coals in the twilight.

"Then you will see him die," he said.

# Chapter Thirty-Six

The Reborn followed the cat deeper into the Lance. She ran ahead, batting at cobwebs—and occasionally her own shadow. A beetle crossed their path and the cat stalked it to a crevice, tail lashing. The moment it vanished, she sprang away again.

Until he came to this place, Will had not perceived color. But the deep crimson Wards glowing along the walls were so bright they penetrated the veil across his eyes. The wrongness of them buzzed in his ears like a swarm of angry wasps as he walked through the endless, winding corridors. Some kind of labyrinth, although Will could not discern its pattern. Then the cat rounded a curve and he lost sight of it.

*Here, brother.*

Noach stood at a small hole where the damp had rotted away a corner of brick. The rest of it was solidly mortared. Will felt a profound despair, almost as bad as the long dark. He'd been so eager for guidance he had latched onto the animal, thinking it was sent by the ley. Hoping it might lead them to the knight. But he had not received another message from Mikhail. And the churning power of this place made his head spin. He doubted he could find his way out again.

*I am sorry,* he sent to the others. *I have led you nowhere.*

Noach studied the wall with a slight frown. *This is new-built. It does not belong here.*

He reached out and pushed with both hands. The bricks tumbled inward in a shower of dust. Will stared in astonishment.

Diamond bodies.

Will had told the light-bringer they had no power, but he had never tested his own strength. It must be why the Red King wanted them for soldiers. He didn't realize that the strength could not be used to harm the living. A wall, on the other hand . . . .

The Reborn stepped through the gap. A circular room lay beyond. A mosaic of a Black Sun with twelve jagged rays stretched across the floor, just like the audience chamber.

The cat had vanished. Will entered and knelt down. He laid his palm on the center of the Black Sun, white light seeping through his skin. The symbol thrummed with power. It tried to block the vision, but in the end the barrier dissolved and Will saw the truth that been hidden away.

Great digging machines sat on the mountainside, surrounded by heaps of earth. A huge scaffold rose up, piercing the clouds. Ropes and pulleys swung great blocks of obsidian stone into place. Men and women in brightly colored robes stood at the bottom, overseeing the construction of the Lance. They were the Praefators. The wizards of old. A terrible war raged across the continent. The Second Dark Age. Only the Praefators saw what must be done if a remnant was to be saved.

A simple but drastic solution to the corruption of the ley.

Will understood it now. The Red King had been tricked. Blinded by his own lust for immortality.

In creating the Reborn, he had sealed his own doom.

The six brothers and sisters joined hands in a circle around the Black Sun. The Red Wards dimmed.

*We are born of the Wheel, but no longer of the Wheel. We are the*

*Wandering Cherubim. We are the Guardians of the Ley. And now we have come home.*

A jagged crack rent the heart of the Black Sun. It split in half. Light filled the chamber, spreading outward in a dazzling starburst.

---

Atop the Lance, Lezarius's eyes flew wide.

He struggled to find a single drop of blue ley. Now, in a single instant, an ocean surged up from the depths of the Lance. He smelled burning flesh as it erupted from his Marks in shafts of blinding brilliance. Panicked, he hurled the ley outward, yet it continued to course through him. He was the metal rod conducting the current and the power would not let him go.

The sky lit with blue lightning. It forked down, striking the Red Wards on the Lance. Still the wave built higher, rolling outward through the mountains and valleys, the glacial fields and boreal forests. Lezarius understood that no vessel could hold such power without being torn apart. He was a mote in the whirlwind, a drop in the tempest. He thought he heard a voice—not the ones that tormented him but a kind voice, telling him to surrender. That all would be well. If the voice was some new form of madness, he still took comfort from it. The pain receded. Lezarius floated on a sea of light.

At last the wave crested and receded. For an endless time, he lay insensible. Then, slowly, the shrieking wind returned. Lezarius opened his eyes. A thin layer of snow covered him. He brushed it away. His shirt was scorched to rags. Lezarius ran a wondering hand over the Mark on his chest. Its lines were raw and red like a brand, yet the heart beneath still beat.

When he saw the snow-dusted mound near the door to the chamber, he began to weep, harsh, choking sobs. The tears froze to his cheeks. Lezarius crawled to Mikhail's body. They were alone on the parapet. The Wards had all gone dark.

"Do not grieve, Lezarius," a voice said. "You were the Martyr. Now you are the Lion."

It was the same voice that had reassured him. But when he looked up at the bloodless creature standing over him, he felt afraid. "What is this?" he whispered. "Who are you?"

A kaleidoscope of colors swirled in one eye. The other was black and knowing.

"We are the ley," the child replied.

# Chapter Thirty-Seven

Alexei was crossing a one-lane bridge when his Marksteed suddenly reared, throwing him into the icy water. Had he been wearing the chainmail hauberk, he would have sunk like an anvil. But it was too heavy to wear all day in the saddle—both for him and the poor horse. He'd abandoned it a few kilometers from Nantwich. The mail wouldn't stop a mage's arrow, only a slash from a sword, and if they got that close he'd be dead anyway.

Besides which, he was not a knight anymore, whatever Clavis believed. Just a priest.

Alexei gasped as he broke the surface. His Marks flared briefly—but not the way they had with Kasia when his mind was in turmoil. That had been a fight to the death. This was akin to the clarity of deep meditation. He stroked to the shore. By the time he got there, his Marks had settled down. Alice was baying and spinning in circles. She seemed undecided about whether to be happy or worried.

The feeling of blue ley flowing through him was common enough. He'd worked it for more than twenty years.

What he was *not* used to was experiencing it in the Void.

He looked around, sodden and shivering. During a natural

surge, the ley would gather in stagnant pools before seeping back into the earth. Now it flowed in swift currents around his boots, just as it did in the cities.

Could the entire Void be gone?

He'd been two years old when Lezarius forged the grid. He had never known a world where the ley flowed freely. The thought was terrifying, even though part of him had braced for this to happen. Perhaps it was only the north. But still, a dire omen. As far as Alexei knew, only Lezarius himself could unmake his work and he did not think the pontifex would do it willingly. Or would he? The man was undeniably mad. Had Falke been right to try to kill him?

A frigid wind swept the riverbank. Alexei realized his cassock was starting to freeze. If he didn't get warm and dry, he wouldn't live long enough to learn what had happened. The horse tossed its head but allowed him to take the reins. He rooted through the saddlebags and changed into a dry cassock. Then he found his way back to the road and took shelter beneath a stand of pines. He unsaddled the horse, gathered dry kindling and got a fire started. There was no sign of snow yet, but he could smell it in the air.

Alexei stared into the flames, feeding them small boughs cut from the pines. The wood was green and gave off clouds of smoke, but he had no choice. Night was falling. *Mox nox,* as the nihilim said. The Morho stretched out around him, silent and still, not a glimmer of light or single birdcall, as if he were the last man on earth. The only sounds were the quiet munching of the horse in her feedbag and the crackle of the fire. A deep chill settled in and he was grateful for Alice's warmth at his side. At least he could use the ley now if he needed to. It gave him comfort, though he wondered what he would find at Jalghuth.

He must have dozed off, because when his eyes opened again the fire was dead and covered in snow. Faint moonlight filtered through the trees. His blanket had slipped to the cold ground. Alexei was reaching for it when a branch snapped in the darkness. Alice leapt to her feet, ears perked. He sensed the rumble building in her chest. "*Sileo*," he whispered. Luckily, he had already shed the wet gloves. He laid a hand on her flank and reinforced the command with a small amount of blue ley. She quieted.

Another rustle of dry leaves. The sounds must have woken him. He rarely slept deeply—and never in enemy territory. His campsite was hidden behind a screen of low branches, but if they kept coming, they'd be right on top of him. He ordered Alice to stay and crept to the bole of a tree. In the clearing beyond, six silhouettes moved through the darkness. Each carried a bow. They were headed on a diagonal towards the road. With luck, they might pass—

The lead figure halted. It wore a cloak. A female voice drifted over. "I smell something." The hood fell back. A Broken Chain glowed redly against her neck.

Her companions came closer. "What, Anaithe?"

"Old smoke. Someone has passed this way." She studied the currents flowing around her feet.

"One of ours?"

"I don't know. We should search."

The group stood six meters away. Alexei's gut tightened.

"There's no time," one of the men said at last. "We are needed to hold the city. The Ravens march."

A laugh. "We will clip their wings soon enough."

"Do you think it's true?" The voice sounded like a young boy. "About the Black Sun?"

"We've all dreamt of him, Trist." The first woman again. "It must be true."

"Will my sister be there?"

"We will find her. But Vergrid is right. We do not wish to meet the rooks before we reach the gates." Her head swung towards Alexei. The Broken Chain glowed like hot embers.

He stilled his mind, drawing deep, even breaths. "Stay close," she said. "I sense a . . . malignancy."

They moved onward, cutting through the clearing. He heard them cross the road, headed west.

*A malignancy*. Is that what he was to them?

Alexei returned to the campsite. Alice stared at him accusingly, unable to understand why he had kept her at bay.

"Little sister," he whispered, "not even you could take a band of mages who wield the ley."

She gave a chuffing cough that expressed polite dissent, but suffered him to rub her scar. The sky was lightening as he saddled his horse and returned to the road.

So they were going to Bal Agnar. Balaur was gathering his forces. Did he hold Jalghuth too? Alexei saw the world he had known teetering on the brink of a precipice. Yet despite all he knew about Falke, he could not think of a better man to lead the Curia now. Clavis was of like mind. Between the two of them, they could hold the north. Luk would have to come around and fight now that the Void was broken. Without him, the balance would be too fine.

His thoughts spun through different scenarios as he galloped northward, but they all came down to the same thing in the end. The Curia had to unite. It was the only way.

The sun was high when he found himself at the outer ring of stelae—or what was left of them. Snow fell thickly as Alexei picked his way through the rubble littering the frozen plain. Half had vaporized to dust. The others were a jumble of broken rock. Alice sniffed around, gave a perplexed bark, then scampered ahead.

He drew up on the shore of Lake Khotang, beset by doubts.

He was Raven-Marked. Key-Marked. There could be no doubt who he was. It suddenly seemed like utter folly to ride into the Beast's lair. Whoever had Lezarius—and it seemed very likely that person was Balaur—had forced him to break the Void. Alexei almost turned back, but the thought of his brother and those poor children made him ashamed of his cowardice. If there was even the smallest chance he could find them before it was too late, he had to try.

He spurred his mount through the stelae towards the blue-gray mountain range that rose in the distance. That such a majestic place could fall to the nihilim angered him, though his Marks soothed it before the emotion even registered. The blue ley flowed swiftly here, gushing from some distant source in the high peaks. The closer he came, the more his resolve hardened. His mind felt clear, supremely rational, the fog of the last weeks lifting at last.

*We are here, Father Bryce. We are well.*

The sending came from the boy, Willem Danziger. It rocked him for a moment, but Alexei gathered his composure.

*What of Lezarius? And my brother?*

*Come to Sinjali's Lance. Come to the Root.*

Alexei let out a taut breath. He rode into the valley at the foot of the Arx. Tall, narrow buildings with multi-tiered curving roofs lined the streets. Yellow and blue were the predominant colors, giving the town a cheerful aspect, but most of the shutters were tightly closed. Other than a dog or two, few people seemed to be about. Presently, he passed a stone fountain with fancifully carved spouts that poured water into troughs. Three women in bright orange tunics with blue sashes stood filling buckets. They cast him wary glances when he drew up, shaking their heads when he spoke Osterlish. He pointed to his Raven Mark and looked around with a shrug. One of the women, dark-skinned and plump with black hair in two plaits, suddenly smiled.

"Arx?" she asked. He nodded. She pointed through the town and gestured that he should keep going. Alexei bowed and rode on until he found a road of frozen mud that led up into a pass. There were no signs of trouble, just an eerie quiet that made him wonder what these people had endured.

Willem's message lifted his spirits, but was the danger truly past? What awaited him at Sinjali's Lance?

When he reached the gates of the Arx, a band of knights in the tabards of the Blue Flame approached. He tensed, but they made no move against him. Alice looked relaxed, her tail wagging. If anything, they seemed to be expecting him. They didn't speak Osterlish either, conveying with gestures that he should continue on. He eyed the walls of the Arx as he trotted past. They had Wards, but the symbols were just cold stone now. The sight shook him. Did none of the Wards work anymore? How far south did the damage extend?

He followed the road higher into the mountains through thick snow. Alice loped ahead, erupting in joyful barks as he rounded the final bend. Alexei reined up, neck craning as he followed the Lance to its peak. The nearly seamless octagonal construction filled him with awe. He couldn't tell what it was made from. Stone? Metal? Some combination of the two? There was the hint of a parapet at the top. He thought he saw a pale speck, but it was lost to streamers of mist.

Willem Danziger ran out from the immense black doors. "Father Bryce!" The boy gave him a sunny, innocent smile that erased the feyness of his appearance. He wore a new pair of sneakers, white with blue stripes. Alexei thought of his room in Kvengard. The half-finished school assignments and neatly polished dress shoes. The racing trophies. A sudden lump in his throat made him turn away.

"Willem," he managed, sliding down from the horse.

The boy crouched down. Alice ran up and licked his hand, then dropped to her haunches and gazed intently at the tower.

"The Lion would speak with you," Will said.

Two knights came out to lead the horse away. Alexei paused to stroke her muzzle.

"She rode hard and long," he said. "Care for her well." They looked puzzled, then smiled and nodded. He glanced at Will. "You told them?"

"I told them, Father Bryce. But there was no need. This is a place of love now, for all of the ley's creatures."

He could feel it, how clean the power flowed, like a river at its source. It wanted to lull him into complacency, but he had not forgotten the mages. Whatever had happened here, the rest of the world was not so placid.

He followed Willem up long flights of circling stairs. At the landings, he could see down into the center of the Lance, which was hollow like a cylinder. The boy didn't seem to tire, but Alexei had to ask him to pause several times. Three days he had ridden with little rest. It was starting to catch up. At last they emerged to a curved landing and entered a bare chamber. Alice went into a frenzy of sniffing, her hackles raised. The stone floor looked freshly mopped, but Alexei could discern traces of blood in the cracks.

"What happened here?" he asked.

Willem Danziger looked sad. "A great sacrifice. But it is not my place to speak of it." He touched Alexei's sleeve. "I am happy you are here, Father Bryce."

The boy's words filled him with dread. He mustered the courage to ask again about his brother, but Willem took off at a run, his sneakers pattering down the stairs.

A second door led out to the parapet he had glimpsed from the ground. Alice trotted to the threshold and stuck her snout out. She didn't seem to like what she saw, for she whined through her nose and lay down just inside the chamber.

"I don't blame you," Alexei muttered as he stepped out on the parapet. Frigid wind bit through his woolen cassock, but bright sunlight broke through the racing clouds. On one side he could see clear across the valley to the Northern Ocean. On the other, row upon row of snow-capped peaks, each higher than the last. A man sat at the edge of the parapet, his feet dangling over the drop. He wore a white robe. Alexei still expected the old man from the Institute and he frowned as the figure turned to look at him. The green eyes were the same, and the kinky black hair, but the features had rearranged themselves to a subtly different face—the one from the triptych in the Iveron Chapel. He grinned with a mouth full of strong white teeth.

"Got a smoke, Fra Bryce?"

Alexei blinked as Lezarius let out a cackle of laughter. "Got you, didn't I?" He slapped the parapet next to him. "Come, join me." The voice, too, was the same, though deeper.

Alexei bent a knee. "Reverend Father."

The chasm below made him dizzy. He sat and inched forward, though he didn't dangle his legs like Lezarius.

"I see you are restored," he said cautiously.

"Yes. The illusion shattered along with my own work." He looked out at the mountains. "I was a geographer, you know. I should have guessed the truth. These are the headlands, Fra Bryce. The snowmelt feeds the rest of the continent. When you drive across the Liberation Bridge in Novostopol, you are crossing water that originated in the Sundar Kush."

"I didn't know that, Reverend Father."

Lezarius waved a hand impatiently. "You may dispense with the honorific. My point is that we always knew the ley flowed like water. That its source lay in the core. Beneath our feet lies a great wellspring. And that is the purpose of Sinjali's Lance. It is a prism that divides the ley into three layers of varying purpose."

Alexei stared at him. "That isn't natural?"

"Not at all," Lezarius replied. "The Praefators created them. It was the only way to tame the corrupted psyches that would destroy the world. They placed the blue on top, to govern the rest, just as the rational mind governs the body's actions. Then the liminal, and at last the abyssal. The subconscious and unconscious. They could not destroy the other layers, nor would they want to. All are necessary for the organism to function, but they must be kept in a proper balance."

Alexei sat in stunned silence for a moment. "And Balaur held the Lance?"

"He Warded it with abyssal ley, disrupting the flow. But the children have set it to rights."

"What . . . are they?"

"They call themselves the Reborn. Sometimes the Wandering Cherubim."

Alexei recalled the book in his saddlebag. *Der Cherubinscher Wandersmann*. He'd thought Angelus Silesius an alchemist, but the man was more of a prophet. His work had been put to evil use, yet in the end, Balaur had planted the seeds of his own downfall.

"They claim the ley put them here to guard the source." Lezarius gave Alexei a wry look. "I am not arguing with them."

A million questions flooded his mind. "Is Balaur dead? How did he force you to break the Void? Can you remake it—"

Lezarius held up a hand, chuckling. "One at a time, Fra Bryce. As to the first, which is clearly the most important, no, I do not believe he is dead." The laughter died. His expression grew deadly serious. "When I came to my senses, he was gone. Until I see his body, I must assume he lives. Two of his foul creations were with him."

"Winged creatures?"

"I see you have already encountered them. Yes, and I fear they spirited him from the Lance. As to the second, I did not mean to unmake the Void, and in fact, it was so polluted by his presence I thought it would be impossible. But I was trying to save your brother when the children broke Balaur's Wards." His face grew haunted. "I am still surprised that I survived. I filled with ley and had no choice but to throw it outwards."

Alexei nodded, though he'd heard little after the phrase *trying to save your brother*.

"Reverend Father," he said, forgetting Lezarius's request. "Please just tell me. Is he . . . is he dead?"

Lezarius raised his shaggy brows. "Saints preserve me, I should have told you straightaway." He looked abashed. "Your brother lives."

A boulder lifted from his chest, though something in the pontifex's tone made him uneasy. "He is injured though?"

"No, he is well. I will take you to see him."

Alexei laughed in amazed delight. "I cannot believe it! I feared the worst."

Lezarius smiled back, but his gaze drifted to Alexei's neck. "You wear Clavis's Mark now?"

"I took it in Nantwich. She sent me here."

"Ah." Shrewd eyes studied him. "You have news of the world. Tell me."

Alexei drew a deep breath. "First, you never answered my last question. The Void. Can you make it again?"

Lezarius shook his head. "I cannot touch the ley at all anymore. The ability was burned out of me." He twisted around to display reddened weals on his neck that traced the Blue Flame Mark. "The rest are the same."

"Saints," Alexei murmured. "I am sorry. Does it hurt?"

Lezarius shrugged. "They are healing. I am still the Pontifex of Jalghuth. Most of my knights are loyal again. Those who were too far gone have already fled." A brief smile. "The Lion has a few fangs yet."

"I expected something like that," Alexei replied heavily. "If you could have repaired it, you would have done so already."

He studied the man next to him. Suddenly, he was weary of lies and deception. If they had any hope at all, he needed to speak honestly.

"Clavis sent me to kill you," he said. "I wasn't going to do it. But she feared you. So did Falke. It was he who sent the priests to the Institute, not Feizah."

Lezarius's eyes darkened. "She didn't know?" he asked softly.

"I am certain she did not."

He raised a shaking hand to his forehead. "We committed murder then."

Alexei remained silent. He had expected denials, perhaps an outburst, but Lezarius seemed perfectly lucid.

"What is done is done," he muttered at last. "I cannot take it back." A spark flared in his eyes. "But now you tell me that both the Eastern and Western Curiae would see me dead?"

"Only to prevent the Void from being destroyed," Alexei said quickly. "I do not condone the decision, but they thought they were averting disaster. That is all."

"Because of my madness?"

He gave a reluctant nod. "I do not see Invertido in that light, but I am the exception."

Lezarius looked angry and Alexei rushed to fill the silence. "What happened is not your fault. They will see the truth. They have to! Mages are gathering. I saw a group of them in the Morho. If Balaur lives, we cannot descend to petty squabbles. A united front is the only hope." He swallowed. "I ask you to look beyond the past and join them now. Send your army to stand with Falke and Clavis at Bal Agnar."

Lezarius scowled. "It is much you ask of me, Fra Bryce."

"Do you trust me?" He held Lezarius's eyes.

The pontifex nodded. "You have always shown me kindness, Fra Bryce. Even before you knew who I was. I believe you are a good man."

"Then make me your nuncio. I will take the Mark of the Blue Flame. Then I will go to Luk and persuade him to fight. If he offers a Wolf Mark, I will take that as well." Alexei had no idea what effect two more might have on him, but it felt right. "I will be a living symbol of the Curia united, as it is meant to be. Of my loyalty to all, not just one city."

Lezarius pursed his lips. "I shall consider it," he said at last. "But there is much to be here first. And while I might trust *you*, Fra Bryce, that does not extend to Falke and Clavis. If they knew the source of power we are sitting on, I wouldn't put it past them to invade Jalghuth themselves."

"But—"

Lezarius held up a palm to forestall further argument. "Enough," he said sternly. "You will not get an answer from me now."

Alexei reluctantly bent his head in deference. "Yes, Reverend Father."

Lezarius regarded his right hand. "Balaur still wears my ring. A meaningless lump of gold, but I want it back." Suddenly, he laughed. "Dantarion would say it reveals my true nature. Covetous and prideful."

"Dantarion?"

"The mage who brought me here. She saved Will and the other children from his vicious grandfather."

"A nihilim helped them?" Alexei asked in surprise.

"And her act of charity got her what she wanted. An end to the Void." Lezarius gave a small half-smile. "I will tell her that if I ever see her again." He slid away from the edge. "I'll take you to Mikhail now. You must be eager to see him."

Alexei helped the pontifex to his feet. "Is he still . . . angry at me?"

"I do not believe so." A sharp glance. "He never brought the children here to fight. They cannot, in any event." A bark of sardonic laughter. "Luk would approve of them. They will not even raise a hand to defend themselves."

"Then you must protect them," Alexei said.

"From what I gather, they cannot be harmed by traditional means. Only alchemical fire." His lips tightened. "And that has been banished from Jalghuth."

Alice jumped to her feet and followed as they entered the chamber. It took a long while to descend the Lance. Lezarius moved stiffly and Alexei wondered how long he had been sitting on the frozen parapet. He seemed saner than the rambling man Alexei had known at the Batavia Institute, but Lezarius had said nothing of his Marks, other than they had burned.

"I haven't yet told the people the full truth of what happened," Lezarius said, as they paused on a landing. "The city was in a wretched state when I arrived. Balaur turned them on each other like a pack of starving cannibals."

"It seemed quiet when I rode through."

"The knights keep order now, though the worst of the poison has already leached away. I am told things are returning to normal. Will says the people remember the last four years as a strange, unpleasant dream, but I owe them an explanation." For a moment, he looked utterly weary.

"When you are stronger, Reverend Father," Alexei said gently. "You have endured a great trial."

"No worse than the others," he replied. "But yes, I must appear strong when I make a public appearance."

Alice suddenly flopped down, paws splayed out and rump arched in the air. The universal dog sign for, *Hello, new friend! Would you care to play?*

Alexei peered along the dim landing. A tiny black cat crouched there, tail low and swishing back and forth. She gave a warning hiss, puffed up like an adder, and swiped at Alice's nose. The dog let out a befuddled yelp.

"Greylight!" Lezarius said sternly, though he looked amused. "The Markhound will not hurt you." He cast a quick look at Alexei. "Will it?"

"No, she likes cats." He laughed. "Though they don't always like her."

Alice tried out another flop, sweetening the offer with a quick shake of her ears. Alexei had to admire the cat. It was roughly the size of the Markhound's muzzle, but it held its ground, yellow eyes narrowed as if to reply, *This is my tower and you shall not pass.*

The standoff lasted perhaps twenty seconds. Alice cocked her head. Then, to Alexei's astonishment, she whimpered and slunk between his legs. Greylight appeared satisfied at this display of submission and streaked away.

"The cat is yours?" Alexei asked with a grin.

"It's the same one Doctor Massot gave me at the Institute," Lezarius said, smiling at his look of surprise. "I still cannot fathom how we both survived the journey. There is more to tell, Fra Bryce, but we will save that for another time."

They descended the second half of the spiral stairs in silence. Alexei's pulse quickened as he thought of Mikhail. The children had purified this place. Could his brother be improved, too? But Lezarius would have told him. Alexei reined in his hopes. Misha was alive. That alone was something to be grateful for. And he had been right to bring the children here, even though it led to the destruction of the Void. If Balaur commanded the very source of the ley, the taint would have infected them all in time.

When they reached the bottom of the Lance, Lezarius led him to a large chamber with a black throne at the far end. Two dozen knights were at work with picks and spades, digging at the floor. Mounds of broken tiles lay scattered about. Alexei studied the half-demolished mosaic and realized it was the remnants of a Black Sun.

Then he spotted Misha. Sweat plastered dark hair to his forehead. He raised a pick and smashed it down. Tiles shattered. A knight moved in with a shovel and began digging out the shards. He must have sensed Alexei's gaze for he turned, lowering the pick. His face split in a wide grin.

"Alyosha!" he called.

The sound of Misha's voice raised gooseflesh on his arms. He had despaired of ever hearing it again. Then Alice gave a low growl. She adopted an aggressive stance, mouth tightly closed, pointy ears erect. Misha's smile faltered.

"*Cessa*," Alexei snapped in irritation. "*Sileo!*"

Alice shot him a baleful look, then continued to stare hard at Misha. She showed what the trainers called *whale eye*, the whites visible all around—always a sign of trouble. He ordered her to go and she skulked to the door, though she looked ready to come bounding back if he signaled her. Clearly, she remembered the beating her master had taken on the cliff.

Alexei's throat tightened as he ran forward and pulled Misha into an embrace. He felt thin, but nothing like he had been. At last, his brother pulled back. His blue eyes glistened with unshed tears.

"Will said you were coming." Mikhail searched Alexei's face. "I'm so sorry for what I did. I had no thought but to find Lezarius, whatever the cost. I hurt you—"

"It doesn't matter." He glanced down at Misha's chest. It was covered by a Blue Flame tabard. "You are a knight again?"

Misha's eyes cooled a fraction. "I always was, brother."

Alexei nodded uncertainly. His dearest wish come true, yet he sensed something amiss. Mikhail tossed the pick aside. His gaze was quick and restless, lit with the fierce intelligence Alexei remembered. He pushed a wavy lock from his forehead and it immediately tumbled into his eyes again. Another familiar gesture.

"Brother," Alexei said quietly, unable to contain the question anymore. "Is it gone?"

Misha shared a quick look with Lezarius, who stood beside them. "No," he said with a touch of defiance.

Lezarius signaled to the knights digging at the floor, speaking a few words in Kindu. They abandoned their tools and retreated from the chamber, leaving the three of them alone.

"Show him," Lezarius said quietly.

Misha held Alexei's gaze for a long moment. Then he lifted the tabard, baring his chest. The Nightmark remained. An image of a blindfolded man with a knife against his throat, face frozen in an ecstatic grimace. But the Mark was no longer Inverted. Alexei stared at it, transfixed. For all the years he had sought a cure, all the sleepless nights he had spent imagining some way out of this devil's bargain, he had never once wished for this. The implications chilled his blood. Made him want to laugh and weep at the same time. He understood now. His brother was sane, after a fashion. He could speak. He appeared to be himself. But in time . . . .

"I can fight it," Mikhail said, his voice low and determined. "I did it before."

Alexei raised his eyes. "Of course you can."

"I am a changed man. You cannot conceive how much I despise the nihilim. I feel perfectly fine now. The same as I was before . . . ." He trailed off, breaking eye contact. "You know what I mean."

Alexei turned to Lezarius. "And you?"

"I am no longer Invertido," Lezarius confirmed.

Alexei nodded absently. "I am glad," he said, silently adding, *But yours are not Nightmarks, are they?* Shame followed on the heels of this thought. Mikhail had taken it for him.

"Brother." Mikhail looked at him pleadingly. "Do you believe me? I must live with this thing, but I will not let it consume me. And if I do . . . show signs . . . I ask that you . . . do the correct thing."

*The correct thing.* Almost the same words Clavis had used when she sent him to murder a Pontifex. Alexei no longer knew what the words even meant. Every time he found solid ground, a fresh tremor pulled the walls down around his ears. Yet Mikhail's halting speech melted the dagger of ice lodged in his heart. He stepped forward and clapped a hand on Misha's broad shoulder, choosing his words with care. "I love you always. Know that. And I never stopped believing in you, not for a moment."

His brother laughed, relief on his face. "If I'm half as stubborn as you are, I think I stand a chance." He bent down and seized the pick. "I will join you later, but not until this heretical symbol is eradicated. Then we can talk of old times. I would hear what brought you to us. I imagine it is a tale."

"It is," Alexei agreed with a smile, watching as Misha hefted the pick and attacked the tiles again.

Lezarius cleared his throat. "Come, let us find you some hot food."

Alexei raised a hand in farewell, but Mikhail was too preoccupied to notice. Tendons stood out on his pale neck as he hacked at the floor with a ferocity that reminded Alexei of his brother's last fight in the ruins of the basilica. He swung the pick as though his life depended on it—and perhaps in his mind, it did.

"Fra Bryce?" Lezarius waited for him at the door.

Alexei blinked. "Yes, I'm coming." He tore his gaze from Mikhail's labors and strode from the chamber, the incessant crack of the pick echoing behind him. Alice fell into step with them. Her hackles still bristled.

How long do we have? he wondered bleakly. How long? Because he knew the truth even if neither of them would admit it. Malach's hook had been set. The line would eventually draw taut again.

And what, he thought, will save us from my brother then?

# Chapter Thirty-Eight

Kasia walked the paths of her wild, overgrown garden, listening to the drone of the bees in the clover. Everywhere, the ley flowed, violet in some places, dark red in others. The blue was not a part of this place.

She never used the ley here because she had no reason to. It was her refuge and no one came unless she invited them. None but—

She pressed a hand to her forehead as the thought dissolved into mist.

Sometimes the garden was large, covering the whole world. Sometimes it was small, a walled oasis with tinkling fountains and emerald lawns. This was the case as she strolled aimlessly, fingers trailing across fragrant blossoms she had no names for. She had not met Alexei here since he left—her own doing. Solitude was what she needed. A reprieve from her confinement at the Arx and the unanswered questions about who she was. For the sweven had given her the meat of it, but not the bone.

She looked up. An old man sat on a bench. She vaguely recalled meeting him before and disliking him. He saw her dark expression and raised a hand. "Wait!"

Kasia strode over. She imagined the bench as empty. The space around it bent, rippled, then snapped back into place. The man was still there.

"How did you do that?" she demanded.

"It is my talent," he admitted. "I will not stay long. I only wanted to talk for a moment."

She scowled. "About what?"

"We are kin," he said simply.

His name suddenly entered her mind. Perhaps she had known it all along.

"You are *not* my kin!"

He shrugged. "Denying the truth won't change it."

Again, Kasia tried to banish him. Their eyes locked. The bubble around him flexed and stretched. His mouth set in a tight line. She glimpsed a face beneath the face, ashen and gaunt, but then it faded and his form grew solid, immovable. A man in his sixties, blond and blue-eyed, still handsome, wearing a rough-spun brown robe. The right hand lay hidden within the sleeve.

"If you had Marks, you would be stronger," he said.

She smoothed her dress, pretending his words didn't cut. "I will never have Marks."

"Never is a foolish word. Now that you have tasted the ley, you will use it again. You will not be able to stop yourself." His words echoed her own fears. "Perhaps if you never had . . . . But it is too late now."

"You don't know me," she snapped.

"I know enough. You have great power." He cocked his head. "Yet you ally with those who would deny it to you. This makes no sense to me."

"Because you think only of yourself," she retorted. "Not everyone sees the world in selfish terms."

"Of course they do. It is the way the mind is designed."

"And what of free will?"

"An illusion. We are governed by instinct."

Suddenly, a coiled serpent appeared at her feet. It reared up to strike. Kasia leapt back, flinging out a hand. The serpent dissolved.

"You see?" he said. "You reacted without conscious thought."

"That's a stupid example. It was a matter of survival."

"My point precisely. The snake wasn't even real, yet your mind made it so and you acted to preserve yourself. All decisions stem from that same basic instinct, even the ones we judge rational and considered."

"Then I should kill you now for sending your hunters after me in the Void!"

He smiled. "The only reason you haven't tried is because you know it's impossible. And I offered you an invitation. I did not try to harm you."

"That's putting a fine point on it. You were going to kill my friends."

"Only if they got in the way. I have nothing against them. I would have spared them if you had agreed to meet with me." A tiny smile. "But you must realize that they are your friends no longer. Oh, they might pretend they don't care what you are, that nothing has changed, but you know in your heart that they revile you now. They think you are less than them, when in fact you are much more."

His pitying tone angered her.

"Don't think to gull me," she spat. "I know your crimes."

"Do you?' He gazed at her mildly. "And I suppose you have spoken with my alleged victims yourself? Or is it that you believe the lies they tell about me?"

"My guardian served in Bal Agnar. She told me enough. And I trust her more than you, to say the least. So tell me. What is it you want?"

He spread his hands. "Nothing. Only to warn you that you cannot deny your own nature forever. You *will* use the ley, Katarzinka, whether your small-minded keepers like it or not.

This is inevitable. And when you run afoul of them—also inevitable—you will have only one place left to turn." He stood. "Know that the gates of Bal Agnar will always be open to you, daughter."

"Don't call me that!" Kasia snapped.

But Balaur was gone.

Her hands shook. She would find a way to banish him. This was her place! To have him come and go when he pleased . . . it was . . . .

She blinked, staring at the stone bench. Kasia snatched at the memory, but it faded to shreds. An uneasy feeling lodged in her heart. Yet within a few moments that too faded. She turned and resumed strolling through the garden, the sunlight warm on her skin.

---

Afternoon light pooled on the drafting table as Kasia studied the stack of sketches Natalya had left. The new cards would take weeks to complete. In the meantime Natalya had managed to find a cheap deck in a novelty shop. Not the quality of her own work, but the basic archetypes were the same. Kasia kept the deck in her pocket. Every now and then, a hand stole down to make sure they were still there, though her attention was focused on the sketches for the new cards. She had a million ideas for details that would make them work better. Signs and symbols to evoke desired results from the liminal ley. Yet the knowledge that the cards would only be used for divination left her feeling hollow.

It was small-minded of Clavis not to trust her, she thought with a trace of bitterness. She had never used the ley except to help others. Now she was being hamstrung at the very moment it could be of the most use. What she really wanted was a war deck—

"You've been avoiding me."

Kasia looked up from the table. Faint purple shadows beneath his eyes were the only sign that Patryk Spassov had been on the brink of death a week before.

"I'm sorry," she said guiltily. "Natalya told me you were recovering well. I kept meaning to visit the infirmary, but there was so much to do."

A lie. She had been perfectly idle for the last six days. No word from the Reverend Mother other than a command that she remain at the Arx—while Natalya was given the freedom to come and go as she wished.

"May I come in?" he asked.

"Of course." She rose with a smile. "It's very good to see you."

Spassov entered the small suite. Despite the fortress-like impression of the Arx in Nantwich, Kasia's rooms on the top floor of the the Villa of Saint Margrit were airy and modern. Natalya had converted the sitting area into an artist's studio, with charcoals and paints lined up on the windowsill. He cleared a stool of more sketches and pulled it up to the table. The seat creaked under his weight.

"The Reverend Mother's aide gave this to me," he said, handing her an invitation on heavy cardstock.

Kasia scanned it. "A party at the Kven legate's house." She looked up in surprise. "They're still throwing parties?"

Patryk smiled grimly. "The mood is strange in the city. Half of them are hunkering down for the end of the world, the other half carrying on as though nothing's happened." His gaze moved to the window. "I snuck out for a pint last night. The pubs are packed. Party while you can, eh?"

The Void had shattered two days after Alexei left. When the Wards died, Kasia hoped it would be like Novostopol. That they would come back. But they hadn't and Natalya reported that messengers from the outer forts said it was like that everywhere.

"Any word from Jalghuth?" she asked, afraid it was why Patryk had come.

"None that I know of." His face softened. "I'm sure Alyosha is alive though. His Markhound will protect him."

Kasia gathered her courage. She'd been steering clear of Patryk for a reason, but she owed him the truth. "There is something I must tell you—"

He shifted on the stool, holding her gaze. "Natalya already did."

"She has a big mouth," Kasia muttered.

"She decided you'd never do it. She also told me that you saved my life."

"I had to use all three layers of the ley together. But it worked, didn't it?" she said with a touch of defiance.

"You are what you are, Kasia. It makes no difference to me."

She scowled in confusion. "How can you say that? You fought them in the Void."

"Them," he said firmly. "Not you."

"They are my kin." The words spilled out. She instantly wished she could take them back.

"Only by blood. In spirit, you belong to Tessaria Foy." He smiled. "I never knew her well, but I think you are much alike."

"Thank you," Kasia said quietly.

He tugged his gloves off and held out a hand. A gesture of trust. After a moment, Kasia took it. His big paw gave her fingers a gentle squeeze. "We're comrades in this fight. Let me be your sword. The Order must know you're here." He glanced at the invitation on the table. "I told the Reverend Mother I would escort you, if you'll have me."

Kasia's throat tightened. In half the scenarios she'd imagined, Patryk viewed her with disgust. In the others, he simply kept his distance. She should have given him more credit.

"I am forbidden the ley, so a protector would be

welcome." A wry smile. "Unlike Natalya, I cannot skewer someone with a blade from twenty paces. And I only have two shoes to throw. After that, I'm helpless."

He eyed her appraisingly. "I doubt that very much. But it will give them pause if I am at your side. Especially with the Wards broken. A nihilim could enter the city and we'd never know until it was too late." He cleared his throat. "Natalya also mentioned your dreams."

"Saints, is there anything she left out?" Kasia muttered in exasperation.

"She says she hasn't had any since we came here." His gaze was intent. "What about you? I don't blame you, Kasia. It was the Danzigers who opened the door to him."

"Well, my rest has been untroubled," she replied honestly. "Perhaps Balaur has bigger fish to fry now that we are at war again."

"Perhaps." Patryk looked unconvinced. "Either way, I am glad to hear it. One less thing to worry about."

She picked up the invitation. Natalya was included as well. "Do you dance, Patryk?"

"Only to club music."

Kasia laughed. "Me, too."

He handed her a second piece of paper, folded. "These are the names the Reverend Mother wants us to look into. They'll all be there tonight."

Kasia took it, but didn't read them yet. "What other news do you have, Patryk? I hear little."

"Someone started a rumor that you foretold the breaking of the Void."

Kasia's eyes narrowed. "Someone? Clavis, you mean."

"One of her underlings, I imagine."

"It would be nice if she bothered to let me know." She tapped a tooth with a lacquered nail. "But clever. It paves my entry into the elite circles. People will cling to any lifeline when the storm hits." He took out his cigarettes with a quirked brow and she nodded. "Just don't ash on Natalya's sketches. She'll murder you."

Patryk scooted the stool towards the window.

"What about the front?" Kasia asked. "Are they shelling?"

He blew out a stream of smoke. "They tried. The mages are using abyssal ley to fuck the guns. A knight told me the nihilim have already set up a line of control around Bal Agnar. Anything that gets too close disappears."

"But Falke still holds Bal Kirith?"

"So far, yes. But it's fluid out there." He sighed. "Alyosha told me a few things in Kvengard. I assume Lezarius is the one who broke the Void."

They had never discussed it, but Kasia felt relieved that Spassov already knew. She didn't relish keeping more secrets from him. "It must be," she agreed.

"So where is he now?"

"The question of the hour."

"You can't tell from the cards?"

"They don't work like that," she replied. "And I haven't tried to do a reading."

"Why not?"

She glanced away.

"You're afraid you'll use the ley?"

"Accidentally, yes," she admitted. "I have to be very careful. Clavis says she trusts me, but that could change in a heartbeat."

Patryk looked around for an ashtray and she pointed at a cup of blue-tinted water. "You can use that."

"You sure? I don't want to get stabbed."

"As long as there's no brush, she won't care. And she never leaves her brushes to soak. It's bad for them."

He dropped the smoldering butt into the cup. "The Reverend Mother is taking a hard line with the Wards gone, Kasia. Six days ago, she suspended civil liberties. Any person can be subjected to a random search of their Marks. If you refuse, you're detained. And anyone found working abyssal ley is subject to deadly force, no questions asked."

"Well, Clavis has no choice, does she?" Kasia said slowly.

"I wasn't criticizing. Just sharing information." He studied her. "Not that it's any of my business, but I don't think Alyosha would have gone north if the Reverend Mother hadn't ordered him to."

Kasia said nothing, pretending to sort through the sketches. In the catacombs, when Bryce said he was leaving, she'd had a desperate urge to claim him, body and soul, one last time. She didn't regret that. But she wished she'd found the courage to tell him goodbye.

"You're wrong," she said at last. "He didn't go for Clavis. He went for his brother."

"Okay. But he did ask me to watch over you."

"Perhaps to ensure I don't cause trouble."

"That's unfair. I don't know what passed between you, but Natalya hinted that it was difficult for him to accept. He'll come around in time, Kasia."

A surge of remorse. "He already did," she said quietly. "It was I who left things poorly in the end."

# Chapter Thirty-Nine

After Patryk left, Kasia took a long shower. By the time she came out, Natalya had returned. Glossy shopping bags lay upended all over the room. The bed was covered with high-heeled shoes and silk stockings, gloves and gowns and cosmetics.

"Where did you get all this stuff?" Kasia asked. She was swathed in a towel, with another wrapped around her hair.

"Did you know that the Arx has expense accounts all over town?" Natalya replied, grinning like a child on Caristia morning. "The Reverend Mother's aide told me to buy something suitable for a formal event."

"I'd say there's enough here for a dozen formal events," Kasia said, eyeing the loot.

"Well, I imagine there will be more parties," Natalya said breezily. "If we're spies, we have to look the part. Can't wear the same thing twice."

"That would be *unthinkable*."

"Exactly," Natalya said, either ignoring or entirely missing her dry tone. "You wouldn't believe the shops. They're much more daring than Novo!" She dangled a backless halter dress that seemed held together by a single ribbon. "What do you think?"

"Tessaria would hate it."

Natalya's face softened. "True, and I wish with all my heart that she were here to express an opinion, but I can't live like a vestal forever. And neither can you," she added firmly.

Kasia rifled through the dresses, scowling. "They're all like that."

"It's what they had," Natalya said innocently. "You can't blame me for the fashion trends in a foreign city."

"But people will know!"

"Don't be silly. Your Marks could be anywhere. Right tit, left tit. Ass—"

"And those things are still barely covered by the outfits you chose!"

"Barely being the operative word, Kiska." She thrust out a hanger. "See! Look at this one. It's practically prudish."

The dress was a long silk sheathe in creamy taupe that left little to the imagination, but at least it didn't have any cutouts. "Fine." Kasia snatched it away. "It's too late now anyway. But I'm going shopping with you next time, whatever the Reverend Mother says."

Natalya grinned. "They have nightclubs, too. Maybe afterwards—"

"Don't push your luck," Kasia growled.

By the time they were both dressed, the room looked like a whirlwind had blown through. Kasia donned a pair of elbow-length silk gloves that matched the dress. Natalya had even found a pair of slingback heels that were almost the same color.

"My nips are showing," Kasia said with a frown, turning to the side in front of the standing mirror. "Can't I wear a bra?"

"Sorry, I forgot what size you are."

"Bullshit."

"Look, it wouldn't work. The straps would show." She rustled in another bag and tossed something at her. "Here."

Kasia caught the shawl, slightly mollified. She wrapped it around her shoulders. "That's better."

"What's wrong with a little nip anyway?" Natalya murmured, applying coral lipstick.

"Says the woman who doesn't have melons for breasts."

"Enjoy them while you can. Soon enough you'll need a crane to hoist those puppies up."

"Thanks." Kasia dragged a brush through her hair. "I must say, you look stunning. They'll be too busy staring at your legs to notice anything else."

"The first rule of being a spy," Natalya replied with a laugh. "Distract the target with partial nudity." She picked up the invitation. "What's a legate?"

"One step down from a nuncio, I think. They handle legal matters."

"Like Kommandant Rademacher's complaint?" she asked shrewdly.

"Well, it didn't stop the Kvens from inviting us. And they can't do anything here."

"I see Patryk came by." Natalya eyed the butt floating in her cup.

"Yes, and I'm not sure whether I should thank you or throttle you for telling him my secrets."

Her friend shrugged. "I knew he'd be fine. You always think the worst of people."

"Not true!"

"Yes, you do. I told you Falke was a good man."

"He is a complicated man," Kasia amended. "They are not the same. But I don't deny the good in him."

"He saved your life." Natalya slid a knife into a sheathe around her thigh. "And your brother's."

"I don't want to think about Malach," Kasia muttered.

"You've never met him, but he tried to strangle me on the roof of our flat. He will never be a brother."

Her gaze drifted to the sketches. The Fool came just before The Mage and The High Priestess. Numbers zero, one and two of the Major Arcana. Malach was The Fool and Kasia herself was the next two, combined. Whether or not she loathed him, the ley had placed them adjacent to each other.

The Hierophant—Falke—was the fifth.

Between sat The Empress, the third trump, and The Emperor, the fourth.

Kasia still didn't know who the Empress was, but she suspected it was someone important—someone who would cross her path eventually, if she hadn't already. A woman of power and authority, but it couldn't be Clavis or Tessaria. The Empress embodied fertility, motherhood, spirit and helter-skelter creation. The scepter in her hand tilted carelessly to the left, signifying intuitive rule rather than adherence to the rigid laws of men. Her other hand clutched a falcon, drawing it close even as the scepter tilted away. A woman who valued love over power.

As for the Emperor, it must be Balaur. Four was a potent number, representing earthly concepts like the cardinal directions of the compass, the phases of the moon, the seasons, and the basic operations of mathematics. But Kasia had spent time doing research in Clavis's archives and learned that it had strong ties to alchemy as well. The four qualities of matter—warm, dry, moist, cold. The four alchemical ingredients—salt, sulphur, mercury, azoth. The four geometrical figures—circle, line, square, triangle. The four humours—sanguine, phlegmatic, choleric, melancholic. And the four elements—earth, air, fire and water.

The sixth trump was The Lovers. Kasia shook her head. What a tangle!

"Does Malach look like you?" Natalya asked curiously.

"A little," she conceded. "He's a few years older. I'm sure he had no idea who I was."

"Maybe he wouldn't have harmed you if he'd known."

Kasia gave her a flat look. "He's nihilim, born and raised. They don't care about anybody. It wouldn't have mattered."

"You're probably right." A pause. "Do you ever wonder what would have happened if I hadn't been sick that night, Kiska?"

She was talking about Doctor Massot.

"Of course," Kasia admitted. "But I wouldn't change it. He would have attacked you instead, I'm sure. He was a pig. And I would rather it was me."

Natalya's eyes went wide—and a little misty. "Now you've gone and made my mascara run," she muttered.

---

Patryk Spassov picked them up outside the Villa at eight o'clock sharp in a sleek black Curia car with acres of gleaming chrome. He blinked at Natalya's outfit—Kasia was ensconced in the shawl—but quickly dragged his eyes away and got out to open the back door.

"I feel sadly underdressed," he remarked, sliding behind the wheel.

Nashka grinned at him in the mirror. "I like you in a cassock, Fra Spassov. It fuels the imagination."

He laughed and rolled down the window, hanging an elbow out. They sped up to the gates, where he spoke briefly to the knights on duty. Then they drove through the tunnel and beneath the portcullis.

"Aren't you on the wrong side?" Kasia asked in alarm as he took a hard left at a traffic circle.

"The rules are backwards here," he replied. "See?"

Indeed, traffic was flowing clockwise. It made her feel acutely disoriented, though Spassov had no trouble adjusting.

He seemed stone cold sober and had even shaved for the occasion.

"Crank that heat up," Natalya said. "I'm freezing back here."

He spun a dial and warmth flooded the vehicle. Nashka trailed a hand across the buttery soft leather seat. "I wonder what happened to your beater, Kiska?"

"It probably has eighteen tickets on the windshield by now."

"And good riddance, I say." She leaned forward. "Can I bum a cigarette?"

Patryk rooted around, swerving to avoid a bus that was changing lanes, and shook one out. He lit it and passed it back.

"Everything looks so normal," Kasia said, eyeing the crowds in the streets and brightly lit restaurants. She did see a few police patrols in navy uniforms with cudgels at their belts, but she'd expected a city on edge, not this vibrant, youthful metropolis.

"We haven't hit the checkpoint yet," Spassov said, lighting another cigarette.

As soon as he uttered the words, traffic slowed to a crawl. A few horns blared, but most people seemed resigned to the delay. After a few blocks, flashing lights loomed ahead. Several official-looking vehicles were parked diagonally across the avenue, reducing it to a single lane. Knights in Crossed Keys tabards questioned the occupants of the cars ahead before waving them through.

"You got that invitation?" Spassov asked.

Kasia found it in her handbag and passed it up to the front seat.

It took another twenty minutes before they reached the checkpoint. An electric torch swept the car. The knight scrutinized the invitation and took a hard look at Spassov's Raven Mark. Kasia's stomach tightened as the torch swept the backseat a second time. Natalya had only one Mark—an amber-maned dragon that that coiled around her left arm from shoulder to wrist. Like Nashka, it was daring and beautiful, with metallic scales rendered in shades of red and green.

"What about you?" The knight demanded. "What's under that shawl?"

Kasia let it slip from her shoulders. "I'm afraid my Mark is in a delicate place," she said, laying a hand on one of the thin straps. The thought of Bryce, gloriously naked, brought a surge of color to her face that she hoped the knight would interpret as embarrassed modesty. "Do I need to . . . ?"

He cleared his throat. "If the priest vouches for you, it's all right, Domina."

He stood back from the window and lowered the torch, signaling Spassov to drive through. When Kasia checked the rearview, he was already bending down to interrogate the next driver.

"See?" Natalya said, blowing smoke out the window. "Nips are your friend."

"I thought the invitation would be enough," Patryk muttered, shooting her an apologetic look.

"If it came down to it, I expect the Reverend Mother would protect me, but I don't wish to embarrass her," Kasia said quietly. "Better no one knows."

"I guess the club is out," Natalya said glumly.

Kasia didn't dignify that with a response. She knew Natalya was joking, though she could be callous sometimes. Which, she thought wryly, is probably why we're such close friends. Birds of a feather.

They hit one more checkpoint, but this time the invitation was enough and they were waved through with a cursory inspection. The party was in the embassy district, a posh area of limestone mansions that would have been a fifteen-minute drive from the Arx if not for the new security measures. Spassov pulled up in front of a five-story townhouse guarded by a contingent of Wolf knights. Happily, none seemed to be from the Fort of Saint Ludolf. A young valet in a white jacket hurried up to take the keys. Spassov flicked his cigarette to the gutter and got out to open Kasia's door. Lights shone in all the windows and she could hear the sounds of merry-making inside.

"Ready to meet the Wolfpack?" he asked softly.

"Oh, I'm looking forward to it," she replied. "More than you can imagine."

Back in Novostopol, she had vowed to be the hunter—not the hunted. Only cowards wore masks to hide their identities. The Order of the Black Sun had made a bad mistake when they messed with her, and a worse one when they murdered Tess and defiled innocent children. If any were here, she would find them. And make them pay dearly.

She tamped down the simmering anger and composed herself as she stepped to the curb. Kasia had decided to leave her hair loose on the theory that it provided additional cover. Natalya sported the skimpy silver lame halter dress, which ended at mid-thigh. Since the attack in the alley on the day of Falke's first public audience, she'd sworn off heels. Now she wore sturdy boots, which shouldn't have fit the look at all, yet somehow did. With her smoky eyeliner and wild blonde curls, she looked the picture of a trendy artist, which was exactly how she was being presented. The Pontifex's new portraitist from Novostopol.

Spassov handed the invitation to a gray-clad woman at the door, who smiled and nodded them inside. About three dozen people mingled in a large reception hall, sipping champagne and chatting in groups as uniformed waiters carrying trays slid through the crowd. Kasia spotted a contingent from the Masdar League in robes and turbans, as well as some Raven-marked emissaries from Falke. The rest looked to be from Kvengard and Nantwich. The hubbub quieted as they entered. Kasia was relieved to see that most of the women wore gowns that would have caused a scandal in Novo. Perhaps Natalya had been telling the truth after all.

"You must be Domina Novak!" An older man in a severely cut dinner jacket with a high, starched collar approached. "And Domina Anderle! Such a pleasure." He gave a courtly bow from the waist. He had the precise, clipped accent of the Kvens. "I am Swen Heitmann, your host for the evening."

"A pleasure," Kasia murmured. "You're the Reverend Father Luk's legate?"

"Indeed." His gaze turned to Spassov. "And you are?"

"Fra Patryk Spassov. The ladies' escort."

Heitmann gave a nervous laugh. "I imagine extra precautions are necessary these days, although the embassy is perfectly secure, you have my personal assurances. Come, I will introduce you to some of my colleagues."

Kasia shared a quick look with Natalya as he led them through the party. She smiled and nodded at the various groups as they passed. All eyed her curiously and she sensed whispering behind her back. The legate trotted them around for a few minutes. They made small talk with various dignitaries, mostly about the news from the front. The topic of Luk and what he might do seemed to be off limits, for all the speculation revolved around Falke and whether the mages would try to take back Bal Kirith. Then someone wondered if Lezarius would break his long isolation and bring the north into the fray. That provoked an uneasy silence. All heads turned to the Kven legate.

"Surely you know something, Heitmann," a woman said crisply. "Luk is the only one he'll talk to."

"I am certain that when our Reverend Father has word from Jalghuth, he will share it," Heitmann replied smoothly. "But I know no more than you do." He laid a gloved hand on Kasia's elbow. "Now, if you'll excuse us, I must steal Domina Novak away."

"Do you have a business card?" the woman asked eagerly.

"Not yet, I'm afraid," Kasia said. "But I can be contacted through the Arx."

Heitmann steered them to a quiet corner. "I have had many requests for readings tonight. We prepared a special room for you." He glanced uncertainly at Natalya.

"I'll go mingle," she said cheerfully. "Perhaps I'll get some new commissions."

He nodded in relief. "Fra Spassov?"

"I would prefer to remain outside the door," Patryk said in a tone that brooked no argument.

"Very good," Heitmann said quickly. He produced a list and handed it to Kasia. "As you can see, your services are in high demand."

She scanned the paper. "It will be impossible to give this many readings in one evening."

His face fell.

"I will start with . . . let's say five," she said. "If there is time, I will do more. If not, I'm sure private bookings are possible."

The legate seemed mollified. "How will you choose who goes first?"

She stared dramatically into space. "The ley will decide."

Kasia swirled her hand above the paper and fluttered her eyelids, then opened them wide.

"All is clear now," she intoned.

She gave him the names from Clavis's secret list. Oddly enough, they had all requested readings from her. Perhaps they were innocent and had nothing to hide. Or one of them wanted to get close to her and was using the reading as a pretext. But she doubted they would try anything in the midst of a crowded party. It was a way to test the waters and she might learn something valuable.

"Would you like to go first, Domine Heitmann?" she asked.

He blinked and smoothed his tie. "Better not, the others

will think I am taking advantage of my status as host. I will go last."

"As you wish. Where is the room?"

He signaled a servant. "On the second floor. You may go upstairs and prepare. I'll break the news that there will be only a limited number of readings tonight." He did not seem happy about it and Kasia suspected he had billed her services as a prime attraction of the evening.

Kasia and Patryk followed the servant up a broad flight of curving stairs. The sounds of revelry faded behind them. A fire burned in a large book-lined study. A table had been placed in the center of the room, with two chairs facing each other.

"Thank you, Domina," Kasia said warmly to the young grey-clad woman. She curtsied and withdrew.

"Let the games begin," Patryk muttered, standing by the door as Kasia sat down at the table.

"What do you have in case of trouble?" she teased, taking the novelty deck from her handbag. "A knife in your garter like Nashka?"

He held up two meaty fists encased in black leather gloves. "These."

"More than adequate, I'm sure," she said, grinning. "Saints, Patryk, they haven't a clue, have they?"

He glanced into the empty hall. "About the true state of affairs, you mean? No, and how could they? It's fucking madness."

"I wonder if Luk knows."

"He must suspect something's amiss with Lezarius. But Luk plays by his own rules. Always has."

Kasia shuffled the deck. Her palms were sweating inside the gloves, but she couldn't risk taking them off. "I hope this works. If I do see something, I can't let on. I'll have to make up a load of nonsense."

"Love, Fate, Destiny," he said softly. "What does the ley hold for *you*?"

She frowned.

"I read your old business card." He smiled. "It's how we found you that night."

They gazed at each other fondly. "I never would have believed it, but I'm glad you did, Patryk," she said at last.

He stiffened. "Someone's coming."

Voices in the corridor. Kasia drew a deep breath and adjusted her shawl. She fanned out the cards, fingertips hovering over the table. Patryk stepped back to allow her first client inside.

"Come, sit down," Kasia said with a smile. "The future awaits."

# Chapter Forty

The char's name was Mila. She'd shared a coffee with Nikola many times when their breaks coincided. Mila had three older brothers, all of them knights, whom she spoke of proudly. Once she had stopped by Nikola's flat to borrow a gray work dress after getting called in for a last-minute shift.

"I fogging hate laundry," Mila had said, yanking the dress on. "I always leave it to the last minute, you know?"

"Yeah, I know," Nikola had replied, looking around at her own messy flat.

"Shit, I'm late already. Do you think they'll dock me? Anyway, thanks a million, I owe you one!" Mila zipped out the door without waiting for an answer.

The two of them had always been friendly. But that was before.

Now Mila forcefully stripped the sheets from the bed, her mouth set in a line. She hadn't returned Nikola's greeting or acknowledged her presence in any way. All the chars were like that. They came in every other day to clean, but they treated her like a stranger. Worse, like she'd committed some crime against them personally.

Nikola sat by the locked window, hands in her lap,

watching the courtyard below the Castel Saint Agathe. Rain poured down, forming puddles on the flagstones. She'd eaten breakfast only an hour ago and she was already hungry again. It wasn't just the child. She was bored out of her mind.

She heard Mila bustle past the two knights guarding the door. That was the other thing that drove her crazy. They never left her alone, not ever. She was watched when she slept, watched when she bathed, when she ate. The chars treated her the worst, but the knights weren't much better. Their contempt was palpable. She carried the child of the mage who had killed their Reverend Mother.

She knew there was no hope of escape until Falke had his prize. But surely he wouldn't continue to watch her so closely once it was done. Her only value lay in the half-nihilim she carried.

Sometimes, when she paced the chamber at night, she caught her reflection in the glass and thought it was someone else. Surely that enormous protruding belly could not be *hers*? Her back ached, her ankles swelled, and she peed constantly. The knights gave her privacy for the last, though there was no lock on the bathroom door and if she took too long they would demand a shouted confirmation that she hadn't tried to drown herself in the sink.

But Nikola Thorn was not a suicide risk. It would take far more than a few weeks of confinement to make her lose hope. She only worried when hours passed without movement from the child. Dark thoughts crowded her mind, images of the other women who had miscarried, but then she would feel a strange fluttering spasm. Occasionally, her whole belly changed shape and she saw the outline of a foot or a knee. It seemed incredible that she had another person inside her.

The knights moved aside to admit the midwife. She was the only one who bore no grudge. Her manner was brisk and without a trace of pity, thank the Saints. Outright contempt was bearable, but pity . . . . There was nothing Nikola hated more.

"How are you feeling today?" She wore her white hair cropped short and glasses with funky purple frames. Strong hands with the nails squarely trimmed, no polish. The first time they met, the midwife told her she'd handled hundreds of deliveries and seen everything there was to see under the sun, so Nikola shouldn't feel self-conscious. Nikola had liked her immediately.

"Same," she said, sitting on the bed while the midwife wrapped a blood pressure sleeve around her arm. "When do you think it will come? Am I close?"

The pump tightened, tightened, then released with hiss of air.

"It's hard to say. Your BP is normal, that's good." She warmed a stethoscope in her palms and pressed it to Nikola's chest. "Deep breaths."

Nikola complied.

"Any numbness in your hands or feet?"

"A little tingling when I wake up."

"That's normal." She placed the stethoscope in her bag and gave Nikola a level look. "I know the uncertainty must be hard. Physically, you're somewhere in the ninth month. The baby's already dropped down, which would put you within two or three weeks of birth. But everything is accelerated."

"So any time now?"

"Let's put it this way. You don't have to worry about a premature delivery. I'd say that kid is fully developed."

Nikola nodded. "Okay."

"I'm standing by." She smiled and pushed her glasses up. "You'll both be fine."

"Can I get some drugs for the pain? Like *all* of them?"

"Let's see how it goes first, eh?"

The midwife left. Nikola lay down for a nap. When she

awoke, rain still beat incessantly against the window. She thought of her last night with Malach, the way he had made love to her with such tenderness, asking constantly if she was well, if he was hurting her. The intense pleasure when he finally allowed her to climax. Sex had never been one of their problems, she thought ruefully. Nikola bit her lip. She'd give her right arm to have him here now, not just to hold her and tell her everything was all right but to touch her like he used to. And Malach would be happy to oblige. Almost *anything* turned him on. She cupped a heavy breast, wondering if she could get away with—

A throat cleared loudly near the door.

She propped herself up on an elbow and frowned.

"Captain Komenko. What are *you* doing here?"

It was the farmboy who had caught her on the beach. He sat in a chair, clad in a simple priestly cassock. A bandage swathed his head.

"Sent back from the front, Domina Thorn."

She sighed. *So much for a furtive afternoon delight under the blankets*. "What happened to you?"

"Concussion. One of the guns blew up." He glanced away. "We are hard-pressed at Bal Agnar. Archbishop Kireyev thought it a waste to station able-bodied knights to watch over you."

She sat up. "So you are to be my new keeper?"

"Until I recover." He eyed her warily. "They say you have not caused any trouble."

"What would the point be?" She cupped her belly. "I can hardly run in this condition."

"Perhaps you hope to be rescued."

"From the Arx?" She laughed. "I think that a very slim possibility, Captain."

"Why?" His blue eyes sparked. "Surely this mage will want to claim his child."

The mention of Malach fueled her own simmering frustration. "Passing the Wards nearly killed him the first time," Nikola said tartly. "He's not that stupid."

And yet . . . if Malach were still on the continent, he *would* come. Maybe it was a blessing in disguise that the witches had him. If they hadn't killed him yet, the captivity might save his life.

Captain Komenko eyed her strangely. "Wards? But they are gone, Domina Thorn."

"*What?*"

"No one told you," he muttered.

"Told me what?" She leapt from the bed and stalked over to him, bracing a hand on her lower back. "What exactly happened?" As an Unmarked, she couldn't see the ley herself. The Wards always looked dead to her.

His handsome face hardened. "It is not for me to say."

"Please." Nikola let her eyes get watery. She lowered her voice. "No one ever speaks to me. They treat me like I'm invisible. Like I'm not even human. My only mistake was to believe the lies of a nihilim who promised to help me start a new life. I won't breathe a word, I promise. Just tell me what happened."

He sighed deeply. "The stelae no longer work as they did."

"You mean . . . the Void . . .?"

"Is gone. Ley flows everywhere. It cost us a great defeat at Bal Agnar."

She feigned astonishment, but part of her had expected it eventually. "Saints," she muttered.

"I thought you would be glad to hear the news," he said sternly. "Since you side with *them*."

"I side with no one, Captain." She moved away. "I want nothing to do with any of you."

"Yet you carry his child." A pause. "Do you love this mage?"

"No! He is everything you say he is." *And far more.* Nikola stifled the unwelcome thought. It just made her sad. "What about you? How did you draw this unpleasant duty?"

He shifted in the chair. "I volunteered. I dislike feeling useless. Most of the others in the infirmary are gravely wounded."

She looked him over. "And you're confident I couldn't overpower you and make a run for it?"

"You could try," he said dubiously. "But you'd never make it past the knights in the hall and that's just the first—"

"I was joking." Nikola's spirits lifted. At least her new guard didn't pretend to be mute. "Does the wound pain you?"

"Headaches," he admitted. "The doctors say they might last for a while."

"Well, I would trade with you if I could. Are you married, Captain?"

A slight flush crested his cheeks. "No."

"So you haven't listened to a woman complain about pregnancy before. We'll be starting fresh!"

To her surprise, he showed no sign of discomfort. "I come from a large family," he said. "Eleven children."

"Your poor mother," she murmured.

"Do you sleep with a pillow under your knees? She always did at the end. Said it alleviated some of the pressure."

"That," Nikola said, "is a fabulous idea. Tell me more."

When her lunch arrived, brought by a wooden-faced char, she tried to give Komenko the chocolate bar, but he refused to accept it.

"That could be considered bribery," he said. "And fraternization."

Nikola couldn't tell if he was kidding or not. The man was strait-laced, though not entirely lacking in a sense of humor. She guessed he was about her own age, middle twenties, though otherwise they had nothing in common. Komenko was a true believer. The first she had ever met. He actually adhered to the sutras of the *Meliora* that preached kindness to one's enemies. Not on a battlefield, perhaps, but to a woman alone in the world.

"You've been talking to me," she pointed out. "Isn't that fraternizing?"

"It's not the same."

"As eating a chocolate bar?"

He frowned. "Sharing food is intimate."

"Okay, Captain." She took a big bite. "Your loss."

He was relieved that evening by her least favorite minder, a vestal who stonily watched her every move. Nikola tried the pillow trick and had the best night's sleep in a week. The next day was the same routine. The midwife arrived, then Captain Komenko for the day shift. He told her more about his family. To her amusement, he *had* grown up on a farm just outside the city. He wanted to attend the Lyceum, but his parents couldn't afford the tuition so he joined the priesthood. He was a strapping lad and the knights had snapped him up. Lucky for him, it was after the Cold Truce was already in place so he'd been spared deployment until Falke's latest foray into the Morho.

They talked about Novo and the best places to eat. It made her hungry and she wondered if there was any chance of a curry takeout. The next morning, he brought her a cold chicken tikka. Nikola ate it with her fingers. He'd finally gotten the bandages off. They'd shaved his blonde hair, but it was already growing in. Everywhere except for the shrapnel scar over his left eyebrow.

He noticed her looking and gave a weak smile. "A centimeter lower and I would've been blind. Lucky, huh?"

Another week passed in this way. Nikola came to look forward to seeing him each morning, and she thought he enjoyed her company, too. But sometimes Captain Komenko would go quiet and she saw shadows behind his eyes. She wondered how many boys like him were being hurled at the nihilim. And how many would come back.

She tried to raise his spirits with dirty jokes. When he

blushed, she nearly died from laughter. The captain was a hard man in many ways, but his rigid sense of propriety tickled her. She was starting to tell him a story about a heroic char who had pulled a prank on one of the bishops, replacing her bedside *Meliora* with a copy of *My Naughty Nihilim,* when sudden wetness flooded her thighs. She stared in confusion at the spreading puddle, but Komenko was already on his feet, bellowing.

He helped her to the bed as the first flutters came. It felt like a menstrual cramp.

"You're doing very well, Domina Thorn," he said calmly. "Just try to relax."

She scowled at him, sinking back on the pillows. "Easy for you to say."

"Do you want some water?"

"No." Nikola gripped his gloved hand. She still even didn't even know his first name, but he was her only friend in this place. "Just don't go, please?"

The captain nodded, his face serious. "If they'll let me."

By the time the midwife appeared, the cramps were stronger. Knights crowded into the room behind her and the midwife cast them an irritated look. "She's stressed enough. She doesn't need an audience."

"But the Reverend Father said—"

"Just wait outside the door," she snapped. "You can leave it open."

The knights exchanged a look, then withdrew to the hall. Nikola held fast to Komenko's gloved hand. "He stays," she said fiercely.

The midwife gave her a strange look. "Do you know this man?"

Nikola winced at a sudden contraction. "He's already seen me naked," she said through gritted teeth.

Komenko's blue eyes went wide. "Not the way you think," he told the midwife, rather desperately. "I was just searching her for Nightmarks. Ah, before she even came here."

"Saints!" Nikola hollered. "Please let him stay. He has ten brothers and sisters. He knows about this shit!"

"It's true," Komenko muttered. "I don't mind helping."

The midwife shrugged. "Fine by me. But not at the bedside. Unless he's a relative or the—" She'd been about to say father, but stopped herself. "Just wait over there. I need to have a look."

The captain strode to the window and kept his back turned as the midwife examined her. "No dilation yet." She drew the covers up. "It'll be a while."

Nikola had hoped the baby would magically fly out, but hours passed. The pain gradually grew worse. Komenko stayed at her side, allowing her to squeeze his hand and offering quiet encouragement. But every time she thought the pain couldn't possibly get any worse, she discovered a whole new sub-level of the torture chamber. Finally, Nikola grabbed the midwife's arm.

"You have to give me something," she panted. "I feel like my spine is breaking."

The midwife lifted the sheet and took another look. "It's too risky." Her voice was even, but Nikola felt a cold prick of fear. "The child has twisted around. Its skull is pressing on your tailbone. Just breathe."

The next hours passed in an agonizing blur. Her back and abdomen were a web of fire. Daggers stabbed into her womb. Komenko's bearded face swam in and out of focus. He stayed calm as she cursed and swore. She closed her eyes and pretended the voice was Malach's, soothing her agony with tender words.

The labor proved to be the worst part. By the time the baby arrived, she was so exhausted, she had no fight left. A sharp sting between her legs and the midwife was urging her to push. There was a tremendous burst of pressure and then . . . blissful relief.

She lay back, slick with sweat, and reached for the baby, but it was already being borne away. "No," she rasped. "Wait."

"You did wonderfully," the midwife said, beaming. "The child is perfect. Now you must recover."

"I want my baby!" Her frantic gaze found Captain Komenko, who had retreated to the window. He held her eyes for a long moment, troubled, then looked away.

"Not yet, but soon, I promise," the midwife said.

"What is it?"

"A girl."

Nikola turned away, a tear trailing down her cheek. Malach got his wish. Yet her heart filled with desolation. Nikola shook them off when the knights tried to lift her from the bloody sheets. "Not until you bring my baby back!" she croaked.

"I can give you something for the pain now," the midwife said. "It will help you sleep—"

Nikola slapped her hand away, but she had no strength left. A needle pricked her arm and then the room was spinning away. The last she saw was the captain's earnest face arguing with someone at the door.

---

NIKOLA WOKE TO THIN DAYLIGHT. She was in another bedchamber, alone for the first time since she'd arrived at the Arx. She wore a clean linen gown—gray, of course. When she hobbled to the bathroom on quivering legs, her urine burned like acid. It was tinged pink. She knew they'd cut her for the birth. The midwife had explained it, saying she would be stitched up afterwards. Two to four weeks before she healed completely.

Nikola had expected the birth itself to be awful—and she hadn't been disappointed. What she didn't realize was how physically wrecked she'd be afterwards. Somehow, she'd foolishly thought her body would just bounce back into fighting shape. But *everything* hurt. She felt like she'd been run over by one of the armored transports.

She staggered back to bed and slept some more. She dreamed of a baby crying somewhere in the Arx. Nikola ran through the dim halls, following the sound. It got louder, but she couldn't find the baby. Yet it had to be close. The wails were loud and lusty. She rounded a corner and found herself at the entrance of a great audience chamber. A tiny figure swathed in crimson lay on the throne of the Pontifex. Knights knelt on the stairs of the dais. One turned, her pretty face incandescent with rage.

"You stole my child!" Dantarion screamed, drawing her blade—

Nikola's eyes opened. Her heart still thundered in her chest. A thin cry.

Falke stood at the foot of the bed. He held her child in his arms, though it was wrapped in a white blanket. Nikola glimpsed a thatch of dark hair.

She held out her arms. "Please," she said, voice shaking. "Let me hold her."

"Of course," he murmured. "You deserve to say goodbye, Domina Thorn."

His words didn't register at first. Had she really believed newborns were hideous? For this one was the most beautiful creature she had ever laid eyes on. The eyes were tightly closed, but she knew they would be golden brown someday, flecked with shards of emerald.

"Look at all that hair," she whispered, drawing the child to her breast. It began to root and she started to draw her gown aside, but a hand with a heavy gold ring seized her wrist.

"The baby has already fed," Falke said.

Nikola frowned.

"We have a wet nurse. A woman who also gave birth yesterday."

She stroked the downy hair with a fingertip. Traced the perfect little seashell ear. When she reached the child's silken neck, Nikola paused. She gently turned the baby's head. A tiny Raven stood out against the caramel skin.

"I Marked her myself," Falke said. "She is a child of the Via Sancta now."

*Marked her.* Nikola stared at his smug face. "How could you? She's just an infant!"

"I will take no chances," he said firmly. "Never again. Now give her back."

"She is mine!"

He signaled to the door. Knights came forward and surrounded the bed. Nikola tried to cling to the tiny bundle, but when it started to cry she let them have it, fearful the child would be hurt. "Marked or not," she screamed at Falke, "she will destroy you someday!"

He didn't bother turning around.

She lay sobbing in the sheets. When her wounded farmboy entered the room a few minutes later, Nikola threw herself against his broad chest. He looked startled, but after a moment, his arms stole around her. If he had said a single word, she would have slapped him. But Captain Komenko seemed to know women for he let her sob on his cassock in silence. By the time Nikola stopped, a very long time later, her eyes were dry.

She had no tears left to shed.

# Chapter Forty-One

The outer wall of Malach's cell was composed of elaborate iron scrollwork that looked out over a white beach. In the mornings, it cast shifting patterns of sunlight across the tiled floor. In the afternoons, a steady sea breeze banished the heat. He listened to the waves and the cries of gulls. Three times a day, a tray came through a slot in the door. He dined on fish and rice and strange yellow fruit that was both sweet and chalky. The portions were generous, the food fresh. It came with a wooden spoon.

He discovered quickly that if he didn't put the empty tray back through the slot, he would not get another one. The witches had learned their lesson.

No one entered his cell, ever.

It was thirty-two paces across, twenty-six wide. Palatial by the standards of a prison. It had a bathroom with clean running water and a flush toilet. No mirror, though he could feel how thickly his beard was coming in. On better days, he scrubbed his teeth with salt and washed in the sink. On worse days, he passed the time masturbating, though even that favorite distraction grew lackluster after a while.

His cell was outside the capital in some distant part of the island of Tenethe. After the ship docked, the witches had bundled him into a rusty antique car and driven along dusty country roads to this place by the sea. A quick glimpse of flaking whitewashed walls, then a long shaded portico, and he was pushed inside the cell. The door slammed shut.

Tenethe smelled of sand and hibiscus and sun-baked bricks. Sometimes he saw dolphins swimming offshore. They passed in long lines, cresting and diving. Sometimes he saw great shoals of silver fish. Birds would come, diving from the heights and folding their wings at the last instant to plunge into the sea. It was a thousand different colors depending on the light and depth and what sort of clouds were passing in the sky above. When it rained, he dragged his pallet away from the open scrollwork.

The agony of not knowing where Nikola was tormented him far more than his own captivity. In his darkest moments, he saw her taken by Perditae. The crazy kind. But these would be followed by fantasies in which she caught another ship and came to his rescue. She was the only person besides Tash who knew what had befallen him.

Would the other mages care if they did know? A stupid question. How many times had he said that if the Perditae allowed themselves to be taken, they got what they deserved?

Malach was starting to think he would spend the rest of his life like a castaway on a desert isle, albeit better fed, when he heard voices on the other side of the door. He looked up from his perch on the pallet.

"You have until high tide, Masdari," a deep male voice said.

Tashtemir stepped into the room, the door locking behind him. "By the Root, Cardinal, you look like a barbarian," he exclaimed. "What have they done to you?"

Malach grinned. "And you look like . . . I don't know what you look like."

Tash made a face. He wore a style of garment that left one

shoulder bare and wrapped tightly around his waist, falling to mid-thigh. "It's called a Rahai. All the temple devotees have to wear them."

"Do tell." Malach patted the pallet. Some childish part of him felt gratified that his friend suffered similar indignities.

Tash hesitated. "It's really not made for sitting down."

"And this is?" Malach glanced at the skimpy loincloth around his own hips.

The southerner laughed. "I thought you would have charmed your way onto a ship by now."

"Hardly. I haven't received any invitations yet. Sixteen days!" The frustration that simmered just below the surface erupted. He pounded a fist against his thigh. "This Mahadeva is toying with me, Tash!"

"Not so loud," he replied, glancing at the door.

"Tell me what's going on," Malach said in a softer voice. "Where are we?"

"I don't know." He leaned against the scrollwork. "They made me wear a blindfold in the car."

"Why did they let you come?" A hopeful note. "Did the witch-queen send you?"

A snort. "Me? Not likely. Perhaps they wanted to make sure you weren't going mad."

Malach barked a bitter laugh. "Not yet, though I'm delirious from boredom."

"Have they mistreated you?"

"No," Malach conceded. "But they tell me nothing."

"How are your wounds?" He peered at the seams of scar tissue on Malach's pale abdomen. "Healing well, I'd say. And you haven't torn them open again." He threw his hands up, gazing heavenward. "It's a miracle!"

Malach eyed Tashtemir, who was deeply tanned. "Are you a slave?"

"Oh, no. They pay me for my service at the temple. I care for the snakes and reptiles."

"Sounds lovely."

"I rather enjoy it," Tash said defensively. "They're mostly tame. And the city is every bit as beautiful as I told you it would be. There are no poor. No rich, either. Everyone lives quite harmoniously."

"What about the men?"

"They're not slaves, either. Not even the Perditae, Malach! The witches buy them from the mages to set them free."

"That's mad." He frowned. "What about their Marks? Don't they use the ley?"

"The witches remove their Marks, Cardinal."

"*What?* That's not possible!"

"I'm telling you, I've seen them."

The hair on Malach's neck prickled. He felt suddenly cold. "Could they do the same to me?"

"I don't know. But the Perditae are treated like everyone else and none have caused trouble. The witches claim it was the taint of the Morho that made them do evil and I'm coming to believe it."

Malach's eyes narrowed. "You sound as if you like the witches."

Tash frowned. "Not what they've done to you, Cardinal. It's wrong. But first impressions aside, there are far worse places in the world." He hooked a finger into the iron grill, staring out at the beach. "The Deir Fiuracha—that is what they call the sisterhood—it has an interesting worldview. They believe a great wyrm coils around the molten core of the planet and its breath is the ley."

Malach filed that away as potentially useful information. "So they worship this wyrm?"

"And its offspring, the cold-blooded scaly creatures. The temples are full of them."

"Bring one with you next time," Malach said darkly. "Something with lethal venom."

"Ah, don't talk like that. You'll get your audience."

"But when? Six months from now? A year?" He shot to his feet. "Why are they holding me here? Why will no one tell me anything?"

"I wish I knew. But they let me come visit you. That's something, eh?"

"Would *you* be free to leave if you wanted to?"

"I haven't asked." Tash's black eyes hardened a touch. "I doubt the answer would be yes, but even if it were, there is nothing for me on the continent. Here, I am safe for now." He sighed. "I will do all I can to get you out of here. But it might take some time."

"Time!" Malach spat. "That's all I have. I would rather be digging trenches in the blazing sun than sitting on my ass all day!"

"Weary of your gilded cage, Cardinal? I don't blame you." A wry smile. "I know how it feels. Bal Kirith was the same to me."

"I thought you were happy there," Malach grumbled.

"I liked Dante when she wasn't on a rampage. And you, of course. But the others . . . ."

"Yeah, I know," Malach said with a heavy sigh. "Enough of my troubles. Tell me about the temple."

Tash stroked his long black mustaches. Neatly trimmed now, Malach noticed. "When I first awaken, I prepare fruit for the skinks. They like a little bit of everything, well-mashed. Mites are the biggest nuisance. They get under the scales and you must kill them with a vinegar solution. Now the snakes are good at catching mice, but they do enjoy their crickets, too."

He listened to Tash talk about his work. Malach learned a great deal about the dietary preferences of various species, their mating habits, and what to do if a baby cobra crawled inside your Rahai. *Hint*: Don't make any sudden movements.

"So that's about it," Tashtemir finally said. He looked around in surprise at the long shadows coming through the grillwork. "Oh, I live there, too, above the temple, but in a much smaller room than this. So count your blessings."

Malach lay with his hands laced behind his head. "Don't suppose you have a blade on you?"

"Why, so you can slit your wrists from tedium?" A white-toothed grin. "I know you stopped listening an hour ago, Cardinal."

"I hung on every word. No, I thought you might cut this cursed Kaldurite from my belly."

Tash gave him a pitying look. "I'm sorry, they searched me quite thoroughly."

"How about that?" Malach glanced over at the wooden spoon.

Tash nodded seriously. "It might serve. If you don't mind your liver coming along for the ride."

Malach laughed. "Perhaps you're right. Tell me, what is the deadliest serpent you work with?"

"The sand snake," Tashtemir replied immediately. "Its venom will kill within the hour if left untreated."

"How is it treated?"

"With antivenin. The witches revere serpents and they will not punish one who bites. But nor do they see it as divine retribution. We keep stocks on hand. If the victim reports it promptly, they will live." His gaze narrowed. "Why do you ask?"

"Just curious. You live dangerously, Tash."

He waved this away. "Not really. I know how to handle them."

The door opened. It was Paarjini. One fist was clenched, no doubt holding a stone should Malach prove feisty. "Ye must leave now," she said to Tash. Cool pewter eyes met Malach's for an instant, then flicked away.

"Goodbye, Cardinal," Tashtemir said cheerfully. "I'll return when I can."

Malach raised a hand in farewell.

The door slammed shut.

Malach scrambled over to his dirty plate. He picked out the largest fish bone and waited for dark to fall.

---

VOICES OUTSIDE THE DOOR.

The slot opened. They were speaking in the witch tongue, but he could guess what they were saying.

*What was that blood-curdling scream? Is he faking again?*

He had timed it so the last rays of the sun would illuminate him on the floor, one arm flung wide. Two pricks near the elbow, oozing blood. He'd squeezed the limb mercilessly until it turned an ugly, swollen red.

Malach twitched. "A serpent," he whispered hoarsely. "It came through the grill."

A long moment passed. Hope withered.

*They will leave me to die rather than take a chance.*

Then the door opened. He kept perfectly still as footsteps approached—though not too close. More whispering. One set retreated, quickly. The other remained. Malach peeked through his lashes.

A tall, well-built man in a Rahai. Malach gave a slight twitch. He should have asked what the symptoms were. The man was staring at him in suspicion. His hand went to a belt knife. He turned to shout something. Malach hurled himself at the man's legs, bringing him to the ground. An elbow to the face and then Malach was out the door, running down a long hall, the ocean side barred with grillwork like his cell. He heard shouts behind and veered around a corner. Another short corridor. It ended at a narrow door. Malach hit it with one shoulder and the flimsy wood shattered in the frame. He'd hoped to come out in front and steal the car, but he was on a veranda above the beach. He leapt down to the sand and sprinted towards the water. The sun had set now, the sand already cooling beneath his bare feet.

Malach hit the sea at a dead run, diving beneath the waves. He surfaced and shook wet hair from his eyes, heart knocking with the sudden taste of freedom. Lanterns bobbed on the shore. No, not lanterns. Glowing stones. Paarjini and three more witches. Another shout. They'd seen him. He dove down and started swimming, long clean strokes. When Malach surfaced again, he was some distance offshore. He could see his prison in its entirety. A round white house with a domed roof, sitting beneath a row of those odd leafless trees. There was nothing else nearby.

Light flared on the beach. He dove down again. This time, when he surfaced, the house was far to his left. He'd been caught in a rip current. All for the better. Let it carry him down the shore. The sandy beach had already given way to low, rocky cliffs, but surely there would be another place farther along where he could leave the water.

Malach alternated between floating on his back and swimming. The moon came out. The sea grew choppier. His muscles ached, but there seemed no end to the cliffs. The waves started pushing him nearer to the shore, where they dashed against shards of black rock. He felt the first hint of panic as a large swell came. He rode it over a shelf that scraped one foot. Darkness loomed ahead. A cave? Malach swam hard, trying to time the swells to bring him closer. If there was any ledge inside, he could hide from his pursuers. They would never find him there.

A final battering wave and he was swept inside the natural cavern. The roar of the sea changed, echoing in his ears. The swirling currents dragged him to the back and Malach crawled out to a crescent of black sand. The cavern was much larger than he'd thought. It formed a natural grotto with its own tiny beach. For a long minute, he lay on his back, catching his breath. By all rights, he should have drowned. His luck had finally turned!

The thought made him laugh. He had indeed fallen low in the world if this dismal place filled him with gratitude. Who knew how high the water would rise? But it was not the cell. He could leave once he gathered his strength. And then . . . and then, he didn't know. But he would find a way off this cursed isle—

Malach's smile died as a sound came from the depths of the grotto. A rhythmic clatter, like pebbles striking stone. It was barely audible over the lap and splash of the waves. Malach licked salt from his lips. "What the fuck?" he muttered, following the sound through a crevice in the rock.

Another chamber lay beyond, this one with a pool in the center. It was lit from below by greenish light. Small waterfalls trickled down the mossy walls. Bats clung to high rock shelves, and from the upper reaches of guano-covered stalagmites. Three nude women sat cross-legged on a smooth section of rock next to the pool. One held a dicing cup. She gave it a rattle and tossed the contents on the ground. Six vibrant gemstones, each of a different hue.

Malach tensed as they turned to him.

"Ah, you have come," said one. "That is good."

She was older than old, seamed with wrinkles, hair a cascade of snow over one bony shoulder. Milky cataracts covered both eyes. Her voice was a husky croak, but resonant with authority. She spoke Osterlish with the barest hint of a musical accent.

"We have waited for you," said the second, a woman of middle years with ample breasts and hips, her hair still dark but greying at the brow. She gave Malach a gentle smile.

"Too long," snapped the youngest, a girl at the brink of puberty with sly, elven features and wild, curling locks. "The aingeal is tardy!" Her accent was much stronger, stressing the first syllable of each word. Like the second, she had eyes of smoke and ash.

All the women wore a dizzying array of rings, bracelets, anklets and earrings, as well as a large pear-shaped ruby on a chain around her neck.

Malach sank to a knee, addressing the eldest. "Your Highness," he said smoothly, hoping he'd guessed right. "I presume you are the Mahadeva Sahevis?"

"*We* are the Mahadeva," the girl said imperiously.

"Mother, Maid, and Crone." The voices overlapped as they spoke in unison. Malach searched their faces. He could see a resemblance. But surely it was some trick, designed to impress.

"He didn't know!" The Maid laughed uproariously, clutching her sides.

"How *could* he know?" the Mother said in a slightly chastising tone.

"Silly aingeal." The Maid sprang to her feet and prowled around him in a circle, nose practically touching his Marks. "We have not seen one before."

Malach bore the inspection with as much aplomb as he could muster. Whatever they were, the complete mastery over the ley it would require to maneuver him to this precise spot . . . . The mind boggled.

As the Maid skulked around him, the Crone returned to her gem-tossing, and the Mother began to braid the Crone's hair with a jade comb.

"We thought it best if you got it out of your system, Malach," the Mother told him briskly. "You're the type who must learn a lesson first-hand, eh?" She winked. "But you see now that escape is pointless."

"Yes, I see that, Mahadeva," he said faintly.

The Maid pinched his bottom and the Mother cast her a stern look. "None of that! We have brought him to speak, not to be your plaything!"

The Maid scowled deeply, but sank down next to the others. "We didn't do it hard," she muttered.

"Soak in the pool if you like, Malach," the Mother said, weaving an elaborate braid. "It is relaxing."

He eyed the luminous green water. "What makes it glow?" It could not be ley, since the kaldurite prevented him from even seeing it.

"Aventurine. It will not harm you."

He cast a quick glance at the Maid, who looked like she was working herself up to another act of mischief. Perhaps he would be safe from her in the pool.

"As you say, Mahadeva," he declared with a brief bow, wading into the water. It was deliciously warm. He found a ledge and sat down. Days of tension leached from his muscles. No doubt they were softening him up for something. Malach resolved to stay on his guard.

"You wonder why we brought you here," the Crone rasped.

"A reasonable question," said the Mother.

"But first, aingeal," and here the Maid stabbed a finger at him, "you will tell us what is wrong with the ley!"

"Wrong?" he repeated. "I don't understand."

"We feel the ripples even here," the Crone said. "A dissonance. The origin is in your homeland. It began four years ago, but grows stronger by the day."

"I cannot tell you," he said truthfully. "I do not sense such a thing myself."

"'Course you don't," the Maid snorted. "You're a *man*. You force the ley to your will instead of allowing it to flow naturally."

"Where I come from, women do that, too," he pointed out. "You could have taken any mage and they would tell you the same." He leaned forward. "But you went to a great deal of trouble to bring *me*. May I ask why?"

The cup rattled. Gems scattered. They refracted the light,

sending colored motes dancing across the ceiling. The Crone's trembling fingers swept them up. "We have seen you in the stones, Fallen One. You are dangerous."

"Only to my enemies," Malach replied with a wink at the Maiden. She grinned back.

"We weren't aware you had friends," the Crone rasped.

He cast a hurt glance at the Mother. "Tashtemir Kelevan is my friend."

"Poor thing," the Maid murmured. Her hand darted out and caught a small blue crab. With a cheeky grin, she tossed it into the pool when the Mother wasn't looking.

So it *was* an act. He made a ridiculous face at the Maid, crossing his eyes and poking his tongue out from the corner of his mouth. Her lips compressed into a tight line to pen the laughter.

The Crone's head swung around. Milky eyes fixed on him. "Do not encourage foolishness, Fallen One. We will not abide it."

Malach blinked. So they *were* three aspects of a single consciousness. The witches worked subtle magic indeed. He would have to tailor his strategy to fit three distinct personalities. A triple seduction! He warmed to the challenge.

"Your pardon, Mahadeva," he said meekly. "You were saying you saw me in the stones?"

"Your Marks," the Mother clarified. She finished the Crone's plaits and turned to the Maid, who scowled deeply as the comb began to untangle her hair. "We gave the description to the Deir Fiuracha and set them to look for you."

"I mean no harm to you," Malach said seriously. "I swear it. I was only on the beach to help a friend escape the Via Sancta. She is Unmarked."

"Arseholes," the Maid muttered, tossing her head.

Malach was coming to like the child.

"That is a crude practice," the Mother said firmly. "She

has our sympathies. And she would be here now if you hadn't foolishly urged her to run."

"Do you know what happened to her?" Malach didn't try to keep the desperation from his voice. "Can you read it in the stones?"

For a long moment, the only sound was the hollow echo of waves surging and withdrawing from the outer grotto.

"She has brought something into the world that will bring the nations of men to their knees," the Crone replied at last.

"My child," he whispered. "They both live?"

"They both live," the Mother confirmed in a neutral tone.

Malach closed his eyes, flooded with relief. "Where are they?"

"That, we cannot tell you."

He raised his head. "Cannot? Or will not?"

"Cannot. The stones are not so precise. They speak only of great events, not small ones."

"But what do the stones say about me? Why am I dangerous to you?" Malach couldn't fathom it. He'd never thought much about the witches until Nikola Thorn came along.

"We did not say dangerous to *us*. We said dangerous." They spoke in unison now. "A king will be reborn. The dragon devours itself. Then it devours the world."

The perfectly synchronized voices of varying timbres raised the hair on his arms.

"You mean my child?"

"No," the Crone replied. "But a Fallen One. That is certain."

"You think it means *me*?" Malach shook his head. "I have no designs to rule anyone! All I've ever wanted is freedom. To have the ley restored to me. You cannot imagine what the Void is like." He addressed the Mahadeva Sahavis as one now, looking from face to face. "It is a bleak place, Your Highness. Imagine if the same had been done to you."

"The Void is gone, Malach," the Mother said flatly.

"What?"

"Shattered. It happened a fortnight ago."

The news stunned him to silence. Malach had dreamed of this moment since he was a boy, never truly believing he would see it. And now here he was, across the sea, with a lump of kaldurite in his belly. Impotent fury drew a red veil across his vision. He did not trust himself to speak.

"We stay out of the politics of other sovereign nations," the Crone muttered. "It is such meddling that brought on the Second Dark Age."

"The continent is in turmoil again," sighed the Mother.

The Maid wrenched the comb from her hair. "And we want nothing to do with it. If they bring a Third Dark Age on themselves, that is none of our concern!"

"Perhaps not," Malach said, reining in his temper. "But it *is* mine. You claim you do not interfere, yet you brought me here against my will."

"If we had not, all hope would be lost." The Crone's milky, unblinking gaze pinioned him. "That is all we know. But it is true."

"How long must I remain, Mahadeva?" he asked tightly.

"Until the stones tell us you are safe."

"But—"

"You have some part to play yet. Until we know what it is, you shall not leave Tenethe."

He swallowed with a dry throat, voicing the question that had haunted him since Tash mentioned the Perditae. "Will you take my Marks away?"

The three women exchanged a quick look. His pulse leapt.

"We cannot, even if we wished to," the Mother said. "The Marks of an aingeal are indelible. They cannot be erased, not by any spell known to us."

Malach felt dizzy with relief. His Marks were as much as part of him as his blood and bone. Without the ley, they were only symbols, but even a frail thread of hope was better than none.

"Cairness spoke rash words," the Mother added gently. "We do not hate you, Malach. But we do mean to keep you safe until the larger pattern becomes clear."

He considered this. "Fair enough, Mahadeva. But I would ask to be given honest labor. Something to occupy me." He pretended to think. "Unloading cargo, perhaps. I have a strong back."

The Maid burst into laughter. "Silly aingeal dian! We already burned the great ships. There will be no more trade with the Curia."

And no way off this isle, he thought furiously.

"But honest labor you will be given," the Crone added. "Perhaps it will do you good. Sweat some of that arrogance out of you."

Malach bowed his head. Defiance would buy him nothing. Not yet. "I serve at your pleasure, Mahadeva."

The Maid splashed into the pool and patted his knee. "You show modesty. That is comely for a man."

"I have no quarrel with your philosophy," Malach replied. "I grew up surrounded by powerful women." A wry grin at the Mother. "They cared little for clothing, too."

She gave him a slow smile. "Come, Malach, we would show you something."

The Maid took his hand. They led him through another crevice thick with dozing bats. It opened to a ledge a few meters above the crashing waves.

"Behold, aingeal," the Maid said, a hint of awe in her sweet, high voice.

Full dark had fallen. A brisk salt wind swept the hair from his brow, raising gooseflesh on his skin. Twin comets rode low over the dark horizon, their long tails of hazy, glimmering light intertwined.

"They are here," the Mother said. "Not one child, but two."

Malach stared in wonder, a powerful stirring in his heart. Always he had clawed for any advantage, existing in the bloody, needful moment, believing he understood the ley. That it was meant to serve him. But he had understood nothing.

It was vaster, deeper than he could even begin to comprehend.

One by one, the Mahadeva Sahevis kissed his cheek and withdrew into the grotto.

But Malach stayed, head tipped back to watch the stars wheel across the velvety arch of the sky.

# Afterword

The third book in the Nightmarked series, **City of Keys**, is now up for preorder on all retailers. Read on for a sneak peek of the first three chapters!

Sign up for my newsletter at www.katrossbooks.com so you don't miss new releases, as well as a free book and exclusive discounts.

# City of Keys (Nightmarked #3)

## CHAPTER ONE

Malach hefted the pickaxe, sweat plastering the linen shirt to his back.

Which witch would it be today?

*Which witch?*

Time blurred in the pit, each day bleeding into the next, but if it was Luansday that meant Darya.

He pictured her cool pewter eyes and plump mouth. Shards of rock exploded as the pick bit into the canyon wall. A seam of jaxite glimmered in the sunlight. He attacked the rock, chiseling a furrow. Six more blows and a sizable chunk of the mineral broke off. Malach tossed it into a bucket. He tipped his last waterskin back, draining it, then resumed hacking. The dull black seam widened as he gouged deeper. Jaxite tended to shatter, but the bigger the pieces, the faster the bucket filled.

Experience had taught him to seek out the nearly imperceptible flaws that would liberate the most jaxite in a single blow. He traced a calloused fingertip along the fine striations, then raised the pick, bringing it down at a precise point the size of his thumbnail.

*Crack!*

Malach leapt back as a head-sized chunk broke free. He hefted it in one practiced motion and thunked it into the bucket. Then he lugged the bucket to the winch site, grabbed an empty one, and returned to the seam. A shimmery, sweltering haze rose from the canyon floor as he picked up the last bucket and hiked out, passing dozens of other dusty men who averted their eyes. Malach buckled into a harness and signaled to a foreman above. The straps creaked tight. He was winched to the surface of the pit, crab-walking along the slanted walls.

A young witch with long russet hair waited for him at the top. She wore a complicated dress made from a single narrow length of silver-threaded cloth. It wrapped around hips and bosom and then all the way down one arm to the wrist, leaving the other arm and shoulder bare. He found the garment erotic—a single tug and it would all come apart—though not on her. Stacked rings adorned her fingers, each set with a different jewel. More shone in her hair and on a gold chain at her throat.

"Hello, Darya," he said with an easy smile, unstrapping his helmet and tossing it on a pile.

The witch smiled back. "You look well, Malach."

All his minders spoke fluent Osterlish, with the quick, lilting accent of Dur-Athaara. They fell into step together, heading toward the barracks.

"The foreman praised you," Darya remarked. "He says you are tireless."

"I find hard work satisfying."

Her fey eyes met his. "Do you? I am glad." Darya fanned herself with a straw hat. "I heard six men collapsed from heatstroke today. It's been a brutal summer."

Lithomancy demanded a steady supply of raw ore, gemstones and crystals. The Mahadeva Sahevis, the witch-queen, had kept her promise of sweating the arrogance out of him, setting him to work at the pit mines that honeycombed the island. The men were well-fed and well-paid—even Malach. He'd started with four days on, three off, six-hour shifts. When it became clear that there was no way off the island, he'd asked them to double his hours. The foreman had raised an eyebrow, clearly expecting him to crumble, but Malach threw himself into the labor, punishing himself until he fell into his bunk like a dead man each day. Gradually, his body hardened to steel. Now he worked five dawn-to-dusk shifts in a row. It was mind-numbing, but at least he had something to vent his frustration on.

When the witches caught him on the beach and brought him to Dur-Athaara, Malach had been confident he'd find a way to escape. But they'd burned every ship and severed contact with the outside world. Three times, he'd run away and stolen fishing dinghies. They all floated straight into the witch-queen's grotto, no matter which way the currents ran. The Mahadeva seemed to find his escape attempts amusing. Like a child allowing an ant to scurry away before scooping it up with a leaf and returning it to the habitat.

"There's shade in the canyons," he said. "Except at midday. But I'm used to it."

Darya nodded, looking pleased. "It is well you have found a useful occupation, *aingeal dian*."

His jaw tightened. Fallen angel, the witches called him. It only reminded him of everything he'd lost. Nikola Thorn was the reason he worked himself to the brink every day. The worry for her was a rat gnawing at his gut. It never stopped. If anything, it worsened with every passing day.

"The Mahadeva is wise. Has she asked about me?"

"She does not need to," Darya replied. "The Crone sees all."

A lie. The witch-queen was powerful—but not a god. She'd admitted that she didn't know where Nikola was or what had become of her. Only that she had borne his child and the two of them lived.

That was months ago. Anything could have happened in the meantime.

"Tell the Mahadeva that I wish to speak with her," Malach said. "Please."

He said the same thing every day. And every day, the witches gave the same reply.

"I will convey your request." Darya witch laid a hand on his arm. He tried not to flinch at her touch. "But when she wants to see you, she will let you know. Be at ease, Malach."

He turned away before she could glimpse the loathing in his eyes and joined a line of men at the outdoor showers. Dur-Athaarans had no modesty about naked bodies. The showers were wide open to public view. He stripped down and let the lukewarm water beat against his skin. Within seconds, the spray sluiced away the dull coating of rock dust. Colors bloomed on the Marks across his chest and arms—bloody red, golden amber, deep greens and blues. All worthless.

He lathered twice with a cake of soap, fingers probing the ridged muscles of his abdomen. A scar above his hip marked the spot where the priest had stabbed him. Malach didn't care about that. It was what the witches had put inside him that made him want to strangle Darya with her own dress. He poked and prodded, but the kaldurite stone was lodged too deeply to feel. It didn't hurt, or interfere with anything but his ability to touch the ley.

The only thing that mattered.

Malach grabbed a towel from a stack next to the showers and dried off. He kept his back to the witch, but he felt her eyes on him. A tingling, itchy sensation that started at the nape of his neck and worked its way down his spine. Somehow, he always knew when a witch was near and watching.

Was Darya attracted? Repulsed? Or did she feel nothing for him?

He wore long sleeves and buttoned his shirt to the neck, but the other men knew he was a mage. They shunned him, which suited Malach just fine. Many were former slaves who'd been given sanctuary in Dur-Athaara. For all Malach knew, he might have sold some of them to the witches himself.

He kept to himself, eating alone in the barracks and going into the city every second Luansday to see Tashtemir. A witch always accompanied him on these expeditions, usually Darya, but sometimes one of her sisters. They treated him with condescension—like a naughty boy capable of mischief but who could learn correct behavior with a little discipline. Since his last escape attempt several months ago, Malach had been unfailingly polite and obedient. Let them think he'd given up.

Darya had no clue that she was about to learn a lesson herself.

"I was thinking of paying a visit to the temple," he said, drying his hair with the towel. He gave her a wry smile. "Would you care to join me?"

"Ah, let me think about." The witch pretended to mull it over. It was a joke he'd started with her a while back. As if they would ever allow him to roam loose unattended. But the small intimacy was another thread he'd tied to her.

"Why, yes, Malach, I would happy to make a devotion to Valmitra." Darya stuck the straw hat on her head and moved to the shade of a date palm. "I will wait for you here."

Malach tossed the wet towel in a bin. He went inside to his bunk, donned a fresh shirt, and knotted a Rahai around his waist. It was one of the few aspects of life here he'd come to appreciate. The simple skirt-like garment was loose and comfortable, much more so than his heavy cardinal's robe. It had no pockets, but he had no belongings, so it made little difference.

He joined the witch at her ancient automobile. It had been sitting in the sun and the leather seat burned his ass straight through the Rahai. Malach rolled the window down and stuck an elbow out as she pressed the starter button. The engine coughed and sputtered to life. They started down the winding road from the highlands at the center of Tenethe. Low, rugged mountains ringed the Pit, but the scenery grew lush as they drove south. Colorful flowers bloomed everywhere, filling the air with heavy perfume.

"How old is this thing?" Malach studied the array of knobs on the dashboard. Few functioned for their original purpose anymore—definitely not the one that promised climate control.

Darya laughed. "Not Second Dark Age, but close."

"How do you keep it running?"

"We have a guild of mechanics that goes back hundreds of years." Her lips quirked. "Why, do you wish to learn?"

"How's the pay?"

"More than you're making now. But I'm afraid the trade is hereditary. Passed from mother to daughter."

"No men?"

"A few. Not many."

"Why?"

She swept an errant lock of hair from her eyes, then took the hat off and tossed it into the back seat. "That's just how it is, Malach."

He was still trying to get a handle on how the witches viewed men. The culture was matriarchal, yet he sensed no resentment at the camp. The witches who came for him were greeted respectfully and he'd never heard a word against them—not even after they were gone.

"Do you think we're too stupid to be mechanics?" he wondered.

Darya frowned. "I do not think you're stupid at all. Obviously, your physique is suited to heavy labor. But men also work in the markets, as you have seen. They are potters and weavers. And they care for the children, of course. It takes great stamina and patience to work in the creches."

"Uh-huh."

"You are skeptical, Malach, because you've been taught

different ideas of what it means to be a man. That is all. The people who founded this land—men and women both—decided to build a society that would not repeat the mistakes of the past. Men are the more emotional sex. It makes little sense for them to hold positions of authority." She glanced at him. "You cannot argue with the fact that while the Via Sancta tears itself apart, we are at peace."

The knot in his chest tightened. "Have you heard anything?"

The car crested a rise and the azure sweep of the sea came into view. An offshore wind farm stood sentinel over the waves, white blades spinning slowly.

"I don't mean to mislead you. I have no news from outside." The witch gave him a *chin-up* smile. "But you're much better off here, I am certain of it. Try to be patient and trust in the Mahadeva's guidance. When you are ready, she will let you return."

How many times had Malach heard the same refrain? Each time, it sounded more hollow.

"Are you a mother, Darya?"

She shook her head.

"Then you can't know what it's like to be a parent yet never to have seen your own child."

"No," she agreed. "I do not know." A sharp glance. "But nor do I pity you. There are those among us who would see you under lock and key. Be grateful for the indulgence you have been given."

Malach bit back a sarcastic retort. "I am. But I cannot help pining for those I left behind."

He lurched forward, bracing a palm on the dashboard as the witch braked for a herd of spotted goats. Her crappy car lacked seatbelts, too.

"I didn't expect a nihilim to be so sentimental." Darya tapped the horn. The curly-haired boy herding the goats shooed them to the grassy verge and the car crept past. "Isn't self-interest your central belief?"

Malach ignored the jab. "If you refer to the Via Libertas, its central tenet is freedom," he said in a mild tone. "Personally, I have no belief in anything."

"You wear the Mark of the Broken Chain around your neck."

"It's given to every mage from Bal Kirith."

"So you have no faith of any kind? I pity you."

Malach eyed her slender neck. If he could snap it before she found a way to retaliate . . . but every stone on her fingers held protective power. And killing Darya, however satisfying, would only gain him an extended stay in a cell.

"You can pray for me at the temple," he said.

Her face darkened. "Do not blaspheme, aingeal. It was your kind who—" She cut off, hands tightening around the wheel.

"Who did what? Why do you hate us so?"

"I do not hate you," she ground out. "You cannot help the sins of your forebears. But I will not pray for you!" She stared straight ahead. "Be silent now."

A tiny smile curled the corner of his mouth. "As you wish, Darya."

# Chapter Two

Malach whistled a tuneless melody as the dirt road widened and the crowds thickened. The capital of Dur-Athaara sprawled at the southern tip of the island. It was a backwater by the standards of Novostopol, the only other city Malach knew, and lacked the frenzied hustle of that great metropolis. People moved at a leisurely pace, pausing to chat with food vendors or rest in the botanical gardens that wound through the landscape like green arteries.

None of the stone buildings had square corners. Every street and wall curved in serpentine fashion, following the canals that allowed the sea to flow in and out according to the tides. The odor of spiced fish mingled with smoke from the pyres along the esplanade, where Athaarans brought the bodies of the dead to be burned.

The practice had seemed grim the first time he first saw it, but as they drove past the wide blossom-strewn steps leading down to the water, Malach sensed the peaceful solemnity of the people gathered there. He turned his head to watch as a corpse wound in bright saffron cloth was set alight and the bier gently pushed into the waves. Voices raised in song. Not a dirge but a joyful celebration of life.

They drove across an arching bridge and the massive Temple of Valmitra came into view. It was circular, the walls carved with overlapping scales, each inlaid with precious metals and glittering jewels. A glass dome capped the structure, bathing the interior in light. Darya parked in the lot reserved for witches and they entered through a side door, pausing to take their shoes off.

The temple looked more like a menagerie than a place of worship. Lizards clung to the vine-covered walls and skittered through the shadows. Serpents of varying sizes slithered freely across the cracked stone floor. Malach counted sixteen witches, along with twelve acolytes whose eyes had not yet turned gray. They all turned to stare at him. Darya smiled, though her gaze was cool.

"You may go visit your friend, Malach," she said. "Find me here when you are done."

She broke off to join a group at the main stone altar, which was fashioned in the image of a serpent with three necks but only two heads. Scented smoke drifted from a pair of fanged mouths. A garland of white flowers draped the severed stump of the third. Dead mice lay on the stone slab. Malach watched in queasy fascination as a cobra emerged from a narrow crevice, spread its jaws, and devoured one of the rodents whole.

The temple was open to all. Besides the witches, devotees of Valmitra came and went, leaving offerings of fruit or bowls of milk. They formed a line, each bowing three times, foreheads lightly touching the floor, a whispered prayer on their lips. The men wore Rahais, the women dresses or loose trousers. A heap of straw sandals sat near the main doors.

Malach made his way through the crowd, eyes locked on the ground. Some of the serpents were harmless. Others less so. The witches kept a supply of antivenin on hand, but he had no desire to test its effectiveness. Tissue-thin wisps of shedded skin rustled beneath his bare feet as he took a flight of winding stone stairs behind the altar down to a warren of rooms below the temple. Malach's steps slowed as he reached the open door of the caretaker's consulting room. He muttered an oath under his breath.

Tashtemir Kelevan knelt next to a python that stretched from one end of the room to the other. Its skin was patterned in gold and black whorls that would blend perfectly with the dappled sunlight of a forest. Malach had run across constrictors that big in the Morho. They weren't fast, but once they got hold of you, it was over.

"Cardinal!" A smile of delight lit the vet's long, mournful face.

Malach returned the smile but kept well back. "What's wrong with it?"

"Fungal infection," Tashtemir explained, moving a damp cloth in gentle strokes along the side of its massive head, where patches of white discolored the skin. "Poor darling. But with repeat treatments, she'll be fine." He laughed at Malach's hesitation. "She won't harm you."

"How do you know?"

"Because she's already eaten." He patted a lump in the center of the snake. Malach didn't ask what the python had dined on, but he mastered his fear enough to enter the chamber.

Tash wrung out the cloth over a bowl and stood. The Rahai was a versatile garment that could be worn in different ways. Tash's draped over one shoulder and fell just above his knees, covering part of a hairy chest.

"The treatment is my own recipe. I found an excellent apothecary at the market, though he's starting to run low on everything because of the embargo." He sighed. "I'll just have to make do somehow. How are you?"

"Eager to be gone," Malach said. He stepped back as the snake lifted its head and slowly slithered out the door. "Did you get the name?"

"I might have." Tash started replacing an array of glass bottles on their shelves. "But I still urge you to reconsider this plan."

"Just give it to me."

Tash turned. His wavy dark hair had grown long, but that wasn't why he looked different. There was a softness to his face. A light in his eyes. It took Malach a moment to realize that the southerner was happy here.

"If it was a matter of simply cutting it from your skin . . . but the stone is deep inside you. I have no idea if this doctor is skilled." Tash glanced at the door, lowering his voice. "A lot of shady people are desperate for money right now, Cardinal. The black market dried up when the Mahadeva banned trade with the Curia. Everyone comes to pay respects to Valmitra and I've gotten to know a few of them, but that doesn't mean they're trustworthy."

"Then you do it."

Tash gave him a weary look. "As I've already told you a dozen times, I don't have the instruments to attempt it. Nor would I even if I did. I can sew up a wound and cure a case of indigestion, but I'm not a surgeon."

"How much will it cost?"

"A lot."

Malach stared at him in silence. Tashtemir finally shook his head. "Six major gems or the equivalent in lesser stones."

Malach did a swift calculation. The most prized gems were diamonds, rubies, sapphires and emeralds. He was paid in lesser stones and had saved all his wages, but the price was staggering. "I don't quite have it. Can you lend me the rest?"

Tash made a dour face, then nodded reluctantly. "There's a commission for the middle-woman. I suppose I can cover that, too."

"What did you tell them about me?"

"Nothing. These people don't ask questions, Malach." He took a folded piece of paper from the waist of his Rahai but didn't hand it over. "If the place looks dirty, promise me you'll call it off."

"I'm not a fool."

"That's debatable." He eyed the scar along Malach's hip. "You just healed from the last impromptu surgery."

Malach gave him a desperate look. "It's worth the risk. I have to find Nikola. And my child. I have to."

Tash's face softened. "I know. Just wait here, I'll get the stones."

Malach leaned against the wall while Tash went to his rooms in an adjacent building. The cloying smell of incense churned his stomach. Or maybe it was the prospect of being cut into again. Unlike his cousin Dantarion, Malach did not enjoy pain. But there was no other way. Once he had the ley back, he could compel one of the witches to help him escape. If the Mahadeva caught him, he'd use it against her. Never again would he allow them to get close enough to force one of those cursed kaldurite stones into his mouth.

Tashtemir returned with a small pouch. Malach tucked it into his boot.

"You look like a wild man, Cardinal," Tash said. "Don't they let you shave?"

Malach scrubbed a hand through his beard. "I'm too tired to shave," he admitted. "And there are no mirrors. I'd likely cut my own throat."

"Well, I would be quite alarmed if I encountered you in a dark alley." He clucked his tongue. "And you used to be so fussy about your appearance."

"Me?" Malach laughed. "You were the dandy. Do you miss your silks and lace cuffs?"

"Not really. The Rahai is sensible for this climate. Do you wear it in the pit?"

"They give us trousers and shirts, but no one except me wears a shirt. Too hot."

"It is a ghastly penance the witch-queen has set you."

"No worse than yours," Malach replied. "I would take the pit over a python any day."

Tash grinned. "Just be glad there are no crocodilians in the isles. They, too, are considered the children of Valmitra."

"How long do you plan to stay here?"

"The Imperator's term expires in one year. Then I shall decide—if the ban on travel is ever lifted."

Malach frowned. "Could they maintain it indefinitely?"

"No one knows. But with the Void broken, the mages must be waging open war against the Curia. I expect the witches will keep their distance until the dust settles." He looked at Malach seriously. "Who do you think will win this contest?"

Malach shrugged. "If I've learned anything, it's that winning is a subjective concept. They have greater numbers. We have greater control of the ley. A conflict like that can drag on for decades. One wonders what will be left at the end."

"Have you become a pacifist?" Tash asked with a laugh. "What happened to the ruthless, bloodthirsty beast I know and love?"

"Oh, he's still here." Malach smiled. "Older, yet seemingly no wiser."

Tashtemir nodded. "Only two things are infinite, my friend. The ley and human stupidity." A rueful grin. "And I am unsure about the first. Come, make yourself useful and refill these jars."

Malach spent the next hour helping Tash in the examining room. He was permitted to treat a cut on a tiny salamander. It was a pretty creature, not slimy but cool and dry. He let it sit on his wrist afterwards, marveling at the vivid orange hue and delicate spots.

"She likes you," Tash said.

"How do you know?"

"Because she hasn't run away." He saw Malach's expression and swallowed. "I didn't mean—"

"It's all right," Malach said dryly. "Nikola was right to leave. And I've no idea if she wants to see me again. But I won't know until I find her, will I?"

Tash nodded. "I think she only did what she thought she had to. But I saw the way she looked at you. She tried to conceal her feelings, but my time at court taught me to read volumes in the smallest gesture. And hers were obvious."

That pleased him. Malach sat very still, communing with the newt, while Tashtemir mixed his elixirs and tidied the examining room.

They'd met three years before when Tash was caught at the docks in Novostopol by three Masdari mercenaries hoping to claim the bounty on his head. Sensing an opportunity, Malach had fought them off, striking a bargain to bring Tash back to Bal Kirith, where even a veterinarian was better than no doctor at all. After some prodding, Malach learned that Tashtemir had bedded the Golden Imperator's wife. Not being the forgiving sort, the Imperator had vowed to see him sorely punished for it. Tash was hiding out abroad until her seven-year term ended, at which point he hoped to return and secure a pardon from her successor. Tash always seemed sad when he spoke of his distant homeland. For the first time, Malach understood the bitter longing of an exile.

"The surgeon is expecting you tonight." Tashtemir laid a hand on his shoulder. "I suppose we may not see each other again so . . . good luck, Cardinal."

Malach had few friends in the world, but the southerner was one of them. He clasped Tash's hand, then pulled him into an embrace.

"Thank you," he said softly. "I know what you're risking for me. I won't forget it."

He found Darya at the altar feeding crickets to a blue-tailed skink. The creature was comically fat, with tiny hind legs that could barely support its weight.

"How was your visit, Malach?" she asked cheerfully.

"Tashtemir is content here. It lifts my spirits to see him."

"You see? It is not as bad as you make out." She seemed to have forgotten their spat. "We are lucky to have you both. My sisters tell me Tashtemir is the best caretaker they've ever had. His experience in the bestiary of the Imperator was invaluable. Now, is there anywhere else you wish to go? The bazaar?"

"No." He covered a yawn. "I'm exhausted."

"Have you eaten?"

He shook his head. Darya made a sound of reproach. "You must take better care of yourself, Malach."

The witch bought him two chicken kabobs from a vendor in front of the temple. Malach ate them in the car as they drove back to the pit.

"You have tomorrow off," she said as they pulled up at the barracks. "Would you like to see some sights? The north end of the island has orange groves with walking paths. Or perhaps an afternoon at the beach?"

"I prefer to sleep."

For four months, since his last escape attempt, Malach had not deviated from a rigid schedule; work like a maniac for five days straight, visit Tash, then stay in his bunk sleeping for two.

A notch creased Darya's forehead. "Are you depressed, Malach?"

The concern in her voice made him want to laugh. "Why would I be depressed?"

She gave him a flat look. "I know you're unhappy. But the sooner you accept your situation the swifter the time will pass."

He smiled. "I thank you for the offer. Perhaps next time. But as you said, the heat takes a toll. Goodnight, Darya."

He walked to the barracks, skin crawling the entire way. As he reached the door, the engine started. He heard gravel crunch under the tires as she drove away.

Malach found his bunk and lay down, lacing his hands

behind his head. The fog of male bodies was potent, but he hardly noticed it anymore. On either side, men snored and sighed in their sleep. He watched the moon rise beyond the line of windows. When it was high and full, he lifted his mattress and took out a fat leather purse. He added Tash's gems to it and stuffed the purse in his boot. Then he crept between the bunks and out the door.

Torches burned in the pit, casting a reddish glow on the rocky ground. The mining never stopped. Night shifts were coveted since they were cooler, but Malach had never asked for one. If he was on shift, there would be no way out of the pit until it ended.

And night was the time for running.

The witches didn't set a full-time guard on the barracks. They were confident he couldn't get off the island, but whatever magic they'd worked left him the leeway to move around Tenethe—for a brief time at least. He steered clear of the pit's rim where most of the activity took place and followed the road toward the city. Driving, the trip was about twenty minutes. On foot, it took him the better part of two hours. But Tash had drawn a crude map and Malach found the address with no trouble.

It was in a quiet area fronting one of the canals. Dr. Fithen lived in a round two-story house with blue and white flowers blooming on the windowsills. Lamplight gleamed on the still, dark water. He studied the house for a moment. Well-kept and respectable with a small plaque on the door bearing the words *Medical Clinic*.

His nerves hummed, but nothing about the place tripped the danger wire in his brain. Malach knocked. The door was answered by a small birdlike woman with a sharp nose and short graying hair. He gave Tash's name and she nodded, admitting him into a reception area with three wooden chairs. A younger woman in spotless whites emerged from a hall. Neither had the eyes of a witch.

"This is Surena," Dr. Fithen said. "My assistant. Did you bring the fee?"

"I'd like to ask some questions first."

"Of course."

"How long have you been practicing medicine?"

She looked amused. "Thirty years. I started as a midwife but received my full training when I was twenty-six. I've performed dozens of surgeries."

"How many were successful?"

"All but one. The patient had a seizure on the operating table. But that was due to a preexisting condition." She looked him over. "You're a healthy-looking man. Unless there's a history I don't know about?"

Malach shook his head. "How long will I be out?"

"A few hours. Then you'll be moved to recovery upstairs. I'll allow you to stay in the room for three days. After that, you must leave."

"How big of an incision are we talking about?"

"With luck, quite small. I'll have to cut through the abdominal wall, but no more than half an inch in diameter. Then I'll use forceps to remove the stone and suture you up."

That seemed acceptable. "May I see the surgery?"

"Naturally." She nodded at her assistant. "I'll go wash up."

Surena took him to a room down the hall. She flipped on a bright overhead light. It held a gurney and IV stand with a bag of clear fluid. There wasn't a speck of dust anywhere. Malach took the purse from his boot and handed it over.

"Wait here," Surena said. She withdrew, presumably to count the gems. He sat down on the edge of the gurney. Steel instruments gleamed on a white cloth. The room smelled of antiseptic. Malach pressed a sweaty palm to his stomach.

He had lied when he told Darya he believed in nothing. The twin comets he'd seen at the Mahadeva's cavern were a sign from the ley. He still didn't know what it meant, but he was not the same man who had first met Nikola Thorn. She had changed him—or simply introduced him to an essential part of himself that he'd never met before.

Malach knew his shortcomings were not magically gone. He had too many for that. But he would protect her to the death. Be loyal to his last breath. She befuddled him and set him aflame in the same moment. She made him laugh.

She terrified him.

Love, he understood now, was greater than the sum of its parts. He could tally up all of these things and they still fell short of the depth of the whole. She didn't feel the same way about him, but it didn't matter. Finding her was worth any price.

He looked up as Dr. Fithen entered the room, now wearing crisp whites. A cloth cap covered her graying hair.

"Where exactly is the stone?" he asked as Surena took a needle from a tray and filled it with liquid.

This made all the difference in how much damage he sustained.

"I'll find it through external palpation, don't you worry," Dr. Fithen said. "Undress, please."

He unbuttoned his shirt and took it off. Then he tugged the Rahai loose and handed that over, too. Fithen's gaze swept across his Marks.

"Lie back." She winked at him. "You won't feel a thing, I promise."

Malach levered himself onto the gurney, a chill sweeping his bare skin. Surena approached with the needle. Her bland expression unnerved him. Tash had told them nothing, yet neither woman seemed surprised at the Marks. His gut tightened. Something felt wrong.

"Wait," he said.

In one quick motion, she jabbed his biceps and depressed the plunger. Malach slapped her hand away. The needle fell to the floor.

"I told you to wait!" he snapped.

The two women stepped back, regarding him warily. "Are you changing your mind, aingeal?" Dr. Fithen asked.

"I . . . ." He raised a hand to his head. Her face blurred, then doubled. "What did you call me?"

Fithen turned away, checking the instruments laid out on the tray. Malach tried to stand, but his legs didn't work. Surena laid a hand on his chest and pushed him flat. Her face swam above him. "Just relax."

Straps cinched around his wrists and ankles. Surena stuffed a cloth into his mouth.

"Shouldn't we kill him now?" she asked.

"No." Dr. Fithen walked over. Her face was a blur, but her voice held a new coldness. "Let him suffer while I cut it out."

"I know he is aingeal, but—"

"If you prefer, you can keep the fee. I'll sell the kaldurite. But you must help me throw him in the sea after. He's too heavy to carry alone."

A sigh. "Yes, doctor."

Malach's eyes slid shut. He dragged them open and managed to raise his head a centimeter from the table. The glint of a scalpel hovered above his abdomen. In an instant, he was back at a stone chamber in the Arx of Novostopol, Falke's priests pinning his arms and legs as the blade bit into his wrist. A muffled scream filtered through the gag.

"I told you we should cut his throat! Someone might hear."

Whatever drug they'd given him, it didn't dull sensation. Every muscle tensed as cold steel touched his navel. With a monumental effort of will, he forced his body to relax. Minimize the blood loss. If he survived the cutting long enough for them to extract the stone, he'd have the ley. It flowed all around him, right there. When he died, he'd make sure they went with him.

Malach fixed his bleary gaze on the circle of light overhead, panting through his nose. A sharp sting—not too bad.

The gentle clink of the scalpel striking the steel tray. A pause as Dr. Fithen chose another instrument. Then pain greater than he'd ever known. It burrowed to his roots. Mist devoured the edges of the room, but he refused to pass out.

*Please please please please find it.*

The instrument finally withdrew.

"It's deeper than I thought," Dr. Fithen said. "Lodged in the lower intestine. I'll need to widen the incision. Get the probe ready."

Malach's heartbeat thundered in his ears. So loud it almost sounded like—

A force rocked the gurney on its wheels. The ceiling spin as he careened across the operating room. The IV stand crashed over. A woman's scream. Pewter eyes stared down at him. Malach turned his face away. Dr. Fithen cowered in a corner. Two witches stood over her. They looked murderous.

Darya's fingers curled in his hair, lifting his head. Her rings gouged into his scalp.

"Ah, aingeal," she whispered, cheeks pale with rage. "I think you'll get your audience with the Mahadeva now."

# Chapter Three

Malach's eyes opened to the sting of saltwater. A heavy weight pressed against his chest. He sucked in a desperate breath. The sea poured in. His fingers scrabbled over the flat stone pinning his chest. It was heavy, but long shifts in the pit—and sheer panic—finally shifted it aside. He sat with a gasp. Water streamed down his face, rattled in his throat. A long minute elapsed before he managed to speak.

"If you intend to murder me, go ahead," he rasped. "But I thought you'd be more creative than drowning." He glanced around. "In a pool less than a meter deep."

The Mahadeva Sahevis started to laugh—all three of them. The Crone had the rusty screech of a gull. The Mother chuckled quietly. But the Maid flailed in helpless mirth, her giggles echoing through the grotto.

"He thinks we're trying to drown him." She eyed Malach fondly. "Silly aingeal!"

"Be silent," the Crone snapped, her own cackles fading. "Valmitra has seen fit to heal you, feckless boy. A little gratitude is in order."

Malach pressed a hand to his stomach. The skin was smooth and unbroken. Even his other scar had vanished. Yet the agony was seared into his memory. He recalled only a fraction of the ordeal at Fithen's house—but that was enough. The woman had gutted him.

"It's not possible," he whispered, staring at them each in turn. "Even the ley cannot heal!"

The Crone shook her head. "How little you nihilim understand." White cauls covered her eyes, but her blind gaze pierced him nonetheless. "Count yourself fortunate that the Great Serpent took pity on you. It is a thing rarely done."

Not for a single moment had Malach believed in their god. The concept was ludicrous. A serpent that coiled around the core of the earth, breathing out ley? But he couldn't deny that an apparent miracle had occurred. He rose from the pool and strode to the rock shelf. A clean Rahai sat there. He unfolded the garment and knotted it around his waist. His stomach growled loudly.

"How long was I down there?" he asked.

"A week," the Mother replied.

"A *week*?"

She dragged a jade comb through her hair. "That butcher you went to inflicted mortal wounds. So we gave you to Valmitra. If you lived, you would surface. If not . . . ." She sighed. "We did check on you periodically."

"What happened to Dr. Fithen?" He hoped it was something terrible.

"Her medical license has been revoked. She will atone for her offense."

Malach nodded thoughtfully. "Tell her I want my money back."

The Maid leapt to her feet, scowling. "Do not jest! You have made us very angry!"

"Have I?" He gave her a cold stare. "And what did you expect? I am not a dog to be leashed and brought to heel. You show me signs and portents. Declare that I am dangerous but not why or to whom. You refuse to tell me how long I must remain here or anything that is happening in my homeland. Where I have not one but *two* newborn children! So yes, I tried to remove the kaldurite. You left me no other choice!"

The three women—he still thought of them as three, although they shared a single mind—regarded him with quicksilver eyes. They resembled each other, more so the Maid and the Mother. Bold nose, thin lips, and high, angular cheekbones. The Maid's hair was a rich mahogany, threaded with silver in the Mother and fading to pure white in the Crone. They wore no clothing, only dozens of jeweled bracelets, anklets, rings and overlapping necklaces that gleamed in the dim light of the grotto.

"If Valmitra saved your life," the Mother said at last, "it is because we were right. You have importance in the scheme of things."

"Then let me meet my destiny, whatever it is!"

The Crone shook a leather dicing cup and tossed the contents between her bony legs. They were not gems, merely rough pebbles that looked like every other rock in the grotto. The Maid and Mother crowded close. They whispered to each other for a minute.

The Crone gave a satisfied grunt. "Valmitra has confirmed our choice."

The Maid grinned impishly. "He will not like it."

"It does not matter what he does and does not like," the Crone said. "He will submit."

Her voice held total assurance. For the first time in his life, Malach felt utterly outmatched.

"Submit to what?" he asked wearily.

"The mines were a poor choice," the Mother said. "They stoked your aggression and failed to stimulate your mind."

"I like the pit," he said, jaw setting stubbornly. "If I must be here, that is my preference."

"And therein lies the problem," the Crone said. "Your judgment is poor, aingeal. We would lock you up before sending you to the pit again. But we do not desire to punish you more than you already have been."

He leaned back on his palms, crossing his ankles. "What are you offering?"

The Maid's eyes glittered. "A challenge, aingeal. If you succeed, we will consider setting you loose."

There were too many conditions in that sentence to take it seriously, yet Malach felt a glimmer of hope.

"Then I will rise to the occasion." His lips quirked. "Shall I slay a monster for you? Seek out a magical sword?"

"You will join a creche," the Mother said. "Rear children."

Malach laughed. "No, really, what is it?"

The Maid scampered over and stroked his hair, toying with the damp locks. "Why do you doubt?"

He opened his mouth, then closed it again. She gave his beard a playful tug, then kissed his cheek and returned to her elders.

"You would trust me around your children?" he asked in disbelief. "Me?"

"Would you harm them, Malach?" the Mother asked.

"No, but—"

"Then it is done."

"I haven't agreed yet!" Unsettled by the swift turn of events, Malach cast about for another excuse. "With all respect, Mahadeva, I don't speak the language. Menial labor is more suitable."

The Crone's thin lips twitched. "*A bheil thu a' creidsinn gu bheil sinn gòrach*?"

He gazed at her, all innocence. "Your pardon, Mahadeva?"

"I say again, do you believe us to be stupid?" She swept the stones up. "Very well. *Glasaidh sinn suas thu*."

"No!" He frowned. "Do not cage me again."

The Maid tossed a pebble at him. "Liar," she growled.

After four months immersed in the speech of Dur-

Athaara, Malach had picked up a good deal. In that way, the witch was right. He'd been so bored at the pit, learning their tongue was the only real challenge. And he'd thought might need it to escape.

"*Dè cho fada 'sa dh'fheumas mi seo a dhèanamh*?" he asked.

"You will remain at the creche for as long as it takes." The Mother's bracelets jangled as she rose to her feet. "Maybe you'll come to like it."

"That's not the point."

She smiled. "The Great Serpent will tell us when you are ready."

"How? Do you speak with it?"

"The pronoun is *them*. And Valmitra will send a sign."

"But if you cause any trouble," the Crone continued, "you *will* be locked away. Consider this a last chance, aingeal dian."

Malach swept an arm across his waist and gave them a bow. "I will take it to heart, Mahadeva. If the Great Serpent has blessed me with their mercy, I shall do my utmost to merit it."

The Crone snorted. "Pretty words mean little. We'll see what you are made of, Malach. If you are a boy who beats his head against granite and wonders why he keeps getting hurt, or a man who faces his responsibilities."

The irony of *that* was too much. He stalked from the cavern. The rhythmic splash of waves grew louder as the passage widened. A dinghy rested on the crescent of black sand. Paarjini, his old nemesis, waited at the oars. Malach gave her a brusque nod and pushed it out, wading to his knees. When the craft floated free, he climbed into the stern. Her arms were slender but strong. She pulled hard on the oars and the boat cut through the swells, turning to take a parallel route along the shore.

"Aren't ye goin' to jump out?" she asked after they'd been rowing for several minutes. Paarjini's accent was very thick, her speech clipped but soft on the vowels. "Make a swim for it? The continent's only a few hundred leagues west. O' course, 'tis against the current. But who knows? Maybe ye'll make it."

The witch's bruises had faded, but Malach doubted she'd forgotten the feel of his chains around her throat. "Are you so eager to see me imprisoned again?"

"Not at all." She tugged on the oars. "In fact, we have wagers on how long you'll last in your new task. My sisters say a week. But I put ten rubies on a year." White teeth flashed. "I'll be a rich woman if I win."

A year? He eyed her sourly. "How did Darya find me?"

"An informant saw ye enter the house. We've been watchin' Dr. Fithen. She's unscrupulous. There are very few people who'd cut kaldurite from a man's belly, but Fithen is one. You're lucky the sisters arrived in time."

"Twenty minutes sooner would have been even nicer."

Sunlight scattered on the sapphire net binding her hair as Paarjini shook her head with a look of disgust. "They dinna stand outside listenin' to ye scream if that's what you're implyin'."

"I never said they did."

"But ye wondered."

He forced himself to hold her gaze. "Yes."

She stopped rowing. "I know I treated ye roughly when I took ye on the beach, Malach," she said. "Ye fought like a devil. But I saw ye when they brought ye out o' Fithen's abbatoir. I would never allow such a thing t' be done to anyone, not even ye."

When he didn't answer, she took the oars again. "If you're wonderin' about your friend, he's too skilled t' be removed from his position at the temple. But ye will not be seein' him again."

Malach had expected this, though he felt relief that Tash wasn't being punished for his own mistakes.

A creche. Did the Mahadeva think that caring for other

people's offspring would be sufficient to soothe his anguish? If so, she was a fool. But after Sydonie and Tristhus, the hellion orphans of Bal Kirith, Malach felt sure he would have no trouble managing normal children.

"Why did you wager so many gems on me, Paarjini?"

Her gaze flicked across his Marks, lingering on the two-headed snake at his hip. Her brow notched. Then she met his eyes with a musical laugh.

"Because ye don't break easily, aingeal."

---

# Glossary of People, Places & Things

**Alexei Vladimir Bryce**. A priest with the Interfectorem and former knight of Saint Jule. Suffers from severe insomnia. Marks include the Two Towers, the Maiden and the Armored Wasp. Enjoyed a successful law career before joining the Beatus Laqueo.

**Alice**. A Markhound and loyal friend to Alexei. Has a scar on her haunch from Beleth and harbors a special hatred for nihilim.

**Arx**. The inner citadels of the Via Sancta, they're akin to small cities and sit atop deep, churning pools of ley power. The Arxes in the two rebel cities were largely spared by the Curia's bombing campaigns, but they've fallen into ruin.

**Bal Agnar**. Situated in the northern reaches of the Morho Sarpanitum, amid the foothills of the Torquemite Range, called the Sundar Kush in Jalghuth, the city was abandoned after Balaur's defeat. Emblem is the Black Sun, a circle with twelve jagged rays.

**Bal Kirith**. Twin city to Bal Agnar, located in the central Morho on the Ascalon River. Its emblem is a Broken Chain symbolizing free will, although slavery and abuses were rampant. Before the war, the city was controlled by a small, vicious oligarchy with the blessing of the Church, led by Beleth.

**Beatus Laqueo**. A specialized Order of the Knights of Saint Jule whose name means *Holy Noose* in the old tongue. Notorious for using extreme tactics against the mages. Motto is Foras admonitio. *Without warning*.

**Beleth**. Malach's aunt and the former pontifex of Bal Kirith. Fond of wigs, powder and decadent parties, she's spent the last three decades writing books of poetry and philosophy that are banned throughout the Curia, as well as a manifesto on the *Via Libertas*, a counter ideology to the Via Sancta that embraces the Shadow Side as inevitable and argues for the rule of the strongest. Despite Beleth's eccentricities, she's cunning and formidable with a sword. Dotes on Malach, whom she raised as her own.

**Balaur**. The former pontifex of Bal Agnar. His sign is the Black Sun. Believed dead since the war, he still has secret followers in every city.

**Cartomancy**. Divination using cards. Kasia uses it to foretell the future with oracle decks made by her best friend, Natalya Anderle. In Novostopol, it's fairly lighthearted entertainment, often done at parties, but also for certain wealthy men and women who are devotees of the occult.

**Casimir Kireyev**. The archbishop of Novostopol, head of the Office of the General Directorate. Widely believed to be the Pontifex's spymaster. Gnomelike and bespectacled, he is one of the most feared men in the Church.

**Clavis**. The Pontifex of the Eastern Curia in Nantwich. The youngest ever to wear the ring, Clavis's special powers encompass doors, boundaries, and crossroads. A keeper of knowledge and technology from the past.

**Corax**. The word for *raven* in the old tongue. Symbolizes Fate's Messenger, a bridge between the material and spiritual realms. In common parlance, coraxes are copper coins given to knights in the field and used to identify bodies burned or mutilated beyond recognition. One side is engraved with the owner's name, while the other side indicates the Order within the Curia.

**Dantarion**. A bishop of Bal Kirith, she is Malach's cousin and daughter of Balaur and Beleth.

**Dark Age (second)**. A cataclysmic period a thousand years before in which the world devolved into violent anarchy. Led to the founding of the Via Sancta and the abolition of most technology.

**Dmitry Falke**. A cardinal of Novostopol and member of the liberal Neoteric faction of the Church. Patron of Natalya Anderle and close associate of Archbishop Kireyev. He led the knights of Saint Jule to victory against the Nightmages and defeated Balaur in single combat, severing three of his fingers. Balaur's signet ring is now encased in a glass paperweight on Falke's desk.

**Dur-Athaara**. Capital city of the island of Tenethe, part of the witches' realm across the sea in the far east.

**Feizah**. The former Pontifex of the Eastern Curia in Novostopol.

**Ferran Massot**. The chief doctor at the Batavia Institute. Marked by Malach. Conducted illicit experiments on his patients, in the course of which he discovered Patient 9's true identity.

**Interfectorem**. The Order tasked with hunting and detaining Invertido. Emblem is an inverted trident. The name means *murder* in the old tongue.

**Invertido**. Unfortunates whose Marks suddenly reverse, causing insanity. Symptoms include narcissism, paranoia, lack of remorse and severely impaired empathy. A genetic component is suspected as it often runs in families, although the condition can be deliberately inflicted using abyssal ley. Generally believed to be incurable.

**Jalghuth**. The capital of the Northern Curia, it's located in the far north. Surrounded by glacial fields with hundreds of stelae to repel nihilim. Its emblem is the Blue Flame. Motto is Lux et lex, *Light and law*.

**Kasia Novak**. A cartomancer with a rare ability to work the ley through her tarot deck. Classified as a sociopath by the Curia, although she adheres to her own moral code and doesn't always act selfishly.

**Kvengard**. The capital of the Southern Curia, it sits on a rocky, windswept peninsula between the Northern and Southern Oceans. Emblem is the Wolf, often depicted running in profile.

**Ley**. Psychoactive power that upwells from the core of the planet. Neither good nor evil, it's altered by interaction with the mind. Divided into three currents that correspond with the layers of consciousness: surface (blue), liminal (violet) and abyssal (red). These opposing currents flow in counterpoint to each other. The ley itself can become corrupted when thousands of people behave in selfish, wicked ways.

**Lezarius**. The Pontifex of the Northern Curia in Jalghuth. Also called Lezarius the Righteous. Creator of the Void and the stelae. A geographer by training.

**Liberation Day**. A holiday commemorating the surrender of the mage cities and the end of the civil war, marked with parades and celebrations in the streets.

**Light-bringers**. Also, **lucifers** and **aingeal dian**. What nihilim were called before Beleth and Balaur led their fellow clergy to disgrace and excommunication from the Via Sancta, they are a species distinct from humans, although the differences all involve the structures of the brain. Light-bringers learned to use the ley and offered refuge to those fleeing the Second Dark Age.

**Lithomancy**. Divination/magic using gems and minerals. Practiced by the witches in Dur-Athaara. Kaldurite, for example, absorbs the ley and prevents it from being used against you.

**Luk**. The Pontifex of the Southern Curia in Kvengard. His unique talent is wielding the ley as an evolutionary force. Luk created the Markhounds and the shadow mounts used by Kven knights.

**Mage trap**. Four interconnected Wards that form a box with no ley power inside the boundary. Can only be activated by someone with Holy Marks. During the war, it was one of the few effective defenses against the nihilim.

**Mahadeva Sahevis**. The witch-queen of Dur-Athaara. Has a triple aspect of Mother, Maid and Crone.

**Markhounds**. Creatures of the ley, bred to detect specific Marks. Invaluable during the war to hunt nihilim in the ruins. Now the hounds are mainly used by the Interfectorem because they sense it when someone's Marks invert and start to howl.

**Maria Karolo**. A bishop at the Arx in Novostopol and head of the Order of Saint Maricus, which enforces the *Meliora*.

**Marks**. Intricate pictures on the skin bestowed by someone with mage blood. Civil Marks suppress anger, greed and aggression and enhance creative talents. They primarily use surface ley. Holy Marks are only given to the clergy. They can use the deeper liminal ley and twist chance to manifest a narrow range of outcomes. People with Marks must wear gloves to prevent accidental use of the ley, which is drawn through the palms of the hands. Each Mark is as unique as a fingerprint. The first one is generally given before the age of eleven.

**Meliora**. The foundational text of the Via Sancta. Written by the Praefators, it has forty-four sutras dealing with the human condition. Its title means "for the pursuit of the better." The *Meliora* argues that form of government is irrelevant and the root of all evil is violence against Nature and ourselves. Technology is a false panacea that creates social disharmony. According to the *Meliora*, the Church itself will eventually become obsolete when society reaches a state of utopia.

**Mikhail Semyon Bryce**. Alexei's older brother. A former captain of the Beatus Laqueo and a patient at the Batavia Institute. Marked by Malach.

**Morho Sarpanitum**. The primeval jungle at the heart of the continent.

**Morvana Ziegler**. A Kven bishop who takes on Alexei's Marks. Formerly Luk's ambassador in Novostopol.

**Nantwich**. The capital of the Western Curia, it sits on the shore of the Mare Borealis. Emblem is Crossed Keys.

**Natalya Anderle**. A free-spirited artist and unrepentant rake. Kasia's best friend and flatmate.

**Nightmage**. Also called **Nihilim**. A somewhat derogatory term to describe light-bringers after their fall from grace. They wear blood-red robes and maintain a church in exile called the *Via Libertas* that espouses a version of extreme free will. In Bal Kirith, they have human servants who've been promised wealth and status when the mages regain power. Motto is Mox nox: *Soon, nightfall.*

**Nightmark**. A Mark bestowed by a mage, distinguished from the Civil and Holy Marks given by the Curia in both form and function. First practiced by Beleth and Balaur, it allows the Marked to tap abyssal ley and to twist chance in their favor more directly and violently. In return, they are beholden to the mage. Nightmarks morally corrupt over time and the images are much darker in tone than regular Marks.

**Novostopol**. Capital of the Eastern Curia. Humid, warm and rainy. A port city, it sits amid two branches of the Montmoray where the river empties into the Southern Ocean. Despite the dreary climate, Novostopol is a lively place, with bustling cafes and nightlife. Thanks to the system of Civil Marks, crime is virtually nonexistent.

**Office of the General Directorate**. The most powerful organ of the Curia, headed in Novostopol by Archbishop Kireyev. Ostensibly, it oversees the other offices and reports directly to the Pontifex. Has a vast intelligence network and used to run covert operations in the mage cities. Emblem is the Golden Bough.

**Oprichniki**. A regular force of civilian gendarmes in Novostopol. Uniform is a yellow rain jacket and stylish cap. They carry only batons.

**Order of the Black Sun.** Human followers of Balaur who have awaited his return. Most bear an alchemical Mark of a small circle inside a triangle, inside a square, inside a larger circle.

**Order of Saint Marcius**. Tasked with enforcing adherence to the philosophy laid out in the *Meliora*, in particular, the tight restrictions on technology. Emblem is a sheaf of wheat.

**Oto Valek**. An orderly at the Batavia Institute. On the payroll of Archbishop Kireyev and the OGD, Oto is a shady mercenary—and a bad penny who just keeps turning up.

**Perditum** (pl., perditae). Feral humans who live in the Void. Once residents of Bal Agnar and Bal Kirith, they were warped by the psychic degradation of the ley before Lezarius created the grid. Some are more intelligent than others, but all succumb to bloodlust when the ley floods. Smart enough to fear and avoid Nightmages (whom they recognize by scent), but anyone else is fair game. Also called leeches.

**Praefators**. Founders of the Via Sancta, they were visionaries who discovered how to use the ley through Marks. The name means *wizard* in the old tongue. Most now comprise the canon of Saints, but due to the tumultuous upheavals of the Second Dark Age, little is known about the first Praefators beyond their names. It is assumed they were all light-bringers.

**Praesidia ex Divina Sanguis**. Protectors of the Divine Blood, in the old tongue. Founded by Cardinal Falke, this secret Order strives to ensure the continuation of lucifer bloodlines in service to the Via Sancta. Motto is Hoc ego defendam. *This I will protect.*

**Probatio**. The office of the Curia that administers morality tests. Emblem is a trident, indicating all three layers of mind.

**Saviors' Eve**. The night before Den Spasitelya (Saviors' Day), a holiday commemorating the building of the Arxes, it has a grimmer theme, with young people donning masks and costumes evoking the evils of the Second Dark Age.

**Sinjali's Lance**. A focal point of the ley in Jalghuth.

**Sweven**. A memory, vision or fantasy shared directly with another person through the ley, as if they're experiencing it firsthand.

**Stelae**. Also called **wardstones**. Pillars engraved with Wards to repel nihilim. Found in the Void at the junctures of the ley lines. Most stelae are emblazoned with an emblem of the

Curia (Raven, Crossed Keys, Flame, or Wolf, depending on the location) and a pithy maxim such as *Ad altiora tendo* (I strive toward higher things), *Fiat iustitia et pereat mundus* (Let justice be done though the world shall perish) and Vincit qui se vincit (He conquers who conquers himself).

**Sublimin**. A psychotropic drug used to bestow or transfer Marks, it temporarily dissolves the barrier between the conscious and unconscious.

**Sydonie**. A young Nightmage at Bal Kirith, sister to Tristhus.

**Tabularium**. A vast archive, it's one of the few buildings in the Arx to have electricity. The Tabularium holds files on every citizen of Novostopol, as well as a separate register for members of the clergy. An even larger Tabularium exists in Nantwich, with records dating back to the Second Dark Age.

**Tashtemir Kelavan**. A veterinarian who serves as the only doctor at Bal Kirith. Hails from the Masdar League.

**Tessaria Foy**. A retired Vestal and godmother of Kasia Novak. Close to Cardinal Falke and Archbishop Kireyev. In her mid-seventies, Tess is an elegant and enigmatic figure. Comes from a moneyed family in Arbot Hills, not far from the Bryce family mansion.

**Tristhus**. A young Nightmage, brother to Sydonie, whose lead he follows without question.

**Unmarked**. Individuals who fail the morality tests administered by the Probatio and are denied Marks. The lowest caste of society, they live by the charity of the Curia since few will employ them. All the chars at the Arx are Unmarked, as proclaimed by their gray uniforms. Unmarked comprise about one percent of the population. In Novostopol, they're relegated to a slum district called Ash Court.

**Via Sancta**. The Blessed Way. A social, scientific and spiritual experiment to improve humanity. Teaches non-violence and beauty in all things.

**The Void**. Also called the **Black Zone**. The region where the ley has been banished. Encompasses the cities of Bal Agnar and Bal Kirith and most of the Morho Sarpanitum.

**Wards**. Symbols imbued with emotional power that concentrate the ley for a specific purpose. Some repel nihilim, others force the ley from a particular area (see mage trap). A surge can cause them to short for minutes to days, but they self-repair. Most use surface ley and thus glow bright blue. Activated by touch.

# Acknowledgments

To Laua Pili, for her sharp eye and even sharper wit. To mom and Nick, always. And to Jacu, who never met a dead, putrefying monster he didn't try to roll around on.

# About the Author

Kat Ross worked as a journalist at the United Nations for ten years before happily falling back into what she likes best: making stuff up. She's the author of the Nightmarked series, the Lingua Magika trilogy, the Fourth Element and Fourth Talisman fantasy series, the Gaslamp Gothic mysteries, and the dystopian thriller *Some Fine Day*. She loves myths, monsters and doomsday scenarios.


www.katrossbooks.com
kat@katrossbooks.com

facebook.com/katrossauthor
instagram.com/katross2014
goodreads.com/katross
pinterest.com/katrosswriter
bookbub.com/authors/kat-ross

## Also by Kat Ross

*The Nightmarked Series*

City of Storms

City of Wolves

City of Keys

City of Dawn

*The Fourth Element Trilogy*

The Midnight Sea

Blood of the Prophet

Queen of Chaos

*The Fourth Talisman Series*

Nocturne

Solis

Monstrum

Nemesis

Inferno

*The Lingua Magika Trilogy*

A Feast of Phantoms

All Down But Nine

Devil of the North

*Gaslamp Gothic Collection*

The Daemoniac

The Thirteenth Gate

A Bad Breed

The Necromancer's Bride

Dead Ringer

Balthazar's Bane

The Scarlet Thread

Made in the USA
Monee, IL
22 July 2022

10161562R00292